Brandishing Beginnings

Devil's Psychos MC Book 1

M.E. Thornwood

Midnight Dreaming Publishing

M.E. Thornwood

Midnight Dreaming Publishing

P.O. Box 312 Elburn, IL 60119

Interior design by Atticus

Edited by: Cantina Book Club

Cover by: RJ Creatives

ISBN: 978-1-962688-07-9

ISBN: 978-1-962688-08-6(e-book)

I F YOU ARE MY family member, thank you for your support, I love you dearly, but DO NOT READ THIS BOOK. This is not for you. We will not be having an awkward conversation about the contents of this book.

Brandishing Beginnings is a dark Reverse Harem/Why Choose romance, meaning the main female character will not choose between her loves interests. There will be group scenes and dark themes including Motorcycle Club Culture, primal play, Shibari, and dubcon scenes. This is a BDSM romance with on screen negotiations and themes that are not suitable for every reader.

For the full list of trigger warnings, please check the author's website. Brandishing Beginnings is book one of a three book series and will end on cliffhanger.

Brandishing Beginnings takes place 10 years before the events of the Ravager Knights series. You do not have to read that to read this one, but characters will show up from that series as it is set in the same world of Mourningside.

Author Note: If you find any errors in this book, please contact the author at m.e@methornwood.com

To Marcos,

Because you were supposed to be one book...

and turned into three.

Part One

Chapter One

Maya

I SMILED AS I took in the party raging around me. Drunken co-eds grinding on the dancefloor, Frat-bros cheered from the kitchen, and next to me, my roommate Terri was flirting with her latest catch: a nerdy chem-major with cute glasses.

It was a standard Friday Night at Northern Illinois University, and I—Maya Henderson—was content to relax, and drink away my stressful week of classes. The first week back was always hard, but it was my junior year and I was quick to settle into my dorm room with Terri. After two years rooming together, we had settled into a routine, so my first week back wasn't as overwhelming as the previous years.

Still, I was glad for the chance to kick back, and the first party of the year always held a magic to it, a promise of things to come.

I glanced around the frat house and smirked when I saw what looked like two freshmen standing awkwardly by the door. Freshmen were always easy to spot, as they had that deer-in-headlight look about them as they took in their first frat party. It usually took a couple months to wear off.

Feeling generous, I walked over to the door and pushed Darren—one of the frat boys—out of the way and greeted the two girls with a smile. "Hey, come on in!" I smirked. "I'm Maya."

"Kara." She had platinum curly blond hair and the brightest blue eyes that I had ever seen. They were keen as she looked around, eyes bouncing from place to place, taking everything in.

"Stephanie." Her auburn hair was pulled back in a tight ponytail that accented her high cheekbones. Her bangs were cut on an angle and swept away from her face. Her green eyes were hesitant and guarded as she swept her gaze over me.

"Freshmen?" I asked.

"That obvious?" Kara asked.

I laughed and nodded. "Come on, let's get you ladies a drink before the idiots drink it all." I glanced to the corner where Terri had been with the chem student moments before, only to find her pressing him against the wall and already making out with the poor boy.

"This place is unreal," Stephanie murmured, voice barely heard over the pounding music.

I laughed and weaved my way through the crowd. "You get used to it!" I called over the music. "Alpha Beta Chi is one of the more laid-back frat houses on campus. They throw regular parties, not like the raggers that Delta Omega throws. Those guys are a whole different level of crazy! Careful if you ever end up there. You might find yourself in some trouble you don't want to deal with," I warned.

Stephanie gulped while Kara just raised an eyebrow, not looking impressed.

I smirked as we reached the kitchen. "Alright, pick your poison. What'll you have?" When both ladies reached for cans of beer, I nodded. "Smart choice at any party. Remember, never set down your drink, and try and keep it covered." I demonstrated by opening my own can of beer, and after I took a quick sip, I covered the opening with my thumb.

Stephanie tried to mimic the move, but struggled, while Kara had already slid her thumb over the top of her beer can.

"Where you guys from?" I asked, feeling a little impressed already by Kara's quick thinking.

"Creekton," Kara replied.

"Galesville," Stephanie said.

"That explains it all." I laughed. "I'm also from Creekton. What school did you go to?"

Kara blushed slightly. "Mourningside Prep."

"Ahh." I nodded. "One of those."

Kara shrugged and took a sip of her beer. "My brother wanted me to have a better life, single mom, you know? So my brother paid for me to go there."

Guilt slid over me as I nodded slowly. "That's admirable."

Kara shrugged and glanced at Stephanie, whose deer in the headlight's expression was slowly melting.

Hours later, the three of us were sufficiently shit-faced. Kara laughed as she climbed onto the mechanical bull in the basement of Alpha Beta Chi. Stephanie and I cheered her on as she settled into position. She had barely locked her knees and grabbed the bullhorn, before the frat-bro manning the controls sent her into a spin.

Dressed in a T-shirt and jeans, Kara wasn't at risk of flashing anyone anything risky, so I cheered on my new friend and called for the bull to go faster. "Fuck you, bitch!" Kara called, broad smile on her face.

I laughed and even Stephanie cheered. This was shaping up to be a night to remember, with new friends that would hopefully stand the test of time.

"Oh shit!" Stephanie swore when Kara was thrown from the bull.

Kara fell back onto the heavy mats surrounding the mechanical bull, laughing hysterically. Stephanie and I rushed over to her, both of us giggling as we fell onto the mat next to Kara. "That was amazing!" Kara yelled.

"So awesome," Stephanie said.

"Yo, we should go get tacos," I said as I tugged Kara to her feet.

"Can we please? Fuck yes, I need a taco, or carnitas, or oh! Tamales!" Kara slipped into a Spanish accent that had Maya chuckling.

"You speak Spanish?" I asked as we left the basement.

"Si, mi madre es de México." *My mother is from Mexico.*

"And your dad?" I couldn't help but ask, as I looked over Kara's blond hair and blue eyes.

Kara shrugged. "I never met him."

"I'm sorry." I sighed. We quickly walked toward the front door of the frat house. I glanced to the corner where Terri had been with the chem boy, only to find them no longer making out, but gone completely. There was a new couple in their spot.

Pulling out my cell phone, I noticed the time—going on 2 a.m.—and a text from Terri, saying she had taken off with the chem boy two hours ago. I frowned and slid my cell into my back pocket. "Alright, Taqueria El Valle is open until 4 a.m. It's a short walk from here, if you guys are down?" I turned to look at Stephanie and Kara.

The two women were having a silent conversation, but they both nodded. "Yeah, okay," Stephanie said softly.

"Tired?" I asked.

Stephanie shrugged. "All of this is not really my scene. I'm kinda pushing my boundaries tonight. I'm a 'in bed at nine' type of girl."

I grinned. "College is all about exploring and pushing those boundaries. Good for you for getting out. First frat party live up to the hype?"

She laughed and shrugged. "It wasn't horrible."

I smiled broadly. "Well, you never end a night of drinking without getting tacos, and Valle's is the best Mexican food around."

"Alright, let's go." Kara grinned.

Maya

"Yo Maya!" I turned to see who had called out my name as I walked through the Quad—the center area between four of the buildings of the university.

Kara hurried after, adjusting her backpack strap on her shoulder.

"Hey girl!" I greeted my new friend with a smile. "How you settling in?"

Kara grinned. "Good, good! Look, I hate to ask, with us just meeting and all, but any chance I could catch a ride with you next time you head back to Mourningside or Creekton?"

I laughed and nodded, knowing it was the way of freshman year. "Yeah, for sure! No problem. I don't head back all that often, though, to be honest. Me and the folks don't get along that great, but I'm always down for a road trip."

"Thanks girl. I appreciate that. Where you headed?"

"Library, you?"

"Same."

"Tis the life." I chuckled.

Music blared, and Kara and I sung along. The sun was shining, and both of us acted like we didn't have a care in the world. I knew that was far from the truth, though. We may have been going home because the campus shut down for the entire week of Halloween, but we were still laden down with homework from professors that thought we had nothing else to do.

The heavy metal song ended and switched to something lighter, a pop-punk band that had been popular when I was in middle school. It had us both laughing and singing along. "I fucking loved this song!" Kara said, before she launched into an off-key rendition, hitting every word.

"Yeah, get it girl!" I cheered.

Kara finished the song with a laugh. She took a sip of water from a bottle she brought with her before she asked, "What are your plans this week?"

I shrugged. "My sister is moving to Chicago this week. She took a job up there. So I'm gonna help her move and hang out in her new place."

"That's awesome. Good for her."

"Yeah, good for her." I sighed.

"Leaves you alone with the 'rents then?"

"Yeah, and we're not always good."

"Are you heading straight back to school from Chicago, or are you coming back down this way?"

"Oh, I'll be back down by next weekend. I'm only staying with my sister until Thursday. She starts the job that night. Night shift."

"Oof, that's rough. What's she doing?"

"She's a doctor. She's finishing her residency. She has a year left. She was doing it down in Bloomington, but wanted more action, you know? Plus, she's hoping to get into the fellowship program up there."

Kara nodded, "I could see that. After law school, I've thought about moving to Chicago for a bit, getting some experience at a big firm, before I head back home. I want to work with families that don't have the means to pay for a lawyer."

I smiled. "That's good of you. So many people become a lawyer for the money, it feels like."

"Yeah, I know. Then growing up in Creekton Villages, you just saw a lot of shit, you know? A lot of heart break, and single mothers, a lot of families just barely getting by. I was lucky. My brother wanted better for me, so he busted his ass to get me into Mourningside Prep."

"He sounds amazing."

"He is...and he's an ass too." Kara chuckled. "Brothers."

I laughed lightly and let the conversation drift off as the song changed again.

"Oh," I gasped, freezing in the doorway as I walked back into the cozy living room of Kara's small apartment. I had gone to the bathroom while I was waiting for Kara to be ready to head back to school, and I came back out to find a large man in the living room who hadn't been there before.

Dressed in a black hoody and dark wash jeans, the man was broad-shouldered and tall. He had a short black hair was buzzed closed to his head and a thick but trimmed goatee that did nothing to hide his chiseled jaw. His brown skin and dark brown eyes suggested he was of Mexican heritage.

His gaze snapped to mine, those dark eyes roaming over my body. I wasn't wearing anything special, a pair of beat-up blue jeans and a purple long-sleeved top that hugged my curves. My curly, golden blond hair was pulled up in a messy bun, but the way he quickly looked me over and then let his gaze roam over my face, sent a shiver down my spine at his intensity.

"Hi, I'm Maya," I introduced myself, trying to break the heavy silence that had descended between us.

"Marcos." He moved forward and held out his hand to me. "I'm Kara's brother."

My heart fluttered in my chest as I listened to his deep voice. His palm was warm in mine and butterflies erupted in my belly as I shook his hand. "Nice to meet you."

There was a spark between them, and I found myself getting lost in his dark eyes.

"Oh good, you've met," Kara said, interrupting the moment.

I quickly dropped his hand and stepped back, looking over my shoulder at my friend. Kara had come out of her bedroom with her duffle slung over her shoulder.

"Marcos, Maya's the one who's been driving me back and forth to Northern," Kara explained. "She's a junior."

Marcos gave a nod of recognition. "Nice to finally put a face with the name, I've heard a lot about you," he said slowly. "Thanks for driving her. It's stupid that freshmen can't have cars on campus."

I smiled. "I know. My freshman year I at least had my sister on campus."

Marcos smiled in return. "You live in Creekton still?"

"Not anymore, my parents moved to Mourningside after I left high school," I explained, brushing a stray hair out of my eyes.

"What are you doing here?" Kara asked her brother.

"I thought I would stop by and see you before you headed back to school," Marcos said.

Kara rolled her eyes. "Then you should have come by yesterday for lunch, like we planned and not have blown me off."

Marcos scratched at his eyebrow with his middle finger, as he tilted his head slightly, watching his sister warily. "I'm sorry, Lil Manita," he said before he continued in Spanish. "Ya te dije que surgió algo con el trabajo." *I already told you something came up with work.*

Kara sighed. "Alright brother, but we're heading out."

He nodded once. "Right. Well here," he reached into the pocket of his hoody and pulled out an envelope, before he handed it to Kara.

I glanced away, not wanting to intrude on the moment between siblings. I gathered up my coat and keys, while Kara spoke softly in Spanish to her brother.

When they finished up, Marcos turned to me and said, "It was nice to meet you. Next time you're in town, we should all get together for lunch."

I glanced at Kara who rolled her eyes, before I said simply, "Sure."

Once we were in the car, Kara turned to me as I started backing out of the parking spot. "So, I totally walked in on a moment back there."

I flinched and quickly looked at her, slowing the car to a stop and shifting into drive. "I uh—"

Kara laughed. "Don't worry about it. I won't be mad if you end up dating my brother, or sleeping with him, or whatever."

"I don't—"

"I'll just warn you that he's ten years older than me, putting him at twenty-eight. And he's kinda a whore."

A startled laugh burst out of me. Too shocked to say anything, and still confused by the moment I had shared with Marcos, I kept my mouth shut and pulled forward in the parking lot, heading for the exit.

A few minutes down the road, I finally asked. "You wouldn't be mad?"

"Oh gross!" Kara groaned dramatically, before laughing.

I couldn't help but laugh as well. "It's college, right? Slut era?"

"Slut era." I held out of my fist and Kara bumped it with hers.

Maya

"Are you going home for Thanksgiving?" Jenna asked, her voice distant, despite the headphones I was wearing.

"I dunno. Are you?" I shot the question back at my older sister.

Jenna sighed. "Probably not. I work that night at eight."

I frowned, sitting back against the headboard in my shared dorm room, grateful that Terri was in class while I spoke to my sister. "Yeah, mom's been extra lately. I'm really not feeling it. I was just there a couple weeks ago for Halloween week."

Jenna laughed. "You were there for like three whole days. You spent most of that week helping me move."

"Three days too many!" I groaned.

Jenna sighed, but didn't say anything. She didn't get it; she wasn't the one Mom nitpicked at. No, Jenna was the favorite, the one that our mother constantly compared me to. It was an unbeatable standard and really drove a wedge between me and my mother.

For as much as Jenna tried to keep the peace, sometimes there just wasn't anything to be done about our mother, other than to keep my distance and try to save my own sanity by not subjecting myself to the crazy.

"Mom said they were going to Aunt Brenda's anyway. I don't really feel like cramming in the car with both of them for an hour drive," I said.

"Yeah, I get it. So what will you do?"

"Maybe, I'll come crash on your couch for those four days."

Jenna sighed again. "I wish, sister. I'm working twenty-four hours starting Thanksgiving. Supposedly the holidays bring out the crazies and they expect us to be busy."

"That sounds horrible, sister." I couldn't help but smile.

"I'm kinda excited to be honest. Busy means surgery."

I laughed and shook my head, despite the fact that my sister couldn't see me. *Leave it to fucking Jenna to be excited about the prospect of slicing people open.*

"You should come by my place for Thanksgiving!" Kara said on the drive home.

In the end, I had decided to head home. Jenna managed to get Sunday through Tuesday off before the holiday, so I would hang out with my sister, before I headed down to my parent's. I'd had made effort of showing up, then made myself scarce with friends the rest of the break.

I glanced over at my new friend. In the last several months, the two of us had grown extremely close, meeting in the library to study almost daily. We also met up with Stephanie and Terri, and a couple other friends at the mess hall for meals.

"It'll be low key, I promise. Literally just me and my Mama, plus Marcos and his two best friends, Jason and Nico." Kara elaborated.

I thought it over, wondering if I could handle sitting through a meal with Marcos, after our *moment,* as Kara was calling it. He was a very attractive man, and there was clearly chemistry there. "I uh—"

"Come on, Maya! It'll be so much fun! We usually play Mario Cart after until we pass out into food comas on the couch."

I laughed, and despite my better judgement, I agreed. "Alright, sounds good!"

"YES!" Kara shouted, throwing her arms in the air. "This is going to be the best Thanksgiving ever!"

I was doubting my decision by the time Thursday rolled around. As nerves rolled over me, I was wishing I had stayed in Chicago, despite my sister working long hours. Being alone sounded better than making a fool of myself in front of Kara's family, her brother especially.

Dressed in leggings and slinky, off the shoulder top, I was classy and casual and still comfortable. I managed to bake some caramel brownies to bring to dinner, so I wasn't showing up empty handed. After finding a parking spot near Kara's building, I shut off my car and took a deep breath. I glanced in the rearview mirror to check that my hair and makeup were still good to go, before I slowly opened the door. I grabbed the brownies from the passenger seat and stepped out of the Honda Civic.

I made sure the car was locked and before I headed up the walkway toward the building. The complex was made up of rows of two-story buildings, and Kara's mom's place was at the end of the building on the second floor.

Moments later, I was knocking on a beat-up front door that was decorated with a cute fall wreath. "Coming!" Kara called through the door. "Hey, Maya!"

"Hey girl, Happy Thanksgiving!" I grinned as Kara stepped out of the way. "Happy Thanksgiving everyone."

A chorus of grunted, "Happy Thanksgiving's," were sent back my way from the three men in the living room, as they looked away from the football game on the TV.

I was met with the stares of the three most beautiful men I'd ever seen, but it was Marcos that held my gaze the longest. He stood up quickly, and walked over. He dressed in a pair of dark washed jeans and a white cable knit sweater, that made my mouth water. "Welcome." He smiled warmly, his dark eyes crinkling in the corners. "Let me get that for you." He reached for the tray of brownies in my hand.

"Thank you." I smiled.

"I'll take your coat," Kara offered.

I kicked off my shoes, before I shed my coat and handed it to Kara. Feeling eyes watching me, I looked back to the two men still staring. Both had blond hair. One was shaggier around his ears, like he was in the process of growing it out, while the other guy's was darker, and short and spiky.

"This is Nico," Kara introduced, pointing to the blond with shaggy hair and blue eyes. "And Jason." She pointed to the one with spiky blond hair and slate gray eyes. "Guys, this is my friend Maya from school."

"Nice to meet you," Nico said, giving me a wide smile.

Jason just nodded in greeting.

"Come on, let's get you a drink," Kara said, pushing me toward the kitchen, just as a short woman with sensual curves and a gorgeous smile walked out. Carlita Candella was as beautiful as she was the last time I met her, with long wavy black hair that reached her trim waist and big caramel-colored eyes that were so warm as they crinkled in the corners and drank you in.

"Oh Maya, good you made it. I'm so glad you're here, *Nena*." Lita wrapped me a huge hug, that I couldn't help but sink into. Carlita had welcomed me into her home with open arms, and immediately treated me with love and affection, more than my own mother ever had.

"Happy Thanksgiving, Lita," I murmured into her shoulder. I had to bend slightly, to hug the much shorter woman, but Lita's hugs were worth it. "Thank you for having me."

"Of course, dear." As we pulled apart, Lita patted my cheek affectionately. "You're always welcome here."

As we ate dinner, I relaxed into the atmosphere. I ended up on the same side of the table as Kara, while Nico and Jason took the other side, leaving the ends or heads of the table for Marcos and his mother.

Conversation flowed easily and I laughed often. The men at the table kept up a solid stream of banter and jokes. Even though I felt like the three men were watching me constantly, I didn't let it affect me. I kept up with their jokes and laughed when they flirted with me. The three of them were being very obvious in their attraction, that even Kara took notice and made her own flirty jokes.

At some point, a pair of feet settled on either side of mine under the table, and they absently rubbed their foot against my own, basically playing footies at twenty-something years old. I left my feet there, letting them do whatever they wanted. I had a feeling that when it came to these three men, it was only the beginning of letting them do what they wanted.

After dinner, all five of us helped Lita clear the table and clean the kitchen. It wasn't until everything was spic and span did Marcos say, "Ma, we're gonna take a walk."

Lita rolled her eyes. "Uh huh."

Kara laughed and pressed a kiss to her mother's cheek. "You could join us."

Lita just shook her head, a smile on her face. "You kids have fun."

"Come on," Kara said to me, passing me my coat.

"Where we going?" I asked, confused.

Jason chuckled behind me; his deep cadence awfully close to my ear. I couldn't help the shivers that ran down my spine. *God damn his voice is fucking hot.* "Don't worry, we'll protect you." His voice was deep and sensual—erotic.

"But who's going to protect me from you?" I glanced at him over my shoulder, watching as the big bad wolf licked his lips, his gray eyes baring into my soul, before a slow sinful smile stretched across his mouth.

"Something tells me, darlin'," he drawled, keeping his voice low as he leaned closer to me. "That you could handle us, just fine."

A gasp left my lips before I could I stifle it.

He winked—*he fucking winked at me*—making my heart pound in my chest.

"Come on, girl." Kara pushed my coat at me, breaking the spell Jason held me under.

I blushed like a fucking schoolgirl and quickly turned to face my friend. Kara was smiling, as she tugged me forward.

I caught Marcos's smirk, as he watched me from the door. His dark eyes tracked my movement. I didn't know where we were going or why, but I would gladly follow them into hell.

A few minutes later we were walking through the parking lot to a spot they apparently all knew very well: behind the dumpsters, along the side of the building. "You could've just said we were going to smoke." I rolled my eyes when Marcos pulled out a blunt.

"Where's the fun in that?" Nico asked. He came up beside me and bumped his shoulder against mine.

I grinned and shrugged. "All about the cloak and dagger?"

Nico smirked. "Something like that."

Jason chuckled softly as he settled on my other side. My panties were soaked. Every damn time the man spoke or laughed, my fucking pussy gushed for him. I met Kara's gaze across from me in the little circle we made. My friend just smiled broadly, and I knew we would be having words later, when no men were around.

Kara might have been OK with something happening between Marcos and I, but tonight was amping up to be a whole different scenario all together. All three of them would not stop smiling or flirting or even touching me at times. The damn passing of dishes had turned into a way to slide their fingers along mine.

"Here." Nico nudged my shoulder with his, before he was pressing the blunt into my hand.

I wrapped my fingers around it and brought it to my lips. I took a deep drag, trying not to blush at the thought that both Marcos's and Nico's lips were on the paper before mine. It was slightly damp, but thankfully neither one of them had saturated the thing. There was nothing worse than someone wetting the paper with too much saliva.

I slowly exhaled the smoke that filled my lungs, tilting my head back so I blew the smoke up and not straight at Kara's face. I turned to hand the blunt to Jason, but he gently pushed my hand back. "Hit it again."

I didn't need to be told twice. I took another quick drag, sucking deeper this time, before I passed it to him. I held in the smoke as long as I could, before I was hit with a coughing spell, smoke exhaled from my lungs as I coughed deeply. I covered my mouth, trying to stifle the noise of my coughs, as to not give away what we were all up to behind the dumpsters.

A hand rubbed my back as I slowly regained my breath. "Fuck," I muttered.

Jason chuckled next to me, blowing out a smooth stream of smoke as he handed the blunt to Kara. A hand on my shoulder, squeezed the tender spot where my neck met my shoulder, and yanked me to the side. I jumped slightly as I was pulled against Jason's hard body. "Easy," he murmured into my ear.

I shivered in response to his touch and the way his voice drove me utterly crazy.

"Cold?"

I shrugged a shoulder and glanced at Marcos and Nico. Both men were watching me intently, as Jason still had his arm around me, holding me against his warm body. Marcos's dark eyes were hungry as they drank me in, while Nico had a playful grin on his face as he let his eyes roam over me—not that he could see much with my coat on.

Kara cleared her throat and I blushed as I pulled away from Jason. He slowly let his hand drop from her shoulder, letting it slide down her back as he let her step away.

"Are you spending the night, tonight?" Kara asked me. There was a knowing grin on her face as she asked the question.

"Yeah," I muttered. "I gotta grab my bag out of my car though." I reached into my coat pocket, feeling for my keys.

"Here." Nico smirked, pushing the blunt toward me. His fingers lingered over mine as he handed me the half smoked blunt; his hands were warm against my skin. I hadn't realized how quick the temps had dropped since the sun went down.

How was it my turn again? I was used to the frat boys I usually smoked with sitting on the blunt for a while. These guys seemed all about the puff, puff, pass. I was already feeling the effects as I took another slow drag, letting the smoke fill my lungs before I sucked in clean air after.

I passed the blunt to Jason, when I felt my phone vibrate in my pocket. I pulled it out and sighed as I saw the face on the screen. "Fucking Tommy?" Kara groaned, having seen my phone screen. "I thought you broke up with that douche?"

I exhaled my smoke and hit ignore on the call, before I tucked the phone back in my pocket. "I did. He won't take the hint."

"'Cause he was whooped on that pussy from day one?" Kara laughed.

I groaned and shook my head. "Dude." My cheeks heated as a blush coated my face. The three guys shifted on their feet, and I could see Marcos's scowl out of the corner of my eye.

Kara, already high, just laughed and laughed. "He's still in loveeeeee," Kara sang.

I laughed at her friend and shook my head. "Dude, it wasn't even like that. It was supposed to be casual." I ignored the men shifting around her. "I told him that up front."

Kara laughed even more.

My phone rang again. "Jesus." I grumbled when I saw Tommy's picture again.

A large, calloused hand slid over mine, warm and strong as it gripped my fingers, pressing them tighter around the phone. I looked up in confusion, giving Marcos the distraction he needed, to pull the phone from my grip. "What are you doing?"

He didn't answer me, instead he hit accept on the call from Tommy and pressed the phone to his ear. "Hello?" Marcos's voice was deep and low as he answered the call, a gravelly growl that had me clenching my thighs together.

"Who's this?" Tommy's voice, while slightly muffled, was still clear as day from my phone.

I was at a loss for words. I didn't even fight him back for my phone, I just waited on bated breath to see what Marcos would say to Tommy. "Maya's now mine. So fuck off."

My mouth dropped open in shock, I was already too high to comprehend what Marcos was saying right now. Kara's giggle didn't help either.

"Who the fuck are you? Put Maya on the phone now," Tommy yelled.

"Listen, shit head," Marcos continued. "Maya dumped you. She's had enough. Now she's mine. So fuck off." Marcos hung up the phone after that.

A deep blush colored my face as my mouth dropped open in shock. I stepped toward Marcos to grab my phone, but he slid it in his pocket. Narrowing my eyes on him, I crossed my arms over my chest and cocked my hip, raising an eyebrow and waiting. "Relax, *Tesoro*, you'll get your phone back. Now hit this." Someone how the blunt was back in his hand. He took a deep drag off the almost finished blunt and stepped toward me.

Oh fuck, is he planning on shot gunning this, right in front of his sister? What's he planning? I had no idea but still found my feet moving toward Marcos.

Marcos smirked down at me before he pressed the blunt between my lips. He held it, as I sucked in a hit. My heart pounded in my chest, and I heard Nico chuckle softly to my right, before his hand slid into my coat pocket. I heard my keys jingle as I turned my head away from the blunt.

I took another deep breath of fresh air, pulling the smoke further into my lungs, all while Marcos still stood inches away from me, looking down at me with a smirk on his face. His dark eyes were mischievous in the light of the parking lot.

"Come on, girl. I'm freezing." Kara tugged my hand, pulling me away from Marcos.

There was a rumble of low laughter from behind us as we walked away. I glanced over my shoulder as Kara and I hit the stairs, to find all three guys—including Nico with my bag slung over his shoulder—standing where we left them, staring after me.

"What the hell is happening?" I mumbled, as we climbed to the second floor.

Kara laughed and shook her head. "Girl. You're so fucked."

I gasped. "What do you mean? Kara?"

"Word on the street is my brother and his friends only date together. As in, *sharing*."

I stopped in my tracks on the stairs. "What?"

"Keep moving, they're watching." Both of us picked up our pace and headed toward Kara's apartment. "Yes, they usually share a girl amongst the three of them."

"Hot damn." My heart was pounding, and my breath quickened.

"Come on, inside." Kara opened the apartment door and led the way inside.

Lita was just setting out the brownies I had brought, along with a tray of cookies and a pumpkin pie. After I shed my coat and kicked off my shoes again, I had to excuse myself to the bathroom. I had a lot to wrap my head around, the idea of being with three men was insane, wasn't it? Kara didn't seem bothered by any of it, not the idea of her brother with me or the idea of me with three guys.

It was all happening too quickly. I barely knew these dudes and they were all over me. I took my time in the bathroom, wishing I had my phone to at least occupy my thoughts, or fucking text Terri, but Marcos still had the device, and I didn't know how I was going to attempt to get that back.

I waited until after I heard the apartment door open and close, and Marcos started a conversation with his mother, before I finally washed my hands, checked that my dirty blond curls were in place, and left the bathroom. As soon as I walked into the living room, the eyes of all three men were on me again. I ignored them and headed straight for the table.

"Dude, are these caramel brownies? They look fucking awesome," Kara grinned, meeting my eye.

I was grateful for the distraction and smiled easily. "Yes. I need like four and a huge glass of milk."

"Milk, coming right up." Lita grinned, immediately walking into the kitchen.

"I can get it," I offered, not wanting Lita to wait on me.

"Sit, sit. I've got it." Lita waved me off.

"We watching a movie?" Nico asked, moving toward the TV.

"Yeah! We gotta watch Encino Man," Marcos said.

I settled back at the table and helped myself to a slice of pumpkin pie and a brownie, not giving a damn about the calories I was about to consume. Jason took a seat next to me, and his foot immediately slid against mine—so that's who my mystery footsie partner was.

"You want whip cream?" Jason asked, his voice low as he leaned over and spoke into my ear, his breath hot against my skin.

I turned my head ever to look at him, our faces inches apart. His eyes were a such a clear light gray color that was utterly beautiful.

His gaze was intense as he took me in. The room around us melted away as I spoke softly. "I love whip cream."

A playful grin tugged at his lips.

"Maya, you good with Encino Man?" Marcos called from the living room area.

Glancing away from Jason's smoldering stare, I turned to find Marcos and Nico waiting expectantly. "Old school Brendan Fraiser? Plus, Sean Astin? Hell yeah, I'm there."

"Let me guess, you're a Lord of the Rings fan?" Nico smirked from across the room. "Samwise for the win?"

I laughed and shook my head. "Huge Lord of the Rings fan, but no, my favorite in Lord of the Rings will always be Aragorn. Nothing hotter than a man in leather."

All three of them smiled dangerously, like they shared the same secret. "Is that so?" Jason murmured.

I turned my head back to him, ignoring Marcos's and Nico's knowing grins, and turned to find Jason's face even closer than before. I gasped, realizing his lips were less than inch from mine.

His gray eyes darkened as they darted between mine.

Was this really happening right now?

"Alright!" Kara called out from the kitchen. "I've got milk with a side of sexual tension!"

I jumped back from Jason. "Fuck my life." I groaned and shook my head.

Kara laughed and I could feel the heat spreading across my face and neck as I blushed deeply.

I shook it off, ignoring the men in the room as Lita and Kara settled around the table again. I took a bite of my brownie and moaned. "Fuck, that's good."

Kara laughed. "Girl, didn't you make them?"

"I'm so fucking stoned, and they hit the spot right now. Stop judging me," I shot back at my friend.

Kara laughed and shrugged.

The sexual tension settled down while we ate our dessert. Marcos and Nico eventually joined us as they finished setting up the movie and rearranging the couches to make room on the floor. They piled the couch cushions on the floor, using the bottom of the couch to lean against, creating a giant mattress on the floor, before they piled sheets and blankets on top of it. It was clear they had made something similar before.

A little while later, Lita was excusing herself for the evening, while I claimed a spot in the center of the blanket nest. Kara took a seat in the recliner off to the left of the room, conveniently near the hallway to her room.

I suddenly recognized my error immediately as Jason and Marcos settled on either side of me. Boxed in, surrounded by testosterone, while my inhibitions had been lowered...I was fucked. Completely and utterly fucked.

Two hours later, the lights had been turned off, the only light in the room provided by the next movie that was playing on the TV. Kara had slunk off sometime during Encino Man, and I honestly had no idea what Nico had turned on after. Jason's hand was rubbing circles into my thigh while Marcos was running a finger over my forearm—seemingly small touches, that set fire to my body.

I was in sensation overload.

I was trying to ignore them and watch the movie—I was trying not to be a total hussy and put out just hours after meeting them. I still didn't understand what was fully happening either. I'd only met Marcos the one time before tonight, and then when I walked in before dinner, the three of them had acted like I'd hung the moon.

I knew I was hot. With my golden curls down around my face, my bright amber eyes that everyone always complimented, and sharp cheek bones, I knew I was attractive. A little short for my liking, but I made it work with heels when I needed to. But these guys were acting like I had walked in naked and promised them blow jobs. It was a little unsettling.

I had to make a damn decision here. "I have to go to the bathroom," I mumbled.

Jason and Marcos didn't say anything as I quickly slipped away from them. I climbed out of the floor-nest and didn't look back as I b-lined it for the bathroom, grateful that it was down the hall past Kara's bedroom.

I did have to pee. So I quickly did my business and washed my hands. I didn't dilly dally in the bathroom like a coward—I didn't want them to come looking for me—no, I left the bathroom and slipped into Kara's bedroom before any of them could say anything. I highly doubted they would come knocking on the door, and if they did, I could easily say I was going to bed.

"Jeeze, girl." Kara laughed as I closed the door softly behind me.

I leaned back against the door and looked at my friend with wide eyes. "I don't understand them. What is this?" I asked.

Kara laughed. "I have no idea what spurred them to act like this, but they obviously are in to you."

I closed my eyes and took a deep breath.

"Are you OK?" Kara asked, softly. "I can tell them to fuck off."

I sighed and opened my eyes. Kara was watching me with a concerned look on her face. "I've never been in a situation like this before."

Kara smiled easily. "You've never had three men want you at the same time, before?"

A laugh broke out of me and I shook my head. "No, ma'am."

"Girl, I would kill to have three men interested in me. That's so fucking hot!"

"You're not mad?" I had to ask. I was worried about our friendship.

"Hell no. Like I said before, that's how my brother and his friends operate. Hell, I'm a little jealous." Kara rolled off the bed and stood up. "You should go back out there. Enjoy the evening."

"You won't think I'm a whore, will you?"

"Girl, it's college. It's all about being a whore and living it up. Trust me, no judgement here."

"Seriously Kara," I stressed. "This is your brother. I don't want this shit to come between our friendship."

"That right there, is all I need to know about our friendship." Kara grinned and walked toward me. Still plastered to the door, I watched and waited. Kara stopped right in front of me and placed her hands on my shoulders. "Listen to me, Maya. There will be zero judgement, this will not ruin our friendship. You have two hotter than hell men out there—"

"Three."

"Two. My brother is not hot," Kara deadpanned.

"Girl, your brother is hella hot," I shot back.

Kara rolled her eyes. "Whatever. Either way, those men are out there waiting for you. Who knows if it'll go past anything more than tonight, but I know for a fact that they won't hurt you. And from the stories I've heard growing up... they know what they're doing."

I didn't know why, but that made me feel better. Nodding absently, I nudged Kara out of the way and stepped away from the door. "Alright," I muttered, and bent over to pick up my backpack from floor next to Kara's bed.

"What's your plan?" Kara asked.

I don't answer, instead I rummaged through my bag, looking for my pj's. Finding the matching set of tiny booty shorts and cropped tank top, I pulled them out and held them up. "Well, it's not lingerie—"

"But its short and little and they'll see it for what it is... a God damn offering." Kara practically cackled with glee.

I can't help but giggle along with my friend. Feeling light hearted, I nod. "Alright. Well, fuck."

"In another hour or two, you probably will be: well-fucked," Kara joked.

I laughed, dropping the PJ set to the bed and pulling my slinky shirt over my head.

"Don't worry about my mom. She has to work early tomorrow, so she's already in bed. She's a heavy sleeper, and I won't leave my room."

I rolled my eyes but turned my back to Kara as I pulled the PJ top over my bra. I was used to changing in front of girls in the locker room, but I also didn't need to flash my friend. I unsnapped my bra under the top and finagled it out from under the tight crop top. Next, I peeled off my leggings and socks, before I stepped into the booty shorts that ended right below the curve of my ass.

"Hot damn, Maya," Kara said from behind me.

I grinned as I folded my clothes and tucked them back in my backpack. "You only live once, right?" It was a rhetorical question, but Kara jumped all over it.

"Hell, yeah girl!"

Nico "Dagger" Gage

"**H**OT DAMN BRO**,**" I groaned as Maya all but ran for the bathroom. Leaning back against the bottom of couch, I eyed my buddies, annoyed.

"Fuck," Jason "Stone" Langford muttered.

Marcos "Killer" Candella shook his head. "Give her time. She'll come back."

"You guys couldn't keep your damn hands off her, all fucking night," Dagger growled, needing them to know how pissed he'd be if they scared Maya off.

Marcos rolled his eyes. "Stop being so dramatic. It's not like we can't get laid."

"Fuck off with that shit," Stone snapped. "You felt it too. Don't brush it off."

"Yeah," Marcos sighed. "There's something about her—" He cuts off as the bathroom door opened.

We waited, listening to Maya pad along the hallway and then entered Kara's room.

"Fuck," Stone muttered again.

I shook my head, my disgust evident.

Marcos sighed. "Give her some time. We came on hot and heavy. She just needs a minute."

"How can you be so sure?" I grumbled.

"Because I'm trying to convince myself too, here. Let's give her a few, and if she doesn't come back out, I'll knock on Kara's door. She'll at least let me know if we spooked Maya, or not." Marcos rubbed a hand over his short-buzzed hair and sighed.

"Kara gonna kick our asses for wanting her friend?" Stone asked.

"Probably," Marcos grumbled.

A few minutes later we were still waiting. I had turned on Bio-Dome to continue the Pauly Shore laugh-fest, even if no one really seemed to be paying attention. Maya had all but zoned out under Jason's and Marcos's wandering hands.

We tuned back into the TV, not really watching, as they waited to see if Maya would come back out. They didn't have to wait long. The three of them stiffened when they heard Kara's bedroom door open again.

A moment later, Maya walked out into the living room, wearing a matching navy-blue PJ set that was tight and short, and showed off all her amazing creamy skin. She walked into the room confidently, smirking slightly when Stone let out a low groan.

She headed back to her seat between Jason and Marcos, but Jason reached out for her before she could turn around to sit down. His hand slid up her bare right thigh and nudged her body to left with enough force that she stumbled toward him.

He grabbed both of her hips and guided her fall so she landed with her legs straddling his lap. It was a smooth move that even I hadn't see coming.

Maya let out a startled yelp, before she grabbed Jason's shoulders to steady herself as she was pulled down. Her cheeks colored red as she blushed so beautifully. "Hi," she murmured seductively.

Jason grinned wickedly, as he slid his hand up her side, his thumb grazing her nipple before as he skated up her body. He wrapped his hand around the side of her head, to cup her face. His other hand left her hip and slid up her back and wrapped around the back of her neck and pulled her toward him.

I had to stifle my groan as their mouths met and parted. I watched my buddy—my brother in arms—kiss the woman we had all been panting for all evening. Maya was utterly breathtaking as she sank into the kiss. Leaning forward, her hands slid from Jason's shoulders as her arms wrapped around him, and her body leaned into his.

The shy and skittish Maya we'd been flirting with all evening was gone, in its place was a vixen that was grinding her pelvis down against Jason's. He groaned low in his throat as his hand left her face and slithered down her body to grip her ass, squeezing it in his palm.

Fuck, I was jealous.

I wasn't about to ruin the moment, though. Maya had been skittish before, so I wouldn't scare her away now that she was finally caving.

She moaned loudly into Jason's mouth before she pulled away panting, her eyes closed as she tilted her head back to give Jason room as he kissed down her jaw to her neck, trailing wet open-mouthed kisses as he went.

Marcos sat up on his knees and moved toward them, settling behind Maya, his knees between Jason's legs. His hands skated up her bare thighs before they circled her hips. Maya's eyes opened as she felt him settle in behind her.

Wanton lust burned in Maya's golden eyes. She was absolutely awe-inspiring as she gasped softly, when she found Marcos so nearby. He took advantage of her surprise and covered her lips with his own.

With Marcos's head in the way, I could no longer see Maya's beautiful face. Feeling left out of the action, I shifted over, so I was sitting beside Jason.

I slid my hand in between Jason and Maya's body, gliding over her smooth belly and dipping under the waistband of her shorts and lace undies. I was met with gloriously bare and smooth skin. She was warm to touch and oh so soft. I had to bite back my groan as I rose up on to my knees to get a better angle, before I dragged my fingers through her soaking wet folds.

"So fucking wet for us," I murmured.

Maya whimpered. Sliding her hands down Jason's shoulders and chest, she wrapped her hand around my wrist and guided my hand lower, pushing me toward her core. "More," she mumbled, her voice thick with need.

Marcos lifted her to her feet in a show of strength. She barely got her feet under her unsteady feet before for Jason was yanking down her shorts and undies. She moaned as Marcos pushed her back down to her knees, straddling Jason once more.

"Shh," I soothed her, before I maneuvered my fingers through her slick heat. Entering her core with two long thick fingers, I set a slow torturous pace as Marcos and Jason continue to pepper her body with kisses.

Jason's hands slid from her face and ass to grab palmfuls of her generous tits, the tight crop top doing little to suppress the voluptuous mounds. He lifted the crop top over her head, tossing it aside, before he's hands returned to her tits. He lifted and squeezed them, as if trying to mold them like dough.

Maya panted as her breathing hitched in her throat as I found that soft spongy spot inside her. She leaned back against Marcos, giving him her weight, as she spread her thighs wider and made more room for my fingers. "Good girl," I murmured softly. A breathy moan left her lips, and I smirked. "Such a good girl for us."

Maya broke the frantic kiss with Marcos to gasp for breath. I circled my fingers inside her, pressing upwards, while I pressed down with the heel of my hand, grinding my hand into her clit. "Ohhh," she moaned softly.

"God damn, you are fucking gorgeous," Marcos muttered. He pressed a kiss against her temple but otherwise let her catch her breath.

"You going to come for me?" I asked.

"Please," she whimpered, her body tensing, going taut, her eyes squeezed shut.

Jason continued to kneed her breasts, occasionally pinching and rolling her nipples between his fingers.

Marcos skated a hand down her back, while the other one slipped around the base of her throat. He held her throat lightly, while his other hand slithered down her ass.

I watched Maya's face as I continued to slowly circle her g-spot with my fingers and rub her clit with my hand.

Her breathing was coming faster and she let out a gasp as one of Marcos's fingers joined mine inside her. Marcos kept his digit shallow, gathering her slickness and slowly pulling it back toward her rear entrance. "Oh fuck." She groaned softly as Marcos circled her rim.

"That's the idea, baby," Marcos muttered.

Maya

I was so high. The damn weed had me floating above my body looking down at the three hot-as-fuck men showering my body with attention. Nico's fingers in my cunt, circling my fucking g-spot were torturous—not to mention Marcos's new attention to my asshole.

I was so fucking close to coming, I never in my life got off so quickly before. "Oh fuck—" I moaned low and deep as Marcos slipped a digit past my tight ring of muscles and my pussy clenched down on Nico's fingers.

My orgasm rolled over me violently, my body shuddering between Jason and Marcos. Nico's fingers kept moving, though, riding me through my pleasure. I whimpered as I shook, the guys' hands gripping me tighter.

Jason gripped my jaw and pulled me in for a kiss, silencing my moans. My hands slid up his neck and held his face against mine and as I continued to ride the waves of pleasure that Nico and Marcos were inducing.

It had been a long time since anyone played with my ass, but I had always enjoyed it immensely. "You like that, Maya?" Marcos asked, his voice deep and low in my ear. "You like being sandwiched between the three of us? Us using your body, and making you come?" He squeezed his hand around my neck, cutting off my air supply.

Jason broke our kiss on a curse, as fluid squirted from me—soaking him—as my body shuddered again, another orgasm rolling over me even faster than the first. My mouth formed a silent scream and was quickly covered by Marcos's mouth. He released his grip on my neck, forcing me to suck in lungful's of air while he ravaged my mouth with his kiss.

I was light headed and limp in their hold, when Nico *finally* slid his fingers from my pussy.

"Hot damn." Nico laughed in awe.

I broke the kiss with Marcos, sliding down his torso, as I could no longer support my sated body. Opening my eyes, I saw the front of Jason's shirt was soaked through, the grey T-shirt slimy with my juices. The devilish grin on his beautifully handsome face was a whole other story though. "Did I squirt?" I asked sheepishly. I could feel my cheeks heating as the blush slid over my face.

"Fuck yeah you did, darlin'," Jason grinned. "Fucking hot."

I ducked my head, unable to meet his gaze. "I've never done that before."

"I've never seen that before, but don't you worry about it. It was the hottest thing I've ever seen," Jason reassured me. He pulled off his shirt and used it to clean my thighs and his abs but left most of my slick on my pussy.

"Talk to me, Maya," Marcos muttered in my ear. "You draw the line tonight. Are you okay with the three of us touching you? Fucking you?"

My eyes fluttered shut as I leaned back against him. I tilted my head back against his shoulder, letting my head fall toward his face as a low breathy moan slipped past my lips. I opened my eyes and looked up at him. "Yes."

"Thank fuck." Nico groaned and leaned in and captured my mouth in a rough kiss.

I groaned when he bit down roughly on my lower lip and reached out, sliding my fingers over the stubble on his jaw as I pulled my lips from between his teeth and kissed him back. It was hot and fast and borderline sloppy—OK it was really sloppy—but I wouldn't change it for the world.

Even after just having the best fucking orgasm of my life, my pussy clenching and dripping—I was aching for more.

Jason's hands slid up my thighs before they pressed between our bodies and worked at the button and zipper of his jeans.

I broke the kiss with Nico, breathless, needing to watch Jason open his fly. He was naked beneath his jeans, no boxers or underwear to be seen. And his cock was fucking glorious. He was thick and long and fucking hard as a rock. I gasped before I could stop myself.

He let out a low laugh. "Like what you see, darlin'?"

I nodded absently, eyes still on his dick.

"Been playing with the little boys at school too long. You ready for a real man?" He shot her a dirty wink.

I laughed, unable to stop myself, it burst from me as his stupid line broke through my daze. "Seriously? That's what you're going with? Some fuckin' 90's porn vibe?"

He grinned lazily, tilting his head back as he winked again. "Gonna work for you?"

"Does it usually work for *you*?" I shot back, grinning incredulously.

He shrugged nonchalantly, while reaching into his jeans and pulling out the monster that lay beneath. It was only after he pulled it out, did I see the piercings: a total six barbells pierced along the underside of his very large cock.

"Is that a Jacob's Ladder?" The awe was evident in my voice; I forced my jaw to shut as my mouth dropped open in disbelief.

Jason's grin was wide and full of male pride. I would have rolled my eyes had I not found the cocky grin so fucking hot. I leaned into him again, pressing my mouth against his. While kissing him,

I reached between our bodies and wrapped my hand around his pierced cock, gripping him firmly.

Jason groaned into our kiss, his massive hand wrapping around the side of my face, holding me to him as he thrusted into my hand. He pulled away a moment later, pushing his jeans over his hips. I rose up on my knees, helping him get the jeans off. It took some maneuvering and a hand from Marcos, but Jason was quickly naked and I was sinking back down onto his bare thighs.

My core throbbed, clenching down as if my body sensed how close it was to being impaled on that gloriously thick cock. I was briefly aware of Marcos and Nico stripping down as well. "You ever dabble in BDSM?" Nico asked from beside me.

I looked over to see his shaggy blond hair pushed out of his face, his blue eyes sparking despite the dim light. His lean body was ripped and tanned, a scattering of blond hair covered his chest and lower abdomen. Nico was kneeling back on his heels, his thick thighs coated in a fine layer of blond hair, with a trimmed patch of hair at the base of his equally impressive cock. "Fucking hell." I muttered the words, feeling a sense of fear for the first time that evening.

Were they all fucking hung like horses?

I looked over my shoulder to check out Marcos. He was shorter than Jason and Nico, but thicker and heavier. His Mexican heritage gave his skin an olive tone, his arms were covered in thick muscles and black tattoos, but his body was hair less, besides the small patch of black curls on his chest. He clearly manscaped everything down below. His cock was equally as impressive as his buddies, thick and long and ready to fuck me.

"Maya?" Nico ran a finger along my jaw, turning her face to look at him. He had a serious glint in his eye. "Did you hear me?"

"Uh, what's the question?" I swallowed thickly, unable to focus as my eyes trailed over him again. His golden skin was flawlessly beautiful.

"Have you ever dabbled with BDSM before?" Nico asked me again, his voice steady and even.

My mouth parted slightly in shock. "No," I murmured. I felt my cheeks heat as a blush rose across my skin.

"Do you know the basics of what it is?" Nico asked.

"Power play, submission and dominance. Bondage and pain." I replied.

Nico gave me a dazzling smile. "And if I told you the three of us were into that?"

I felt my heart racing in my chest. Marcos's hands slid around me, warm against my hips before they skated along my belly. "You want to tie me up and hurt me?" I asked, fear racing down my spine.

"Not tonight." Marcos murmured in my ear, his breath hot against my skin. "Maybe another time...pain can be sensual and enhance the pleasure."

A shiver slid over my body as the heat from his breath and hands mixed with the dirty words he spoke, clashed with the cool room around me.

"No, nothing so advanced tonight." Nico shook his head. "Tonight, you would just listen to us, move where we tell you, do what we say."

I licked my lips as his words drifted over me. Power play is what he was implying—they wanted to take control of me...and I wanted nothing more than to give it to them. "OK." I agreed.

A slow grin spread across Nico's sexy face. "No safe-words tonight. Tonight, you say no to something and we stop, OK?"

I nodded slowly, my mind racing a mile a minute trying to comprehend everything happening. It felt like everything was moving a million miles an hour, yet too slow at the same time. Marcos hands on my belly were rough and calloused as they rubbed against my smooth skin. His warmth embraced me as I leaned back against him as he pressed opened-mouth kisses down the side of my neck.

"Need to hear your words, darlin'," Jason said. His voice was low and gravelly, sending shivers down my spine. He gripped my thighs, rubbing his hands up and down my legs.

"Yes." I breathed shallowly, my breath catching in my throat. It was all almost too much. I needed them to really touch me, not just skate around it.

"Yes, sir," Jason corrected.

"Yes, sir." I immediately repeated.

"Good girl." Jason smirked.

Groaning, I jumped forward and kissed him again, my lips barely reaching his, as Marcos held me tightly against him.

Jason met me halfway though, his large hand cupping the side of my face again as he opened for me and kissed me passionately. My eyes closed as I lost myself to my senses. Jason's hands slid up from my thighs to my hips, before he slid my body forward. Marcos eased up on his hold, letting his buddy move me forward, so my bare pussy slid over the barbells of his dick.

"Oh fuck," I gasped, breaking the kiss.

Jason laughed wickedly before slid me forward further, my slick folds sliding over his piercings. My hands braced on his shoulders and ground down on him, my body's lubrication assisting me. "That's it, darlin'," Jason intoned. His voice a low spicy timbre that just drove me utterly wild. "Use my cock to make yourself come."

I whimpered, but did as he said.

"Have you ever had one back here?" Marcos asked. His fingers trailed over my back entrance, circling my puckered hole.

"Just once." My voice was breathy as I continued to rock on Jason's cock.

"Mm, baby, we're going to rock your world tonight." Marcos chuckled.

I couldn't respond. Nico wrapped his hand around my jaw again, and pulled me into a kiss. Marcos's hands were on my tits, squeezing them and tweaking my nipples. Jason's hands were heavy on my hips as he guided me back and forth over his pierced cock. Nico held my face to him, kissing me passionately, and stealing my breath away.

It was all too much, yet my body craved more. Needed more. I pulled away from the kiss, panting. "More. Please, more."

Jason let out a low chuckle before he guided me over the tip of his cock, before he notched himself in my cunt. Just the head of his thick dick was stretching me open. "Oh," I moaned and pushed down onto him. "That's it darlin', good girl."

I whimpered, my hands squeezing his shoulders as my body stretching to accommodate him.

"You're doing so well." Jason pulled my body down slowly over his cock, his hands on my hips guiding my way.

I was lost in the sensation of my body sliding over those piercings, that I didn't even notice when someone grabbed a bottle of lube, until I felt them squeeze a dollop onto my asshole. Shivering from the cold liquid hitting my back side, I dropped down the last several inches onto Jason's cock and groaned.

He hissed, his head falling back on his shoulders, clearly as effected by me as I was him. "So fucking tight," he bit out.

I was having problems breathing; I squeezed my eyes shut and tried to relax as the tip of Marcos's finger slid past my ring of muscles and inside me. His fingers, combined with Jason's cock was enough to drive me to the edge. I was barely hanging on to my senses as Marcos slid another finger into my back side and began to scissor open my hole.

"Fuck." I let the word out on a soft breath.

Marcos chuckled darkly behind me. "We're just getting started, baby."

Moaning softly, I swiveled my hips and Jason groaned loudly. "I'm not gonna last if you keep doing that," he grumbled.

I smiled and opened my eyes. The blatant need in Jason's eyes made me gasp. I had been feeling bold and sure of myself after my little hip swivel, but the lust in his gaze made me feel like I was going to self-combust. I shifted my hips, readying to swivel again, when someone slapped my ass.

"No," Nico said from my left.

The sting of the slap had my mouth dropping open in shock. "No?" I questioned.

Nico grinned wickedly and shook his head. "No, Maya. You aren't in charge here. You will wait patiently while Marcos preps your ass before they both will fuck you."

Still in shock, my mind not comprehending what I was hearing. "But—"

"No," Nico said again. He leveled me with stern expression that made me close my mouth and listen. "Good girl." He gave me a nod when he realized that I wasn't going to speak further.

Butterflies fluttered in my belly from his praise, something I'd never understood before—why praise made me feel so good.

Nico moved closer to me, taking a seat on the couch next to Jason—now low to the floor without the cushions on it—and spread his thighs. His impressive cock jutted out from the patch of blond hair and stood waiting for attention. "Come 'ere." He motioned for me to lean forward.

I licked my lips, my mouth watering, already knowing what he expected from me. His hand caressed the side of my face before he slid his fingers into my hair and guided me toward his cock, all while Marcos continue to scissor and twist his fingers in my ass.

"Good girl," Nico murmured.

Wrapping my lips around the head of his cock, I licked his tip, wetting it and tasting the salty precum already leaking from him. I moaned deeply when Marcos pulled his fingers out of my ass and squeezed more lube into and around my hole. A moment later the blunt head of his cock slipped inside me.

I gasped around Nico's dick, as Marcos thrusted, propelling me forward, causing me to swallow several more inches of Nico. "Fuuuuck," the three men groaned together.

I shivered as I thought about how I might look, pinned amongst them, in the middle of the living room where Lita or Kara could walk out and see us at any moment. It made me feel dirty, like a whore, and *that* made me come alive. I moaned low and deep around Nico's cock, hoping to spur the men into moving.

I desperately needed them to fuck me, and fuck me *now*. They took the hint, Jason and Marcos began to move. And it was heaven, utter fucking heaven. They moved slowly at first, figuring out a rhythm, before they picked up speed.

"Fuck, I can feel each fucking barbell," Marcos grunted.

Jason chuckled darkly. "You're welcome."

I was a moaning mess, barely able to contribute to Nico's blow job as he wrapped his fist around my hair and thrusted his hips up, and fucked into my mouth with little assistance from me. I only gagged once before I took a deep breath and opened my jaw wider, letting him slip into the back of my throat.

When my face was nestled in the patch of hair at his base, he groaned before he began to fuck me fully. I had one hand on his thigh and one hand on Jason's shoulder for support, but I was quickly losing my strength.

My orgasm ripped out of my body before I even felt the tingling in my spine. My entire body jerked and shuddered as the intense waves of pleasure rolled over me.

"Fucking hell." Jason grunted as I clamped down on both him and Marcos.

"Oh fuck." Marcos swore, his fingers on my hips clamping down.

"So fucking good. Don't stop." Nico panted, his fingers tightening in my hair.

I was lost to my pleasure, barely realizing when his dick twitched in my mouth. He pulled back far enough for me to breathe before he came with a groan, flooding my mouth with his cum. Moaning, I swallowed him down, lapping at his slit for more.

I swiveled my hips and smirked as both Jason and Marcos swore again, before they sped up their pace. It wasn't long before the both of them were tensing and jerking with their orgasm. Nico finally let go of my hair and I slowly pulled off his cock, licking my lips.

I swayed, unsteady, as I tried to sit upright.

Jason's and Marcos's hands were there to steady me, as I swayed. "Easy," Marcos muttered.

I leaned back against his chest and sighed.

"You were fucking amazing," Jason murmured.

I smiled lazily and closed my eyes. I could easily fall asleep between them. Groaning as Marcos slowly pulled out of me and pushed me forward against Jason. I snuggled into him, resting my face in the crook of neck, while he wrapped his arms around me and held me gently.

"So fucking good for us," Jason whispered into my ear. He pressed a kiss to my temple and ran his hand down my spine.

A moment later, Marcos returned to the living room with a warm washcloth in his hand. The guys helped me slide off Jason's cock and sprawl out on the cushions. Marcos cleaned my folds before he tossed the rag at Jason, to clean himself with.

Exhausted and feeling good, I rolled to my side, facing Jason and promptly passed out.

The next morning, I woke feeling beautifully sore and rested. It was still dark in the living room, and I was nestled between a still sleeping Jason and Nico. I glanced around, finding Marcos asleep on the other side of Nico. My bladder forced me out of the cocoon of warmth I was surrounded in.

I moved carefully, as to not wake the sleeping men, and found my clothes folded on the arm of the couch. I scooped them up and walked quickly into the bathroom. I used the facilities before I eyed the shower. Looking around, I found extra towels in a linen closet and decided a shower was in my best interest.

Sweaty, sticky, and sore from the night before, I reveled in the hot water cascading over my body. Using the products in the shower, I washed quickly with a clean washcloth I had grabbed when finding a towel. I was just rinsing off, when the door opened and Marcos walked in.

His dark eyes were hooded as he closed the door behind him. Only wearing boxers, he quickly shed them before he slid open the glass door and stepped into the shower with me. I kept quiet, not moving from under the stream of water as he stepped toward me—only to hiss in pain and jump back.

I smirked.

"Jesus fucking *Christ*!" he whisper-yelled. Thankfully he kept his voice down and didn't wake up Lita or Kara.

"It's barely even warm, you big baby," I shot at him.

"Fucking spawn of Satan."

I laughed quietly and tilted my head back in the warm water, enjoying the feel of it loosening my stiff muscles.

Marcos stepped into me, using my body to shield himself from the scalding water, he reached around me to turn the temperature down. I didn't move as he pressed against me, wrapping his arms around my back. Leaning over me, he bent his head down and pressed his lips against mine in a gentle kiss.

I sighed and leaned into him, sliding my hands up his now wet chest and around his neck. Moaning softly as he opened his mouth and our kiss turned more passionate, I reminded myself to keep quiet. I did *not* want to wake Lita. How embarrassing would that be? It was bad enough that I fucked three guys on the living room floor, where anyone could have walked in on. But waking up Marco's mom while I was in the shower, naked with her son... not on my list of things to do for the day.

Marcos on the other hand, had his own agenda. He picked me up and I immediately wrapped my legs around his waist. I had to stifle a gasp when my back hit the cold wall of the shower. Marcos snuck a hand between our bodies to slide a finger through my folds, checking my wetness, before he grabbed his cock and slowly slid inside me.

I moaned softly, digging my nails into his shoulders as I clung to him. I was still swollen and sore from the night before, but his cock was caressing all my most intimate places, and drove me wild. "Fuck," I gasped, breaking our kiss.

He kissed his way down my jaw to my neck, sucking wet kisses into my skin. He fucked me slowly, sensually, setting a lazy pace that was quickly pushing me toward the edge. My breathing picked up, as the tell-tale tingle gathered in my spine.

Marcos captured my lips again, just as my walls clamped down on him and I came with a low groan into his mouth. He swallowed down my cries as his hips thrusted faster, chasing his own orgasm. It wasn't long after he was following me over the edge, his knees almost buckling, as his release reared out of him.

We broke our kiss, panting for air. I leaned my head back against the shower wall and watched him. He slowly opened his dark eyes and rubbed a hand over his dark buzzed hair. "Maya, you're amazing," he murmured in awe.

I blushed slightly and had to look away when the reverence in his stare was too much. "Do the three of you do that often?" I asked, changing the subject.

"Do what?"

"Fuck women at the same time?"

His fingers wrapped around my chin, guiding my face up to look at him. "Yes, there's been others," he admitted, his eyes serious. "But never like that."

I wondered what he meant by that, but someone was knocking on the door. "You about done in there?" Kara asked softly from the other side of the door.

"Yeah," I replied. I pulled away from Marcos, ignoring his probing stare. I grabbed my towel and quickly wrapped it around myself.

Marcos shut off the water while I dressed quickly into my pjs. I tossed Marcos a clean towel from the linen closet and used mine to wrap my hair up. Once I was sure the two of us were covered, I snuck out of the warm bathroom and across the hall to Kara's bedroom.

Kara gave me a sleepy grin when I walked in. "Have fun?"

I sighed and leaned back against the door, feeling star-struck. "You have no idea."

Kara just laughed. "My mom will be up soon. I just wanted to make sure you guys were decent and covered before she got up. Nothing like walking out to a pile of naked bodies in the living room."

I giggled and moved away from the door.

"Come to bed." Kara patted the mattress next to her. "It's too early to be awake."

I grinned and took a seat next to her. Grabbing my backpack off the floor, I pulled out my hair brush and quickly brushed out my long locks. From the hallway I could hear Marcos leaving the bathroom and heading back out to the hall. "We weren't loud last night, were we?"

"Girl, I put in headphones and have no idea."

I yawned and put my brush away. With my hair brushed out, I wrapped it up like I was going to put it in a clip, then laid down next to Kara, using a spare pillow. I'd only gotten a couple hours of sleep, I could use some more, and maybe avoid an awkward morning after with Marcos, Jason, and Nico. I didn't know where I stood with them, and wasn't about to get my heart broken over a one-night stand.

Thankfully, that wasn't the case, because when me and Kara woke up several hours later and headed out to the living room, we found it empty and cleaned up, the cushions put back to rights and the blankets put away. On the coffee table in the middle of the room, there was a folded piece of paper with my name on it. Opening it, I found a short note saying, "Had a great time." Next to the scrawled chicken scratch was their names and numbers, all three of them.

I tucked the note in my pocket, deciding I'd figured out what to do with them later.

Maya

I DECIDED NOT TO call or text the guys after our night together. I left things as they were and went back to school feeling like a million bucks. I'd had a great Thanksgiving break, and despite my parents being the usual dicks, I was in great spirits.

Kara invited me to Christmas, but I declined. My sister had managed to get time off, and the two of us were heading to Florida for some fun in the sun.

The second semester of school flew by for me. I started my nursing clinicals, and between that, work, school, and time at the clinic, I barely had time for friends. I caught up with Kara, Stephanie, Arturo and Karma every other Friday night when my friends dragged me out of my dorm room. Terri went out most nights without me, but still it was nice catching up with her without the stress of cramming homework between our conversations.

By the end of the school year, I was ready to be done. Even though I had signed up for eight weeks of summer school to put me on track to graduate on time and not need an extra semester like so many other students usually did, I still got three weeks of freedom between my semesters.

It was the last day of living in the dorms for most, so many students were moving out and packing up. Me and Terri had already signed the papers to keep our dorm for the next year, and I paid for my summer tuition so I didn't have to move out for the summer. It made things so much easier and gave us time to hang out with our friends while they packed up.

I was down in the freshman floor, helping Kara pack up. Marcos would be coming down with a truck to help her take all her stuff home for the summer break. I wasn't sure how I felt about seeing him again, after everything since Thanksgiving. I never called him or his friends after our night together. Kara had assured me he was fine with it, but I still felt bad.

I hadn't wanted to cause any drama between me and Kara, nor did I want to cause any drama between Kara and her brother. Truth of the matter was, I just didn't have the time for a relationship right now, not with how packed my schedule was. I barely even had time for my friends.

There was a knock on the dorm door, startling Kara and I out of our conversation of summer plans while we packed. I continued packing Kara's books, while she opened the door. "Hey," Marcos's deep voice said.

I looked over my shoulder to find not only Marcos but also Jason and Nico standing behind him in the doorway. My heart leapt in my chest as I forced a smile to my lips and stood up to greet them properly. "Hey guys."

Marcos smiled easily at me as he moved into the room. He hugged his sister, before he moved on and hugged me warmly. "Hey, Maya."

"Hey, Marcos." I savored his hug, loving every moment of being back in his arms. Glancing over Marcos's shoulder, I found Jason watching me with an eyebrow raised, his gray eyes giving nothing else away.

Nico was smiling broadly though, as he entered Kara's dorm room. It was a tight fit with the five of us already in there. Stephanie had moved out the day before, but she and Kara would be back on my floor when they returned in the fall.

I pulled away from Marcos's as Nico barreled past Jason, pushing him out of the way, and wrapped his arms around me, lifting me in a bone tight hug. "Hey," I murmured, holding him just as tight.

"Hi, beautiful." Nico's voice was soft and right next to my ear. "You've been a bad girl."

I chuckled softly. "Punish me later?"

"Careful," Jason warned, his gaze stern. "You don't know what you're asking for."

"And sister is still in the room!" Kara exclaimed, shaking her head.

Marcos laughed and smacked my ass. I jumped, startled, and yelped.

Kara groaned and grabbed a box. "I'm going to the car. Don't fuck on my bed."

I immediately blushed, my cheeks going hot as embarrassment rolled over me.

Marcos laughed again and pressed against my back, pushing me into Nico. "Fucking hell, you smell amazing."

"I just want to eat you," Nico groaned. He bit down gently on the side of my neck, making me groan low in my throat.

"Did you get our note?" Jason asked.

"Straight for the jugular, huh?" I asked, eyeing him warily.

"Darlin', you have no idea," Jason muttered. He still looked stone face, and I wondered if he was pissed that I hadn't called or texted.

"Note received, but I didn't think we were doing anything more than having fun," I said, trying to deflect his anger.

"Can't have fun if there's no contact," Jason shot back.

I smiled, "You miss me?" I pulled away from Nico and Marcos and pressed myself into Jason's chest. "You wanted to see me again?"

Jason rolled his eyes, but his hands rested on my hips, holding me tightly. "I didn't say that."

"But you did, without using the actual words." I grinned up at him. "Am I in trouble, big guy?"

He growled before he captured my lips in a filthy, passionate kiss. I moaned and wrapped my arms around him, holding on tight as he lifted me. Wrapping my legs around his waist, I fiercely kissed him back.

I felt my phone being tugged out of my back pocket and didn't even care. They would find that I did indeed add their numbers, but never texted them.

Clinging to Jason as he took a seat on Kara's bed, I found myself straddling his lap once again. "This feels familiar," I murmured, breaking their kiss.

"Too many clothes for it to be familiar," Jason shot back.

There was a loud knock on the dorm door, before Kara yelled out. "Are you decent?"

"No," I called back, before I slowly slid off Jason's thighs.

"Too bad, I'm coming in," Kara grinned wickedly as she walked in the room.

I blushed but rolled my eyes at my friend's antics.

Two hours later we had packed up all of Kara's stuff into Marcos's Chevy pickup truck. "Come on, Maya, we're getting lunch," Marcos called to me as he finished tying down the boxes in the bed of the truck.

Nico wrapped an arm around my shoulders before I could back out. He led me around the side of the truck. He opened the backdoor and waited for me to climb up into the crew cab truck. When Jason climbed in the other door, and Nico followed me in the back, I was surprised, yet not surprised, to find myself sandwiched between the two men on the bench seat.

On cue, as the doors shut, they both spread their thighs out, taking up all the available space in the back. I rolled my eyes at their predictability, but decided to play with fire, setting my hands on both their thighs and squeezing just above the knee.

"Shit," Nico yelped, flinching away.

Jason jumped as well, but kept quiet.

I smirked as I suddenly had all the leg space available to me, and spread out.

"No hanky-panky in the back seat," Kara said.

"Wouldn't dream of it," I replied.

By the time we reached the bar Marcos wanted to have lunch at, I was a dripping mess in my jean shorts. There was no way I was going to be able to sit through lunch with one of my best friends and not flirt back, or touch, the men around me. It was going to be torture on another level.

Marcos parked the truck and everyone started climbing out. As I turned to get out on Nico's side, Jason snaked a finger through my belt loops and yanked me back. I let out a quiet yelp, and Nico smirked as he shut the door in my face.

Jason pulled me back, so I was on my hands and knees on the bench seat with my ass in the air. "You've been naughty, haven't you, darlin'?"

I gasped as the sound of his deep voice sent shivers racing down my spine. *God damn this man's voice.*

His fingers slid up my thighs and into my shorts, pushing my thong to the side, he sunk two fingers into my sopping core in one hard thrust of his wrist.

"Oh fuck."

"Dirty, dirty whore," Jason muttered. "I bet you've been thinking about taking us all day, haven't you? This greedy little cunt has been crying for attention since we showed, hasn't?"

"Yes," I whimpered, unable to deny it any further.

I heard the hit before I felt the pain—the sharp smack to my ass—as Jason growled. "You'll address me as, sir."

"Yes, sir," I replied immediately. I moaned as his hand rubbed over my stinging flesh, soothing away the pain.

"You're going to let me fuck you in this truck."

It was a statement, not a question, yet I found myself answering anyways. "Yes, sir."

He chuckled darkly before he pulled his hand from my cunt. His other hand slid around my waist and started unbuckling my shorts. I quickly helped him, my core clenching for his pierced cock. My shorts were yanked down to my knees a second before he slammed into me.

The way my soul left my body as each and every piercing dragged over my clit and then my g-spot upon entry—and the silent scream I let out as I dropped to my elbows. He didn't give me a moment to catch my breath or get accommodated to his size before he pulled back out and pounded into me.

"Jason," I cried out.

The smack to my ass should have been expected, but I jumped all the same. "Excuse me?"

"Sir," I mumbled.

He spanked me again. "Don't forget it again."

I whimpered and fell from my elbows to my chest on the back seat, leaving my ass in the air and at his mercy. His fingers dug into my hips as he used my body as he pleased, pistoning in and out like a god damn jack hammer.

"So fucking tight," he grunted.

I was a mewling, whimpering mess. Tears poured down my face. Never in my life had I felt such pleasure—besides my last time with them. Jason knew exactly how to touch me. His pierced fucking cock stroked every damn erogenous zone inside me. I could feel myself leaking down my thighs—I was so fucking close.

A keening wail left my lips as slammed into me harder. My orgasm crashed over me, my body shaking as my cunt clamped down on him.

He groaned, following me over the edge, his hips stuttering to a stop.

We panted as we caught our breath, Jason still inside me. I sighed as my entire body relaxed into the seat cushion. Jason rubbed a hand over my back, before he slowly pulled out. I groaned as each piercing rubbed against my delicate skin. "Fuck."

"You're so fucking beautiful." His voice was soft, sending shivers down my spine. "I want to live inside your cunt."

I huffed out a laugh and slowly sat up. I could already feel his cum leaking out of me. The bathroom would need to be my first stop inside the restaurant. Balking at the thought of pulling up my thong through the mess that Jason left behind, I pulled off my jeans and thong entirely and used the scrap of fabric to clean myself up the best I could. I dropped the thong to the seat of the truck, I'd have to grab it when they took me home, but I couldn't wear it any longer. Wincing when I was put back together, I sighed and ran my fingers through my hair.

"Ready?" Jason asked.

I looked over to see him sitting there, calmly watching me. I shrugged a shoulder. "As ready as I'll ever be."

He gave me a winning smile that lit up his gray eyes, making him utterly breathtaking.

I was so figuratively and literally *fucked.*

The restaurant was busy with families of students having one last meal before they hit the road home for the summer. Beelining for the bathroom, I waved at several friends in the crowd before I ducked out of sight.

In the bathroom, I hit a stall and used the facilities before I mopped things up more than I'd been able to in the truck. The short walk into the restaurant had already soaked the inseam of my jean shorts—nothing that'd be noticeable from the back but sitting with the seam pulled taunt against my own seam, was going to be the most uncomfortable hour of my life. I prayed that lunch would be fast and that I could go back to my dorm to change.

When I finished in the bathroom, I washed my hands and headed back out to the bustling barroom. I was stopped a grand total of five times, before I made it to the table where Kara sat with her brother and his friends. I could feel their eyes on me as I moved around the room, but I was sad to see friends go for the summer, or forever. I had several friends that had graduated already, and who knew when or if I'd see them again.

By the time I made it to the table, there was already a vodka sprite sitting at the open spot of the table, nestled between Nico and Marcos. My smile was wide as I took my seat and reached for my drink.

"I ordered for you already. Your usual." Kara smirked at me.

I blushed. "Thanks."

"No worries," Kara replied.

A hand came down on my bare thigh, making me jump. Looking down, I saw it belonged Nico, his devious grin was panty-melting and set my core on fire all over again. I'd never been so horny immediately after fucking before. These three men would be the death of me, and they weren't even mine.

Just get through lunch, then you can go home and change.

Nico left his hand on my thigh throughout lunch, not moving it besides the gentle caressing of his fingers. It was distracting. I tried to keep up with the conversation between Kara and Marcos, who were laughing and carefree as they spoke of their summer plans. Kara's relationship with her brother was usually a little more tense, but it was great to see them both in good moods and joking with each other.

Jason kept shooting me sexy smirks that drove me wild, paired with a wink every time I shifted in my chair.

Our food came and as everyone started digging in, Marcos turned to me. "Maya, what are your plans for the summer?"

I shrugged and sipped my drink, grateful for the distraction. "I'm staying here for the summer semester, work as many clinical hours I can get, along with class. It should put me on track to graduate on time next year."

"Would you not be on time?" Nico asked.

"The nursing program is just so grueling, it's not uncommon for most nursing students to take another semester to finish. I'm hoping by cramming this summer, I won't have to do that."

"What kind of nurse do you plan on being?" Jason asked.

"Either trauma or critical care."

"Where would those put you?" Marcos asked.

"Trauma would be ER, and critical is ICU."

"What are you leaning toward?" Nico asked.

"Most likely critical. The ER is rough and lot of gunshot wounds, especially in Mourningside…" I trailed off, not wanting to go deeper into it. I had a crazy amount of respect for ER nurses, but they were a different breed. Critical care would offer a little more stability especially when it came to scheduling.

"Aren't you planning to do travel nursing?" Kara asked.

I nodded. "Yep. I'll probably do a year or two locally, then sign on with an agency. Travel nurses pay so much better, and you can pick your contracts, and travel and see the country."

"Sounds like a beautiful plan, Little Dreamer," Nico said softly, his eyes almost sad.

A blush spread across my face at the nickname. It was insanely sweet, and I didn't know how to respond to him. A lull fell over the table as we ate our food. I savored my burger and fries, knowing it probably would be a couple months before I would be back at the bar/restaurant. All too soon we were filing back into the truck and heading back to the dorms to drop me off. "Thanks for lunch," I said when Marcos pulled up near the door.

"No problem," Kara grinned cheekily, knowing her brother paid. "I'll text you this week."

"Yep," I agreed. "See you guys." I jumped out of the truck before the three men could say anything. I didn't want things weird between them. I had a feeling I'd be seeing them a lot in the next year or so, as long as me and Kara were friends.

I was just closing my dorm room door behind me, when it got caught on something. Looking down, I found someone's foot kicked between the door and the jam—fucking Nico was grinning back at me when I met his gaze. "You forget something?" I asked him.

"Yep. Sure did." He grinned cockily and pushed his way through the door. He closed it and locked it behind him. "Stone's not the only one who's getting laid today."

"Stone?"

"Jason. It's a... nickname." Nico shrugged and stalked toward me.

I smirked. "And what is your nickname, hotshot?"

"Dagger."

I laughed. "And Marcos?"

"Usually just Marcos, but sometimes he goes by Killer."

I froze, licking my lips, feeling my grin slide off her face. "Seriously?"

Nico wasn't smiling. He was serious.

I frowned, but didn't have time to respond before Nico wrapped his hand around the back of my neck and hauled me into him. The kiss was passionate and demanding. It was different than our first time together, just as Jason had been different than our first night together. "Nico," I gasped, when he broke the kiss and began undressing me.

"You smelt of sex the whole time we were in the restaurant. All I wanted to do was sink balls deep into this glorious cunt."

Nico shoved my shorts down my thighs, before he spun me around and bent me over the side of my bed. He sheathed himself inside me in one powerful thrust that rocked me forward.

I gasped at the bite of pain, despite still being wet from Jason, Nico wasn't small by any means, and I was still swollen from before. "Fuck," I groaned.

"That's the plan, Little Dreamer." His thrusts grew more frantic, hard and deeper than before.

Curling my fingers into my bedspread, I pushed back against him, fucking him as well.

"Fuck, you're so good," he mumbled, his breath hitching. He was hitting my g-spot with every thrust, making me moan and cry out as he fucked me harder.

"Nico!" I shouted as my orgasm rolled over me.

"Fuuuuck." He groaned a moment later, his body jerking to a halt as his own orgasm rocked him. "Fucking hellll."

I chuckled softly as I collapsed onto my bed, my body no longer able to hold me up. Nico placed a gentle kiss to the side of my neck before he slowly pulled out of me.

"I've gotta go, they're waiting in the truck."

I laughed and stood up slowly, my knees still weak. I sat down on my bed, facing him, watching as he buttoned up his pants. My heart was still beating wildly in my chest, but I felt light as he bent down to kiss me.

"Answer us when we text you." Nico's face was inches from mine, his orders clear.

I tucked my hair behind my ear and shrugged. "We'll see... I'm busy you know."

Nico nipped at my bottom lip, gripping my chin between his thumb and forefinger, holding my mouth to his. "Make the time, Maya."

"Bossy," I shot back.

"You have no idea, Little Dreamer."

My heart pounded in my chest and butterflies danced in my stomach. *This man is sex on wheels and he fucking knows it.*

He kissed me again, before he left my room, leaving my heart and body a mess.

Maya

"LET'S GO! FIRST ROUNDS on me!" I yelled to my friends as they walked into the hole-in-the wall bar in Rockwell. The Squirrel Cage was a local townie bar that we had found when Arturo and Karma had bought a house in their hometown of Rockwell, located about an hour from the school.

So many weekends we found ourselves out in the country, enjoying the small-town life around Arturo's and Karma's. The Squirrel Cage also didn't card, which was great for Kara and Stephanie, who were in their second year of college—only nineteen years old—and couldn't get in most bars we went to. The bar was also down the road from our friend's house, so we could walk back and pass out on the floor or couch, or if you were lucky enough, the guest bedroom.

After drinks were ordered, Stephanie, Karma, Terri, and Arturo hit the dance floor, leaving Kara and I behind to sip our drinks and watch our friends'. "Hey, Marcos mentioned he hadn't heard from you in a while. Everything OK?" Kara asked.

I glanced over at her, trying to gauge her thoughts on things. Shrugging, I sighed and said, "I dunno. It's fun talking to them, but I don't want to lead them on. Like the sex is good, but I don't plan on being in Mourningside long term."

"So tell them that! So they leave me alone!" Kara gave me an annoyed look.

I laughed. "They've been that bad?"

"Girl, you have no idea. Like fucking whooped."

My heart sunk to my stomach. "Fuck."

"Yeah. Girl, I told you I don't care either way. You do you, boo. My brother and his friend's obsession aside—you have plans for yourself. Don't let a little dick get in your way."

"The dicks aren't little," I shot back, smirking.

"Oh gross!" Kara yelled and reached for her drink. "I need to wash out my ear drums!"

I laughed and tossed back my own drink, feeling great. Summer break had been long and grueling, and having my friends back with the fall semester was just the rejuvenation I'd needed. School had been back in session for two months and it was quickly nearing the Thanksgiving break.

Marcos, Nico, and Jason had been texting me all summer, randomly or nonstop at times. I enjoyed talking to them, but I never made it home over the summer break like I planned, instead I headed to Chicago and spent my time off with my sister. I'd only gotten three weeks before and after summer school, and I wanted to soak up as much time with my sister as I could.

The guys seemed to understand, but they weren't dating either, so I didn't feel the need to explain it to them. Dorm move-in day had fallen on a Tuesday, and I was working at the clinic as a CNA—certified nursing assistant—so I had missed Marcos, Nico, and Jason when they helped Kara move into the dorm.

Marcos:

Where are you?

Maya:

At work, why?

Jason:

Cause we're here, and you aren't.

Nico:

We were hoping to see you.

Marcos:

What time you get off?

That had been the extent of their conversation, and I hadn't heard from them since then, and that had been two months ago. I hadn't been bothered. Life was busy. School, work, and clinicals took up most of my time. When I wasn't studying, I was squeezing in as much of the *college experience* as I could with my friends. It was my final year, I'd be graduating in the spring, and I just needed to buckle down and concentrate for a little bit longer.

I hit the dance floor when Arturo came back to our table. He'd watch our drinks while I had fun with our friends. I fucking loved nights like these, where everyone was together. There was a loud cheer from my friends when Kyle and Travis walked the crowded bar. They had another man with them, one I hadn't met yet, but by the looks of him, I was hoping to.

Hunter was his name, and he was lean and muscular, with black shaggy hair and piercing green eyes. He had a rugged jawline covered in a hint of a beard. He was pre-med and had met Travis and Kyle in biology.

It was all I needed to know to wind up in Karma's guest room with the dude, after the evening spent drinking. The sex had been decent, hard and fast, and he'd gotten me off—which was better than most of the guys I'd slept with—but something had been missing.

It was good enough for me though. We met up a couple of times after that before we both agreed that life was too busy for anything more than casual, but we also didn't feel the need to see other people. So I felt it was only fair I gave the guys a heads up.

Kara:

I met someone.

It didn't surprise me when I didn't hear anything back from them.

Kara had invited me home for Thanksgiving again that year, but I had to decline. My clinical hours were ramping up, and I was working every day during Thanksgiving break. I wouldn't have time to go home for the Holiday.

Instead, Hunter threw some turkey legs in the crock pot, and heated up some Stove Top, and we did our own low-key version of Thanksgiving together in his dorm room. The food had only been alright, and the company decent. I sorely missed Lita's homecooked meal, and the company more.

I was surprised though when the group chat had lit up, late that night.

Marcos:

You should have been here.

Jason:

Don't think you're not in trouble.

Nico:

We're cooking up your punishment.

My heart had hammered in my chest as I read their messages. Even after telling them that I was seeing someone, they still wanted me.

Playing with fire, I texted back.

Maya:

Yes, sir.

Maya

THE WEEKS BETWEEN THANKSGIVING and Christmas were always busy and chaotic as hell. I hadn't heard from the guys since Thanksgiving, but I hadn't reached out either. Things with Hunter had been decent enough, if not a little boring and predictable. He was great, and things were easy, but I'd be lying if I wasn't missing the spark that was between me and Marcos, Jason, and Nico.

It was the weekend before Christmas break and all through the campus people were partying...

I laughed at my own joke, even if it were true. Everyone *was* partying, including me and my friends. We were a little more low-key though, compared to the rest of the campus. Out at Arturo's and

Karma's house, my group of friends were drinking and playing cards, smoking weed and eating munchies, all while laughing and having a good time.

The small ranch style home Arturo and Karma had bought over the summer was a simple two-bedroom starter home. Both of them were a year older than me, but I had met Karma in the nursing program and had learned a lot from her over the years. Her and her husband Arturo were high school sweet hearts, who everyone thought would be pregnant by now. Karma had rolled her eyes every time someone brought it up, but she had no plans of being pregnant any time soon. Arturo was on his last year of Architect school and Karma was working full time at Mourningside General already, driving the hour south three days a week.

New adult life was tough, but we made it work and still managed to keep in contact with old friends. Our group and I tried to visit every other weekend. With Arturo and Karma living an hour south of campus, we all had to make an effort to spend the night, or someone had to suck it up and be the designated driver.

Regardless, the evening was everything I wished for and more when I got time to hang out with my friends. Terri and Travis were dancing around the living room, while Kyle and Kara headed outside to smoke. Stephanie, Karma, and Hunter were in the kitchen making more drinks, or snacks as was the case for Karma. She was making me a snack, since I'd drawn the short straw and was the designated driver for Kara, Stephanie, and Terri.

Sitting at the table with Arturo, my good buddy, I laughed as he told me the jokes he was considering for his stand-up comedy gig. He finally going to hit the stage at school for amateur night and see how a crowd of strangers reacted to his jokes vs his best friends. "I don't know man," I laughed shaking my head. "You're funny, anyone will see that."

The phone on the table beside me rang, but I ignored it, it wasn't mine.

"You say that, but I think you're biased." Arturo shook his head and ran his hand over his face.

"Bullshit dude, you have all of us rolling every time we see you!" I argued.

Arturo shook his head and ran his hand through his short black hair, slicking it back before he pulled his hat over his head.

Kara's phone continued to ring on the table beside me.

"You should answer that," Arturo said, nodding toward the phone.

It had already stopped ringing, so I shrugged. I was stoned and feeling lazy. "Not my phone. It's Kara's."

"Bet it's important," Arturo said.

When it rang again, I picked it up. Turning it over, I saw it was Marcos and frowned, answering it quickly. "Marcos, hey, it's Maya."

"Where's Kara? I need to speak to her." Marcos's voice was thick with emotion, his words rushed.

"She's outside. Is everything OK?" I quickly stood up; phone pressed to my ear.

"No. I need—" Marcos choked up, like he was stifling a sob.

My heart plummeted to my stomach as a chill went down my spine. *Something was wrong.* "Hold on, let me find her." Rushing toward the back patio door, I heard Marcos sniff and clear his throat.

Opening the door, I looked around the back porch, cursing when I didn't immediately see Kara and Kyle. "Fuck," I grunted. Turning around, I closed the door and rushed to the front door.

I threw open the front door, startling Kara and Kyle mid make-out session. They jumped apart as I rushed forward. "Kara, it's Marcos." I pushed the phone at her, knowing I probably looked frazzled—because I was.

I'd never heard Marcos sound like that before, and it tore at my heart.

"Marcos?" Kara asked.

I hovered, not giving my friend space to speak to her brother. I needed answers.

"What do you mean? Mom?" Kara choked out.

My heart broke as I watched Kara's face fall, before her whole body fell as her knees buckled and Kara collapsed onto the front porch.

"Shit," Kyle swore, swooping in to catch Kara before she could hit the concrete.

I jumped with him, grabbing the phone as it ground. "What happened?"

"Mom's—" A sob tore out of her.

Carlita is gone. I just knew it in my heart, the panic in Marcos's voice, Kara's knee-buckling reaction—I just knew it.

I wrapped my arms around Kara and held her tightly, "I've got you." I looked down at the phone in my hand and saw the call with Marcos was still connected. "Hey Marcos," I murmured softly, "we're going to call you back in a little bit, OK?"

Marcos cleared his throat. "Yeah, Maya. Thanks." His voice was thick, the tears evident.

I ended the call and tucked the phone in my back pocket. "Come girl. Let's get you in the house."

Kyle and I helped Kara to her feet, sobs wracking her body as we guided her in the house. Kara was inconsolable, and I felt helpless. Our friends were startled as they took on the scene, as everyone realized that something serious had happened after I had rushed outside.

"What happened?" Stephanie asked, her eyes wide, as she rushed to Kara's side.

I shook my head and mouthed, *her mom.*

Stephanie's eyes widened in shock. Karma gasped from the dining room.

"What happened?" Arturo's deep voice carried from the dining room of the open concept layout.

I ignored them as I held and rocked my devasted friend.

Eventually Kara's sobs slowed and she pushed away from me. "I need to go home."

I nodded, jumping to my feet. "I'll drive you."

Kara didn't respond, just stood from the couch and headed to the door without saying goodbye to our friends.

I quickly grabbed my coat. "I'll text you guys later," I said, glancing at my friends as I stuffed my feet into my shoes.

"Are you guys going straight south?" Stephanie asked.

"Probably. I'll text later." I rushed out of the house, heading straight for my car at the end of the driveway.

The drive south to Mourningside from Arturo's and Karma's only took an hour. In the middle of the night, I made it in forty-five minutes. I had called Marcos from Kara's phone once we hit the road. Kara hadn't spoken once on the drive; silent sniffles and occasional sobs filled the car. I kept the music low and the peddle on the floor.

When we pulled into the parking lot of Carlita's apartment complex, I immediately saw Marcos, Jason, and Nico standing in front of the building, smoking cigarettes. I turned the car into an empty spot right in front of them. I barely had the car in park before Kara was throwing the door open and rushing to her brother.

I sighed, watching the siblings embrace. My heart hurt, tears prickled my own eyes as I shut off the car. I slowly unbuckled my seat belt, wondering if I should stay, or just head back to school.

Nico came around the driver's side and opened the door for me. I slowly unfurled my body and stood from my Honda Civic. Nico pulled me into his arms, holding me tight. Leaning into him, I let him take my weight and bear some of my burdens. My body was wound tight after my tense drive, my belly an anxious mess of nerves. Holding onto him, I let out a deep breath, savoring his warmth in the cold night.

"Come on, let's get inside," Nico murmured.

I pulled away, glancing over my shoulder at Kara and Marcos. Neither one was paying attention to anyone but each other, and they deserved their privacy. Nico patted me on the back and pulled away. I followed him and Jason toward the stairs, briefly recognizing that Nico's hair was much longer than the last time I'd seen him—now reaching the middle of his back.

After two years of coming to Kara and Lita's apartment, it was like coming home. It certainly felt more like home that living with my own parents did. We let ourselves into Lita's apartment and I glanced around the living room, expecting Lita to come walking out of the kitchen, drying her hands on a dish towel—like she'd greeted me so often in the short time that I'd known the women.

A sob tore out me and I tried to stifle it, but it was too late. Jason reached for me before Nico could, pulling me toward him.

He wrapped me in his arms before he scooped down and picked me up bridal style. He walked over to the couch and sat down, arranging me in his lap and holding me tight as I was overcome with emotions.

I buried her face into the crook of Jason's neck and let out all the emotions I had bottled up on the drive there. I had been strong for Kara on the way there, Kara had needed her family, but now that I was able to relax, I felt like I had come home too. I let the emotions pour out of me, my tears soaking Jason's neck and shirt collar. I didn't care. His arms around me were the safe space I needed, along with Nico's heat as he took a seat beside us.

A while later, I heard footsteps outside the door before it swung open. I scrambled to ease my breathing and wipe my tears as the door opened and Kara and Marcos walked in the living room. Kara rushed for her bedroom, but Marcos stood in the doorway, stoic and staring after his sister, looking utterly lost and helpless.

I rose from Jason's lap and walked around the couch to greet Marcos. He took one look at me before his face crumpled and he wrapped me in a tight embrace, pulling me into him. "I'm so sorry." My voice was broken, but I had to say the words, even once, even if they were meaningless in the grand scheme of things. Being sorry would not bring his mother back, being sorry would not cure the pain.

Marcos sobbed into my shoulder, his arms almost bruising me with how tight he was holding me. I didn't move though—wouldn't move—until he pulled away first. I stood there in the open doorway, letting in cold air, for as long as he needed me.

Someone—Nico I thought—got up and closed the door behind us.

"Come sit down," Nico murmured from behind Marcos.

Marcos sniffled and pulled away slightly, just enough so he could see where he was going as he carried me to the couch. Sitting down between Jason and Nico on the sofa, with me in his lap, Marcos leaned back and cradled me against his chest.

I let him position me however he needed to feel comfortable. If he needed a human blanket at the moment, I'd gladly be that blanket. "What happened?" I asked softly.

"Drunk driver. She was hit head-on, by a drunk driver." Marcos's voice was hoarse and broken.

Tears poured down my face, my heart broke for him and Kara, and what they had lost. "I'm so sorry," I murmured again.

He squeezed me tighter, burying his face into the crook of my neck. I gave him a few minutes before I sighed. "I should go check on Kara."

Marcos nodded and I slid off his lap and walked into the Kara's bedroom. Shutting the door behind me, I found Kara laying in her bed, holding a stuffed bear and crying silently. "Hey, babe. Maybe we should get some sleep?"

Kara shrugged solemnly. "I can lend you some clothes."

I nodded.

Maya

THE NIGHT BEFORE THE funeral, Kara had gone to bed early. She hadn't been sleeping well and had crashed right after dinner, leaving me to fend for myself with Marcos, Jason, and Nico. Despite the fact that the three of them had their own places, they had all but moved into Lita's apartment, setting up a bed of cushions on the floor. Marcos had changed the sheets in his mother's bedroom and had taken her bed, leaving Jason and Nico on the floor.

I didn't think they minded as I settled into the nest of blankets they had created. The guys had thrown on an action movie, something with lots of explosions and little plot with bad guys vs good guys. I enjoyed the mindlessness of it as I relaxed, feeling some of the tension leave my body.

I was sandwiched between Jason and Nico, like I had been that fateful night we'd been together, only this time I felt awkward knowing I had a boyfriend—even if we weren't serious.

Halfway through the movie, Jason slid his hand over my thigh and left it resting there. Tired from a long week of remote learning and helping Kara plan a funeral, I ignored his hand while secretly enjoying the warmth of it. I would not cheat on Hunter, but I wasn't immune to Jason's touch.

When his hand started sliding up my thigh, I shook my head and shifted away, so his hand slid off my leg inside. "Don't."

"Come on, Maya," Jason groaned. "You've refused to touch us all fucking week."

"Because I have a boyfriend. I told you that." I shook my head, annoyed that I even had to explain it to him.

"Well, he's not here," Jason said.

I sat up and quickly got to my feet. "Fuck you, Jason. Fuck you."

"Maya," Nico sighed.

"Fuck you too, Nico," I shot out, looking down at them. "Cheating's a hard limit for me; it's not something I'd ever put up with or do to someone. I have zero respect for cheaters, so you two can fuck off. I'm done." I turned on my heel and walked away.

Once I was in Kara's bedroom, I had to be quiet, as Kara was sleeping, but I was pissed. It took me a long time to fall a sleep that night.

The next morning, I woke up feeling like shit. I barely slept the night before and a headache was already pounding behind my eyes and my entire body ached. I took a quick shower and got ready for the funeral, packing up all the shit I had at Kara's.

After the initial mad dash to bring Kara home following the news of Lita's death, I had gone back to the dorms the following morning and packed bags for both of us. The week since then had been busy with helping Kara plan the funeral, while still managing to attend my classes online. Rescheduling my clinical hours had been a bitch, but I'd done it for Kara.

Dealing with Marcos, Nico, and Jason all week, had been a test of my fucking nerves. The three men had been overly friendly and touchy-feely, something I could ignore due to the circumstances, until they drew the line.

My heart was hurting, while anger still roiled through me. I couldn't believe they'd try to pull something, knowing I was seeing someone. It really made me question their integrity—and made me question if I'd even want anything further with any of them.

It was the last thing I wanted to deal with, on top of feeling like utter crap while I packed up my things and got ready for the funeral.

The sun shone brightly in the sky, though the air was crisp, when Kara and I finished packing my car, and headed to the Church together. Marcos, Nico, and Jason had gone home sometime in the night—probably after I told them off—and left a note in the kitchen, stating they would meet us at the Church.

Kara was pissed, but I kept my mouth shut. I didn't want to add onto the drama of the day. I'd eventually tell Kara about it some other time.

Hunter and all of our friends were waiting for us outside the church, armed with coffee for both of us. I smiled weakly, pressing a kiss to his lips as I accepted the coffee. "Thanks, babe."

Hunter pressed a kiss to my temple and wrapped his arm around my waist, pulling me against him. Kara and I greeted all of our friends, grateful for the support. It had been a long stressful week, and I was so happy to see our little ragtag group.

Armed with coffee and Hunter's arms wrapped around me, I was beginning to feel a little better, despite my still pounding head. That was until Marcos, Jason, and Nico each showed up to the funeral with a woman hanging off their arm.

"What the fuck?" Kara muttered, watching as the three men climbed out of Marco's F150, and each looped an arm around a leggy slut in various shades of fake-and-bake tans with sky high heels and too short skirts. Fake tits poured out of plunging neck lines. It was utterly disgusting.

I felt my heart shatter in my chest. We weren't together by any means, and I was even dating someone else, but the fact that they had never once mentioned seeing anyone, in the last five days that I'd basically been living with them day and night, killed me, especially after the bullshit they had pulled the night before.

We might not have been sexual in the five days I had stayed with them, but the lingering touches and gentle caresses had been too familiar if they were each seeing someone. And if they weren't seeing someone, and this was payback because I turned them down the night before? How fucking petty. I didn't have time for childish antics from grown men.

They walked toward the church entrance, not glancing over at me even once. Marcos snagged Kara's hand as he passed, and tugged her along with him. I had to stifle a sob, and turn away, my heart in shambles as utter disbelief washed over me.

Hunter tugged me closer to our group of friends, and turned toward the church to follow Kara and her brother inside. Kara glanced back only once they'd been seated up in the front pew of the church, to see that our group of friends and I had opted to sit further back, giving the family space.

The funeral was a small and quick affair. A simple Mass with readings, celebrating the life of Carlita Candela. One of the women from Lita's church group stood up and delivered a beautiful eulogy, along with Lita's sister, Mary.

After Mass we had bundled up for the gravesite memorial. I held Hunter's hand tightly and purposely avoided looking at Marcos, Jason, and Nico. Decked out in mirrored sunglasses, I had no idea if they even glanced my way, but it didn't matter to me. I was only there for my friend—Kara.

Later, during the repast at a local restaurant, the women had draped themselves over the laps of what I was considering *my guys*. Marcos, Jason, and Nico didn't seem to mind, as they chatted with friends and ate their meal.

My head was pounding, a stabbing pain between my eyes. The noise of the restaurant wasn't helping, and the screeching laughter from the whores on my guys' laps was nails on a chalkboard for me. "You, OK?" Hunter asked. His hand came out and felt my forehead—gloriously cool. "Shit, babe. You're burning up."

I sighed. I had a feeling I was coming down with the something when I woke up that morning, aching all over. Stress had a way of knocking you down though. "Can we go? My head's killing me."

"Yeah, of course." Hunter immediately stood up and I handed him my keys. He had ridden down for the funeral with our friends, so he could easily drive me back to the dorms. He reached out and grabbed my hand, helping me to my feet.

I swayed, unsteady as my vision swam around me. "Wait," I murmured, gripping his hand. I blinked as my vision went blurry and an aura arched across my eyesight. "Fuck. There's an aura." I gripped Hunters hand tighter and slowly sat back down.

"Migraine. We need to get you somewhere dark and quiet," Hunter said.

"Maya, you good?" Karma asked, from where she was seated next to me. Cool hands reached out and cupped her forehead. "Fuck, girl. You're burning up."

"My head's killing me," I mumbled, unable to talk loudly. I needed to get out of the restaurant, it was too loud, everything was too loud.

"Come on, let's get you outside," Hunter said. He lifted me into his arms, bridal style, and carried me to the door.

Karma scrambled next to us, stopping to say good bye to Kara. Hunter kept moving though, so I only heard Karma say, "Hey girl. We're gonna go. Maya's not feeling well."

By the time Hunter got me outside the restaurant, my stomach was rolling as the nausea settled in. I fucking hated migraines. It had been a long time since I had one, and I'd completely missed the warning signs. Now here I was, unable to see, about to puke my guts up with a pounding head, when I should have been making sure my friend was OK in the aftermath of her mother's funeral.

"Babe, I'm gonna set you down to unlock the car, OK?" Hunter's voice was soft and gentle.

I moaned softly, unable to speak. The cool air was working wonders on my blazing skin, but my stomach still rolled. Once Hunter set me down, I immediately squatted down and put my hands on my head. The thought of getting into a moving vehicle and then having to drive for two fucking hours back to the dorms made me queasy.

"Maya, are you OK?" Kara's voice was soft.

I could only groan. I was going to puke, and soon. Movement behind Kara caught her eye, Marcos, Jason, and Nico had walked out of the restaurant. I moaned and squeezed my eyes shut. I did NOT want them to see me like this.

Karma nudged Kara out of the way and pressed a cool wad of paper towels to my forehead. "Have you taken anything yet?"

"No." I barely got the word out before her stomach clenched hard and I was expelling my breakfast all over the pavement—Karma and Kara jumping back to avoid being hit. I hadn't eaten that morning though, so all I threw up was water and coffee. Someone pulled my hair out of the way as my stomach revolted again.

"What's going on?" my voice was soft and accented, coming from close behind her, as if he was the one holding her hair back.

"She's got a migraine and fever, said she wasn't feeling well this morning," Karma answered.

Tissues and a water bottle were pushed into my hands, and I gratefully wiped my lips and nose before I rinsed out my mouth and spat on the ground again. I reached for another tissue and mopped up my tears and makeup the best I could without a mirror.

"Thanks," I murmured. I looked up to find Hunter squatting down next to me. "I'm OK."

"Did that help?" Hunter asked.

"My head's still killing me, but not as bad. Can we go?"

"Of course." He nodded and slowly stood up. He reached down and gently helped me to my feet.

I groaned softly as my head swam with the altitude change. Swaying on my feet, someone's hand landed on my back, between my shoulder blades, to steady me. Looking over my shoulder, I found Marcos there, with a concerned expression on his handsome face. Still annoyed with him, I turned back to Kara and forced a smile on my face, though it was more of a grimace. "Sorry girl. We're gonna head back to the dorms."

"No worries at all," Kara immediately said. "Are you sure you feel up to the drive? You can always go back to my place."

I shook my head. "I'm OK, promise. I just really want my bed right now."

"I'll ride with you guys," Karma said, glancing at Hunter.

I could feel Jason and Nico's eyes on me, as I moved away from Marcos. "I'll text you later," I said to Kara.

"Sounds good. I hope you feel better."

Ignoring everyone else, I climbed into the backseat of my Honda Civic and closed the door. Hunter and Karma said their goodbyes to our friends, before they too got in the car. Thankfully, I had already planned on going back to the dorms after the funeral, so my car was packed with my stuff. I grabbed my pillow and arranged the backseat so I could lay down across the bench.

Karma passed me a hoodie from the front seat and I used it as a blanket as Hunter started to pull out of the parking spot. Curling up in the back seat, I closed my eyes and was quickly dead to the world for the drive back to the dorms.

Jason

I FELT MY HEART constrict as Maya climbed into the back-seat of her car. Her boyfriend said goodbye to Kara and their friends before he got behind the steering wheel. Another girl, one of her friends, climbed into the passenger side, and then they were gone.

I stood motionless with Nico, as Marcos slowly walked toward us. The three of us stood watching Maya's car until it was out of sight. "We fucked up," Nico mumbled.

"Yep," I said.

"How did we not notice she was sick this morning?" Nico asked, as Marcos reached them.

"We were all in our own heads." Marcos sighed, running a hand over his buzzed hair.

I shook my head. "We shouldn't have had the sluts come today."

Marcos jerked his head to the side to meet my gaze. "You think we had something to do with her being sick?"

"Not what I'm saying." I shook my head again and sighed.

"Stone's right," Nico groaned. "We were too focused on being petty because she's dating someone else, and didn't see that she was barely holding things together today."

"We should be the ones taking care of her," I said.

"She shouldn't be driving two hours just for a bed," Nico tacked on.

Marcos sighed, rubbing at his brow. He nodded slowly, realization sinking in. "So what do we do?"

"We text her later, apologizing about the skanks," I suggested. I ran hand through my messy blond hair, messing it up further. "And pray she forgives us."

"We'll make her forgive us," Nico said.

Marcos shook his head. "She's not some skank we can just throw money at. Maya has integrity. She's a badass, she won't take our shit."

"Which makes our fuck up even worse. We shouldn't have invited the skanks today," I shot Marcos a glare.

"I know, OK, I know! I was hurting, and she wouldn't fucking touch us!" Marco exclaimed.

Kara and her friends walked over at that moment, Kara pausing to glare her brother. "What the fuck?" she asked him.

Marcos whirled around and flinched when he saw his sister. Kara had been strong all day, only shedding tears while at the gravesite service. She'd held Maya's hand while Marcos clung to the slut at his side. Now I could see how that had affected her as well.

"You invited those fucking skanks to my mother's funeral ON PURPOSE! To HURT my best fucking friend? You stupid motherfuckers!" Kara spat, glaring at the three of us. "I can't fucking believe you would intentionally hurt MY BEST FRIEND!"

Nico and I winced, hanging our heads in shame as Kara scolded us.

"Kara—" Marcos started.

"Don't," Kara snapped. "I'm so fucking disappointed in the three of you. After I encouraged her to be with you, after I practically *pushed her into your arms!*" Kara was shaking with rage.

"Kara," Marcos tried again.

"Don't you fucking say a god damned thing, *brother*!" Growing even more enraged than possible, she was practically growling the words she spat the three of us. "I'm going tell her exactly what you did, then I'm going to warn her to stay the fuck away from the three of you."

I flinched again.

"Kara, please," Nico tried. "We weren't trying to be malicious—"

"Bull fucking shit!" Kara snapped again, turning on Nico and me this time. "Of course you fucking were! Why else would you purposely invite those hideous fucking skanks to my mother's funeral?" She was growing more inconsolable by the moment. "Too fucking butt-hurt over the fact that Maya met someone else? Had to act like petty ass little bitches?!" She turned back to Marcos, tears pouring down her face. "I fucking NEEDED you today!"

Guilt settled hard into my stomach. Nico shifted uncomfortably next to me. Neither one of us had thought of Kara in all of this. Every damn word she'd flung at us had been the truth. Marcos hung his head, shame rolling off him.

A blond with glasses chose that moment to walk out of the restaurant, looking warily around at us. "Kara, come on." The blond waved Kara toward the door.

Kara's face crumbled, as a sob tore out of her. She rushed to her friend, not bothering to look back at the three men.

Anxiety rolled over me as the reality of the situation fell on me. Marcos had to wipe his eyes and quickly turn and look away.

How the hell were we going to fix this?

Later that night, shame and guilt continued to eat away at me and my buddies, my brothers in all but blood. We had fucked up good and bad, not only with Maya, but with Kara as well. We hadn't even thought of how their actions would affect their sister, or how it would look to invite skanks to a funeral.

Marcos was laying on the floor at my feet, as I sat on the couch. Nico sat off to the side, leaning back in the recliner. The three of us had headed back to our cramped apartment, not wanting to upset Kara further at Lita's.

A ping of text coming through had Marcos reaching into his pocket for his cellphone. I looked over my buddy's shoulder and read the message from Kara.

Kara

> I'm going back to the dorms tonight with my friends. I packed up my stuff. Let me know what you want to do about the apartment.

Marcos

> Lil Manita, I'm so sorry. I'll take care of the apartment until the end of the lease. Don't worry about it. We can talk more about it this summer.

Kara

> I'm probably going to stay at the dorms for Christmas.

Marcos crumbled, a sob breaking out of him as he read Kara's words. I sighed as Marcos rolled onto his side, and tried to stop the tears. He slowly stood up and headed for his room, not saying a word to either of them.

"What happened?" Nico asked.

"Kara said she's going to stay at the dorms for Christmas break."

Nico's face fell as pain etched into his features. "Dude, we fucked up."

"Tell me about it." I shook my head, fucking disgusted with myself.

"We should have fucking talked Marcos out of the stupid plan," Nico said.

Shaking my head, I sighed. "We tried. He wouldn't listen."

"Well now it's all fucking shot to shit!" Nico exploded, jumping to his feet. He stalked the living room, pacing as he ran his fingers through his shaggy, shoulder length hair.

Deciding to take matters into my own hands, I pulled my own phone and sent Kara a message.

Jason

I'm sorry about the skanks at your mother's funeral. Everything you said today was right, but you know that already. I'm sorry I wasn't a better friend and brother to you today. I'll work on that, lil sis.

Kara

Do better.

I had to smile wryly at her reply.

Jason

Yes, ma'am.

Jason

> Any chance I can convince you to come home for Christmas?

I had to wait a while for her reply, pacing the living room as Nico pulled out his own phone and began typing.

Kara

> Sorry. It was something I was already planning. Christmas just isn't the same without Mom. I can't try and put on a happy face this year. I just want to be alone.

Jason

> I get that, Kare Bear, I really do. But we'd feel better if you at least came home. You can stay at our place.

I threw the offer out, knowing our small apartment was cramped enough as it was. Three small ten by ten bedrooms with a twenty-by-twenty kitchen, living, and dining room. It would be tight, but Kara was family.

Kara

> I'd probably catch a disease from your couch, no thanks.

Jason

> Come on, we aren't that bad.

Kara

Skanks at my mother's funeral?

Ok we are that bad.

I sighed and rubbed a hand over my messy hair. I was trying here.

"She still pissed?" Nico asked.

"Yeah. But she's talking to me." I shrugged.

I am really sorry though.

I know.

Unsure of what else to say after all that, I tossed my phone to the couch and pulled at my hair. I had to think of a way to make shit up to both Maya and Kara.

"Who are you talking to?" I asked, as Nico was fully concentrating on typing on the small keyboard of his cellphone.

"Maya," he murmured.

I moved around the back of the recliner and read over Nico's shoulder as he typed out a paragraph to Maya.

Hey, just wanted to check in… make sure you're ok?

> Maya, I'm so sorry for what happened today at the funeral. We never should have invited those girls. It was a family affair and we should have left it at that. I'm so sorry for alienating you today and not realizing you were sick. We should have taken care of you.

Nico

> I'm sorry if I hurt you. It was never my intention.

Maya

Yes, it was.

I sucked in a breath. I hadn't expected her to respond at all. I looked at my own text messages to see if Nico had texted her in the group chat or not, only to be disappointed that he hadn't. Not that it really mattered, we all had to apologize to her, because we had all fucked up.

No time like the present, I thought and opened a new chat for Maya.

Jason

> I'm so sorry, darlin'. I know we fucked up with the skanks. It was stupid and petty. We were jealous that you started seeing someone else and wouldn't mess around with us this last week. It hurt and we lashed out. That's on us. I deeply regret that our petty actions hurt you today.

I paced the room, breathing hard. It wasn't like me to apologize to a woman. I never cared enough before to feel the need to. My chest was tight as I thought of all the ways I had hurt Maya today—how hurting her had fucking hurt myself in return. I'd never felt like that before.

"Anything?" I asked Nico.

"No," he muttered, clenching his phone.

A moment later we both looked at our phones as they beeped with an incoming text: the group chat.

Maya

> The fact that you guys pulled some high school fucking bullshit and invited skanks to your mother's fucking funeral, all because I wouldn't fool around with you this week, tells me more about your character than I ever needed to know. Please stop texting me. Whatever we had is over. It shouldn't have gone further than a one-night stand. I don't believe in cheating. It's a hard no for me, and a huge red flag that you three have zero issue with it. I'm no longer interested in pursuing anything further with the three of you. If you see me with Kara, please leave me the fuck alone.

I sucked in a breath and stumbled to the couch as my knees buckled beneath me.

"What the fuck did you guys say to her?" Marcos's voice a gravelly growl as he stalked into the living room.

"We tried to apologize," I muttered.

Marcos barreled into me, his fist swinging and catching me in the mouth before I could even react. I leaned back into the couch as Marcos snatched up my phone. He read the texts I had sent Maya before she responded to the group chat and shook his head in disgust, but his anger deflated slightly.

Nico handed Marcos his own phone and waited while Marcos also read Nico's messages to Maya.

Marcos sighed and tossed Nico his phone back before he collapsed onto the couch next to me.

Despair and anguish settled around us. There was nothing more we could do, but respect her wishes.

Maya

THE MONTHS FOLLOWING LITA'S funeral were both long and yet fast as the seasons changed from winter to spring. I hadn't heard from the guys since then. I had spent Christmas in Chicago with my sister and my sister's new boyfriend, while Kara had eventually gone home for Christmas.

We had texted during break, and Kara admitted to going off on her brother and the guys again. I told her not to worry about it, and leave it be. The last thing I wanted was some fling coming between me and Kara—our friendship was too important to me.

For spring break, Kara, me, and all of our friends—Hunter included—had gone down to Panama City, Florida for all the spring break shenanigans. It was my last year of school and I had wanted to go out with a bang.

It had been a blast, and every day I took advantage of living in the moment with my best friends. Whoever said high school was the best years of your life never went to college, because my senior year was everything I had hoped for and more.

By the time Graduation rolled around, a sense of melancholy settled over me. Everything was changing, our little crew of friends would all be headed in different directions. Terri would head to her parents' new home in Florida and Maya would have to move back in with her parents in Mourningside.

Stephanie and Kara still had two years left of undergrad before both were headed onto more schooling. Karma had graduated the year before, while Arturo was graduating from the architect program. Hunter was heading to the west coast for med school, while Kyle and Travis headed east.

Our little group was breaking up—and so did Hunter and I. I had done it last night, but Hunter hadn't been blindsided by it. The two of us were never serious, though we had agreed to be exclusive, we knew we didn't have a future. We agreed to be friends, and weren't going to stop hanging out just because we were no longer fucking.

The mature relationship I had with Hunter meant the world to me. The way we could talk about things and be comfortable about our time together, gave me hope for the future. We might not have been each other's happily-ever-after, but we weren't each other's worst nightmares either.

Graduation day was a sunny and hot day in early June. Terri and I were nervously pacing the school's gymnasium, waiting to be told to line up before we headed out into the football stadium where the ceremony would take place.

"Are your parents out there?" Terri asked me, already knowing my relationship with my parents was rocky at best.

"I don't know," I said, not wanting to think about it. It was depressing to think that my parents probably weren't in the stands, despite the fact that I invited them. "Are yours?"

"Yeah. They got a hotel room last night." Even after moving to Florida, Terri's parents made sure to both be their when she walked across the stage and graduated.

My heart clenched at the thought. It made me upset, so I forced it from my mind. My phone pinging in the pocket of my Graduation gown, pulled me from my thoughts. I pulled out my phone and saw the notification of a text from a group chat.

Assuming it was my friends talking about our plans for dinner and dancing that, I opened the group chat only to freeze when I saw it was from Marcos, Nico, and Jason. And it wasn't just one message; it was multiple messages. Each one of them sent me an apology after apology, and congratulations on my graduation.

Marcos:

Hey Maya, I never apologized for my actions that day back in December. I am so sorry that I hurt you and that I wasn't the man you deserved. I'm sorry that I was petty and childish, and not able to see past my own selfish desires. You were right in everything you said to us that day. We don't deserve you for a moment, and probably never did. I'm sorry I forced both Nico and Jason to listen to me that day and invite those women. It was my own selfishness that hurt you, and for that I'll never forgive myself. I just want to tell you how sorry I am, and that even now, months later, I can't stop thinking about you. Good luck today, and congratulations on graduating.

Jason:

Hey Darlin'. I know you asked us to stay away, and we have. But I wanted to apologize again and let you know I still care about you. I haven't been able to stop thinking about you at all in the last six months. Good luck today. Hopefully next time you see us, you won't completely hate us.

Nico:

Hey Little Dreamer, I just wanted to say how much I miss you, and how sorry I am that our actions drove you away from us. You deserve so much better than us. You deserve the world. I just hope that one day you can

> forgive us. I'll always miss you. Good luck today and congratulations.

I choked on a sob as I read through their messages. I tried to get myself together, as not to mess up my makeup, but it was hard. Terri took one look at my face and wrapped her arm around my shoulders. "What happened?"

I showed her the phone and let her read the messages herself.

"Well, damn." Terri huffed out a breath and handed me back my phone. "What are you thinking?"

I shrugged a shoulder and wiped my eyes.

Terri shook her head slowly. "Maybe it's time to forgive them?"

I jerked my head up, my mouth falling open in shock. Terri had been my biggest supporter in the last six months, but she'd also been the most vocal against me ever getting back together with either of the three men. She'd been vehemently against the very *idea* of Marcos, Nico, and Jason.

"Look girl. I know things have been hard for you the last six month. Their betrayal really hit you. I'm not saying to jump back into their arms, but I guess I'm also not saying not to, either. You and Hunter broke up, and you guys were good together, but you never had that same spark, you know?"

I nodded, wiping my eyes.

"And you are about to be back in Mourningside again. It's practically Creekton. You'll probably run into them a lot."

Again, all I could do was nod.

"I say give them a run for their money if they make an effort to try again."

A whistle blew, signaling it was time to line up, saving me from answering her. There was a scurrying of activity as everyone in the gym formed our lines to walk outside. Then we were on our way, walking into the blazing sun and heat to march across the stage.

Two hours later, the ceremony was complete and I was joining my friends in a circle, knowing I didn't have any family in the crowd. I was too happy and excited to be done with school to be upset that my parents hadn't shown up.

"Maya!" a female voice yelled for my attention.

I whirled around to find the beaming and smiling face of my older sister, Jenna. Bright blond hair and my same curls, Jenna was as beautiful as ever. "Oh my god!" I cried and jumped at my sister, hugging her tightly. "What are you doing here?"

"You really think I'd miss my only sister's college graduation? Are you out of your mind?" Jenna's matter-of-fact tone was like aloe on a sunburn, healing my heart after my parent's blatant dismissal.

"Thank you!" I cried, hugging her tightly.

When we pulled apart, both of us with tears in our eyes, I turned and introduced my big sister to my group of friends. Even Kara and Stephanie had showed up to celebrate with us, despite the fact they had moved out of the dorms the week before.

After an hour of heartfelt reminiscing and tearful good-byes—despite the fact they'd be meeting up at the bar later that night—my friends finally departed. Jenna and I walked with Kara and Stephanie back to the gym so I could grab my purse and change out of my graduation gowns.

"What the hell?" Kara said as she stopped walking.

I looked up to see three men, dressed in sharp black suits with ties, looking hot as fuck, just a few feet from the gymnasium. Students eyed them as they streamed by, wondering who the hell the three tattooed and pierced, rough and tumble looking men were.

"Hot damn," Stephanie muttered.

"What's going on?" Jenna asked, looking from the three women to the three men.

"Kara?" I questioned.

"This wasn't me. I swear." Kara shook her head.

My heart pounded in my chest. I could feel my cheeks heating as Jenna looked at me. "Maya?"

"I uh—it's them." I nodded toward the men.

"The three guys?" Jenna asked. I had told my sister over Christmas break everything that happened between me and my guys.

Jenna had been properly pissed off for me, but she had also been very supportive of me doing whatever I wanted when it came to them. "Oh, sister. They are fucking hot."

"Yeah." I let out a breath, my voice strained. Each man held a red rose in his hand and was watching me patiently. "Why are they here?"

Jenna laughed and said, "I'd say they're here for you, sister."

"Kara?" I asked again.

"I uh—yeah. I'd say so. They've been asking about you nonstop the last several weeks, seeing if I'd agree to help them with some plan. I told them no." Kara had always supported my decision to cut ties with those three, despite them being her family. "But if they're going through all this effort... the choice is yours, babe. I won't tell you not to."

"You could just see what they say," Stephanie reasoned.

"Hear them out," Jenna agreed.

"And if you don't like what they say, tell them to fuck off," Kara added.

I felt dazed as I nodded and slowly walked over to where the three of them were standing. It was so odd seeing them in suits, granted they were all black, even their shirts and ties were black. The three of them seemed to stand up taller—straighter—as I grew closer.

Nico's long blond hair was no longer shaggy, instead it was sleek and shining in the summer sun. Reaching the middle of his back, his hair was pulled back into a neat ponytail at the back of his neck. His bright blue eyes sparkled and his face was covered in a thick trimmed beard. He looked like something out of a wet dream.

Next to him, Jason looked a little more hardcore with his neck tattoos rising over the collar of the black shirt, his spiky blond hair styled in a purposely messy look and his pierced eyebrow and a new lip ring glinting in the sunlight—a circle ring in his lower lip that made my mouth water. His piercing gray eyes tracked every move as I slowed to a stop in front of them.

Marcos looked the same as always, if not a little thicker in the arms and shoulders—more muscles bulked on his already thick frame. His dark hair was still trimmed short against his skull, his dark eyes deep pools of sin that pulled me in.

Standing before them, I could already feel myself flagging in my resolve. Did I really want to tell them to fuck off again? Instead, I asked, "What are you doing here?"

"We wanted to congratulate you," Marcos spoke up, stepping toward me. "Congratulations on graduating." He handed me his rose.

I did my best not to blush or show too much emotion as I took the rose from him, but it was hard with them so close. Especially with how fucking hot all three of them looked.

Jason was next, stepping forward and handing me his rose. He stared down at me with all the emotions clouding his gaze. His gray eyes shining, like tears were welling, as he pressed the rose into my hand. "Congratulations, Maya. I'm proud of you." He stepped back before I could respond.

Nico swooped in and kissed the corner of my mouth, as he handed me his rose. I was stunned as he pulled away, his lips pulling up at the corners. "Congratulations, Little Dreamer."

"We know we fucked things up bad," Marcos said, drawing my attention back to him. "And we're sorry for hurting you. Is there any way you'd see yourself being able to forgive us?"

I sucked in a breath. This was the moment of truth. I honestly wasn't sure what I was going to say either. "I don't know—"

"We can work with that," Marcos said immediately, steamrolling over anything else I might've said.

"Just like that?" I shot back, annoyed. "You don't even know what I was going to say."

"You didn't say no, though," Nico smirked. "So we can work with that."

"You don't know about us," Jason added. "That's fine. We can change your mind."

I huffed out a breath of annoyance. "Just like that?" I asked again.

"Yep," Marcos said.

I narrowed my eyes on them, not trusting them entirely, but also intrigued as to what they might to do to *convince* me.

"We'll be seeing you, Darlin'." Jason smirked and turned away from me.

"See you, Little Dreamer," Nico said.

"Be safe tonight," Marcos said.

I nodded mutely, watching as they turned and walked away from me.

"Hot damn," Jenna crooned as she walked over to me.

I was startled out of my thoughts as my sister and friends surrounded me. "So, what's the verdict?" Stephanie asked.

"I told them I didn't know." I shrugged a shoulder. "They didn't give me a moment to speak. The second I said I didn't know, they pounced, basically. Said they could work with that."

"What does that even mean?" Jenna asked.

"You didn't say no, so it gave them an opening," Kara explained. "Not an outright *no*, means they have room to try to convince you."

"They could try to convince me any day," Jenna laughed.

I groaned and shook my head. "Let's get out of here. I'm dying of heat exhaustion."

"So dramatic," Jenna shot back.

Maya

"YEAH, I'M OUT FRONT. I'll be in a few." I hung up with Terri just as the rideshare pulled up in front of the bar, Satan's Palace.

Graduation night had finally come. It had been a long day of celebrating with friends and Jenna, and now it was time to party it up. I was officially done with nursing school and already had a job offer. I started my new nursing job a week from Monday.

All of that was the furthest thing from my mind as I stepped out of the car. Dressed in a skintight red sequin dress that dipped low in the front, showing my ample cleavage, with skinny strings that held the dress up. It laced down my back in a crisscross pattern, displaying miles of smooth skin. Ending at midthigh, I had to be careful not to flash anyone my thong when I slid from the back of the car.

I rocked a pair of matching red sky-high heels that were sure to kill my feet after a couple hours of dancing, but I didn't care—I didn't care about anything tonight.

I showed my ID to the bouncer, a tall man wearing a black leather cut with a patch of a devil on the left, the name Devil's Psychos patched on the right. I had a feeling this was a biker bar that Terri had chosen. Scantily clad women serving drinks to women dressed in even less—my dress was conservative in comparison. The place was packed, music bumped from the speakers, and people yelled over the music. The dance floor was hopping and I couldn't wait to grab a drink and let loose.

In the corner, near the bar, a group of leather clad bikers congregated around a table, surveying the busy bar around them. In the center of them all, three all too familiar faces had their eyes glued on me. It was almost comical the way Jason's gray eyes widen as they roamed over my body, or the way Nico licked his lips as his bright blue eyes hungrily checked me out, and even Marcos's mouth dropping open when he saw me standing there.

My heart pounded in my chest. *What the fuck are they doing here?* I had no idea.

"Maya!" My name was screamed across the noisy bar turned dance club.

I smiled broadly and headed for my friends, ignoring the three bikers at the table full of leather clad brothers.

"They keep watching you," Terri grinned at me as we washed our hands in the bathroom.

I blushed slightly and shrugged. "Let them."

Terri laughed. "Kara really doesn't care?"

"Dude, you heard her. Shit, you asked her yourself! She really doesn't care. She's more worried about me getting hurt than anything," I said. I frowned at myself in the mirror slightly, thankful that Kara and gone off with Kyle tonight, and wasn't at the bar to see whatever might happen between her brother and me.

"I mean, you could get hurt in any relationship. Why hold yourself back from love, when its right in front of you?" Terri shot back, raising an eyebrow.

"Who said anything about love? You think three bikers are looking for love and commitment and forever? No. They're looking to fuck. End of story." I rolled my eyes and leaned toward the mirror to wipe a smudge of makeup from under my eye.

"What's wrong with fucking?" Terri laughed. "Three, hot as fuck bikers wanna get down for a night? Sign me the fuck up."

I chuckled and shook my head at my friend's antics. After four years of sharing a dorm room with Terri, countless parties, and endless nights of baring our souls during girl talk, I was feeling nostalgic. This might be one of the last nights we partied together. Terri's parents had moved to Florida in the last year of school, and without a home base in Illinois, she would be moving in with her parents again while she job searched. "I'm going to miss you."

Terri gave me a wide grin. "Bitch, you ain't getting rid of me. There's still phones and social media."

I rolled my eyes at my friend's blasé attitude.

"But same, bitch." Terri walked over, wrapped an arm around my shoulders and planted a big wet kiss to my cheek.

"Ewwww," I grumbled. I tried to push Terri off me, but she was like a bad smell, still hanging on.

"You fucking love me."

"Whatever." I rolled my eyes, but grinned widely, watching my friend in the mirror.

Yeah, I was definitely going to miss nights like these.

After the bathroom chit chat, I headed for the bar and quickly ordered another round for my table. I was feeling far too sober after that little show of feelings with Terri. I had just settled onto a stool when I felt them come up on either side of me.

Marcos and Jason to my left, and Nico to my right, making it impossible to look at all three at the same time, without turning my back to one of them. It left me vulnerable, and knowing those three, it was an orchestrated move to make me feel unsettled.

I rolled my eyes at the thought. This wasn't a chess game, there were no moves to be had. While I didn't like anyone behind me, I figured Nico was mostly harmless, compared to the other two, so I gave Marcos and Jason my attention as I let my gaze roam over the leather cuts up close.

Black leather with the devil character on stitched the left side. On the right side, were two embroidered patches: the name Devil's Psychos on top, and the patch below it read Enforcer, on Jason's and vice president on Marcos's. I frowned slightly as I slowly surveyed them, taking in every detail from the way their shirts hugged their chests, to the way their heavy black boots were scuffed beneath their jeans.

I didn't say anything as I frowned. I studied their solemn faces—such stark contrast to their confident smirks they bore earlier that afternoon after graduation. They clearly hadn't expected to run into me here. Both Marcos and Jason looked more than a little unsettled at the moment. "I take it Kara doesn't know?" I raised an eyebrow and watched Marcos expectantly.

Marcos sighed and ran a hand over his hair, seeking comfort from the closely buzzed locks. "No. I'd like to keep it that way, please."

I ignored him, studying Jason instead. His gray eyes were hard as stone, almost emotionless, like the nickname I often heard Marcos and Nico call him. I could see it in his eyes how he was trying to push me away, trying not to care that I was in possibly *his* bar, on his turf, and seeing him *clearly* for the first time ever. It made him vulnerable and I could see how much he didn't like it. Again, the fucking opposite of how he was earlier that afternoon.

I turned away from Jason and Marcos, giving them both my back, as I turned to look at Nico. The blond adonis, with his bright blue eyes, blond hair back in a ponytail, and tanned skin, he was smirking playfully when I turned my attention on him.

I gave him the same slow inspection, letting my eyes drift over every inch of him, noting the way the leather cut looked damn good on his muscular frame. Shit, it had looked good on three of them. "Like what you see, Little Dreamer?" Nico crooned.

I pursed my lips.

I was saved from answering, though, when the bartender set down a tray ladened with drinks in front of me. Ignoring the three men, I grabbed the tray and slid off my barstool, and sauntering back to my friends without a backwards glance.

I could feel their eyes burning into me all the way... and if I danced extra provocatively in the following couple of hours, so be it.

After I said goodbye to my friends later that evening, I slid onto a barstool and waved to the bartender, motioning for another drink. The man nodded and I settled in to wait, turning my back to the leather clad bikers in the corner and facing the rest of the barroom, to take in the still raging party.

Once again, I felt them before I saw them. It was like the air shifted around me before I was surrounded by muscled men in leather cuts. Nico behind me, Marcos in front of me, and Jason to my left, leaving me boxed in with the bar to my right.

"Jesus Christ, Little Dreamer." Nico groaned from behind me. As I went to turn my head to look at him, Marcos grabbed my knees and forcefully spread my thighs apart, so he could step between my legs. My skirt was tight around my hips, stretching as he opened my legs wide.

"What do I gotta do to get you to come home with me tonight?" Nico groaned, pressing open mouth kisses along the column of my neck. I tilted my head to the side, letting it fall back against his shoulder as he melded his body against mine. His hands slid down my sides, grazing sensually over my breasts, before he dug his fingers into those sensitive spots right above my hip bones. His kisses turned into nibbles, before he was biting down on my jaw bone just below my ear.

A breathy whimpered moan left my lips.

Jason slid his fingers through my messy hair, fisting his hand through my locks. He yanked my head further back, forcing me to look at him. "You look good enough to eat tonight, darlin'."

A shiver shook my body as his damn gravelly voice went straight to my core. *Fuck his voice man.*

I gasped at the devilish glint in his gray eyes. Jason lowered his head and took advantage of my open mouth, dipping his tongue in and immediately kissing my mouth how he wanted, his new lip piercing adding to the pleasure.

Nico sucked on my jaw, soothing the bite he'd placed there. His hands slid up my tummy, slow and heavy as they caressed my body through my silky dress.

Marcos pressed against my front, his mouth completely covering a nipple through my dress. His wet hot mouth around my nipple had me bucking against him.

Nico slid his hands down my belly again, past my hips to my bare thighs. He gripped them tightly and spread me open further. I was practically laying back again Nico now, with him supporting my weight, while the back of the barstool was between me and Jason.

Jason continued to ravage my mouth as Marcos attacked my nipples, sucking on one, while tugging and rolling the other between his fingers.

I was a writhing, moaning mess in the middle of the three of them. My hands gripped the opening of Marcos's leather cut, holding him against me. I didn't even give a damn that I was in the middle of a bar and anyone and everyone could be watching—in fact that turned me on more.

I broke the kiss with Jason, gasping for air.

"I wanna take you home, tie you to my bed, and never let you leave." Marcos growled.

"So do it," I dared, meeting his dark gaze. *It was now or never.* I decided right then in there, that I wanted more from them. Tomorrow when I was sober, I would lay down the ground rules, but tonight... tonight I wanted to play.

"Darlin, you have to know what you're getting yourself into, before we go down that road." Jason spoke soft, near my ear.

"We play for keeps, Little Dreamer," Nico said into my other ear. "You come home with us tonight, that means you're ours, we don't fuck around. So make sure you're clear in your decision. There's no 'I don't know' this time around."

A breathy whimper left my lips. "Like forever?" I was dumb-founded.

"Forever and ever, *Mi Vida*," Marcos murmured before he captured my mouth. His kiss was slow and sensual as he pushed his hips against my core. Nico's hands were still on my thighs, holding me open. Jason's hand was still in my hair, holding my head in place.

My body quivered with need as I wrapped my legs around Marcos's hips and gripped his cut to hold him in place.

Marcos groaned into my mouth as Nico's hands slid between us. My dress was hiked further up my hips, and my lacy thong was pulled to the side before Nico's fingers were gliding through my slick folds.

I was a mess already, the scrap of lace did nothing to soak up my juices as they coated my thighs, pooling on the leather barstool beneath me. I had a vague thought that I hoped my friends were all gone, so they didn't see me slutting it up with three men in front of everyone.

Marcos's mouth was relentless. Every time I tried to break the kiss and come up for air, Jason's fist tightened in my hair.

Nico's mouth latched onto the side my neck and sucked in deep, while his fingers toyed with my cunt.

Jason leaned down and kissed along my jaw, until he found a place just behind my ear that drove me wild.

I bucked against Marcos, moaning loudly as Nico slid two fingers inside me.

Marcos drank in my moans as he ground his cock against me.

"Should he fuck you right now? Right here? Should I open his fly and guide his cock into you?" Nico whispered into my ear.

I moaned again, trying to break the kiss with Marcos. I was breathing hard, my chest heaved, and still Jason's hand held my head in place, while Marcos continued to fuck my mouth with his tongue. His fingers tugging painfully on my nipples.

Jason's other hand slid over my tits, brushing over Marcos's hand before his hand skated up my chest to wrap around my neck. His grip tightened around my throat as he yanked my hair, pulling my head back.

I huffed, my chest heaving as I sucked in lungful's of air before Jason's hand tightened around my throat.

"What's it going to be, darlin'? You comin' home with us?" His gravelly voice sent shivers down my spine and I didn't even try to muffle my moan at how it made my fucking cunt clench around Nico's fingers.

Nico's other fingers circled my clit.

Jason's hand tightened further around my throat.

Marcos pinched and tugged on my nipples.

"Yesss!" I came so violently, I would have jackknifed off the chair, if it weren't for the three men holding me in place. My loud moan was quickly silenced as Jason sucked my tongue into his mouth and squeezed my neck tighter.

I was floating, fucking high as a kite, as my orgasm rocked my body. Pleasure rolled over me, tears pouring down my face as I sobbed into Jason's kiss, my eyes squeezed shut.

"Shh, Little Dreamer," Nico murmured, pressing a kiss to my temple. "We've got you."

Marcos eased off my nipples, massaging my swollen buds instead of torturing them.

Jason's grip on my neck loosened and turned into a gentle caress as his thumb smooth circles against my overheated skin.

Nico slowly pulled his fingers from my cunt, and I shivered as cool air hit my bare pussy.

Jason slowed our kiss to a lazy battle of tongues, as the hand in my hair gently let go of my curls.

"So fucking hot," Marco muttered.

"Mmmhmm," Jason murmured against my lips. He pulled away slightly, pressing a chaste and gentle kiss to my mouth, before he stepped back.

My eyes fluttered open to take in the scene around me. I was still in the middle of the bar, but the three of them blocked me mostly from view. The bar was to my right, and thankfully the bartender was occupied further down the bar, and didn't seem to have seen me in the throes of passion as it were.

My heart began to race, as panic rose within me.

"Shh, *Mi Vida*. We've got you. Nothing is going to happen. No one saw a thing," Marcos spoke softly.

"Let's go home," Jason suggested. He glanced around, and for the first time, I noticed a wall of leather clad bikers between my three men and the rest of the bar. A wall of Devil's Psychos patches greeted me, as their backs kept me from seeing out to the barroom beyond them.

Nico and Marcos made quick work of tugging my thong back into place and smoothing down my dress. They pieced me back together while Jason nuzzled my throat. "You were so good for us, baby." Butterflies fluttered in my belly as his nose rubbed against my neck. "We're going to take you home and never let you go."

"Come on," Marcos said, before I could even think about what was happening. He helped me slide off the barstool before he grabbed my hand and laced our fingers together. Turning away from me, he tapped the biker in front of him, and the man moved forward.

As one, the crowd of bikers around us moved forward, keeping pace with Marcos, Jason, Nico, and I as we walked toward the back of the bar to the exit. The wall of bikers protected me from prying eyes of those in the bar, and from making even more of a spectacle of myself, as I could feel the wet spot soaked into the back of my dress from where my fluids had pooled on the bar stool.

I was an utterly *fucked* mess. And I loved every fucking minute of it.

Shivering slightly as the cool air hit my overheated skin. Jason pressed in behind me, wrapping his arms around me. "How'd you get here?" he asked, voice low.

"Ride-share," I mumbled, feeling drunk and tired, and utterly blissful.

"Ever ride a motorcycle before?" Nico asked, chuckling to my right.

I shook my head minutely. "Never."

"This isn't the time for your first ride," Marcos said gently. "Not tonight." Just as he spoke the words, a beat up old pick-up truck pulled up behind the bar.

I pouted slightly, but was grateful for the truck. I was too unsteady on my feet, too fucking out of it still, to fucking balance on the back of a motorcycle. I felt like I was going to pass out at any moment.

"Come on, *Mi Vida*. Let's get you home."

Chapter Twelve

Maya

WHEN I WOKE UP, light streamed in from an open curtain, hitting me across the face. My head was pounding as the hangover kicked in, and my bladder was screaming at me to get out of bed. I groaned; my stomach grumbling was the last straw. Looking around the small unfamiliar room, I slowly sat up in the queen-size bed.

The bedroom was mostly sparse, save for the bed and a dresser. The dresser didn't have any personal items on it besides a pile of dirty laundry. I couldn't see any family photos or knickknacks anywhere.

Sliding out of bed, I looked down and saw I was in an oversized T-shirt, and my red dress was hanging from the closet door—someone had changed me last night. I didn't remember anything past agreeing to go home with my guys and following them out to the pickup truck. I must have passed out on the way.

Feeling unsettled, and the need to pee overwhelming, I padded out of the room and looked around for a bathroom. Thankfully, across the hall from the bedroom I'd slept in was a bathroom. Down the hall, I could hear the deep voices of my guys and the clinking of dishes.

I took my time in the bathroom, even going as far as to use their shower after I found it was clean enough. After living in the dorms full of women for four years, my standards were pretty low. Thankfully, my boys were relatively clean when it came to bathroom upkeep.

Smiling when I checked out the shampoo selection and finding shampoo *and* conditioner—which had to be Nico's—I managed to wash my curls and not worry about them going haywire. When I finished, and dressed again in the borrowed T-shirt, I used Nico's hairbrush to part my curly hair and used my fingers to comb out the locks. I had to be careful with my curls, or they would rebel and drive me crazy all day.

Feeling better after the shower, I left the bathroom and went in search of my guys. I found them in the open concept kitchen, dining, and living room, sitting down at a small rickety table, eating breakfast. All three of them had yet to get dressed, still in sweatpants and T-shirts. "Morning," I murmured as I stepped into the small open living space.

Three sets of eyes turned to meet my own. I tried not to blush as three hungry stares devoured me. The T-shirt hung off my shoulder, and my wet hair cascaded down my back—I could only imagine how they saw me if their stares were anything to go by.

"Good morning, Darlin'," Jason greeted with his low timbre that made me shiver.

"How'd you sleep?" Marcos asked, reaching a hand out to me.

I moved toward him slowly as Nico stood up. "You hungry?" Nico asked.

I nodded and smiled as I slid onto Marco's lap. He wrapped a heavy arm around my waist, holding me to him as he ate his breakfast.

Nico set a plate of food down next to Marcos's plate, pushing his plate over to make room, before Nico handed me a fork. On my plate was a full set up of biscuits and gravy with hashbrowns and bacon on the side.

I didn't want things to be awkward this morning, and I wasn't sure where I stood with them. Sure, last night when I'd been drunk, they had said *forever*, but did they actually mean that in the morning? If this morning was anything to go by though, they had meant what they said. I was amazed by how easily they had just slotted me into their morning routine.

"How you feelin, Darlin'?" Jason asked.

I shrugged a shoulder as I chewed my food. "Alright. I've got a slight headache."

Nico shot up again and headed for the counter. I heard the pill bottle rattle before I could look over. "Coffee, Milk, Water?" Nico asked.

"Coffee, please," I murmured.

A moment later, two blue liquid-gels and a steaming mug of coffee were set down beside me. I beamed as I reached for the mug of black coffee. "Thank you."

Nico grinned at me as he returned to his chair at the small table.

"So about last night," Jason said.

I reached for the pills and raised an eyebrow at Jason. I tossed back the pills with a sip of the burning coffee, relishing in the taste of the strong, fresh brew.

He waited until I was done before he continued speaking. "We were serious about this being real for us."

I slowly set down my coffee and nodded. "We going straight into it then?"

"Let her eat, first," Marcos grumbled.

Jason shrugged. "You can eat and talk." He smirked.

I rolled my eyes and took a bite of the biscuits and gravy and moaned low in my throat. "Oh my goooood."

Nico chuckled, "Fucking hell, Little Dreamer."

Marcos adjusted me on his lap as his cock kicked beneath me.

I giggled around another mouthful of food, not sorry in the slightest. "You were saying, Jason?" I smiled coyly over at him.

Jason's gray eyes had gone stormy with desire, his eyelids hooded. He was looking at me like he wanted to throw me down on the tabletop and eat me instead. And I was OK with that. "What do you remember about last night?" He questioned me instead.

"All of it, until the truck. Did I pass out?"

Jason's hooded gaze narrowed on me. "Yes, you passed out. Which had it been anyone else—"

"Had it been anyone else, it wouldn't have happened. Save the lecture, Dad, before it's not you either," I snapped off, rolling my eyes before he could really get into it.

Nico whistled under his breath, looking almost gleeful.

Jason's eyes narrowed on me further.

Marcos shifted beneath me. "Let's back it up here," he spoke up, intervening. "Maya knows how to take care of herself."

Stone barely glanced at his buddy, before he turned his gaze back to me.

I watched him suspiciously, waiting for him to say something else that might piss me off. I was NOT a morning person, and I was still mad at him—all of them. And as I didn't remember what happened after they got me in the truck, I had to ask. "Did you guys, sleep with me last night?"

"What? God no. You passed out," Nico exclaimed.

Relief washed over me, as I took in their horrified expressions. "What the hell do you take us for?" Jason snapped.

I glared at him. "As you said, I passed out. And as I really don't even know you guys..."

"We'd never touch you without your permission, Dream Girl," Nico said, shaking his head.

I shrugged, unsure what else to say after that.

"Alright, so last night," Marcos said. He rubbed his hand over my bare thigh, soothingly. "We said we play for keeps, meaning you come home with us, you're ours."

"I remember," I said.

"That means something different to us, Maya," Marcos continued. "Last time we played together we talked a little about BDSM and the lifestyle we're into."

I nodded slowly. "So that would apply to our relationship then?"

Nico nodded. "We wouldn't expect you to go twenty-four-seven. But in the bedroom, yes, that's what we'd expect."

"And when we meant for keeps, we'd want you to move in," Marcos clarified.

I froze, my fork halfway to my mouth. "No." The word was out before I realized I even spoke it.

Marcos's body stiffened beneath me, like he was shocked at my answer. "No?"

I set my fork down and stood up, shaking my head. Marcos's hand trailed down my body as he let go of me. I walked a few steps away to the counter and leaned back, crossing my arms over my chest as I surveyed the three of them.

"What do you mean *no*?" Marcos asked.

"Just what I said. You want me to move in here? Just like that? No." I shook my head again. "For the record, I'm still pissed at the three of you. I'm not just letting that shit go and moving in here, not just cause we slept together a couple times and you said so. Fuck that."

Their heads lowered, gazes on the table, before they slowly got to their feet, chairs scraping on the cheap linoleum. "Alright. We deserve that," Marcos nodded, as he turned toward me.

I gave them a look that screamed 'Duh' in return. I hated when men tried to validate my fucking feelings, like they were only acceptable if men deemed them so.

"So, that's it?" Jason asked, crossing his own arms over his chest, his T-shirt pulled tight across his muscles, his biceps popping. He had that stone-cold expression on his face, locking down his emotions, but I knew better. I could see the hurt in his gaze.

"I didn't say that." Shaking my head, I ran my fingers through my damp curls. "BDSM is all about negotiations, correct?"

My men froze, their eyes on me cautiously. "Correct," Marcos agreed, the hint of approval his dark gaze.

"So, I'm open to negotiations," Maya conceded.

Jason smirked. "Good girl," he murmured.

Heat bloomed across my cheeks and I had to fight the smile that threatened to spread across my face. I needed to keep the upper hand here, stand my ground. "Don't, Jason Langford. Not right now, I'm not in the mood."

"She's right." Marcos sighed. "We fucked up, and we're not in the position to be making demands here."

I nodded solemnly. "I don't like the idea of moving in with anyone without dating. We've only fooled around. I want actual dates. I'm not talking fancy dinners and roses bullshit," I said, when I could see their faces clamming up. "I'm talking about doing things together, going places. I'm not a fancy chick. I don't care about that bullshit, but we do need to get know each other before I make a decision."

My men nodded slowly. "Dating," Jason said, testing the word, like he'd never heard it before.

I smirked. "Dating."

"Agreed," Marcos nodded.

Nico flashed me a smile. "You're gonna be falling head over heels before you know what hit you, Little Dreamer."

If he kept up the nicknames like that, I didn't doubt him.

"What else?" Jason asked.

"Besides dating for an undetermined amount of time? Before I agree to *maybe* move in here?" I asked incredulously.

"Yes," Jason said. "What else are you negotiating for?"

I paused, unsure. I honestly had no idea what else I to negotiate for. This was all so new to me. "I uh—"

"This is new, so we're not in any rush, and negotiations are ALWAYS open for discussion, at any time. Just because we agree to something, doesn't mean we can't revisit the conversation at a later date if things aren't working for you or us," Marcos said.

I nodded slowly, my mind whirling.

"We should each fill out a check list and Maya there's a questionnaire and online quiz you can take. Those should help you understand your likes and dislikes, and what we should talk about as a group," Nico suggested. He reached for his phone and started typing. "I'll send you the links."

"I've got a couple blank check lists in my room," Jason said, his voice gentle. "We should all take them again, so Maya can read them when she gets time."

"That sounds good." I nodded, hopefully sounding braver than I felt.

"Alright, come eat," Marcos said, reaching for me again. He pulled me into his arms, holding me close. He pressed a kiss to my forehead before he pulled back and guided me to the table again.

We ate breakfast in a companionable silence.

Chapter Thirteen

Maya

OVING BACK HOME AFTER four years in the dorms was awful. Every day I was home I struggled to get along with my mother. My father, as usual, was mostly silent, but why would he ever speak up for me when my mother berated me every moment of the day.

I was used to living on my own, not having to account for my whereabouts, being spontaneous and carefree when I wanted, and knowing when I needed to bust my ass to finish homework. I was twenty-two years old, not a damn child—but according to my mother, I couldn't even wipe my own ass.

It was bad enough that my parents didn't come to my graduation, but living with them since then, was wearing on my nerves.

In the week I had off between school and starting my new job, I had barely dumped my things in the bedroom I had claimed, when my parents had moved into this new house. They had moved out of my childhood home in Creekton, and moved into this newer house in Mourningside while I was away. The bedroom still had the random band posters hanging on the walls that I had hung up one summer while I'd been home from school.

In the end, it was just a room for my belongings until I could move out. Instead of being stuck at my parents' house during my week off, I spent days catching up with old friends and even spent a whole day with one of my oldest friends, Slade Cooper, getting every damn tattoo I'd wanted while I was away at school.

After Slade had pierced my belly button, I had relaxed back in a tattoo chair for the remainder of the day. Slade tatted me in between her other scheduled appointments. We chatted and caught up on everything that had happened since the last time we saw each other, the summer before.

"Girl, same old shit really," Slade grinned, her bright green eyes dancing in the sunshine. She had black hair down to her waist the last time I saw her, but was now cut short and choppy around her face.

Slade and I had been neighbors growing up in Creekton. While Slade was four years younger than me, that hadn't stopped our friendship. She was like the little sister I never had, and just tagged along with me and Jenna or my friends where ever we went. At eighteen, Slade had graduated high school the year before—graduating just before her father had succumbed to his lung cancer.

Slade now ran her dad's tattoo parlor, Skin of a Different Breed, all by herself. She employed a handful of workers and had a steady stream of clientele. Slade had a good head on her shoulders and I was proud of her. "How's modeling going?"

Slade laughed whole heartedly. "A totally different world. Oh man." She shook her head. "It's fun at times. The money is great, but that world is *not* my world. I don't need all the glitz and glamor, and those chicks don't eat anything all day, then drink and do drugs at night." She shook her head again, her smile dimming. "It's not really my scene, you know? You can get lost in that life."

Once again, I was reminded that my friend was an old soul and our age difference didn't matter. "That's good you know that. So many people get swept up in the glitz and glamor, especially when they come from small towns."

"Creekton is a lot of things, but we didn't grow up in the bad areas. We saw it, but our home lives were decent enough." Slade sighed.

I smiled sadly. "Have you talked to your mom in a while?"

Shaking her head, Slade grumbled. "Not since the funeral. She sent a wedding invite to some new guy she's with in Florida, but I'm not interested."

I winced, "That's rough girl."

Slade shrugged a shoulder and bent back over my side, continuing her work on a large butterfly piece that spread from boob to hip on my right side—the wings curling around my front and back with bright multi-color designs interlaid. Slade was working it free hand as we spoke, bringing a gorgeous masterpiece to life.

I was lounged back in the tattoo chair in my bra and panties, to give Slade the room to work without clothes getting in the way. Thankfully Slade had adjusted the air conditioning, so I wasn't freezing my ass off. Comfortable and alone in the shop with one of my oldest friends, I hadn't minded when Slade only moved the privacy curtain to our view of the door.

Wednesdays at the shop were slow, Slade had said, until the evenings—that's when things picked up. It had been just the two of us throughout the day, until she had the occasional customer, but her staff and appointments didn't start until that evening, when most people got off of work.

The door chimed, signaling a walk in, before a familiar male voice called out. "Yo Slade, you here?"

"Give me a minute," Slade called back as she was finishing a line she was shading.

"Yeah, no problem," he replied.

"Nico?" I asked.

"Little Dreamer, that you?" Nico walked around the curtain and grinned broadly. Dressed in his Devil's Psycho's cut, with a white T-shirt and blue jeans, he looked hot as hell. His blond hair was pulled back into a ponytail and his blue eyes shone in the sunlight. "Hot damn, pretty lady."

I giggled and reached a hand out to him.

"You guys know each other?" Slade asked, a cheeky grin on her lips as she looked up from her work.

"Something like that," I murmured, before Nico took my hand in his and bent over to give me a kiss on the lips.

"She's ours." Nico told Slade as he pulled away from the kiss. He kept his fingers laced with mine and grabbed a rolling stool from the next tattoo station, taking a seat next me.

"Whaaa?" Slade looked up from her work, dumbfounded. "Bitch, you didn't say shit! All fucking day!"

I blushed immediately. "It's new... it's—I don't even know how to describe it."

Nico chuckled. "You're cute, Little Dreamer. It is new, I'll give you that. But you came home with us, and you agreed, you're ours."

"As in Jason's and Marcos's, as well?" Slade raised an eyebrow, smirking.

I blushed scarlet red, covering my face with my free hand, while trying to drop Nico's hand.

"Yep," Nico said, popping the p for emphasis.

"Hot damn, Maya!" Slade grinned.

I shrugged, rolling my eyes. "They grow on you... like mold."

Nico laughed deeply and squeezed my hand.

"Well, good for you! And Nico, I'll kick your fucking ass and never tatt all three of you again if you hurt my girl here. She's my sister from another mister."

Nico's laughter ceased immediately as a look of horror passed over his face. "What the fuck?"

"You heard her." I smirked up at him.

"I—you don't have to worry about that with us, babe." His eyes were so earnest as he spoke. He lifted my hand to his lips and kissed my knuckles.

My heart pounded in my chest and butterflies erupted in my belly. *God damn, I was so fucked.*

"Whatcha here for, Nic?" Slade asked, changing the subject and returning to her work. She was only doing the black outlining on the butterfly today. I would have to come back for multiple sessions to finish the coloring and shading, but it already looked amazing. Paired with the two other smaller tattoos Slade had done earlier that morning—I had finally put a dent into the list of tattoos I had wanted done.

"Was going to see if you had free time to work more on my back," Nico said.

Slade glanced up at a clock on the wall and shook her head. "Sorry, dude. I've got an appointment at five."

I looked up, *it's already a quarter to five?* "Damn."

Slade laughed. "Time flies when you're having fun."

"How long you've been here, Little Dreamer?" Nico asked.

"All day." I laughed.

"We got breakfast at like eight?" Slade said. "Then we came here. Couple tattoos, a new piercing, and voilà! My girl is even hotter than before!"

Nico's grin turned wicked. "I'd say."

I rolled my eyes, despite the blush coloring my cheeks again.

"And you've got an appointment, Slade. Sounds like I came just in time to take Maya out to dinner."

The buzzing of the tattoo gun stopped and Slade put down her gun. The next few moments Slade slathered my tattoo with ointment before she dressed and wrapped it. Then I carefully pulled on my jean shorts and tank top. My shorts, once buckled, cut in a little too tight around my new butterfly tatt, irritating things, so I unbuttoned the jeans, and arranged my flowy tank top over it, so it wasn't noticeable.

Nico's blue eyes were dark, as he watched me dress. "Fucking hot, Little Dreamer."

I smiled coyly up at him. "You're taking me to dinner?"

He nodded and stalked around the tattoo chair, coming for me. I held my ground and waited, smile still on my face as I tilted my chin up. His finger traced down the side of my jaw, before he hooked it under my chin and pulled me closer. His kiss was slow and sensual, gentle.

I moaned when he pulled away, cutting the kiss entirely too short.

"No sex in my shop," Slade called from the back room.

"We won't," I called back. "What do I owe you for today?"

"Dinner!" Slade yelled.

"That's it?"

"Yep! Double cheeseburger with bacon and extra cheese from Jimmy's." Slade lowered her voice as she moved closer.

Nico and I walked around the curtained off area and met Slade near the cash register. "Are you sure?" I asked, not wanting to take advantage of my friend.

"Absolutely, girl! I already ordered it; you just need to pick it up and pay. Then bring it to me. My next appointment is only forty-five minutes, but my six o'clock is four hours long. I won't have time to eat."

"Shit girl," I shook her head. "We should have stopped hours ago."

Slade grinned. "We were having fun. Plus, I missed you." Slade leaned and hugged me tight. "Today was on the house. The rest, you pay for."

"Alright," I nodded. "Come on, pretty boy. Let's go pick up her dinner."

We spent the next hour or so picking up Slade's dinner and dropping it by her, before we dropped my car at home. Then I changed into more appropriate clothes to ride a motorcycle in. I picked out a pair of faux leather pants—because the waistline was elastic and didn't bother my new ink like my jeans had—paired with a sexy red tank top, black combat boots, and red lip stick. I looked fucking fantastic.

I put my long curly hair up into a ponytail, pulling out my longer bangs to frame my face, before I grabbed a red bandana and tied it over my hair. Making sure my bangs fell around my face still in front of the bandana. I nodded to myself in the mirror before I walked out of my bedroom.

I walked through the empty living room and had just reached the front door when my mother called after me. "Where are you going, dressed like that?" My mother's disapproving voice called out from the kitchen.

"Out, mom," I called over my shoulder, not stopping.

"The hell you are! You look like a whore!"

I walked out, slamming the front door behind me. I headed down the long driveway, to where I had told Nico to wait. Stopping by my car, I grabbed my sunglasses for the ride. Having never been on a motorcycle before, I was nervous and was trying to anticipate all the things that I might need. Nico had already told me that pants were required, as well as sunglasses.

Nico was off his bike and leaning against it, smoking a cigarette, when I walked over to him. He looked like a fucking God, with his long hair, arms covered in tattoos, and the black leather cut over his white T. So fucking hot. The smoldering heat in his gaze, though, as his eyes trailed leisurely over my body, had my pussy clenching with need. How the hell was I going to sit through dinner with his man?

"Hi," I murmured, feeling shy, as I slowed my steps.

"Hot damn, Little Dreamer." Nico stood up, tossed his smoke into the road, and pulled my body into his. "You gonna slap me if I ruin this lipstick?"

"It's smudge-proof." I smirked.

"Sounds like a challenge." The words were uttered in a deep growl, before he grabbed my jaw with his finger and thumb, tilting my face to claim my lips in a bruising kiss.

Dinner alone with Nico was a magical thing. He took me to a dimly lit and very romantic Italian restaurant on the border of Mourningside and Creekton. Sera's was close to my house, and one of those places that had a waiting list that was booked out for months. It was also the kind of place with a dress code, and was frowned upon to show up in leather and denim.

And yet, Nico walked right in, dressed in his Devil's Psychos cut and acted like he owned the place. He said a few words to the Maître D, and then we were escorted to one of those coveted tables near the window, overlooking the Evermore River and the beautiful sunset that painted the sky.

It was the most unexpected and romantic dinner of my life, and I was sharing it with a long haired, rough and tumble biker, that had a devious smile and trouble on his mind. "How?"

Nico laughed and held my hand across the table. "It's my cousin's restaurant."

My mouth dropped open. "Your cousin is Leonardo Seratelli?"

Nico nodded and shrugged. "My mother's maiden name is Seratelli. My mother and Leo's father are siblings."

I closed my mouth slowly, as what that really meant dawned on me. "Nico, is your uncle the Mo—"

Nico's smile slid from his face, but he was saved from answering when their waiter, an older Italian gentleman with a cultured and smooth accent greeted them and asked for their drinks.

I dropped the subject, but the thought was never far from my mind. The Seratelli family was a notorious in Creekton. Some said they were Mafia, others refused to speak about them, but everyone knew not to cross them.

They owned a handful of businesses in and around both Creekton and Mourningside, and were said to have their hands involved in City Hall and the mayor's office, but the most notable of their business dealings was the river boat casino they owned and operated out of: Stella's. Located on the Evermore River, not far from the restaurant we sat in, Stella's was conveniently placed right on the border in the area known as The Edges, where jurisdiction lines were blurry. Not quite Creekton, and not quite Mourningside, but on the edge of both. It had been common knowledge growing up in, that even someone as far removed from that life as me, still knew it to be true.

After we finished our meal—the most decadent tasting pasta I'd ever had—we chatted quietly, holding hands and sipping on cocktails. A hushed murmuring around the room garnered my attention and had me looking around for the source of the activity, only to be surprised when a man around Nico's age and dressed in chef's whites walked over, carrying two plates of what looked to be tiramisu.

My mouth dropped open in shock, as the Chef stopped by our table and smiled brightly at us. "May I offer you both my famous tiramisu?"

"Yes, please!" I grinned, pulling my hand out of Nico's grasp and sitting up straight to make room on the table for the Chef to set down the plates.

"You slick bastard." Nico chuckled.

"Coming from the biker that name dropped to score a fancy meal for a first date?" The Chef shot back, raising an eyebrow. He had black hair and was deeply tanned, with the same bright blue eyes as Nico. He had a very stereotypical look about him, but when his eyes crinkled in the corners and he smiled broadly at Nico, I could see their family resemblance.

"It's not a first date," Nico countered.

"It is a first date," I shot back.

The Chef laughed and held out a hand to me. "Leonardo Seratelli. This bastard's cousin."

"Maya Henderson. This bastard's date." I beamed and shook Leonardo's hand.

Leonardo laughed. "I like her, Nic. It's nice to meet someone who keeps him in check." Leonardo squeezed my fingers gently before he dropped my hand.

"It's nice to meet you too, Leonardo. You have a beautiful restaurant. Everything was delicious."

"It's Leo, please." He smiled easily. "I'm glad you enjoyed everything. It's always a pleasure to receive a compliment from a beautiful lady."

Nico shook his head, smile plastered on his face. "Thanks, cousin."

Leo laughed and clapped Nico on the shoulder. "It's been too long, cousin. You should come to dinner, Sunday. You know the family misses you."

Nico's smile slipped a just enough for me to wonder why, but when he just shrugged a shoulder and said, "We'll see. I'll have to check my calendar." I knew the family dinner was the last place Nico planned on being.

Leo turned back to me with a smile. "It was nice to meet you, Maya. I hope you like tiramisu, it's one of my specialties."

"You too, Leo. I'm sure it'll be amazing." I shook his hand again.

"It was good to see you, cousin." Leo clapped Nico on the shoulder again, before he turned back to the kitchen and walked away.

I waited until Leo was behind the kitchen doors, before I took Nico's hand in mine again. "You, OK?"

Nico's smile seemed forced, but he squeezed my fingers affectionately. "Just great, Little Dreamer."

I let the topic go, instead I turned to my dessert and dug in, moaning loudly. "Oh, that is amazing."

"Jesus Christ, Maya." Nico groaned. "You're killing me here."

I just laughed and dug into the dessert whole heartedly. It was the best thing I'd ever tasted.

After the amazing dinner we had at Sera's, it was dark when we mounted the bike. Both of us were stuffed from our meal and lost in thought. We drove around seemingly aimless, until he turned up the hill that led to Dead Man's Pointe. Located on top of Dead Man's Bluff, it overlooked Quinnlyn Beach and the crystal-clear waters of Lake White Buffalo below. It also happened to be a popular make out and party spot for local teenagers.

A silly smile graced my lips as Nico slowed the bike to a stop at the top of the bluff. There was an empty parking lot and wooden guard rails along the edges to keep people in. Nico pulled his

Harley into one of the spots, but didn't move to dismount. As he cut the engine off, I slid off the back of the bike and waited. "You, OK?" I asked softly. I ran a hand over the back of his neck.

He slowly turned to me, pulling his night riding glasses off his face. Desire burned in his gaze as he reached out to me, as he wrapped his large hand around the side of my face. His fingers were on the nape of my neck, with his palm along my jaw, and he pulled me toward him slowly.

I smiled as I stepped into his body, seeking his heat. With the sun down, the early June heat of the day had receded to cooler nights and I already regretted not bringing a sweatshirt.

Nico pulled me into a slow and sensual kiss, nothing like the heat that had been smoldering in his blue eyes. He was gentle and soft, so I pressed against him harder, wrapping my arms tighter around his neck, and kissed him back with more fire and passion. He groaned immediately and tried to pull away from me. Locking my arms around his neck, I smirked into the kiss before I bit down gently on his lower lip.

His groan was immediate. His hand slid down to my ass, palming my cheeks roughly before he dropped his hands to my thighs and lifted me. Holding me tightly against him, he slowly lowered me onto the bike in front of him, so I straddled his thighs as he sat me down on the gas tank.

I slid forward so I was sitting in his lap, facing him on the bike. Our kiss grew sloppier, more passionate. He sucked my tongue into his mouth and I moaned loudly. "Fuck." He groaned, breaking the kiss.

Laughing, I nipped the underside of his jaw.

"I really didn't bring you up here for this. I thought maybe we could sit on the ledge, watch the water for a while. Get to know each other."

"We can still do that. After you fuck me, on this bike," I murmured softly, leaving wet open-mouthed kisses down his jaw and neck.

"Fucking hell, Little Dreamer." He groaned, his fingers digging into my hips as he pulled me down on his denim covered cock and ground against my core.

"I should have worn a skirt."

He chuckled low in his throat, "As hot as that is, it's not fucking safe. And if you're riding with us, you're gonna ride safe."

I twisted my hips and thrusted them up, grinding on him.

"Fuck baby." He groaned and yanked my pants down.

I shifted and helped him, lifting my ass and propping my foot off the back seat behind him so I could slide backwards on the gas tank, giving him more room to work. I bent my knees so he was able to pull my jeans down—until they got stuck on my combat boots. "Fuck!"

Nico laughed and stood up with me in his arms. He set me back on my feet before he turned me around and roughly pushed between my shoulder blades, shoving my chest down onto the bike.

I moaned loudly at the rough treatment, my core clenching as the need to get fucked rolled through me. I heard his belt jingle, then a moment later the blunt head of his cock nudged at my entrance, before he was gripping my hips tightly, and slamming home in one fucking stroke.

My back arched and I cried out, feeling the burn of his cock stretching me. He didn't give me time to get used to him either, he grabbed a fistful of my hair with one hand, while the other dug into my hips. He set a brutal and bruising pace, our bodies clapping together loudly with each thrust.

All I could do was hold on and arch my back as he fucked me hard against the motorcycle. A chill ran down my spine at the thought that anyone might be able to see us, watch me being used so thoroughly, and the idea turned me on.

They had mentioned their own checklists and a quiz they wanted me to take, but I still hadn't gotten anything from them. I had started on my own research though, and everything I had already read had turned me on immensely. I was so ready to learn whatever they wanted to teach me.

Moaning and panting, I held onto the motorcycle as best I could as Nico ravaged her pussy. "Oh fuck." I gasped, feeling my climax building quickly. A keening wail broke out of me as my pleasure rose and my orgasm tore out of me. My pussy clenched down on

Nico's cock and my body went ridged, before I shuddered with pleasure and moaned loudly again.

"Fucking hell," Nico grunted. He tried to fuck me through it, but I was clenching him too tightly. He held me tightly through it, and when I finally calmed down, he resumed thrusting, slowly this time, giving me a few moments to adjust to the sensitivity.

Boneless, I was draped over the bike as Nico let go of my hair and grabbed both of my hips. His slow, deep, thrusts pulled a moan out of me with every thrust. When his thrusts came hard and faster, he let a low groan, and I knew he was close. I swiveled my hips and he swore, his knees shaking before he groaned deep in his chest and exploded inside of me.

We stood there, braced over the bike, catching our breaths for a long time. I felt like every time I slept with one of my guys, I had a life shattering orgasm that changed everything I knew about myself and sex. If this was a taste of what they had in store for me once we started digging into the BDSM lifestyle that they enjoyed, I could only imagine what the sex and orgasms would be like going forward.

Eventually Nico slowly pulled out of me, leaving me feeling empty and messy. My juices were sliding down my thighs, mixed with his cum as it slowly leaked out of me. He slid his fingers through my folds and pushed his cum back inside of me. He growled low, his voice deep, right next to my ear. "You'll keep that inside you, if you know what's good for you."

A shiver ran down my spine at his implied words. My pussy clenched, already feeling the need to be fucked again.

Nico did up his own jeans, before he pulled up my thong, pulling the strings higher than they needed to go, up over my hip bones, so the string was taut through my folds, rubbing at my wet and swollen flesh. I cried out, trying to shift away from him.

A sharp smack landed on her bare ass cheek, and I yelped.

"Be a good girl. You'll wear the thong as I put it."

"Yes, sir," I replied softly, my heart beating wildly.

Nico pulled up my faux leather pants next, but my thong was well above the hem. I moaned as the fake material rubbed over my damp skin. I prayed to God I didn't have to walk much tonight, or I'd end up completely chaffed.

Nico pulled a bottle of water out of one of the back saddle bags on his bike and handed it to me. I cracked the seal and took a long drink of the cool water before I handed it to him. He took a sip and then nodded toward the cliffs. "Let's sit."

I took his hand and let him lead the way.

Once we were seated with my body cradled between his legs and my back against his chest, he wrapped an arm around my waist and pulled out his phone with his other hand. I watched the waves crest over Quinnlyn Beach down below. The view from Dead Man's Bluff was amazing, there was hardly any light pollution around us, so the stars were breathtaking.

"I'm sending you the kink check list the three of us use, and a questionnaire. I'll also send you the link to the online quiz we found. It's a pretty good way of determining where your limits lie, and learning about yourself." Nico's voice was soft in my ear and it sent shivers down my spine. For as much as I thought he was easy going and fun, I was also learning he was very dominate and sensual.

"Have you guys done this a lot?"

He sighed and his arm wrapped around me tighter. "We're accustomed to BDSM ourselves, from our own past relationships. We've shared women in the past, mostly one-night stands, and always incorporated D and S. It makes it easier to keep emotions out of it."

I thought about his words for a minute, sitting quietly. "Have you guys ever dated someone together, before? Like you plan to with me?"

He set his phone down and wrapped his other arm around my waist, pulling me backwards against him even tighter. "There was one girl. It only lasted three months. She ended up meeting someone else, though."

"She cheated?"

Nico nodded.

I sighed and laced my fingers through his. "How long ago was this?"

"We were probably nineteen or twenty? So it was nine or ten years ago. It doesn't matter; she wasn't anyone we saw ourselves with long term."

"How old are you guys?" I laughed, realizing it never came up before. Kara had told me Marcos age at one point, but I had forgotten, 'cause it hadn't mattered.

"Twenty-nine." Nico chuckled and nuzzled my neck. "You worried you're dating a group of old men?"

Laughing, I shrugged and nuzzled him back, rubbing my cheek against his. "Nah, seven years isn't bad."

"Tomorrow, I want you to print out the documents I sent you. Take the online quiz, then print out the documents and fill them out. Take your time, research things if you don't know about them. Really decide if something on there is too far out of your comfort zone, or if you're unsure. Even if you're unsure about something, and you end up not liking it later, we can always talk about things."

I smiled softly as my heart pounded in my chest. I loved how understanding and gentle he was. "Alright."

He pressed a kiss to my neck. "You're already so good, Little Dreamer."

"I like that you call me that."

He hummed and kissed me again.

Maya

THE NEXT DAY, I did as Nico had asked. I started with the online quiz he sent. It asked me over a hundred different questions all about sex, from 'do you enjoy getting tied down dominated in the bedroom', to 'do you enjoy causing your partner pain'? By the end of it, I had learned that I was most definitely a sub, with a pain and rope fetish. The idea of being chased through the woods had intrigued me, and being watched while have sex or being used degradingly was a turn on for me.

I also learned that I needed to be cared for, and the idea of someone taking care of me and making me their priority, sounded good to me. Shit, that sounded good to anyone in any relationship, but I also knew all relationships were different, and not everyone received the same attention from their partners as others.

I doubted I would have any lack of attention from dating three men, in fact, I often wondered if I would get any alone time at all. This week we were taking things slow. They wanted me to read about the lifestyle and ease into things. I'd had one date with Nico already, and when he took me home last night, he'd mention that Marcos would be taking me out Friday night.

That gave me two whole days of research. I knew Marcos was nothing like Nico. He wouldn't be gentle when I saw him. Marcos had an intensity about him. He wouldn't ease me into anything when he finally had me to himself.

After I took the test, I printed out my results three times. I figured I would give them to the guys and let them know I was serious about things. The test had definitely been eye-opening for me—I had learned a lot about myself in a very short amount of time. I moved onto a very long and detailed check list.

I took my time with the check list, pausing to look up things like *sounding* and *golden showers*, neither of which I thought I was into. The check list had columns for me to check either hard yes, soft yes, maybe – let's talk about it, soft no, or hard no. Feeling like I really evaluated the list and myself, I made sure that if there was anything I was really on the fence about, I checked the *maybe – let's talk about it* column, hoping my guys would be understanding and not condescending if I really didn't know something.

There was so much more to BDSM and kink that I ever knew about. I ended up researching most of the day, falling down rabbit-holes on the internet and getting sucked into things I'd never heard of before.

By the end of the night, though, on Thursday, I was a horny mess and needed to get off. Feeling almost bold, and intrigued about asking for permission from my Dom's, I reached out to the group chat I had with my three guys and texted.

Maya

> I've been taking quizzes and checking boxes all day. I feel like I've done more research today than I did all last semester. I'm so fucking turned on right now.

I didn't have to wait long at all, before the three little dots popped up and someone was typing.

Marcos

> Is that right, baby. You need something?

Jason

> Is your little cunt dripping for cock?

Nico

> Such a good girl for us. I can't wait to read your answers.

Maya

> I'm aching. So fucking wet. Can I come please?

I expected the three little dots to pop up immediately again, but was shocked then they didn't. Were they going to leave me hanging?

Finally, I received a reply.

Jason

> Good girl. You should always ask us before you touch that cunt. It belongs to us.

I waited, wondering if Marcos or Nico would respond. Jason didn't technically say I could, he just praised me for reaching out to them.

My phone rang with an incoming video call. I silenced the call quickly. It was late and my parents were sleeping. I didn't want to risk waking them by talking on the phone late at night. I answered the phone, keeping my voice soft. "I can't talk loud," I explained as I answered the phone.

On the screen, all three of my guys were huddled together in what looked like the living room of their small apartment. Dressed in plain T-shirts, they looked like they were winding down for bed for the evening. "God damn, chica," Marcos muttered.

I smiled and glanced down at what I was wearing: short booty shorts and a tight cropped tank top. I'd been home all day alone while my parents were at work, there had been no reason to get dressed. Now, in front of my guys, I could see how much skin was on display, especially my new tattoo that I was letting breathe for a little while.

"Dagger said you were friends with Slade Cooper. She does great work." Stone's voice was a soft rasp that sent shivers down my spine.

I must have closed my eyes and shivered, because his deep chuckle had me opening them to look down at my phone screen. "Please." I moaned low.

"Prop your phone so we can see you," Jason commanded.

It took me some maneuvering, but I finally propped my phone against a couple pillows at the foot of my bed, and laid back, propped up against a couple more. "Good girl," Jason murmured.

My eyelids fluttered at the tone of his voice. *I swear to God, this man can get me off from just the sound of his voice alone.* "Please," I whimpered.

"Take off your shorts," Nico ordered.

I slid my fingers under the waistband of my booty shorts, grateful to not have panties on underneath, and pulled them down my thighs. I carefully guided them down my legs, mindful of my phone perched precariously on a pile of pillows. Tossing them aside, I bent my knees and let my thighs fall wide, leaving my wet cunt on display to the three men on my phone.

"Jesus," Marcos breathed.

"Gorgeous," Nico murmured.

"Slide your fingers through that wet cunt," Jason ordered.

I did as I was told, throwing my head back against the pillows as I slowly slid my fingers through my folds.

"Pull your tank top down, shove your tits over the top." Marcos's voice was raspy as he commanded my moves.

Quickly shoving the top of my tank below my tits, I palmed them both, pulling them up and over the crop top, before I slid one hand back down to my dripping pussy, mindful of the new bellybutton piercing I had received the day before.

"Pinch a nipple," Nico said.

Pinching my nipple with one hand and circling my clit with my other, I slowly swiveled my hips as my body amped back up, edging closer to orgasm. I'd been hanging on a precipice for so long, before I even reached out to them.

"Tell me something you learned today that you want to try?" Jason said.

Groaning, I struggled to think. "Clamps," I muttered, pinching my nipple harder, gasping as pleasure shot from my nipple down to my clit.

"Fuck yeah, baby," Marcos muttered.

"Please, I'm so close," she begged.

"Such a good girl, Maya." Jason spoke low. "Doing your research and following direction, taking the initiative to ask permission, even when we haven't negotiated yet. So, so, good for us."

I whimpered, my fingers circling and pinching faster, tighter. My eyes clenched tight. "Please."

"Come for us, darlin'. Let's see that needy cunt clench and beg to be filled with our cocks," Jason murmured.

I moaned low, gasping, as my orgasm crashed into me, my pussy clenching on nothing, begging for more, just as he said. I took a shuddering breath, my hands dropping to the side, as I came down from my high.

"So beautiful," Nico murmured.

I slowly sat up, fixing my tank top before I picked up my shorts and shimmied back into them. Grabbing my phone, I fixed up the pillows and then slid under the covers of my bed. "How you doing, darlin'?" Jason asked, his voice even softer than before.

"Good." I sighed as I laid down, resting my head on a pillow and propping my phone on another.

"You going to sleep now?" Nico asked.

"Soon." I yawned, covering my mouth.

"What are you doing tomorrow?" Marcos asked.

"I've got some running around to do in the morning. What time are we going out?"

"Why don't you come here around five, then we can leave from here together. And you'll have your car for the morning," Marcos said.

I smirked sleepily. "For the morning? Am I spending the night?"

"Yes." All three of them responded immediately.

I laughed softly. "Alrighty then."

"I mean, if you want to, of course," Marcos added.

"Mmmhmm," I replied, my voice growing thicker with sleep as my eyelids drooped.

"So sleepy, Little Dreamer," Nico murmured.

"Close your eyes, darlin'," Jason said.

I closed my eyes, a smile on my face. "I can't wait to fuck you, Mi Vida," Marcos muttered.

It was the last thing I heard, before I drifted off to sleep.

Chapter Fifteen

Maya

FRIDAY FLEW BY, I managed to get all of my running around done early, even squeezing in a waxing appointment, before I pampered myself in the afternoon with a manicure and pedicure. By the time I pulled into the guy's parking lot, I was feeling both relaxed and excited.

I had packed a duffle with more clothes than I needed, but I figured I'd leave some over at their place. I bought brand new bottles of my shower products: shampoo, conditioner, body wash, loofa, razor. Being prepared was something I had learned in college. Having a travel bag in the trunk in my car, ensured I never did that walk of shame the morning after.

"Moving in already?" Nico smirked when he saw my stuff.

Smiling, I shook my head. "You're not that lucky, yet."

He met me with a kiss and took my grocery bag with my toiletries in it. Glancing inside he laughed and headed for the bathroom. "But I'm not wrong, either."

I just shrugged. He was probably right, it was inevitable, really. I'd never felt so strongly about anyone before meeting them and things with them were hot and heavy immediately. I wasn't complaining, the chemistry was amazing. I just hoped that in a year from now, we still felt the same.

Marcos walked out of the bedroom a moment later and I smiled at him. Dressed in a pair of dark jeans and a black button-down shirt, he looked sophisticated and dangerous. It was a breathtaking combination.

Thankfully I had texted Marcos earlier in the day and asked what I should wear. When he said dressy, I opted for the little black dress I kept on hand for these sorts of occasions. It hit mid-thigh and I briefly wondered how I might sit on a motorcycle, but figured Marcos wouldn't tell me to wear a dress if he planned on taking his bike.

"You look beautiful," Marcos said as he walked toward me. He smiled and pressed a gentle kiss to my lips.

"Thank you," I murmured as we parted.

Dinner with Marcos was not what I had expected. We hadn't ended up at some fancy restaurant, no. Instead, he took me out for pizza at a local family-owned place, one of those places that had been in the neighborhood for decades. Afterwards, we hit a club and danced the night away.

Marcos was a surprisingly amazing dancer. God, I loved every minute of dancing with him, from the dips to the spins, to grinding against him. When the music changed to something more Hispanic, Marcos smirked and grabbed my hands. "Ever danced merengue?" His accent thickened as he leaned into speak over the music.

"At a quinceañera, a long time ago."

He nodded and led me through the moves. It was a series of hip swinging steps while also moving close together before spinning away and back in to each other again. I let him guide me through it all, a smile on my face. His sultry gaze was sinful as he watched my hips sway as I kept up with him. My heart was pounding in my chest every time he pulled me in close and the scent of his cologne was a spicy mix that I knew I would imprint into memory for the rest of my days—along with that night.

After dancing the night away with Marcos at Starlight, he took me back to his place. Jason and Nico were already in bed and the lights in the small living room were dimmed low. Holding my hand, he led me through the apartment, to one of the small three bedrooms in the back. Overall, the apartment was a tight space and I couldn't see how I would be able to 'move in' like they kept talking about—there wasn't enough room for all my stuff.

I still didn't understand their zero-to-one-hundred thought process on our relationship. We barely knew each other past being friends with Kara for the last two years, and they had demanded everything from me, immediately. No, 'hey let's date', it gone straight to: you come home with us, we keep you forever.

It set my heart pounding every time I thought of that night—graduation night. Apparently, I had celebrated so much more than just graduating college, as it was the night I had given into their demands.

Following Marcos into his bedroom, I blinked against the bright light as he flipped the switch. "Do you need to wash your face or brush your teeth?"

"Can I shower?"

"Yeah. Whatever you want. Treat this place like your home." Marcos smiled at me before he started unbuttoning his dress shirt.

My mouth watered as I watched him. "Do you know where my bag went?"

Marcos pointed to the black duffle on the bed.

Grabbing the bag, I turned for the door and headed quietly across the hall to the bathroom. Nico already unpacked my toiletries and there was a fresh towel folded on the counter. They really were trying to move me in and make me feel at home.

I took my time in the bathroom, making sure to fully remove my makeup before I slipped into the shower. I didn't need to wash my hair just yet, so I washed the sweat and grime from the club away and washed my face. When I finally climbed out of the shower, my limbs were relaxed and my movements languid. Brushing my hair and teeth quickly, I moisturized my face and body, before I slowly dressed into the satin nighty I had bought for spending nights at their apartment.

When I was done, I walked out of the bathroom with my clothes bundled in my hands and my duffle bag slung over my shoulder, and headed across the hall to Marcos's room. His door was shut, so I quietly opened it, to find his room only lit by the table lamp. Already lying in bed, Marcos has the blankets draped over his chest. Opening his eyes as I closed the door behind me, he smiled softly. "You look beautiful," he murmured, his voice rough and gravely.

I smiled back and set my dirty clothes on the floor next to my duffle bag, before I climbed over Marcos, and onto bed between him and the wall. The queen size bed was pushed against the wall, and Marcos took up most of the mattress, leaving me enough room to shimmy in next to him. I was surprised that he hadn't initiated sex by now. Was he just going to go to sleep? Expect me to sleep next to him?

"Relax," he murmured.

Lying beside him, unsure of what to do, I giggled. "Are we not having sex?"

Marcos chuckled softly, before he rolled toward me. Sliding one arm under my head and wrapping the other around my hip, he turned me toward him, and pulled me in close. He kissed me softly before he pulled back. "Get some sleep, babe."

Tucked under his chin, I wrapped an arm around his waist and sighed contently. Feeling warm, safe and secure, I drifted off to sleep with thoughts of love already flitting through my mind.

Marcos

I woke in the middle of the night to a mane of curls suffocating me. Sometime during sleep, Maya had rolled over, so her luscious ass was pressed against my rock-hard cock. She'd come to bed in that silky nightie that drove me wild and I'd had good intentions when we came home—I'd wanted to cuddle and not sleep together on our official first date—but it was hard to hold myself to that resolve now that those plump and juicy cheeks were cradling my dick.

My cock and balls were aching as I shifted them against Maya. Sliding my hand up her thigh, I nearly groaned when I found she wasn't wearing any panties. I rubbed her bare, warm skin, watching for any kind of reaction from her. She was dead to the world and her nightie had slipped up and over hips as I ran my hand over her thigh and hip. Taking a gamble, I rolled away from her and quickly shimmied out of my boxers, trying not to shake the bed too much as I got naked. Flinging my boxers off the side of the mattress, I rolled back against Maya's backside and slid in close.

Maya, for her part hadn't moved. Her breathing was slow and steady, unchanging. I continued where I left off, sliding my hand down her thigh to behind her knee. Pushing her knee and leg forward, I bent her knee, opening her legs. Sliding my fingers through her folds, I found her warm and wet already.

I fingered her slowly, spreading her juices before I slid my cock between her folds. Soaking myself in her slick, I slowly pushed myself inside her, all the while monitoring her breathing and reactions.

Her breath hitched, when I was finally fully seated inside her warm and slippery cunt. When she didn't stir, I slid my hand over her hip and around her belly, resting my hand over the small swell of her tummy. "One of these days, *Mi Vida*, I'm gonna breed you." I pressed a kiss to the crook of her neck and slid my other arm under her neck, settling in close. "I'm gonna give you my baby and watch this belly swell with my seed."

Maya's breathing stayed steady, her chest still rising gently as I vowed to her and myself that I would make that happen one day. The idea of her carrying my child just struck a chord within me, it felt *right* on so many levels that I knew I would have to make it come true one day.

Thrusting my hips, my bare cock fucking into her, I had to stifle my groan as her wet hot heat sucked me in, her body begging for more. "I almost want to wake you up so you hear all the filthy things I'm gonna do to you." Almost.

I made love to her slowly, continuing to whisper the dirtiest things I could think of, making a promise to myself to fulfill each one of them.

When I came, my body shaking as I laid besides her, I made sure not to jostle her as I monitored her breathing: still slow and steady. I pressed a small barely-there kiss to her temple, before I slow pulled out of her.

"Fuck baby, we're going to have so much fun together." I settled back beside her. I would need to put my boxers back on before she woke up in the morning, but for now, I would savor the feeling of her sleeping peacefully in my arms.

Maya

"Good mornin', Darlin'," Jason greeted me with a smile. Walking into their kitchen, I smiled sleepily at my three men. Seated around the small kitchen table, that only had three chairs, Jason held an arm out to me. I went to him easily, leaning into his body as I stepped between his legs.

"Hi," I murmured. Perching on his thigh, I rested my head on his shoulder, and turned my face into the crook of his neck.

Marcos got up and made me a cup of coffee, before setting it down in front of me.

Jason's arms wrapped around my waist, holding me tight against him.

I moaned softly and nuzzled the scruff under his jaw.

"My turn tonight." Jason's voice was deep and gravelly as he spoke directly into my ear.

I shivered as the heat of his words and breath skated over my skin. "'Kay," I murmured.

Jason's chuckle was a deep rumble in his chest that vibrated through my side. "Not a morning person, Darlin'?"

I mumbled under my breath. Hadn't we already had a conversation about this the last time I'd spent the night? Ignoring him, I reached for my coffee and brought it to my lips, cupping it with both hands.

Marcos and Nico laughed while they watched me.

"I asked you a question, Maya," Jason said, his voice stern.

I mumbled under my breath.

"Use your words, please."

I tried to sit up straight and pull away from Jason, annoyed with his questions first thing in the morning, but his arms tightened around me, keeping me in place. I didn't like his *directness* first thing in the morning. "No, I'm not," I snapped.

"That attitude will earn you a spanking really quick, darlin'." Jason's voice was commanding and low as he reprimanded me.

"No, it won't," I snapped again, struggling in his hold. "We haven't negotiated shit. I'm not listening to you trying to tell me what to do. Let me go."

His arms were like steel bands wrapped around my waist, despite my struggling, I wasn't able to get away from him.

"We may not have negotiated yet, brat," Jason retorted, sounding angry. "But you are still a guest in my home and you will treat me with respect. And that means using your words like an adult and not grunting or whining when you speak to me."

I froze, staring down at the table. I didn't like what he was saying. I could understand it, but I didn't like the disappointment in his voice. Jason pulled me back against him and I let my body go pliant, letting him lean me back against his chest.

One of his hands came up and wrapped around my jaw. Turning my face toward him, he said, "Look at me."

My breath caught in my throat and it took everything I had in me to raise my eyes to meet his. The storm that raged in those steely gray eyes set my heart racing. His mouth was pressed into a tight line that had me pursing my own lips. I didn't like this feeling, like I was being scolding like a child.

"Are you done?" Jason asked, his voice deep and stern.

"Yes," I murmured, looking down at his chest and not meeting his eyes.

"Look at me when you speak to me," Jason said. His hand was still wrapped around my jaw, so he lifted my chin and forced me to gaze up at him.

Heat bloomed across my cheeks and I had to bite the inside of my cheek to keep from lashing out. There was something uncomfortable about being forced to look at someone who was reprimanding you. My core clenched, as heat pooled in my belly. I was painfully aware of just how turned on this was making me, and I wasn't sure how I felt about it. It was humiliating in a sense, especially as I could feel the heat of Marcos's and Nico's gaze on Jason and me, watching our every move.

"Now, I asked you a question," Jason said. "Are you not a morning person, Maya?"

I narrowed my gaze on his, "No."

A smug smirk pulled across Jason's lips. "I can see that." He chuckled low in his throat, a sensual sound that sent shivers down my spine. His fucking deep voice—God damn, his voice turned me on. I bet I could listen to the man read a fucking grocery list and I'd be dripping wet.

I glared at him, keeping my eyes on him as he hadn't said I could look away yet, and his hand was still wrapped around my jaw, holding me still.

He chuckled again. "And what does your morning routine usually consist of?"

"Quiet," I snapped immediately. I heard Nico and Marcos stifle laughs behind me, but I couldn't turn to look at them.

Jason shifted beneath me, spreading his legs more. I could feel his thick cock harden beneath my ass and had to force myself to concentrate on those stormy gray eyes. "We're going to talk about that attitude of yours, one day."

I swallowed thickly as Jason painfully squeezed my jaw again, before he abruptly let it go. I didn't dare move, though. Unable to look away, I continued to watch him, warily.

"What do you need?" Jason asked.

My heart skipped a beat in my chest. Furrowing my eyebrows together, I narrowed my eyes on him, waiting. Was this some kind of trick of his? Was he setting me up? What did he mean?

"Maya." Jason spoke softly, his stormy eyes calming as his harsh stare softened. "What do you need when you wake up in the morning?"

I bit my lower lip before I answered. "Uh, quiet," I muttered again. "Like you guys can talk to each other, but I don't like to talk until I'm ready. Most of the time I don't like to eat until later, but if there's bacon, I'll probably eat it. At home, I like to sit and drink my coffee while staring out the back patio door into the yard. In my dorm room, my window over looked the forest, so I would sit in the window and drink my coffee there. I just like to zone out, and slowly wake up without pressure."

Jason stared at me even after I finished speaking. Understanding dawned on his handsome face, and his eyes softened while I spoke. "Good girl," he murmured.

Blushing, I ducked my face, unable to meet his gaze for a moment longer.

Again, he chuckled, but he reached out and grabbed my coffee and handed it to me. I barely wrapped both hands around the still warm mug, before he slid his arm under my knees and lifted my legs onto his lap. Cradling my coffee mug against my chest, I let Jason arrange me in his lap so I was seated sideways across his legs, leaning against him, almost in the fetal position with my knees bent and resting against his chest.

I sighed contently and rested my head on his shoulder, savoring the heat from both my mug and his chest. I nuzzled my face under his jaw and closed my eyes. This was all I wanted, why couldn't he have just left shit as it was before?

Either way, it had been a learning lesson for both of us. It had opened my eyes to our potential future, too. I would have a lot of to think about... later. After my coffee.

I vaguely heard Nico start up a conversation, but I ignored them all and took a sip of my coffee, enjoying the peace that had settled around me. Even Jason seemed more relaxed than he had a few minutes ago.

Ten minutes later, after I had finished my coffee quietly, I spoke up. "What are you guys up to, today?"

Nico smiled at me from across the table. "We've got some club business to take care of today, but you're free to stay here, if you want."

I frowned, my eyes darting between his and Marcos. Both men watched me as I shifted on Jason's lap.

"What's on your mind, Maya?" Jason asked.

"I dunno. That seems fast," I admitted.

Marcos chuckled softly. "So what? We're not evening going to be here. You can relax and watch TV."

I sighed. "No." I shook my head. "I'll head home. It's OK." I dropped my feet to the floor and sat up straight on Jason's lap. Turning to him, I ran my fingers over his stubble covered jaw. "What time are you picking me up?"

"Not sure how long today is going to take. Let's aim for five, and I'll keep you updated throughout the day, so have your phone handy, alright?"

"Yes, sir." I nodded before I leaned forward and pressed a kiss to his lips.

"Good girl," he murmured against my lips.

Maya

I SIGHED AS I pulled my Honda Civic into my parents' long driveway. It was just after ten in the morning and after a wonderful night sleeping securely in Marcos's arms, I felt great. The idea of walking into my parent's house, though, was enough to sour my mood.

Things had always been rocky between my parent's and I, mostly between my mother and I, as my father usually let my mother rule the roost. The two of them not showing up to my graduation had only been the latest form of contention between us, and it was just another strike on a lifetime list of disappointments.

I got out of my car and headed inside, leaving my bag behind. I didn't need to showcase the fact that I'd spent the night away from home, despite being a grown adult that could make my own decisions. My mother still thought I was a harlot.

Sure enough, when I walked through the front door, my mother was in the kitchen, reading the newspaper at the kitchen table. She looked up with air of contempt as she ran her eyes over me, studying me, like I hadn't made sure to come back with my hair combed perfectly, or clean clothes on. The jean shorts and tank top—my usual go to in the summer—were not out place in the slightest. When my mother could find nothing wrong with my appearance, she sniffed haughtily. "And where have you been?"

Stifling the urge to roll my eyes, I sighed and said, "Good morning, mother."

"Don't give me that attitude. I asked you a question."

Now I really did roll my eyes. Ignoring her, I headed through the living room to the hallway on the right.

Nico had tried to get me to stay at their place for the day, even though they had to be at the clubhouse most of the day. I had felt awkward and turned them down, plus I knew my mother would have a field day when she saw me next. Now I wished I had stayed, instead of enduring my mother's contempt.

My bedroom was still filled with boxes that were still packed up from my dorm room. Somehow Jenna and I had packed up both our cars—Jenna's SUV—with all the belongings I'd accumulated over my four years at Northern. Besides hanging up my clothes in the closet, I hadn't bothered to unpack anything else. In my heart

I hoped I wasn't staying long. The goal was to work as many hours at the new job as possible and save enough for a deposit on an apartment of my own.

My phone pinged in my back pocket with a text message. I pulled it out as I closed my bedroom door behind me.

Nico

Little Dreamer, it's a shame you didn't stay at our place. We could have watched you on the cameras and been able to see your beautiful face all day.

Maya

Your place has cameras?

Nico

Safety first

I smiled, seemingly not surprised by his response—they were bikers, after all. From my years growing up in Creekton and driving past their clubhouse down on Main Street, I knew they valued their privacy and security. The clubhouse was covered in cameras on the outside, and it only made sense that any home they lived in would be the same.

Maya:

I wish I had stayed too. My mom's in a tiff.

Nico

Should just move in, Little Dreamer.

Jason

It would have been nice to be able to check in on you throughout the day. Would have kept you naked, so I could watch you play with yourself all day.

A shiver ran down my spine as a blush colored my cheeks. Glad I was safely behind a closed door as I giggled softly. I still couldn't believe that all three of them wanted me, that three men in general were OK with sharing like this. Desire and lust poured through me. It was a heady feeling and I was enjoying every minute of it.

I wasn't sure how long they would last, if the three of them would grow bored with me, but I wasn't going to worry about it. I was young. I was going take life by the horns, and have my cake and eat it too. I'd been the responsible adult. I'd gone to college, gotten my degree, and graduated. I was starting my new job in two days. I'd done everything I had needed to without the support of my parents. I was allowed to have fun now.

Maya

That sounds hot.

Marcos

We'll get you a key tonight.

I didn't know how to respond to that declaration, so I chose not to. Instead, I changed the subject.

Jason, what are we doing on our date tonight?

Shooting.

My mouth dropped open in shock. I had never fired a gun before. I had never even been around guns before. I knew my guys valued safety and security, but was teaching me to shoot really necessary?

My phone rang a moment later, Jason's name flashing across the screen. "Hi," I answered immediately, knowing that's what he expected.

"Hi, Darlin'." His voice was a gravelly growl in my ear, that sent my heart racing. "You ever shot a gun before?"

"No," I murmured, blushing.

"That's good. That means I can teach you the right way, and you don't have any bad habits that need correcting."

"I think you enjoy correcting me," I said, and I immediately regretted the words the moment they left my lips.

His laugh was deep and rich, it was fucking music for my ears, sending my heart racing and butterflies fluttering in my belly. God damn. "Oh, baby girl. You have no idea how much."

"What should I wear tonight?" I asked, coyly.

"Jeans and boots if you have them. Nothing fancy darlin', we're going shooting and maybe dinner," Jason said dryly.

I couldn't help but smile at his matter-of-fact tone. "Sounds good to me."

"Pack a bag too. You're staying with us again tonight. I'll pick you up around five."

"Yes, sir." I chuckled.

His answering growl sent shivers down my spine and would live with me throughout the day.

I couldn't help but be nervous for my date with Jason as I dressed into a pair of blue jeans. I had laid out several options for shirts on the bed, knowing I was likely to be warm in the jeans and boots. I had a basic black t-shirt, which would be practical; a spaghetti string black tank top, which would keep me cool and was a little sexier than just a t-shirt; then I had a red low cut halter top that would put a lot of bare skin on display.

I texted Slade a picture of my options, to get her input.

Maya

Date with Jason tonight. He said he's taking me shooting. Only said to wear jeans and boots.

Slade

Then clearly no shirt required.

I laughed while another text from Slade came in immediately.

Slade

Go with the red halter. It's still sexy, and wear that leather jacket you picked up the other day.

I grinned, thinking back to the mini shopping spree I'd gone on while killing time while the guys were busy. The leather jacket had been on a manikin in a window display at the mall. I had just been walking by, when it called to me. I ended up buying several more outfits and the black combat boots from the new edgy store I had stumbled across.

Maya

I finished getting dressed quickly, knowing I was running out of time. I kept my make up simple, eyeliner and mascara and bright red lipstick. I pulled my long curly golden-brown hair up into a high pony, leaving a couple tendrils down to frame around my face. Draping my leather jacket over my arm, I quickly left my bedroom, hoping to slip out of the house unnoticed by my parents—rather my mother.

My father was sitting in his recliner watching TV as usual, but thankfully my mother was nowhere to be found. "Night dad. I'm staying with a friend tonight, so I'll see you tomorrow."

"Night, honey." He barely even glanced away from the TV to look at me.

I ignored the pain in my heart at his easy dismissal and walked out the front door. Walking down the long driveway, I was right on time as Jason came riding down the road on his bike, the rumble of the Harley going right to my core. I fucking loved motorcycles.

I grabbed my bag out of the back of my car and slung it over my shoulder.

Jason pulled up beside me and I quickly slipped into my leather jacket. He popped open the large side compartment of his motorcycle and I stuffed my bag inside. Then he handed me an extra helmet without a word and I put it on. Before I could start looping the strap through the rings, though, Jason slapped my hands out of the way.

I grinned up at him, but his intense gaze was looking down under my chin. Deft fingers worked the straps of the helmet, grazing my skin and making me hot. Feeling a little out of place under his scrutiny, I reached up at slapped down his visor, in a childish move.

His answering growl, though, as he jerked my body forward by the straps of my helmet, made me whimper a moan. Fuck, that had been sexy. His eyes flashed to mine, the warning in those steely gray eyes only half-deterred me from trying something else bratty. If that was how he was going to respond, then brat I would become.

"You gonna say hello to me?" I asked saucily.

"Hi."

Once he finished with my straps, he slid his hand around my throat and squeezed sensually. "Oh, my little, little, brat. You play with fire, you're gonna get burned." His voice was low, a gentle croon that sent a shiver down my spine.

I swallowed audibly. "I like fire." My voice a soft rasp.

There was a storm brewing in his gray eyes, a sinister gleam that promised retribution. "We're going to have fun with that another time, darlin'. Tonight, you're going to listen to me, you hear me?"

"Yes, sir," I replied immediately, keeping my eyes on his.

Twenty minutes later we pulled up to a nondescript warehouse on the far south side of Creekton, in an area I didn't dare venture into alone, as it wasn't safe. I knew different gangs liked to claim these parts of town and crime was high. Knowing there was a shooting range over this way, was not surprising.

I eased off the back of Jason's Harley when he shut off the engine, and I slowly looked around. I didn't like the look of the area; it made me feel unsettled, so I stuck close to him.

Jason stood and swung his leg over his bike, as I stepped out of the way and started undoing the straps on my helmet. Jason made quick work of his, and we both placed them on his motorcycle. He opened one of the bags on the back of the bike and pulled out a hard case that was locked, along with a ridged looking duffle bag.

He slipped the strap of the duffle over his shoulder, grabbed the case, and closed up the bag on the Harley, before leading the way toward the building. Following him as he led the way into the range, I focused on my breathing. Trying to steady my breathing so I don't freak out from nerves. Having never done this before, I don't know what to expect. I knew it was dangerous and someone could get hurt.

Jason opened the door and walked through, reaching his left hand back for me. Taking the hint, I quickly followed him and entwined my fingers with his. Thank God, he was in tuned with my nerves.

We spent the next ten minutes filling out paperwork, before we're finally told a bay number. "Put on ear protection before entering," the man behind the counter advised them.

Jason opened the duffle bag and pulled out two sets of heavy-duty over-the-ear, ear muffs. His were all black, but the set he handed to me were a bright magenta pink. Grinning, I accepted them and settled them over her ears, fixing my hair to stay out of my face.

Jason led the way through one set of doors that buzzed as the attendant unlocked them. We went down a short hall to another set of doors where another worker in a polo nodded at us as we passed.

Following Jason passed the bays full of other shooters; I felt my heart rate skyrocket. We were really here. I was really about to shoot a weapon for the first time in my life. Once we got to our bay—a narrow stall with thick metal walls and a small wooden counter—Jason sat down the hard case and duffel bag he was carrying.

I watched him pull out a black gun and a magazine from the case and set them out on the counter. Then he closed the case and set it out of the way, under the counter on the floor. Next, he pulled out a box of ammo from the bag, along with two sets of safety glasses, before the bag also went on the floor out of the way. Glancing over his shoulder at me, he turned his body and said, "Come here," motioning for me to step between him and the counter.

I did so, taking a breath as he wrapped his arms around me and centered me against his chest. My senses were in overdrive as he cradled me in his arms. His woodsy scent engulfed me and the heat of his body was comforting as my nerves threatened to make me flee.

"Easy," he murmured softly. His breath was warm against my ear. "I've got you."

Closing my eyes, I let myself melt back against him. Resting my hands on top of his on my waist, I laced our fingers together. He rubbed his nose against the side of my neck, before pressing a soft kiss there. "Come on, Darlin', it'll be ok. You'll see. We'll go through it step by step."

He slid his hands from around my waist and I let my own hands drop to my sides. He picked up the empty gun in front of us and held it sideways in his large hand. "First thing to know is the model. This is a Tauras TX22. It's a standard twenty-two caliber pistol. It has a lighter recoil than a 9mm, so it'll be easier for you to learn with."

I nodded, listening intently.

"This is the safety," Jason continued. Holding the gun sideways, his thumb taps the switch on the side of the weapon that looks like a small lever. "Up means the safety is off, and down means it's on."

I continued to listen as Jason went through the basic mechanics of the gun. From the barrel, the grip, the striker, the magazine, and the trigger, he led me through it all slowly, so I would understand. He did it all while standing behind me, giving me the space to learn without being overbearing.

When it came time for me to shoot, Jason went first. He showed me how to stand and how to position my shoulders. He explained to me about the iron sights on the barrel and how some people were able to aim well with those. Then he flipped on a laser that was mounted under the barrel, and a bright green laser light shown down the range, aimed at the target. "For learning purposes, we'll use the laser sights instead."

I nodded. When it was finally my turn, Jason stepped back, giving me space. I had to take a deep breath as I picked up the weapon. The safety was on, as it should be whenever not in use, so I flicked if off and squared my shoulders and aimed down the range. Using the laser sight, I lined up my shot and squeezed the trigger.

"Good," Jason said from behind me. "Now you know what to expect. Try correcting your aim this time."

For the next twenty minutes I went through magazine after magazine, as I shot down the range to the target. Each time, my aim and confidence grew a little better, and after every new magazine I put into the gun, Jason moved my target just a little further bit away. After a while, I took a deep breath and rolled my shoulders. "How are you feeling?" Jason asked.

"I'm getting sore," I admitted.

"Alright. One more magazine and we'll call it."

"You're not gonna shoot?" I looked over my shoulder at him to make sure I understood him right.

He shook his head. "I don't really need the practice. Maybe next time we'll get two stalls and you can try reloading everything on your own."

I grinned brightly at the thought of returning. "This is fun."

Jason laughed and kissed my temple as he handed me a newly loaded magazine. He had been an angel and reloaded each magazine for me while I worked on emptying them. He had shown me how—and I tried a couple—but my fingers grew tired quickly, and the more bullets I loaded into the magazine, the harder it was to push them down. It would take time and practice for me to get the hang of it.

I was confident, though, that I would get the hang of it. It was just another thing in my life with them that I would learn and master.

I was hot and bothered as I rode on the back of Jason's Harley. That shooting session had been hot as fuck and I was so fucking keyed up. My core *ached* with need. I fucking needed him *now*. The vibrations of the bike running through me had me clenching my thighs tighter around him.

I wonder if I could come on the back of this thing? I thought. *Would he notice?*

My panties were soaked. The damn material did nothing to protect my clit from the seam of my blue jeans. Add in the vibrations of the motorcycle, and I was sure that if I added just a little bit of friction, I would be able to come almost immediately. Now how to do it without drawing too much attention to myself.

I arched my back, sitting up straighter, as if I was trying to get more comfortable. My tits pushed into Jason's back and my grip around his waist tightened. I dug my fingers into his leather cut. The new position helped; my clit pressed even harder against the seam of my jeans. I had to stifle a gasp, but I doubted he could hear me over the roaring of the engine.

I swiveled my hips, then rocked forward. A low moan slipped out as my body almost cooperated. *So fucking close!*

Jason's hand dropped from the handle bar to my thigh and squeezed. I didn't know if it was in warning or permission, but I didn't give a fuck. He could punish me later.

Chasing my orgasm, I swiveled my hips again, all but humping him as I rubbed my wet pussy against his leather-clad back. My body tensed and I cried out as my orgasm finally washed over me. I let out a heavy sigh and slumped forward against him, letting Jason take my weight for a moment.

His fingers loosen on my thigh and he rubbed my leg.

I took a deep breath before I glanced around. We were in my neighborhood, but he was currently driving past my parents' street. I tapped his chest and then pointed toward the road as it flew by.

He tapped my thigh and shook his head.

Confused, and with no way to really communicate besides yelling, I could only wait it out. I didn't have to wait long though, as a few minutes later he took a right turn down a different street, before he slowed down. He turned into the driveway of two-story blue and white farmhouse. Set back on just over an acre of land, it had a large wrap around porch and a detached garage on the right side of the house.

My confusion only grew further as I took in the two Harley's parked in front of the garage. Jason followed the long driveway past the house and parked alongside the two other bikes, which upon closer inspection, I recognized as Marco's and Nico's.

Thoroughly confused, I didn't move right away as Jason shut off the bike. He tapped my thigh to get my attention and I jumped out of my thoughts. Sliding off his bike, I stepped out of the way so Jason could get off as well.

My fingers moved slowly as I tried to undo my straps on my helmet. I was still in a bit of a daze from my orgasm. Hands knocked my fingers out of the way, and I looked up to find Nico grinning down at me. His sparkling blue eyes, lit up with desire. "Hi, Little Dreamer."

"Hey Nic," I murmured.

Once my helmet was off, Jason pushed Nico out of the way and wrapped his hand around the back of my neck, tugging me into him. My hands landed on his chest as I stumbled slightly. He didn't give me a second to gather my bearings though. He crashed his lips against mine, crushing my body to his, as his fingers tight around the back of my neck.

I moaned loudly as his tongue pried my lips open and swept into my mouth. Gripping his cut, I kissed him back just as passionately.

"Um, hello?" Nico said from behind me.

Jason's other hand wrapped around my throat, just below my jaw, holding me in place. I couldn't move, even if I wanted to. I was completely at his mercy.

Someone stepped in behind me, a warm body pressed tightly against my back, pushing me into Jason. "Was someone a tease?" Marcos's deep voice skated over me and rumbled through me. His hands wrap around my hips and slip under my shirt immediately. Rough callouses skimmed across my belly, before gliding up and cupping my heavy breasts.

Another moan pulled out of me as Marcos sharply pinched my nipples.

Jason abruptly pulled away from me, leaving me dazed. He glared over my shoulder at Marcos. "My date." He practically growled the words at his buddy.

Marcos chuckled deeply, but back away, leaving me feeling cold.

I shivered slightly, despite the heat, and Jason wrapped his arm around my waist, and held me against him. I snuggled into him and sighed. I was so in love with these fucking men, it wasn't funny.

"Alright, brother," Marco said, amusement in his voice. "We're taking off. Enjoy the rest of your date."

I turned my head to Marcos and Nico—or rather I tried too, but Jason gripped my jaw and claimed my mouth again, distracting me.

"See ya, Mi Vida," Marcos said, before pressing a kiss to the side of my neck.

"Have a good night, Little Dreamer," Nico said. He also kissed the side of my neck after Marcos backed away.

All the while, Jason held my jaw and clamped his arm around my waist, holding me in place, possessively. I melted into him, my mind a mush of post-orgasmic bliss and a new need amping up inside me. This damn man was all about owning me, and I didn't even care. I was going to melt into him and let him.

Let him own me. Let him possess me. We belonged to each other. For tonight, I would be his alone. Tomorrow, I would remind him that he had to share.

When Marcos and Nico started up their bikes, I jolted out of my haze and managed to break away from Jason. Panting, I looked over at my two other men and smiled. I blew them both a kiss and both men grinned cockily before they revved their engines and gunned it down the driveway.

"What are we doing here?" I asked, looking up at Jason.

He pulled me back against him, claiming my mouth again before he picked me up. I wrapped my legs around his waist as he started walking. Closing my eyes, I let him carrying me as he continued toward the house.

I broke away from his kiss as he struggled to open the door. Glancing over my shoulder, I grabbed the handle of the screen door and managed to get it open for him. Jason grabbed the door and carried me inside, shifting my weight as he got a better hold under my ass. "You could just let me down," I muttered.

He chuckled under his breath. "And where would the fun in that be?"

I rolled my eyes, but pushed his chest, looking around what appeared to be a mud room with and laundry room in one. He kept walking through the space though and into a kitchen. "Let me go." Reluctantly, he let me slowly slide down his body, pressing me into his very hard cock as I went.

I looked around the house in shock. There were boxes everywhere, stacked on the counters, the floors, even the kitchen table—which looked familiar, like the one from their apartment. "What's going on?" I asked.

"Welcome home," Jason murmured into my ear. Standing behind me, he wrapped his arms around me and pulled me back against his chest.

"What do you mean?"

"This is what we did today. We signed the lease this morning and moved all of our stuff today. The three of us."

My mouth dropped open, my eyes widening as I really looked around the old farm house. The kitchen has been updated at some point in the last century, rocking Formica counters and a fresh coat of paint on the cabinets. While slightly dated, it wasn't horrible. Everything was clean, despite the boxes littering the space.

I pulled out of Jason's arms and started walking around.

The two-story home had an eat-in kitchen with a formal dining room just off an arched opening attached to the kitchen. The living room was through a large cased opening, that if one were to knock down the walls, could make a seriously large open concept great room. Down the hall from the kitchen was an office and bathroom. In the living room, were the stairs leading up to the second floor. I didn't say a word to Jason as I toured the house and headed upstairs to check things out. I found four bedrooms in total, including the master bedroom that already had two brand-new king-sized beds pushed together.

"What's this?" I asked, needing him to clarify where my thoughts were headed.

Jason came up behind me again, wrapping me in his arms before he spoke. "It's your room, with space for us, if you choose to invite us in. The three of us took the other bedrooms, but figured this would be your space, and probably our space, but you have the right to kick us out at any time."

I was speechless, utterly flabbergasted by what he was saying. "What do you mean?" I asked, my voice soft.

He turned me in his arms, then cradled the side of my face in his large hand. "We're asking you to move in with us. I'm asking you to move in with me."

Again, my mouth dropped open in shock. "I don't know what to say."

"Say *yes*."

"I don't—it's too soo—"

"It's not too soon." Jason shook his head. "Not for us. We know how we feel—all three of us. We want you here. We got this place for you, so we'd have a place for *you*. A home for you to feel comfortable in."

I licked my lips, my thoughts racing a million miles an hour. *They did this for me? Rented an entire house, for me?* It was almost too much, but the same time, it was fucking perfect. I had already fallen head over heels for my three guys. I couldn't imagine life without them.

"It's ok if you aren't ready just yet," Jason said softly. "We don't have to rush into anything right now, we just wanted you to know, we're ready, whenever you are."

I launched myself at him, jumping up onto my toes and reaching for his face, pulling him down to claim his lips in a fiery kiss. He lifted me into his arms effortlessly and carried me to the massive bed. I had no idea how I was going find sheets big enough to cover it, but I wasn't worried about it right now.

Right now, all that mattered was Jason and I, and this moment. I was going to take full advantage of my one-on-one time with him too. He laid me on the bed and broke our kiss to pull his shirt and cut over his head. I followed his lead and quickly started stripping my clothes. I kicked my boots off and shimmed out of my leather jacket, before I whipped my red top over my head.

Jason was fully naked by the time I reached for the button on my jeans. He slapped my hands out of the way and proceeded to undo my jeans, before he yanked them down my thighs. Flinging my pants out of the way, he licked at the center of my core through my damp lace panties. "Fucking hell, darlin'," he huffed against my skin. "You smell divine."

Grinning, I looped my fingers into the thin straps of my undies and tugged them off me. Jason got with the program and helped me, throwing them aside before he dove head first into my pussy. I cried out as he immediately went to work, licking and sucking my clit. "Jason!" I yelled, as I went over the edge a moment later. I was still so keyed up from our ride home and all the teasing touches all evening at the shooting range.

"I should have made you worked for that," Jason grumbled, smirking as he pulled away from her. "After all, you were a bad girl."

I huffed out a laugh, still panting. "Not gonna lie, coming on the back of your bike like that was hot as fuck."

He laughed and wrapped his hands around my hips, lifting me. My hands went around my shoulders and he cradled my body against his as he kneeled his way up the bed, before he laid my body beneath his. He immediately sank down on top of me, covering me completely.

Looking up into his stormy gray eyes, I felt my love for him expand in my chest. My heart was beating rapidly as I reached up and slid my thumb over his sharp cheek bone. His eyelids fluttered at my touch, so I did it again, marveling at how I could get this hard as stone man to lower his defenses around me.

He didn't give me a moment to relish in my achievement, though. He thrusted his hips forward and slammed into me without warning. Crying out, I arched against him. He pushed down on my hips and held me in place. "My turn." His voice was deep and gravely as he rasped out the words. "My. Fucking. Turn."

He set a brutal pace. It was all I could to do hold on to his shoulders or back as he pummeled his hips into mine. The loud smacking of flesh on flesh filled the room along with my keening wails. I wrapped my legs around his waist and dug my nails into his back as I held on tight.

"Oh fuck!" I yelled as I was thrown over the edge again, my orgasm racing through my body.

"That's it, my little slut. Mine to fucking ruin." Jason panted and thrust his hips harder if possible as he rode me through the waves of pleasure. "Fuck. Yes." He groaned low as he came, his hips stuttering to a standstill as he slumped against me.

We lay still, panting heavily, a hot sweaty mess.

"Well, that's one way to break in the new mattress." I laughed lightly.

Jason's booming laugh vibrated through my chest, making my heart swell. I was so utterly in love with this man.

Maya

First days on the job were always stressful, filled with paperwork and orientation, tours and training, my head was ready to explode by the time I pulled into my parent's driveway. It was hard to think of it as my home, when I hadn't spent much time there—or was fully welcomed there.

It was a little after six-thirty and I was starving. I'd found out quickly that I probably wouldn't be getting out of work on time—ever—not when I had to catch up the night shift nurse in my area, then chart my patients—not that I'd done any of that today. But it would be my routine eventually.

Grabbing my lunch box and purse, I climbed out of my car and headed for the house. I could only pray that my mother had made dinner. With any luck, I could just heat up a plate, and eat before I took a shower and fell into bed.

"Where have you been?" My mother's shrill voice cut through my exhaustion and had my metaphorical hackles rising.

Looking up, I found my mother standing in doorway between the kitchen and the living room. Elaine Henderson was short and petite with short graying blond hair that she still dyed and a pinched look permanently on her face. "Work. I told you; my hours are from nine to six during training."

Her mother narrows her eyes at her. "I expected a phone call that you'd be home late."

"I came straight home from work. Literally. Traffic was hell."

"Don't get an attitude with me. You want to live in my house, you can abide by my rules. A phone call when you're going to be late is common curtsey."

"I'm not late, though. I told you my hours, and with traffic this time of night—"

"Enough with the attitude," my mother snapped.

"I don't have an attitude," I said, shaking my head in disbelief. "You're not listening."

"You, ungrateful little brat," my mother ranted. "You think you know it all? Well, you can do it all then too. I want you out of this house."

My mouth dropped open in shock, my mouth practically hitting the floor. "You're kicking me out?"

"Sure am."

"For what? Exactly?" I ground the words out between clenched teeth, as my body began to shake. I gripped my bags tightly, my knuckles white as I waited for my mother to speak again.

"For being rude. I won't have you talk to me like that in my own home." She crossed her arms over her chest.

I looked into the living room, noticing my father for the first time. Sitting in his recliner watching TV, he had heard everything and had not said a word. "Dad?" I asked him, hoping for back up.

"You heard your mother." His voice was gruff, no-nonsense, leaving zero room for debate.

Tears welled in my eyes, but I blinked them back, refusing to justify my mother with any emotion. "Bad enough you couldn't come to my college graduation, now you're kicking me out, because of traffic? What did I ever do, to make you hate me so much?"

My mother didn't respond, instead, she turned her back to me and walked away, leaving me to gape after her. Turning to my father, I walked around the recliner, so I was between him and the TV that he cared more about, than his own daughter.

His caramel eyes, eyes that matched my own, flicked from the TV to meet my gaze. "Don't look at me like that," he sighed. "You know how your mother is. Give her some time, she'll calm down."

I just shook my head as disappointment raged through me. "One day, you're gonna look back and wonder just how you lost me, and you're going to realize you did nothing to stop it."

Emotions flickered across his caramel eyes. "Don't be like that, sweetheart."

I just shook my head, fighting to back the sob that was bubbling in my chest. Abruptly, I turned away and headed for my bedroom. I needed to pack; I needed to leave before I broke down. I would not give my mother satisfaction of seeing my pain.

In my bedroom, I grabbed my two large suitcases—that I still hadn't unpacked in the week I'd been home from school. In fact, all I needed to do, was pack up my bathroom, grab my dirty clothes basket and my suitcases and I would be set for a while. I could come back and grab my mountains of boxes later, but I'd at least have enough to get me by.

I took the time to slide my laptop into my pillows before I placed those into the dirty clothes bin as well. I wheeled my suitcases out of my room, to find the living room empty—my father gone.

Shaking my head in disbelief, I wheeled my suitcases out the front door and left them on the porch. It only took me two trips to get everything important I owned out of my parent's house.

Once my car was loaded, I drove away without glancing back. When I was out of sight and around the corner, I pulled over and parked. "What the fuck?" I sighed, making sure my doors were locked before I pulled out my cell phone and called my sister.

"Hey boo, how was your first day?" Jenna answered on the second ring.

"Mom kicked me out," I said in greeting.

"What the fuck?" Jenna snapped.

"Yep."

"Dude, what happened?"

"I told her my hours for the week several times. Today I got off at six, technically. I didn't get out of there till almost 6:10, and with traffic I walked in the door at maybe 6:45. She said I need to call her when I'm going be home later than planned. Because you know traffic is plannable."

"What the actual—where was Dad?"

"Oh, he was sitting right there in the living room, watching TV while I stood right behind him. He didn't say a word."

"Fucking bastard."

"Yep."

"Where are you?"

"I'm sitting in my car around the block. Thankfully I hadn't really unpacked yet. So I threw my clothes back in my suitcases and grabbed them, my dirty laundry basket, pillows, and important stuff like my laptop and that in the car."

"Jesus," Jenna groaned. "What's your plan?"

"Well," I hedged. "Remember I told you my guys were wanting me to move in with them?"

"Yeahhh," Jenna hedged.

"Well, after my date Saturday night with Jason, he brought me back to a rental house that him and the guys just got. They just signed a lease on a house just a couple blocks away from mom and dad."

"Wow," Jenna murmured. "I—that's—wow." She laughed. "That's amazing. Honestly. Wow."

I laughed, hearing my sister so utterly speechless was a first. "Yeah. I haven't told them yet. But that's where I'm going to go now. I'm gonna ask them to get the rest of my boxes and stuff."

"That's amazing! Yes, absolutely, sister! Go live your best life! Damn, if I had three hot-as-sin men after me, you know I'd be there."

I laughed loudly and heartily, immediately feeling better after talking to my sister, like a weight had been lifted off my shoulders. "Yeah, so I'm gonna go do that."

Jenna cackled like a witch. "Alright, sister! Call me tomorrow night and we'll talk about everything."

"Sounds good, Jen. Love you."

"Love you too girl. Sorry mom and dad suck."

"Thanks."

"Talk to you tomorrow."

"Yep. Bye."

"Bye."

Smiling, I hung up and set my phone in the cup holder. I made sure it was safe to drive, before I pulled away from the curb and drove the three blocks to the house Jason, Marcos, and Nico had rented. The two-story blue and white farmhouse was something out of my dreams, set back on just over an acre of land, it had a large wrap around porch and a detached garage.

The long driveway ran down the right side of the house the house and ended at the open garage doors, where three black Harley's were lined up inside. I pulled my car to a stop in front of the doors, and barely shut the car off before I saw my guys walking out of the backdoor of the house, toward my car.

After quickly unbuckling, I climbed out of the car before my boys could reach me. "Hi." I smiled broadly as I looked them over.

"Hi, beautiful," Nico said, walking right into me, pressing his body against mine. His hands cradled my face as he pulled me into a mind-blowing kiss.

"Hi," I murmured against his lips. My hands came up and gripped the lapels of his leather cut, holding him against me.

Someone squeezed behind me, their warm body pushing me against Nico. "God, you look amazing," Marcos muttered into my ear, before he sucked a wet open-mouth kiss into my neck.

I moaned and leaned back against him. Nico used my distraction to angle my head and devoured my mouth again.

"Alright, numb nuts, give her a minute to breathe," Jason grumbled.

Nico ended our make out session with a gentle a chaste kiss to my lips, before he stepped back and gave me space.

Marcos didn't move, his open-mouthed kisses led up to my ear before he said, "As lovely as this surprise is, what are you doing here?"

I sighed. "My parents kicked me out."

Marcos pulled away, dropping his arms from around my waist. "The fuck?"

"What happened?" Nico demanded.

"Are you OK?" Jason asked.

I took a moment to really think about how I felt about it all, the hurt and the anger that simmered inside me. "No." I shook my head slowly, grimacing. "Not really, but I think I will be."

A smirk tugged at Jason's lips before he slowly walked toward me. "Yeah, Darlin'," he murmured, stepping in close to me. "You're in good hands. We've got you from here."

A soft whine, low in my throat, tore out of me as his mouth descended on mine. The kiss was slow and sensual, passionate. Jason poured his heart and soul into me as his hands wrapped around my hips and tugged me against his hard body.

Marcos moved away, giving us space, and I sighed as I leaned into Jason and one of the most passionate kisses I'd ever experienced. I was dizzy and breathless when he pulled away. He kissed my forehead as his hands slid around my waist to my back and he hugged me tightly.

An unexpected sob tore out of me. The unexpected comfort and security I felt just by being in his arms, allowed for the emotions that had been bubbling at the surface to finally boil over. Clinging to him, I buried my face into his chest and let it all pour out of me, all while Jason rubbed my back and murmured soothing sounds as he held me tight. "It's alright, darlin', we've got you."

I gave myself a sold two minutes to bawl my heart out. When I pulled away, I took a deep breath, wiped my eyes, and shoved down the hurt and pain. I straightened my shoulders, cleared my throat, and took charge of my life. "I packed what I could in my car, my clothes and important stuff. I need to get the boxes still, but it was all still packed from college."

Marcos pulled out his phone and started typing. "We'll get the prospects out here. We'll grab everything tonight. No reason for you to have to go back there."

I smiled, feeling the weight of the world lifted off my shoulders. "Thank you."

Marcos turned to me and cupped my cheek. "We've got you, Mi Vida."

In the end, I went back to my parent's house with the guys. They had four prospects and two pickup trucks and I didn't have to lift a finger. My mother was livid when I walked back in the house, but I directed the men to my bedroom and instructed them to take everything but the furniture.

It took twenty minutes to pack up my life and remove any trace of me from my parent's home. Twenty minutes, and my parents never said a word to me. My father sat in his recliner, watching TV and didn't bat an eye as leather-clad bikers stomped through carrying boxes and bags of my belongings.

Thankfully, my mother kept her mouth shut, and we were able to get out of there as fast as possible.

Now, standing inside the bedroom my boys had given me—the master suite of the rental house—I looked around the chaos. My guys had already furnished the large room over the weekend, purchasing two king beds and pushing them together so the four of us could sleep together easily. Dressers lined the walls, and two nightstands framed the two beds.

My suitcases and dirty clothes bin littered the floor, there were bags of toiletries covering the counter in the ensuite bathroom. The bed was covered with odds and ends we had grabbed from my bedroom along with my laptop. We had left most of my boxes downstairs in the dining room, out the way for me to go through and unpack when I had more time.

It was getting late, and I still needed to eat dinner and shower. My first day had gone from being long and stressful, to utterly exhausting and heartbreaking. I forced the thoughts from my mind as Jason walked into the bedroom. "How you doin'?" he asked softly.

"I'm fuckin' drained," I answered honestly.

He nodded, as if he already knew. "Go shower and get ready for bed. Nico's cooking dinner, it'll be ready in a bit."

Relief washed over me—I wouldn't have to make any more decisions; they would take care of everything. Nodding, I reached out to open my suitcase when Jason moved behind me and wrapped me in his arms.

"You're safe darlin', we got you." He murmured the words into my ear as he pulled me back against his chest.

"I'm sorry I'm such a mess," I muttered.

He chuckled softly. "You're not a mess. This is just a bump in the road, you'll see. You were meant to be with us."

I smile softly. "This place is beautiful. I'm so happy you guys got this place."

Jason only squeezed me tighter, before he spanked my ass once. "Go on, shower."

"Yes, sir," I smiled.

Jason chuckled again. "Easy now, we haven't negotiated yet."

"Right," I sighed.

"Don't worry about it just yet. We'll talk this weekend. Go on, shower."

I nodded and headed into the attached bathroom, feeling lighter, despite my exhaustion. My men would take care of everything. I didn't have worry. They would take care of me.

Chapter Eighteen

Maya

THE REST OF THE week went by as if in a dream. I got up and went to work every morning and after a day of training and learning at the hospital, I came home to one of my guys cooking dinner. The four of us ate together before either sexy time began, or we snuggled on the large sectional couch in the living room, binge watching TV.

It was finally Friday night and I was chilling on the couch, watching TV while Nico was cooking dinner. "Are you sure you don't want to come to the party tonight?" Nico called from the kitchen.

"I'm good," I said, snuggling further under the blanket. "It's been a long week. I'm probably passing out early."

A cell phone rang upstairs and moment later Marcos's deep voice answered. I couldn't hear his words, just the cadence of his voice.

Jason walked in the backdoor through the mud room, just off the right side of the kitchen. He walked into the kitchen and took a seat at the table to undo his boot laces. "I changed the oil on the Civic," Jason said, meeting my gaze across the open concept room.

Warmth spread through my chest and I smiled easily. "Thank you."

"You're due for a tune up. We'll bring it by the shop tomorrow and give it a work over."

I nodded, before my eyes snapped to Marcos, who was walking down the stairs from the second floor. Fresh from a shower, he had on a pair of dark washed jeans and a black button up, with his leather cut over it. "Kara called. The lease is about to end on my mom's apartment."

"Well shit," I said looking around. "We could put a door on the back den and turn it into a bedroom."

"That makes the most sense," Jason agreed. "No sense in paying for an apartment when she's living in the dorms nine months a year."

"Yeah," Nico nodded. "I'm cool with that. It'll just be for the summer aways, then she'll go back to school."

Marcos smiled down at me, as he wrapped his thumb and forefinger under my chin and gripped it gently, "You'd be OK with my sister moving in here?"

A soft smile spread across my face as I nodded. "Yeah. She's my best friend and your sister, of course she can stay here. We'll have to set some ground rules of course, the last thing your sister wants to hear is us going at it like animals."

A wicked smirk spread across Marcos's face. Tightening his grip on my chin, he pulled my face closer to his. "When we negotiate, I'm going to ask for punishment measures."

The blood drained from my face as her my parted, and my jaw practically dropped to the floor. My eyes widened as my heart skips a beat. "Wha—"

"I'm going enjoy spanking this luscious ass and watching it bounce with every hit." A wicked grin pulled across his face, making my breath catch in my throat. "I think you like the sound of that."

Speechless, I couldn't answer him, unable to form a coherent thought. I could only stare up at him with my mouth open.

"Close those pretty lips, Maya, or I might find something to stick between them."

Blushing, I snapped my jaw closed and turned away from him, forcing him to drop his hand from my face. "This is the shit I don't want to happen in front of Kara."

"Well then bring your best negation skills to the table." Marcos's God forsaken smirk sharpened, if possible.

"I'm already going to be outnumbered." I shook my head. "What's to say I'll even get a say in these negotiations, and the three of you won't just steamroll over me?"

Immediately the smirk dropped from his face and he shook his head. "Never, Maya. We would never do that. The whole point of this is to hear each other out. If at any point you don't feel comfortable with any of it, we stop immediately. And nothing we agree to is set in stone, ever. We can *always* renegotiate at any time if anything isn't working out."

Frowning, I stand up, needing space.

"The whole point of negotiations is communication. It's the number one thing we value, darlin'. Just be honest with us," Jason said as he stood up from the kitchen chair.

"Right." I nodded and sat back down on the couch.

Marcos squatted down in front of me, cradling my face between his large hands. "It'll be alright, you'll see. Tomorrow then, after breakfast. We'll pull out all of our check lists and compare notes. We'll make a new one for the things we're willing to try and discuss as a group."

"OK." I nodded and sighed. "And if there's something I don't want or like?"

"Then we don't do it, ever," Jason said sternly from the kitchen. He stood up and walked over to me, stopping when he was a foot from me. "We never want you to feel uncomfortable with us."

I loved how seriously they were taking this, and nodded slowly. "OK," I agreed again.

My heart was pounding as I read through the questions once again. I'd read through both the check list and the questionnaire a dozen times in the last several days. I'd printed them out and answered everything I could to the best of my ability, and noted things I had questions about. I'd gone over each answer multiple times until I could recite both the question and my answers verbatim. Even when I was confident in my answers, that they wouldn't change or that I wasn't confused about anything, I still reread them.

Now, sitting out back around the fire pit, I was rereading everything *again*, while waiting for my guys to get back with breakfast. I had spent the day before googling everything I didn't know, then writing questions on the papers for my guys, for a more detailed look at how something might work within our relationship.

It wasn't long before I heard the telltale sound of Harley's in the distance—a sound I had grown to love. I was still rereading everything when a shadow fell across my papers. "Come on, Little Dreamer. We'll talk after food."

"I don't know if I can," I admitted.

Nico crouched down beside my chair and reached for my chin. Pulling my gaze toward his, he gave me a reassuring smile. "Don't worry about it so much, Maya. We'll still love you no matter what."

I gasped, my mouth dropping open in shock. "You love me?"

Nico's smile was radiant and breathtaking. He pulled off his sunglasses and tucked them into his shirt collar. "Of course I love you, Maya. I told you already, you're mine. We play for keeps."

"I love you too, Nico." I leaned forward and pressed a kiss to his lips.

His hand slid from my jaw to around my neck as he kissed me passionately. I moaned when his hand squeezed gently around my throat. His laugh was rich and full as he pulled away from me. "Come on my Dreamer love. Let's do this."

He stood up and held his hand out to me. I grabbed it and let him pull me to my feet. Holding hands, we walked into the house where Marcos and Jason were setting food out on the kitchen table. The Styrofoam containers from the local diner contained all our favorite breakfast foods.

"Change of plans guys," Nico said as we entered the kitchen. "We're gonna negotiate first, then eat. Maya's too nervous to eat."

I squeezed his hand.

Jason and Marcos immediately stopped what they were doing and looked up at me, both of them examined me carefully. "Alright. Let's go in the living room," Jason said.

I swallowed thickly and let Nico pull me into the living room. He dropped my hand as he rounded our massive sectional couch and pulled me sideways across his lap. He pulled the throw blanket off the back of the couch and wrapped it around my shoulders, before he tucked me against his chest.

Feeling snug and secure, I felt my heart rate slow as I started to calm down. I didn't know why I was so damn nervous, but being bundled like a baby against Nico had immediately calmed me.

Jason and Marcos took a seat on the couch in front of me, both of them holding sheets of paper. I realized I was still clutching my own papers tightly in my fist and slowly pulled them out from under the blanket.

"No need to be nervous, darlin'. Let's just do this, so there's no more build up." Jason grabbed my papers and set them in his lap. He snatched the top two sheets—his and Marcos's—and placed them on the coffee table before grabbing Nico's. "We'll just go down the list. It's mostly alphabetical per category, so it's simple. Marcos, grab that blank one and we'll check off things we all like as we go."

I took a deep breath and kept my eyes down on the papers in Jason's hands.

"First category: bondage and suspension. Blindfolds: everyone said yes," Jason said.

Marcos marked off on the blank paper.

"Does that mean you like them on yourselves or on me?" I asked.

"For most of these, we chose for you, but there's some we went both ways on. You'll see," Marcos said.

"Bondage heavy and bondage light," Jason continued. "Maya said yes to light and maybe for heavy. That's valid. We'd work you up to anything heavier. See where your comfort levels are." He gave me a soft smile.

I grinned in return, feeling my heart skip a beat. This was going easier than I expected. I really didn't have to talk much; he was just reading off our answers.

"To make this go a little faster, we'll do your answers unless I know it's something one of us has an issue with, OK?" Jason asked.

I nodded.

"Bondage multi-day, maybe. Bondage public under clothing, willing to try. Leather restraints yes, chains maybe, ropes maybe. I'm assuming you put maybe for things you're willing to try?" Jason asked.

I nodded. "Yes. Most of that I won't know until I try them."

"Good girl," Nico murmured in my ear.

"Lots of maybes for immobilization, arm and leg sleeves, harnesses of all material types: chains, ropes, leather. Cuffs of leather were maybe, but metal handcuffs, manacles, and irons were listed as 'unsure', do those worry you more than the others?" Jason looked up from the paper to meet my gaze.

I nodded slowly.

"Something else we can work up to? Is because it's harder to get out of? Or the symbolism?"

"Both maybe? I just kept thinking of handcuffs or like manacles as being a kidnapping type of situation and it brought things to a different level."

"Something else we work towards, maybe?" Marcos asked.

I nodded and smiled. "I'm open to that."

"Alright," Jason said, before going back to the check lists. "Gags of all kinds, cloth rubber, tape, phallic, ring ball, mouth bits were all maybe with a smiley face." He chuckled. The phallic one has a little heart."

"Let me see that." Nico leaned forward to see her papers and laughed heartily. "Wanna gag on my cock, Little Dreamer?"

"Sure, or a replica." I laughed.

"Full head hoods are listed as tentative no. Mumification/saran wrapping was a maybe along with strait jackets and all forms of suspension. What about the full hood has you saying no?" Jason asked.

"I think it's too many senses taken away at once. If I get too hot, I get claustrophobic almost immediately and my anxiety skyrockets."

Jason nodded slowly, while Marcos looked concerned. "Do you usually have issues with claustrophobia?" Marcos asked.

"Not really, but being too hot is sometimes a trigger. It can set off my anxiety more than anything," I admitted.

"OK. That's good to know," Jason said. "Next section is impact play and percussion. Spanking and flogging are yes." Jason smirked. "Canning is a tentative no, which is valid. Belts and leather straps and riding crops, all tentative maybes. Wooden paddles, hairbrushes, all tentative maybes. I like where this is going, darlin'." Jason shot me a wicked grin.

Nico laughed. "Our girl does love a good spanking."

"Hair pulling yes, face slapping no—"

"Good," Marcos said.

My eyes shot to his as he ran his hand over his buzzed head. "I don't like the idea of slapping your face baby. It feels too much like abuse to me."

I smiled and held my hand out to him. He reached across Jason and laced our fingers together. He kissed my knuckles before he dropped our hands so Jason could continue.

"And we're on to sexual activity. I think we're all on board here," Jason laughed. "Anal sex obviously, triple penetration, been there done that."

We all laughed.

"Vibrators, masturbations, cunnilingus." Jason rattled off, his deep voice a soothing balm for my nerves. "Fisting, yes?" He looked up a shocked smile on his face.

"Fuck that's hot." Nico groaned.

I blushed. "I wanna try. Maybe try two of you in my pussy at one time."

"Fuck, baby doll. You're fuckin perfect," Nico sighed.

Marcos shot me a saucy wink that made me blush more.

"Outdoor sex, yes. Orgasm control yes, anal plugs yes. Sounds like we're gonna have some fun," Jason commented. "Moving on to sensation play. First up abrasion, no. Scratching, No. Biting maybe, tickling kissing, ice cubes, wax play all yeses. Alright. We've got maybe on clothes pins and zapping. Moving along to breath play. Asphyxiation is a not sure, slash maybe, but breath control and choking are a yes. Alright, so we work up to complete asphyxiation? Toy around with it?"

I nodded. "Slowly."

"Of course." Marcos nodded.

"Next up is humiliation. I see this whole section had you on edge. Want to talk about it?"

"I uh—" I sighed and reached down for the blanket and tugged it closer around myself.

"Your mom?" Marcos asked. Sympathy darkened his eyes.

I nodded immediately, feeling tears well in my eyes. "She's not nice to me. My sister has always been her favorite. I don't want you guys to be mean to me. I don't want anything humiliating to remind me of her."

Nico hugged me tighter. "I don't want do anything ever, that reminds you of your mother."

I had to laugh at that. Grinning brightly, I wiped my eyes and nodded. "There are some things under that category that I am interested in though. The clothing, the outdoor scenes, maybe objectification to a point. Not sure on public exposure, but I'm not opposed to small things maybe under the table at dinner or something."

Jason smile broadly. "And here you thought you'd be bad a negotiating."

I grinned, blushing slightly.

"Alright, on to the fun stuff. Body part torture." Jason grinned wickedly.

I laughed. "Yeah, but the category only had nipple stuff. I'm fine with those."

"So nipple clamps, weights and suction cups are a go." Jason nodded. "Under the fetishes section, you have a big question mark. So for example, if I punish you and make you kiss my boots, is that a problem for you?"

I blushed. "Kissing the top, maybe not. I draw the line at licking anything."

"Valid." Marcos smirked.

"Chastity devices were a yes question mark?" Jason asked, drawing her attention back to him.

My blush heated my face and I tried to look away, but Jason was faster than me. His hand shot out and wrapped around my jaw, forcefully turning me to look at him. "Don't hide from me." The order was clear in his voice. "Do you like the idea of us plugging your holes and locking you up? Only unlocking your device to pump you full of more cum?"

My blush had to have been scarlet as my cheeks heated further. "Yes, sir," I murmured.

"Good girl."

I was so unbelievably turned on and we weren't even done yet.

Jason let go of my jaw and picked up the papers again. "Role-playing. Hmm," he hummed. "Marcos, you'll be happy. Our little dare devil wants to be chased through the woods and kidnapped."

"Fuck yes," Marcos crooned.

"A little primal play, fear play, kidnapping, interrogation, rape fantasy, gang bang, prison scenes," Jason rattled off. "Oh baby. We're going to have so much fun together."

I could only lick my lips in anticipation.

"Next we have service and restrictive behavior. I don't really like these terms and your answers were mostly maybes. Following orders is a given. You will be our sub and listen during a scene. We'll have rules to follow and we'll talk about that in a bit. Forced servitude? No one is making you do twenty-four seven d/s relationship. We're busy people and don't have time for that. Restrictive rules on behavior? Not really our style, but it could fall under club rules and again, we'll get to that in a minute. Wash room restrictions, you wrote no and we agree, that's not something we're into. Kneeling, yes. Agreed. Begging, maybe." He nodded thoughtfully.

"The rituals, standing in the corner—again not really our style," Marcos said. "But some of this, the rituals and protocols that might come up are regarding the club—if you ever visit there with us. We'll discuss those before we go, they're mostly safety precautions."

"But the learned postures are something we—I like. We'll go through them later. There will be kneeling involved. Are you OK with that?" Jason asked.

"Maybe. When we get there, we can discuss," I agreed.

"Massage, given." Jason continued reading my answers. "Alright, onto voyeurism and exhibition. Forced nudity in private yes, around others no. Exhibitionism in front of friends is no, but strangers is a maybe. Modeling for erotic photos or filming is a hard, no?"

"My job is important to me. I don't want my career put in jeopardy because of leaked videos or photos."

"Can we keep one or two of you on our phone?" Nico asked.

"Maybe one or two," she sighed. "I don't really like the idea."

"That's fair," Marcos agreed.

"Voyeurism goes with exhibitionism. Thoughts on someone watching us fuck you?" Jason asked.

"What do you think of, when you think about that?" I asked.

"I dunno, maybe fucking you on the pool table in the middle of the clubhouse during a party?" Marcos asked. "There's usually other people fucking all over the room, it wouldn't be unusual and no one else would touch you but us."

My mouth dropped open in shock as heat pooled in my lower belly. "Um."

Jason laughed. "Not completely opposed. Alright." He continued with the papers. "Then watersports was a no, which completely valid. Well, that's the checklist. It doesn't cover everything, so we're going to go a little off the cuff here. Let us know if you're uncomfortable."

I nodded slowly. I had a feeling the easy part was over and now they were onto the really nitty gritty of our relationship, things I might not like.

"One of my hard limits," Marcos started slowly, his eyes watching me carefully. "Something that really is a hard no for me: you can't tell Kara about the club."

My mouth opened, not expecting those words to come out of his mouth. "Never?"

Marcos shook his head. "No. One day, she might find out, but it will not be from you, understand?"

"She's my best friend, Marcos. You can't expect to me to outright lie to her." I shifted on Nico's lap.

"I'm not telling you to lie to her. I'm saying don't talk about it. If she has any inkling or suspicion, you avoid the conversation. If she outright asks you a question, and you have no other choice but to lie, then I'll understand if you have to tell her. But Maya, don't let the conversation get to that point."

I swallowed thickly. I don't like how serious the conversation had suddenly become. Nor did I like the idea of keeping something from my best friend.

"It's not likely to come up," Marcos said, shaking his head. He tried to smile. "We're used to keeping the club life away from Kara. She's planning on being a lawyer. She doesn't need to know the kinds of things her brother gets up to."

I nodded slowly. "OK," I finally agreed.

"OK." Marcos nodded.

"Changing the subject back to the checklist. A couple things not on this particular list... how do you feel about somnophilia?" Nico asked.

I frowned, my mind struggling to keep up with the conversation. Going from Marcos's intensity to Nico's question, almost seemed comical. "Like fucking me while I'm sleeping, you mean?"

"Yes." Jason nodded.

I shrugged. "I guess? I never thought about. I really don't like my sleep fucked with though, especially on work nights. So if you can do it without waking me up? I guess sure."

Jason laughed and nodded, slapping Marcos on the shoulder. "Thoughts about drug use or sedation?"

Maya's mouth fell open in shock before she quickly closed it. "What kind of drugs?"

"Nothing addictive. We'd be careful with what we use, but sleeping pills. Maybe an injected sedative or a Xanax, something to take the edge off," Marcos answered.

I shrugged my shoulder slowly, shaking my head in disbelief.

"Is that a, no?" Nico asked.

I shook my head again. "No. I'm not saying no. I'm just a little shocked, to be honest. I uh... Yeah, I'm not saying no."

Marcos laughed darkly. "I'll take it."

"We need to discuss safe-words," Nico said.

"I've been reading about those," I admitted. "I like the idea of the traffic lights. Red to stop, yellow to slow down or I'm feeling nervous. Green for good."

My men all nodded. "I was going to suggest that, it's great for beginners," Jason said. "I'm glad you're doing your own research too."

I blushed at his praise, a smile spreading across my face.

"Titles during a scene?" Marcos prompted Jason with a nod of his head.

Jason nodded once, "Yes. During a scene you will refer to us as Sir, unless we tell you otherwise."

"Yes, sir." I smirked.

"Cheeky brat." Nico chuckled.

"How do you feel about name calling during a scene?" Marcos asked. "I know you don't want anything that reminds you of your mother, but if I call you my little slut during a scene will that trigger you?"

My mouth dropped open in shock. "Uh..."

Jason laughed. "I think you broke her."

Nico squeezed my side and I jumped, snapping out of my daze.

"I don't know. I'm intrigued though."

"Alright, a maybe, it is." Marcos laughed.

"Alright, moving on to rules. We have a few simple rules that we want you to abide by in this relationship," Jason said. He paused until he had my attention on him. "One, most important: Never lie. You don't lie to us ever. Honesty and communication are the only way a relationship like this works. You don't lie to us, and we don't lie to you."

I nodded my head. "I can agree to that."

"Good. Because it non-negotiable. Two, you always text the group chat when you're leaving work. I don't care if its three in the morning, you text when you're on your way home." Jason gave me a stern looking, as if he was waiting for me to answer.

"OK."

"If you go out drinking without us, you *always* call one of us for a ride. You don't ride share anymore, darlin'. One of us will come get you."

I licked my lips, frowning slightly. "I'm a big girl, I can handle a ride share by myself."

"Non-negotiable, Maya. You will be punished if you don't follow these rules," Marcos said.

I frowned. "What are punishments?"

"We'll get to that," Jason replied quickly. "Do you agree? You don't ride share and you call us?"

"Yes," I nodded.

"Next is my personal favorite." Nico snickered. "No panties ever."

"Wha—"

"Unless you're on your rag," Nico continued. "No panties, unless you're bleeding. Then you can wear what you need."

I sat there dazed a moment as the thought of never wear panties again washed over me and I found myself soaking my current panties. The idea was a turn on, but I wasn't sure it was feasible. "I can try."

"You'll do more than try, Mi Vida," Marcos smirked.

"Alright," I nodded, conceding.

"Last rule," Jason said. "No speaking in a scene unless given permission."

Once again, my mouth dropped open in disbelief. "What?"

Jason shook his head. "During a scene, you will do what you're told. You will trust us to guide you. We will make sure you know what we want. But besides moaning, you will not speak unless given permission."

I bit my lip as I thought it over. "And you'll know if I have questions?"

Jason smirked. "We'll know. Don't worry about that. You trust us?"

"Yes," I answered immediately.

"Then trust us," Jason said.

"OK."

"OK," Jason repeated.

My stomach grumbled and I shifted on Nico's lap, uncomfortable. "And what are the punishments for breaking these rules? I'm new at all this, it's going to be complicated and hard for me to get used to." I turned to Marcos. "You mentioned wanting to negotiate punishment measures."

Marcos grinned wickedly. "Oh yes, I believe I stated I wanted to spank your luscious ass if you disobeyed me."

I blushed and nodded.

"That's a start. Other things could include edging you until you're crying for release. Or too many orgasms until you're crying for us to stop," Marcos said.

My mouth dropped open shock once again.

The guys laughed. "Punishments will fit the crime. Spankings will be a primary go to," Jason said. "We'll discuss each punishment before its administered, and we'll talk about why you earned it. Again, we're not asking for a twenty-four seven relationship, outside of the ground rules we're enforcing for your safety."

I nodded slowly, my mind whirling.

"I think that's a pretty good start for now," Nico said. "Let's heat up our food and feed our girl. We can talk about positioning and scene expectations later."

"Alright," Jason agreed.

"How does all that sound, Maya?" Marcos asked.

I smiled faintly. "Sure."

Nico squeezed me tightly before he finally let me go. "You'll be OK, Little Dreamer. Don't worry about it. We got you."

"That's what I'm afraid of," I admitted. "I just walked into the lion's den and I'm about to be their next meal."

My men laughed deeply, almost ominously.

I had a feeling that I just sold my soul to the devil, or a group of them.

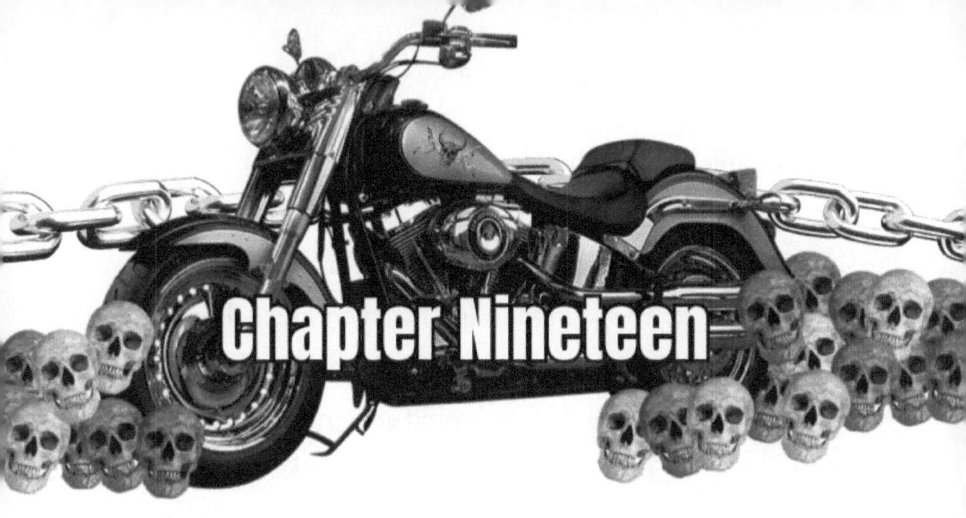

Chapter Nineteen

Maya

SUNDAY AFTERNOON, I WAS helping Kara settled into her new room in the house I shared with the guys. We had packed up Lita's apartment with the help of the Devil's Psychos prospects—who had been told not to wear their cuts and not to talk about the club at all in Kara's presence.

It had been an emotional weekend across the board. Packing up Lita's apartment had been hard on everyone, even more so for Marcos and Kara. I couldn't imagine the heartbreaking pain they must be in.

The last several days had been a whirlwind of activity and I was pretty drained. The negotiations had gone well and I was glad they were mostly over. The rules I agreed to, hadn't seemed unreasonable. I liked the idea of them caring enough about my whereabouts to want me to check in regularly.

We hadn't discussed punishments further than spankings, nor had we discussed the *positions* Jason had mentioned, but my mind had been put to ease over the stress of the big stuff. I had started reading books about BDSM and could imagine the positions Jason was inferring to, things like kneeling with my legs under me and back straight while I waited for directions. I had a feeling these scenes would grow more intense as time went by with my men.

It was oddly comforting, knowing there'd be structure of some sort. Knowing what to expect, eased my anxiety and allowed me to relax into our relationship.

"Girl, you seem lost in thought today," Kara commented as we put sheets on her bed.

I blinked out of my daze and shrugged. "I guess I am."

"What's on your mind?"

I chuckled softly. "I'm not sure you wanna know."

"About my brother, huh?" Kara smirked.

"Not just him. All of them. What do you know about BDSM?"

"Just what I've read in romance novels. That something you're doing with them?"

"Yeah." I paused, wondering how much to tell Kara, but decided my best friend could tell me when or if she got uncomfortable. "We negotiated yesterday. Kinks we're into, things were not. We discussed a lot and they laid down some rules."

"Rules? Oh hell no." Kara barked out a disbelieving laugh. "Let's hear them."

"Simple things really, like text them before I'm leaving work. No more ride shares, if I go out drinking without them, to text them and one of them will come get me. No underwear ever."

Kara let out an outrageous laugh and doubled over. "Never?"

"I mean, besides that time of the month, but otherwise, nope."

"And how do you feel about that?" Kara sobered up, watching me.

I blushed. "I uh... I don't have a problem with their rules. I kinda like them, honestly. Just the idea of having someone to be accountable to... I've been on my own for so long. Even when Jenny was around, she wasn't worried about when I'd be home—just assumed I'd be there."

Kara gave me a sympathetic smile. "Well, now you've got three overbearing hot heads to report your every move to."

I laughed.

"No undies though?"

I smiled and shrugged at her. "Again, I don't really mind it. Does talking about this bother you?"

Kara shrugged. "I mean, we've always told each other everything about our sex lives, so not really, but I don't need to know about my brother's cock, alright?"

"Valid." I laughed.

The days started to fly by as I settled into my new job and life with my guys. It had been two weeks since we all moved in together and a week since we'd negotiated our relationship, and we still hadn't *played*. I was growing antsy and wondering when we might take things up a notch. What was the point of talking about all sorts of primal play and paddles, if we weren't going to do any of that? Our nightly activities had mostly been vanilla by the checklist standards.

We had been talking at length about a primal scene they had in mind—chasing me through the woods, tying me up and suspending me from a tree—but that's all it had been: talk. We walked through the woods in the evening, checking things out, but besides the hint of that being something they were into, we mostly talked of other things while taking those walks.

It had been distracting and hard to keep up with.

I heard the rumble of Harley's down the street and looked up from my book, noticing how late the evening had gotten. The sun was already going down behind the trees of the forest in the back of the yard.

I had a fire roaring in the firepit, despite the late June heat, as dusk was settling in for the evening. I'd had the day off work, so I hadn't bothered to get out of my PJs all day. A cropped tank top and short booty shorts was all I wore. I had kicked off my flip flops when I curled up on the lounge chair far enough away from the fire, to not feel the heat.

A moment later the raucous laughter of my men could be heard over the roaring of the engines in the driveway. I smiled as I read my book, another spicy book about BDSM—something my guys had given me, this one about primal play and Shabari. I assumed they were hinting at my future with them, so I devoured them happily. They had encouraged me to do my own research regarding the lifestyle, and I had dove head first into anything I could get my hands on.

I didn't move as the bikes shut off and my men dismounted. With my back to the driveway, I didn't see them as they creeped toward me.

A hand wrapped around my throat and squeezed tight.

I startled, dropping my book as I was lifted out of the chair by a steel band of arm wrapping around my waist.

"Bad girl, Darlin'," Jason crooned in my ear, his breath hot against my skin. "You should always be aware of your surroundings."

I struggled as he clenched my throat tighter, cutting off my air supply. His arm around my waist squeezed tighter. Despite my fervent struggles, I was unable to fight him off. "Run, little lamb."

Jason pushed me violently away from him. I stumbled to my feet before I took off running. I didn't look behind me to see where Marcos and Nico were...I had a feeling I would pay for that.

Barefoot and crashing through the forest, I only had a vague idea of where to go. Thankfully we had spent several evenings after dinner walking through the woods in the last week, that I managed to familiarized myself somewhat with the forest surrounding the back of our rental home.

None of that seemed to matter now, though. My heart pounded in my chest as my breathing labored. I tore through the under-brush, wishing I had my flip flops even, to protect the bottoms of my feet. Branches scratching at my arms and belly, but I barely felt them.

Not hearing anyone behind me, I risked a glance over my shoulder. No one was there.

I wished I had paid closer attention on our evening walks. The boys had distracted me thoroughly with conversation each night. Familiarizing me enough with the woods around us, but kept my mind focused on them and not my surroundings, as to keep me from memorizing the layout of the woods.

It was utterly frustrating.

And downright scary.

A branch snapped in the distance and I took off running again. Away from the fire, I realized how chilly the night had grown, my bare skin pebbled as goose bumps covered my flesh.

Out of the corner of my eye, I caught a black shape lunging toward me from the right. I yelled and darted the opposite way. The sound of crushing leaves and snapping branches crashed behind me and I pumped my legs faster.

I was panting so hard I could barely hear anything but my own labored breaths. I needed to slow down and focus, needed to get my wits about me and figure out where I was.

The sun had fully set and it had grown dark around me. The air was cool on my bare skin, and I was kicking myself for my lack of clothing. The short shorts and cropped tank were not a wise decision—neither were the bare-feet.

I pushed myself further though, losing track of how long I'd been running. I slowed to a walk, before I stopped all together and bent over, holding a stitch in my side, while I gasped for breath.

Only pausing for a second, I stood up straight and glanced around the dark forest. I was lost and growing colder by the second. My feet were torn up and I wondered just how much longer I would be able to hold out, before I allowed myself to be *caught*.

We'd had several conversations regarding this scene this week. Several conversations about what would happen once I was *caught*. I almost wanted to end this right now and give in, let them have their dirty way with my body.

But I wasn't a quitter—and where was the fun in that?

I quickly discovered how much I enjoyed being a brat. Jason's growly remarks of what he'd do to me if I kept pushing my luck only spurred me on. It made my pussy clench, just thinking of it. I could feel my juices damping my shorts—the lack of undies apparent.

Looking around, I listened to the quiet forest, straining for any sounds of my men closing in on me. It had grown too dark to see much through the trees, and I was still struggling to hear over my labored breathing.

The whiny gasp that left my lips as a heavy hand wrapped around my throat, was a turn on to even my own ears. I'd never made that sound before in my life. The hand around my throat tilted my head up and forcefully pulled me backwards into hard wall of muscle. Heat immediately engulfed my back, heating my chilled skin.

With my head tilted back, I saw the black ski mask of the man holding me, and realized I had no idea which one of my guys had caught me. Another whiny gasp left my lips, as I panted for breath.

He snaked his other hand around my waist, sliding his gloved hand sensually over the bare skin of my belly. A low growl rumbled through his chest, vibrating through my back, sending a shiver down my spine.

My eye lids fluttered close as his gloved hand slowly slid up my belly and under the loose crop top of my jammies. The slow sensual play mixed with the low growl and utter terror of the scene were such a contradiction of feelings and emotions, it had me on edge, unsure of how to feel.

His gloved fingers pinched my nipple, making me gasp again. "Such a naughty little thing, running half naked through the woods where anyone could find you."

They'd done something their voices—distorted them somehow—I couldn't make out which one of my guys was holding me. My heart pounded in my chest, this was so hot, so unlike anything I'd ever done before. My body was achy with need; my breasts heavy and nipples hard. Every breath made my chest heave.

I took a step forward, trying to get away, and was roughly pulled back. The arm around my waist tightened into a steel band and the hand around my neck clamped down, cutting off my air supply.

Immediately, I stopped moving, freezing in place.

He let out a low, deep chuckle, his breath hot against my ear. "That's right, little lamb. I'm in charge here." He slowly released my neck, just enough for me to gasp in a breath before his grip constricted again. "I control you; your movements." He let go of with both hands long enough to grab my arms and pull them behind my back, wrapping one hand around my wrists, before his other hand gripped my throat again. "Your breathing." His hand squeezed my neck. "Your body." He kicked my feet apart, stabilizing me, causing me to fall back against his chest, relying on him for support. "Your mind."

A soft blind fold fell over my eyes, making me jump. Someone else was there. I never heard them walk up. But with both of my captors' hands on me, there was no other explanation. "You're ours, little lamb."

My heart was racing a mile a minute, my chest heaved as I sucked in gasping breaths through my constricted throat. Shivers raced across my skin, pebbling it, in the cool night air. I was so fucked, and for the first time all evening, I wondered if I bit off more than I could chew. I was in over my head, but found I was loving every minute of it.

"Little lamb," the voice crooned behind me. "Once again you were not aware of your surroundings. You walked right into our trap."

Low, deep laughter seemed to come from all around me. My eyes were wide as I tried to look around the dark for the other two men. I found nothing. "Please," I murmured, not even sure what I was asking for.

Another low chuckle of hot breath in my ear. "Oh, little lamb, you beg so prettily."

I whimpered. The deep voice and hot breath lit my body on fire, sending tingles of arousal straight for my core. "I need—"

"You need to stop speaking," the man said, squeezing my throat again, tilting my head back so I rested against his shoulder.

My mouth fell open in a silent moan.

My booty shorts were pulled gently down my legs, softly skating over smooth skin. The hand around my throat loosened and I barely hissed in a breath before a hot wet tongue parted my folds and lapped at my cunt.

Then hands were moving everywhere over my body, caressing my legs, my arms, my belly and breasts. I was gasping for breath and so fucking turned on. I needed more, needed to be fucked, to be owned, to be fucking worshipped.

Abruptly, the hands roaming my body retreated and I was left panting, still leaning back against the man behind me, before scratchy ropes brushed over my skin. I gasped, as the rope was looped around my ankles. My arms were pulled over my head and my crop top was lifted off my body, before my arms were positioned in front of me, just below my naked breasts.

Ropes wrapped around my arms and torso; knots being formed every so often as a harness was created around my body. My legs were likewise encased in rope and knots, another harness that would leave each leg free to move on its own and still be encased in rope.

I let out a breathy whimper at the thought of how hot I must look in that moment.

"Oh, little lamb, you are absolutely dripping right now." The deep voice crooned in my ear. Smooth leather gloves parted my folds, barely brushing my clit and making me cry out. "Taste yourself." A moment later, smooth leather was penetrating my mouth, and I could taste my own arousal mixed with the warn leather.

I moaned and sucked on the fingers in my mouth, needing more of my own juices from the leather, needing more of everything.

Ropes were being fed through the harness wrapped around my body, and I gasped as the fingers abruptly left my mouth and I was lifted off the ground. A chill ran over me as I was pulled away from the body heat of the man who had been behind me. Suddenly suspended, my body rotated in the cool night air, naked and on display.

"God damn," Nico groaned from somewhere in front of me, his voice apparent.

"So fucking hot." Jason's deep crooning voice sent chills down my spine. His voice always having an effect on me—even more so now.

"Beautiful," Marcos murmured, his voice low, barely there.

And I felt it, beautiful. Never before in my life had I ever felt as beautiful as I did in that moment, with my men around me and strung up like an animal. I was theirs to do with what they wanted. I was completely at their mercy, and I never wanted anything more in my life.

"Please," I whimpered.

"There she goes, begging so prettily," Jason murmured.

"How you feeling, Little Dreamer?" Nico's voice was soft and gentle, coming from right in front of me.

"So good," I answered, my voice coming out in a soft moan. "So green," I added, knowing exactly what he was looking for. It was one of those things we had spoken about on our walks around the forest. How to answer in a scene, when asked how I was doing.

"Good, little lamb," Nico groaned, before his mouth descended on mine in a bruising kiss, forcing my lips open immediately. His tongue swiped through my mouth, opening mine further, owning me as he sucked my tongue into his mouth.

I moaned loudly, barely able to breathe as he owned me with his kiss.

The ropes shifted and I was pulled away from Nico as my front half was lowered toward the ground. My body hung parallel to the ground, my breasts swinging freely while my legs were bent and spread open, my ankles tied loosely to my hips. For as contorted as my body was, I wasn't uncomfortable. I felt secure and safe in the rope harness, even with my head hanging loosely below my body.

Hands slid through my messy ponytail, pulling my head up. Groaning, my mouth dropped open, only to immediately be filled by a very hard and naked cock. I sucked it into my mouth instantly, without being told what to do.

"Good girl," Nico murmured.

His praise made my body grow hotter.

"We're going to paddle this ass until is a pretty shade of red, then we're going to fuck you in every hole you have." Marcos's voice was a deep gravel that sent shivers down my spine.

It made me want to answer him with a *yes, sir,* despite the cock in my mouth. As if reading my mind, Nico pulled out of my mouth. "Yes, sir," I responded.

Marcos chuckled darkly. "Like you have a say in it, dirty whore."

I whimpered. God damn, being degraded never felt so good.

Nico pressed his cock to my lips again and I quickly sucked him back into my mouth. Hands ran up my thighs, caressing them gently, warming my cooled skin. My mind was gloriously blank as they continued to massage and caress my body, moving higher toward my core. My aching pussy clenched down on nothing but air as I waited to be fucked by them.

Swirling my tongue around the head of Nico's cock, I sucked him further into my mouth. His hands landed on either side of my face, holding my head in place. Two fingers pushed abruptly into my cunt, thick and long, and they immediately curled to find my g-spot. I groaned loudly around Nico's cock, as he began thrusting into my throat, fucking my face while those two thick, glove-covered fingers spread me wide open.

Lips wrapped around my clit, a tongue lapping and sucking at my bud while those glove-covered fingers pressed into my clit from the inside. I screamed as the orgasm ripped out of my body so fucking fast, and stars covered my vision.

Nico pulled out of my mouth, leaving me gasping for breath as my body shuddered with pleasure. "That's one."

I didn't know what he was talking about, didn't care. All I knew was that was fucking hot and my body was on fire.

The glove-covered fingers left my cunt, leaving me clenching and shaking in the aftermath. "We're going to push to past your limits tonight, little lamb," Jason murmured, his voice right next to my ear, his hot breath fanning across my skin.

Then I was sent spinning, one of the ropes tugged and sent me spiraling through the air. Dizzy and disorientated, I was not expecting the first smack to my ass as the heavy thud of impact was felt throughout my whole body.

The gasping moan that left my lips was high and startled out of me. When the second thuddy hit fell on my opposite butt cheek. I was better prepared, but a low moan still escaped my lips. "That's a good girl," Marcos murmured. "Let us hear how much you like it."

I let out another low moan as the third hit to my backside thudded loudly around us. I breathed deeply, trying to catch my breath as each and every smack to my lower ass and upper thighs radiated through me.

After the fifth hit, I was moaning loudly and writhing in my binds. When the paddle caught the side of my foot, that had been bound near my hips, I hissed, and a hand immediately wrapped around the injured flesh, holding it to remove the sting.

A mouth wrapped around my clit again, distracting me from the minor pain in my foot as fingers—bare this time—entered my core. "Please," I whimpered, pain forgotten.

"So needy for us." Jason chuckled.

Fingers plucked at my hanging nipples, pulling and tugging on them.

"Ahh," I moaned breathily. "I need—"

"We know what you need, little lamb. And you were told to stop speaking," Marcos said, his mouth leaving my cunt just long enough to chastise me.

I whimpered as he dove back into my dripping pussy with passion, licking and nipping at my cunt, making me moan more.

Liquid was poured over my backside, startling me and making me jump as fingers massaged my ass, pulling the globes apart to expose my hole. My skin was warmed from the flogging, hot to the touch as the cool liquid—lube I assumed—was poured over me.

Fingers probed at my ass, entering slowly, as the fingers in my cunt swirled in a circular motion, rubbing me throughout. Nico's cock pressed against my lips again and I quickly swallowed him down. There was too much happening, too much to keep up with, so I let my mind go blank and focused on giving Nico the best blow job I could.

My ass was scissored open slowly, one finger, then a second, working my hole. I gasped around Nico's cock, his hands gripping my face to hold me where he wanted. He began thrusting his hips, fucking my face leisurely—a slow rolling tide he was building toward.

I was breathless and barely able to keep up, vaguely running my tongue along him as he used my mouth for his own pleasure. The fingers in my ass retreated as a small silicone plug was pressed in, popping into place behind my ring of muscle, held in place by my body.

I groaned as my body adjusted to plug.

"So fucking sexy for us," Jason murmured.

Marcos swirled his tongue around my clit again, pressing his fingers back into my g-spot, circling them as he applied pressure. It was like a fucking honing beacon to my orgasm, a damn button to press whenever they wanted to make me come.

And come, I fucking did.

Screaming a keening wail around Nico's cock, I cried out as waves of pleasure rocked my body, making my shake and shiver.

"That's two, darlin'." Jason chuckled.

They were counting my damn orgasms?! My mind blanked out. *Is that what they meant by five?*

Marcos pulled his fingers out of my core, as Nico's grip on my face tightened and he began thrusting harder into my throat, gagging and choking me.

I sputtered around his cock, spit dripping from my mouth.

Nico groaned deep in his chest as he only fucked my face harder, each thrust pushing my body backward, only for his hands to pull me forward again, a fucking pendulum for him to use. "God damn, your fucking mouth." Nico grunted in time with his thrusts.

I was helpless to it all, as Nico pounded into my throat.

"So. Fucking. Good." He moaned softly before his cum coated my tongue, he pulled out painting my face with his load. Thankfully the blindfold covered my eyes, because he made sure to get his cum *everywhere*.

I swallowed what I could, but was left panting and painted, in the wake of his pleasure.

My guys didn't give me a moment of reprieve, though. They immediately began unknotting the rope holding my ankles to my ass, only to reposition my legs, while massaging them and folding them under my body—pulling them straight, like I was trying to touch my toes.

I moaned softly, as my body was repositioned. I was pulled up, so I was sitting up with my back straight. My arms were untied from my torso, then pulled above my head and retied to the suspension ropes. "Such a good girl for us, Maya," Marco murmured into my ear as his hands tied me where he wanted me.

My legs were pulled apart and a warm body stepped between them. The feeling of floating—because I actually was—was overwhelming. My head listed to the side before a calloused hand wrapped around my jaw and angled my face so he could capture my lips in a wet and slopping kiss.

Our tongues tangled together. I moaned into his mouth, still unsure of who was between my legs and kissing me.

"God damn," Jason gasped, breaking the kiss. "You're so fucking hot." His voice was gravely, rough and gutted. It sent shivers down my spine.

I was already so fucking close, just the sound of his voice could put me on edge. I whimpered, needing more, needing to come again, but knowing better than to ask for it.

"Shh, darlin'," Jason murmured. "I've got you."

The warmth and the emotion he poured into that simple sentence made my heart clench in my chest, wrapping around it and squeezing. I had to push it to the back of my mind. I would re-exam those emotions later, when I wasn't so keyed up.

Jason's hands slid over my body to my breasts, where he roughly kneaded them, pushing them together and massaging them.

I moaned as tingles shot straight for my core, my pussy clenching.

Jason's fingers left my breasts, instead they began plucking and pinching my nipples. He tugged and pulled on them, pinched and plucked, punishing them beyond relief.

I yelped and twisted, trying to get away from his methodical torture. Each fucking tug was like a lifeline to my clit—making my pussy throb while trying to clamp down on nothing. I needed something inside me. I needed to be *fucked*.

"These nipples are so fucking beautiful, darlin'," Jason crooned. "They'd look fucking hot with some barbells through them."

I gasped, throwing my head back. I was so fucking turned on and his words only added fuel to the fire. It wasn't the first time Jason had mentioned wanting to pierce my nipples, but it was the first time I felt like agreeing with him—felt like giving in.

He tugged me again, forcefully pulling my suspended body forward by my nipples.

I cried out, my head thrown back in pain and ecstasy.

"You gonna come, just like this, darlin'?" His deep voice skated up my spine, mixing with the pulling pleasure of my nipples. "Dirty little whore, coming from just having her nipples play with."

"Ahhh!" I yelled as I came hard, my body shaking as my orgasm rolled over me. Tears pooled beneath my blindfold, as pleasure wracked my body.

"Good girl. That's three," Jason murmured. He finally released my aching nipples, only to step back, leaving me to hang and swing in the cool night air.

My chest heaved as I caught my breath. I was so utterly blissed out, I didn't even know what day it was, let alone cared.

I felt like I was flying—high through the sky—a million miles from home. There was not a care in the world for me.

Hands smoothed down my sides, slowly bringing me back to earth. I tilted my head back, only for it to fall against a hard chest.

I moaned softly as a gentle kiss was pressed to the column of my throat. "So pretty, Mi Vida," Marcos's deep growly voice whispered in my ear.

I smiled lazily. I could get used to this praise. These men already owned my heart, but damn were they burrowing into my soul too.

Marcos

I PRESSED MY BARE chest to Maya's naked back, my hot skin warming her instantly. She moaned softly at the contact, but otherwise didn't say a word. Her rules during a scene had been made clear during negotiations: no talking. She'd broken that several times already tonight and we'd been lenient so far. It was her first major scene, after all.

But now she was beyond words, falling into subspace and mostly going nonverbal. It was glorious.

My hands slid over her body, caressing her belly and grazing over her tortured nipples. I massaged her breasts gently while I scattered open mouth kisses to the side of her neck.

A lazy smile pulled across her lips as she tilted her head to give me better access. "So good for me," I murmured. I slid my hands down her back, cupping her ass and pulling her cheeks apart.

A shiver ran down her spine—she knew what was coming.

My fingers toyed with the edges of the plug inside her, gently pushing and prodding it, making her gasp with pleasure. "Uhh," she moaned softly.

I sucked a bruising kiss into the side of her neck, marking her, while one of my hands snaked around her body to rub at her clit.

She was over sensitive, her body burning with desire, and every new sensation was pushing her toward the edge. I tugged on her plug, pulling it gently past the ring of muscles holding it in place, before I thrust it forward, fucking her ass with it.

A whimpered gasp left her breathless.

I toyed with her clit while I fucked her with a butt plug. She was simply breathtaking. She whined and writhed, her body aching.

"Such a good little slut for us," I murmured into her ear. I was so damn proud of her. Her first hardcore scene with us and she was doing fantastic.

She whined.

"Shh, Mi Vida," I murmured, before I switched completely to Spanish. "Confía en mí para llevarte allí." *Trust me to take you there.*

I turned her head and kissed her softly, lazily, as I continued to toy with her.

She gasped into my mouth, trying to move closer to me, arching her body to get what she needed from me.

It was no use though. I was methodical in my approach, and as soon as she tried to take control of the kiss, I backed away, chuckling softly. "Be good, baby girl," I murmured and twisted the plug in her ass.

She groaned, letting go and leaned back against me, surrendering to his control again.

"That's it," I said and fucked her harder with the plug, as my fingers pressing harder into her clit.

"Ohhh," she moaned softly. She was close, so on edge.

"That's it," I repeated. "Give in to me." I twisted the plug and pinched her clit roughly.

A loud wail left her lips as her body arched and her orgasm crashed over her. Her pussy squeezed and throbbed, while her ass managed to push out the plug that I had barely left inside her. Shaking and whimpering through her orgasm, I held her tight. "Good girl," I said. "That's four."

She had no words; she was utterly breathless and spent. She hung limp against me.

Maya

"You're doing so good for us, darlin'. Think you hold out a little longer?" Jason asked, his voice coming from in front of me, as someone stepped between my legs.

I licked my lips in response.

Jason's hands skated up my thighs softly, ghosting over the ropes that held me suspended, and around my waist. His thumbs found the sensitive spots above my hip bones and dug in.

I moaned low in my throat.

Jason pulled my bare pussy against his very naked cock and rubbed against me, soaking himself with my juices before he plunged into my pussy.

Gasping, I arched my back, thrusting my hips as much as I could against his protruding member.

"So fucking good for us, darlin'." Jason groaned.

All I could do was moan.

Marcos's fingers started playing with her asshole again, sliding in and out, prepping me again, while Jason settled deeply into my cunt while he waited. "Fucking perfect, Maya," Marcos muttered.

I jolted forward as cool liquid was poured down my ass crack and rubbed into my hole again. There was a squelching sound as Marco notched the head of his cock into my ass and slowly slid in.

"You're so fucking hot like this, Little Dreamer." Nico groaned softly, his face inches from mine. I licked my lips before he claimed them in a soft and sensual kiss. His tongue parted my lips, sliding against mine.

I wished that I could reach out and touch him, wrap my hand around his cock. I didn't know how long it had been since he came down my throat, but I was sure all of this was turning him on.

Marcos bottomed out in my ass and Jason swiveled his cock in my pussy. I groaned deeply into Nico's mouth as hands came up to play with my tits.

I wasn't going to last much longer—there was no way. I broke away from Nico's kiss, my breathing ragged as Jason pulled out of me and slammed back home.

"Fuu—" I groaned, almost swearing and breaking their no talking rule. A rule I'd found I actually enjoyed, as it put me into a different headspace—something more sensual and primal.

"Good girl," Marcos muttered, pulling out and snapping his hips forward again, driving in deep.

My heart beat frantically in my chest. My breathing was ragged—harsh panting gasps—that did little to bring oxygen into my lungs. I whimpered as I realized I was struggling to breath.

A heavy hand landed on my chest, pushing me back against Marcos's chest, while another snaked up my side and wrapped around my neck. "Deep breath." Marcos's voice was deep and command demanding. He growled right into my ear as his hand squeezed around my neck, applying just enough pressure to remind me that he was in charge.

I took a deep breath, breathing easier under the weight of their hands, than I had been before.

"Again." Nico this time, his hand caressing over my cheek.

I forced myself to listen to my Dom's as their hands caressed my skin, trusting that they would take care of me. I hadn't realized how tense I had grown, until I eased backwards against Marcos's chest, falling limp.

"There's a good girl," Jason crooned.

"Much better, baby," Marcos whispered in my ear. His hand slid from my neck and down my side, gliding over my sweat-soaked skin till he spread his palm open over my belly.

I smiled faintly, but I was fading fast. It had been a long night and my arms were starting to ache.

"Just little bit longer, Little Dreamer." Nico pressed a kiss to my lips.

I moaned and then Jason and Marcos began moving again. They quickly found a rhythm, as Nico pressed butterfly kisses to my lips and whispered how beautiful I was. It didn't take long for my orgasm to build. The gentle back and forth motion between Marcos and Jason, the constant praise and kisses from Nico, I was crying out in pleasure soon after.

"Fuck." Jason grunted as he picked up his pace, pounding into me, chasing his own release. Jason's fingers on my hips dug in harder, his own hips snapping once more before he thrusted one last time. He gasped out another curse as he came before he fell against me, trembling and breathing hard.

"Mi Vida," Marcos groaned. His hips shuddered to a halt as he growled out his release. Marcos's head fell into the crook of my neck as he panted. He took a moment to gather himself before he pulled away, placing a gentle kiss to my temple and slowly pulled out of my ass.

Jason followed his lead and I groaned at the loss of them. My body began trembling and shivering as the cold night air surrounded me.

"Such a good girl, Little Dreamer." Nico turned my swinging body and lifted me bridal styled into his arms. Jason and Marcos made quick work of the knots and ropes, and when my arms were lowered from their suspended hold above my head, I breathed a sigh of relief.

Nico gathered me close to him, cradling me against him as he lowered us to the ground, then wrapped me in a thick fluffy blanket.

I tucked my head under Nico's jaw and closed my eyes. The blindfold still blocked my view, but I didn't care. I was too lethargic to care.

"So good for us, baby girl," Nico murmured.

I breathed in his woodsy scent and sighed peacefully. I floated in between consciousness and sleep, only halfway paying attention to my men moving around me. Each knot was untied and each rope slid off my body. They spent time massaging my limbs and soothing my skin, all while whispering sweet praise to me.

I drifted off to sleep, safe in my lover's arms, as the three of them placed kisses along my body, making me feel more loved than I ever had in my life.

Chapter Twenty-One

Maya

L IFE SETTLED INTO ROUTINE as the summer flew by and my relationship with Jason, Marcos, and Nico developed into a stable and steady foundation. Communication was key, and we had learned we thrived best when the four of us were on the same page.

They had even developed their own little rituals and protocols for how they greeted me, and in return, I learned how they wanted me to address them when Kara wasn't around. It was funny how easily we fell into a twenty-four-seven dynamic, despite them telling me that I didn't have to live that way if I didn't want to.

More than anything, I found that I enjoyed it. It was so simple to address them as Sir, or to kneel in the bedroom waiting for one of them to get out of the shower, or to kiss them good morning after I made a pot of coffee—something I only did on mornings I got off the night-shift. Otherwise, I was still not a morning person and didn't like to deal with anything more than sitting on their lap while I sipped my coffee.

The routine of it all is what I loved the most. Life was chaotic enough; knowing what to expect from my three lovers was a relief. Especially while we shared the house with my best friend.

Kara living with us was an added challenge, but not all that bad. There was a layer of sneaking around that made things fun, not that we had to hide things from her, but we also didn't want to make her uncomfortable with public displays—she was Marcos's sister after all.

Kara didn't seem to mind though, besides rolling her eyes every once in a while, when the boys were especially sappy, she seemed to be very happy for us—and I would know, I'd asked her a million times.

"This isn't weird for you?" I asked for probably the tenth time in the last two months.

"I mean, I don't want to see you guys making out on the couch or nothing," Kara laughed. "But I'm totally fine with it. You're good for them." She shrugged a shoulder. "You're good for my brother. It's good to see him happy."

Kara's words may have seemed happy, yet despite her smile, I could see something was bothering her. There was still a sadness clinging to her, that only surfaced when it was just the two of us. "How are you doing?" I asked.

Kara shrugged her shoulder, staring off into the distance. Her eyes were unfocused as she took in the woods surrounding the property. "I've been thinking about my father a lot lately."

Surprised by the admission, I chose my words carefully. "Do you know anything about him?"

"No. I only found out his name because I was cleaning out Mom's papers recently. Marcos doesn't like to talk about it; we don't have the same father." Kara sighed and ran a hand through her blond hair, the humidity made it stick to the back of her neck. She pulled it up and into a messy bun, tying it off with a hair band that had been around her wrist.

"So what'd you find out?" I asked, dying to know.

"His name is Vincent Carmichael."

"She gave you his last name at least."

Kara nodded. "I googled him. He's some hotshot lawyer in Mourningside."

I gasped. "So he's practically local."

"Yeah."

"Shit, girl. That's rough."

"Yeah." Kara sighed again. "I have half a mind to go down to his firm as ask him why he didn't want me, you know?"

I watched her solemnly, watching the melancholy wash over her. "Did you ever ask your mom about him?"

"Yeah, and she never really answered. Just said that he wasn't a nice man, and I shouldn't look for hope when there was none."

I pressed my lips together, biting back a retort. I didn't want to seem insensitive to a dead woman, but not being open to a child about their birth father was cruel, even if you were trying to protect them. They deserved to know, even if that parent was a shitty human being, it only spurred on hope otherwise. "Maybe your mom was just trying to protect you."

Kara shrugged. "I guess we'll never know."

"Does it bother you, finding out he's a lawyer?"

Kara barked out a laugh that sounded sarcastic but otherwise didn't respond.

"I mean, you've been planning on being a lawyer practically your whole life. Kinda ironic, huh?"

Shaking her head, Kara stood up and started pacing in front of the fire pit. She tugged at her ponytail before she finally responded. "It's such fucking bullshit! I had to find out his name from my birth certificate. She clearly cared enough about him to write his name there. Why couldn't she have given me more to go on? Tell me he's an asshole, or that he cheated on her. Or SOMETHING! Not the blasé *'he's not a good guy'* spiel she gave me. Then I find out he's a lawyer? Not some criminal like I thought!"

"Girl, just cause he's a lawyer, don't mean he's a great guy," I shot back. "Lawyers can be crooked as fuck. They know how to manipulate the law to their advantage."

Kara sighed and stopped pacing. Tugging her ponytail again, she nodded. "True."

"Let's say you reach out. Then what?"

Crossing her arms over chest—like she was hugging herself and not being defensive—Kara stared out into the forest again. "I don't know. It's stupid, you know? Like I'm some orphan needing validation from a parent or something."

Empathy rolled over me, as I watched my friend pace. "Maybe you should talk to Marcos about it all. I know he doesn't like talking about it, but maybe he knows more, something your mom told him and not you. He is quite a bit older than you; he would remember the time before your birth. Maybe he met your father."

Kara paused and seemed to consider it, her head tilted to the side, lost in thought.

I heard the rumble of bikes down the street and knew my alone time with my best friend was coming to an end. "Sounds like the boys are home."

Kara sighed and took her seat again, staring out into the surrounding forest.

A few minutes later, Jason was bending over me and pressed a kiss to my lips. "Hi darlin'."

"Mmm, hi." I smiled against his lips as he kissed me again, this time more passionately.

"Sister sitting here," Kara said.

Jason chuckled and pulled away, leaving me breathless and panting.

"Hi, sister." Marcos laughed before he bent over me and kissed me just as thoroughly. "Hello, Mi Vida."

"Hello." I laughed when we pulled apart.

Nico pushed Marcos out of the way before I could say another word. "Little Dreamer," he greeted, before he claimed my lips.

"What are you girls up to?" Marcos asked his sister.

"You know, just chillin'," Kara replied.

I pulled away from Nico slowly and gave him a smile, before I turned to Marcos. "Actually, we were talking about Kara's father."

Marcos froze slightly, his dark brown eyes turned toward his sister, watching her carefully. She was still hugging herself and ignoring them for the most part, staring out into the forest.

I decided to help my friend out. Reaching for Marcos's hand, I laced our fingers together and squeeze his hand. "Kara found her birth certificate in a bunch of Lita's papers, and found her father's name. She looked him up. He's some lawyer in Mourningside. Did you know him?"

Marcos squeezed my hand tightly. "No. Mom never brought him around the apartment. If she was meeting him, she either did it at the club or a hotel or something."

Kara's head dropped to look at the ground in front of her.

My heart broke for her. I couldn't imagine the pain she was going through. To have such a loving and caring parent and to lose them so young, it was heart breaking.

"Mom did say that she loved him at one point, but she found out he wasn't the man he portrayed himself as." Marcos sighed and rubbed a hand over his buzzed head. "I dunno, Lil Manita, do you think you want to reach out to him?"

Kara shrugged and I could see the tears welling in her eyes.

I tugged on Marcos's hand and he glanced down at me. I nodded my head at Kara and Marcos nodded slowly. Running his hand over his head again, he stepped away from me, letting go of my hand and walked over to his little sister.

Marcos crouched down in front of Kara, resting his hands on her knees. "Lil Manita, I'm so sorry," Marcos murmured. Kara's eyes slowly looked up to meet her brothers. "I wish I had the answers you're looking for, but I don't. I'm sorry, chaparrita, but I'm here for you if you want to reach out to him. Whatever you need." *Shorty.*

Tears fall from Kara's eyes and she sniffled softly. I turned away, giving my friend some space with her brother. Privacy was hard to come by when you lived together and I could grant my friend that space.

Summer faded away into fall and soon Kara was back at Northern Illinois University for her junior year, leaving me and my boys plenty of privacy in our rental house. Living a twenty-four-seven dom/sub dynamic fell naturally to me. Our group chat was a constant stream of chatter, so texting my boys when I was leaving work became as natural as breathing. I was eager to get home to them after a long shift at the hospital, and knew they were excited to see me.

As for my other rules, I found the no panty rule to be oddly freeing. I liked knowing my men could slip inside me easily if I wore a skirt. I also liked how sexy and naughty it made me feel under my scrubs. Let's face it, scrubs were not the sexiest pieces of clothing, but they got the job done. Feeling sexy and desirable only made me more confident in myself.

I was finding there were many things now that made me feel more confident and sexier, and I felt stronger over all, since I started submitting to three men. It sounded absurd, I knew, but it was the truth nonetheless.

I had never felt freer in my life.

"Alright, Little Dreamer," Nico started as we sat around the dinner table. "Tonight's the night."

My heart skipped a beat and a nervous smile pulled across my lips. "I'm ready."

"Good." Jason smirked.

"You're riding with me tonight," Marcos said. His hand slid across my knee under the table, drawing my attention to him.

I nodded. "Yes, Sir."

"You're not to be alone tonight. You'll stay with one of us at all times, at least the first couple visits to the clubhouse. We're claiming you as our old lady tonight," Marcos continued.

I swallowed thickly. None of this was news to me, we'd been talking about it for weeks now, but knowing it was happening tonight, and not some far off date, was still unsettling. They had been waiting for Kara to go back to school, though. They didn't want to raise any suspicions with her, so it had been easier to wait.

"There's an outfit laid out on your bed for tonight. Generally, it's unsafe to ride in a skirt, but we'll make an exception tonight. Going forward, we'll bring your clothes with and you'll in one of our dorm rooms at the clubhouse," Jason said.

I nodded, slowly taking in the information they were telling me.

"Tonight, you won't speak to any patched brother unless asked a direct question and you will look to us before you answer them, you got me?" Marcos asked.

I nodded. "Don't speak unless spoken to and look to you guys first."

"Good girl." Marcos smiled. "I know it's a lot. It won't always be like this. Once you're around the club more, after everyone knows you're *our* old lady, it won't be as strict. Eventually you'll be able to talk, but protocols have to be followed first."

"Once you're inked as our old lady, things will calm down," Nico added.

I bit her lip. "Inked?"

"With the Devil's Psychos logo." Jason pointed to the patch on his leather cut that they wore all the time now that Kara was no longer living in the house. "Then you'll also tattoo our names around it."

My mouth dropped open in shock. "That's a big step."

"It is," Nico agreed. "It's the equivalent to marriage in the biker world."

I swallowed thickly, my heart falling to my stomach. We'd been dating roughly four months now; this was moving too fast for me.

"Relax, Mi Vida," Marcos murmured. "That's not what's happening tonight and we're not expecting that of you any time soon. We're just telling you what to expect and how things run in this world. Old ladies are considered property of the patched brother. One day, we'll do your official inking, but tonight we're just announcing it to the club that you're ours."

Butterflies fluttered in my belly at the thought of these three men *owning* me. They practically did already, because I gave them that right, but knowing in the eyes of their club, that's all I was—was their property—it turned me on.

"We should also speak about that exhibitionism *maybe* that you checked on your list," Jason said.

I licked my lips, "You mean, when Marcos said he wanted to fuck me on the pool table during a party?"

"Fuck yes." Marcos growled.

"Can we see how I feel in the moment?" I asked.

"Always, Mi Vida, always. And you can safe-word out at any moment," Marcos reminded me.

I smiled and placed my hand on top of his on my knee, squeezing it. I loved that about them, that no matter how intense things got between us, they always reminded me of my safe-words and to use them if needed, that I should never feel ashamed to use them. "Alright then."

The outfit that was laying on my bed, was the hottest thing I had ever seen, let alone worn. Thigh high black leather boots that came up over my knees, a black pleated leather skirt that ended several inches above my boots, showing lots of olive skin, paired with a red leather crop top that hugged my tits and laced up the front, displaying ample cleavage and miles of smooth skin. My belly button ring had a rhinestone skull and cross bone dangling from it.

The new tattoo Slade had started in the beginning of the summer had been completed. The massive piece that spanned the right side of my body from my boob to my hip—butterflies with wings curling around my front and back and bright multi-color designs inter-pieced had turned out beautifully. After several sessions with her, it was finally done and healed and looked magnificent. I could understand why my boys wanted me to show it off at my first official club meeting.

Recently, I'd added chunks of black to my curly golden-brown hair, giving it an edgier look. Tonight, I straightened those curls and tied a black bandana around my head to help prevent my hair from tangling during the ride. I slid some chunky leather cuffs around my wrists and stood in front of the full-length mirror, taking it all in.

I looked fucking hot.

Better yet, I felt fucking hot. I felt on top of the world.

"You are beyond words, Little Dreamer." Nico leaned against my bedroom door frame, taking me in.

I smiled easily. "Thank you, Sir."

"We're spending the night tonight, so pack a couple things for morning." Nico stepped into my room and went to my closet. Even though he told me to pack something, I knew he would do it himself. He liked dressing me. Even if he didn't outright say it, it was something I had learned in the last couple months being together, and I wasn't complaining. His outfit choices were always hot, always something I'd pick out myself, and it made me feel less self-conscious knowing my men already thought I looked hot.

He pulled out a pair of my more ragged and holey blue jeans and slipped a black tank top off the hanger—it had a black rose printed on it. Simple and bad ass in its own right, it would be a good morning after outfit. Nico bent over and grabbed my black riding boots from the floor before he walked over to my dresser and grabbed me a pair of socks.

Deciding to help him out, I pulled a small duffle bag out of my closet and set it on the bed, before I headed into the master bathroom and pulled my travel toiletry kit out from under the sink. I double checked that my mini shampoo and conditioner bottles were full, before I closed everything up and walked back into my bedroom.

Nico had just finished placing my clothes in the duffle bag, when I handed him my toiletry bag to add to the mix.

"You nervous?" he asked, glancing up at as he zipped up my things.

I shrugged a shoulder. "Kind of? Nervous, anxious, kinda excited really."

Nico grinned brightly, his blue eyes shining. "Remember, you're ours. We're not going to let anything happen to you. And tonight is about having fun. We'll have some drinks, play some pool, maybe even dance."

"Yeah, pretty boy. You gonna dance with me?" I smirked up at him.

He laughed and wrapped an arm around my waist, pulling me against his rock-hard body. "Little Brat, I might dance with you or I might bend this tight little ass over on dance floor and fuck you for that little comment."

I blushed as Nico's hand slid around the side of my face and tilted it to meet his lips. I opened for him immediately, his hot tongue sliding across mine. Moaning, I gripped the sides of his leather cut and held him to me. "I love you," I murmured against his lips.

"Back at you, Little Dreamer." He chuckled and claimed her mouth again.

The ride the clubhouse hadn't been long, maybe twenty minutes, but it had been long enough to rile up my nerves. The Devil's Psychos clubhouse was in the heart of downtown Creekton, just off the main street, and in a not-so-great part of the city anymore. Not that Creekton really had a great part anymore—it was slowly turning into a crime infested city.

I vaguely wondered if the Devil's Psychos had anything to do with that—but it wasn't the time to ask her guys about it, because they were pulling to the clubhouse.

Bikes lined the street in front of the rundown building that used to house an old motel. Marcos pulled in Harley into the line-up, somewhere near the middle of the pack. I could assume there was some sort of hierarchy to the parking order, as I knew Marcos wore an Enforcer patch on the front left side of his cut, below the Devil's Psychos patch.

Jason and Nico backed their bikes in further down from Marcos, so he clearly held more rank than did. I would have to ask later, when we were in the privacy of one of the dorm rooms and not with so many eyes watching us.

Men stood around the outside of the clubhouse, drinking and laughing. From the open doors of the building, I could see a barroom filled with people. Loud music pounded over the roaring of the motorcycle engines. Only when Marcos shut off his bike and patted my bare thigh, did I slide my hands from around his waist, to his shoulders to steady myself as I stood on the back peg and swung my leg over the back of the Harley and dismounted with ease.

I stepped out of the way, giving Marcos room to swing over his leg over the bike. He wrapped an arm around my waist and pulled me against his front. "Ready for this?"

I gave him a wry smile and tilted my head up toward his. "Yes, Sir."

"Good girl." He nudged my hip and I turned and stepped aside. Lacing his fingers through mine, he led the way to the main door of the clubhouse, Nico and Jason falling into step behind us.

It was loud and hot inside the clubhouse. I tried to keep up with Marcos and look around the main barroom to take in as much as I could. There was a bar lining one wall and peeling wallpaper, but there were too many bodies to see much else. Lots of half-naked women and big burly, leather-clad bikers.

Marcos led me to the bar, his fingers tight on mine as he tugged me along. Jason was right behind me, his hand on the small of my back as he guided me forward. I wished Nico was closer as well, but I knew he wasn't too far behind.

At the bar, Marcos motioned for the bartender and shouted at the scantily clad women dressed in a barely-there silvery bikini top that hardly covered the nipples of her very large fake tits. She preened up at Marcos with a huge smile that had me narrowing my eyes on the woman. It was too loud, so I couldn't hear what Marcos said, but a moment later the woman was smiling was pouring several drinks and setting them on the bar in front of Marcos: three glasses of Whiskey and one Vodka Sprite with a lime wedge.

Jason pushed against my back to grab two of the glasses and passed one back to Nico. Marcos dropped my hand to pick up the last whiskey and vodka soda before he turned away from the woman without another word. He handed me my drink and grabbed my hand again. "Come on." He nodded at Jason, who's fingers slid across the bare skin of my lower back before he turned away.

I turned and followed Jason as he led the way toward the corner of the room where Nico was standing with a group of men, near one of the pool tables. It looked a little too official for my liking. I squeezed Marcos's fingers between mine and took a sip of my drink, hoping for a little liquid courage before I walked into whatever meeting the boys had planned.

Marcos stepped in front of me, pulling me to his right side, so I was positioned just behind him. I had to shift my drink and switch hands that were laced with his, but we did it quickly and seamlessly. "Pres," Marcos shouted over the music. "I want you to meet my old lady. This is Maya Henderson. Maya, this is our president, Larry Buckley."

I took in the one Marcos called president, seeing a man in his fifties with a paunchy belly and salt and pepper hair. He had leathery skin and crow's feet in the corners of his hard eyes. His arms were crossed over his chest, resting on his beer belly, as he turned and roamed his gaze over me. There was something off about the look, more derogatory than calculating, like he was thinking of all the ways he was picturing me naked, rather than to scare me off. Maybe that was supposed to scare me off. I bet a man like him weren't used to being told *no*.

I plastered a smile on my face and glanced at Marcos—who nodded—before I addressed their president. "Nice to meet you, sir."

President Buckley's smile was oily—there was no other way to describe it. It didn't sit right with me—gave me a bad feeling. "Beautiful name for a beautiful woman," Buckley said, almost mockingly. "So this is the woman, three of my best men have been sharing."

I kept my mouth shut, grateful that Marcos had at least stepped slightly in front of me to block my body a bit and Buckley let his gaze roam over me salaciously, not bothering to hide his arousal. Disgust swirled in my belly at his blatant leering.

"Maya," Jason spoke up from Marco's left. "This is my father, Jerry Langford."

I turned my head to one of the other men in the circle, to the left of Buckley. The blond-haired man was almost the spitting image of Jason, only twenty years older. Buzzed dirty blond hair, flecked with gray, the same steely gray eyes as his son, and a hard face weathered from sun and age. He had a kind smile, though, his eyes crinkling in the corners when he greeted me, holding a hand out to me. "Nice to meet you, Maya."

I glanced to Marcos—who was already nodding—before I smiled easily at Jerry and shook his hand. "Nice to meet you too."

"Well trained, already?" Buckley laughed mockingly patting Marcos on the shoulder.

Marcos fingers tightened on mine the second my fingers slid back between his. I took a sip of my drink to keep myself from saying anything back to their president. I hated men like him, who thought they were god's gift to women and openly treated them like dirt. I may have signed up for this dynamic between me and my guys, but I didn't sign up to be disrespected by other men.

"She's our Old Lady," Marcos said evenly. "She'll be treated as such."

Buckley laughed easily and patted Marcos on the shoulder. "Of course, of course. My bad, boys. You've got a beautiful woman there." He laughed again before he walked off.

I couldn't help but breathe a sigh of relief when he was finally gone, leaving me alone with my boys and Jason's father.

Jerry gave me a reassuring smile. "Stay away from Buckley if you can and don't wander off from these three."

I nodded slowly.

"It's alright, you can speak freely around Jerry," Marcos murmured into my ear.

I smiled and nodded again. "Thank you, I don't plan on going anywhere."

Jerry grinned and changed the subject. "I hear you're an RN."

I nodded and relaxed a little as Marcos let go of my hand. My boys ease up a little, now that Buckley was gone, spreading out to create their own little circle and I fell into easy conversation with Jason's dad.

After the introduction to Buckley, I had calmed a little and settled down. Sipping on drink after drink, I started to enjoy my evening as I played round after round of pool with my guys. I wasn't half bad, so I managed to keep the guys on their toes.

When pool turned into making out between shots, Marcos picked me up and carried me out of the barroom. Once we were behind closed doors, he set me down on my feet and cupped the side of my face, gazing down at me intently. "I might share you with my brothers, but I won't share you with the club. They don't get to see us fuck you." His voice was rugged and gravely, his stare so damn intense, that my stomach fluttered with butterflies.

These fucking men always knew what to say and do to make me fall head over heels for them every damn time. A slow smile spread across my face, "Yes, sir."

Jason growled from behind me and crowded against my back. His hand slid through my hair, grabbing a firm hold at the roots and pulled my head to the side, forcefully, so he could suck open mouth kisses in to my neck.

I moaned loudly as my eyes fluttered closed immediately. God, they knew how to work my body.

Marcos pressed in closer, pushing me back against Jason's hard body, before he claimed my mouth in a biting kiss. I whimpered, wrapping a hand around his while my other hand gripped his cut and held him against me, all while I fought him for control of our passionate kiss.

Hands slid down my body, across my bare belly and under my red leather crop top, while more hands slid down my thighs to the bare skin below my short-pleated skirt. Fuck, had I felt so hot all night. Nico had great tastes when it came to dressing me.

My lack of panties made access to my pussy too easy. And my arousal had been dripping down my thighs all fucking night from being touched and kissed in front of others. I was glad Marcos had been possessive and brought me back here, though. I wasn't comfortable around their club, having just met them, and Buckley gave me creepy vibes. I may be dating and fucking three men, but I still wanted respect.

Fingers parted my folds and slid through my slick heat, plunging inside me, pulling me out of my musings. Jason's hot breath fanned my skin, before he sucked a bruising kiss into the side of my neck, making me throw my head back and moan loudly, breaking the kiss with Marcos.

"That's it, Mi Vida." Marcos chuckled. "Let them hear you."

I knew they couldn't, knew the music was way too loud, but the idea of others possibly hearing me, made me even hotter. We would have to figure out a safe way to explore my exhibition kink.

"Get her naked," Nico said from across the room.

I jerked my head to the side to find Nico sprawled across Marcos's queen-sized bed. I had no idea how we were all going to fit on that thing, but I didn't care, as long as they were fucking me.

And fucking me, they did. They spent half the night switching positions and manhandling me around, flipping my body like I weighed nothing, all the while they thoroughly used my body and took what they wanted from me.

I lost count of how many times I orgasmed and when we finally collapsed into a sweaty heap with me sprawled across Nico's body, and Jason and Marcos crammed together on the mattress, I let out a soft sigh, smiling contently.

If this is what life would be like with my guys, then I'd live a happy life, forever with them.

Part Two
Two Years Later

Chapter Twenty-Two

Marcos "Killer" Candella

I LOOKED AROUND THE club house, taking in the club whores and my brothers in arms fucking them. It was late at night and the party was raging around us. Maya was dancing her ass off in a tiny ass skirt with fuckin Stone plastered to her back while he ran his hands over her scantily clad body—lots of skin and ink on display.

Half our club was three sheets to the wind, so I didn't mind the show the two of them were putting on in the middle of the make-shift dance floor.

I still couldn't believe we had landed ourselves a chick like Maya Henderson. All curves and attitude—she was one bad ass bitch—and she was all ours.

In the two years we'd been together, life had never been better. Maya had really grown into herself and found her place in our relationship, even accepting her place as our old lady. While she wasn't inked, she wore a property patch with pride. She was an easy girl to get along with, communicated her needs well, and rarely got angry—but also wasn't afraid to throw down if a club whore got too handsy—like tonight when she punched out one of the sluts that had sidled up to me, trying her luck.

Maya had also turned into an amazing submissive to play with—who *mostly* followed our rules to the letter. She did like to brat at times, and I loved it every time she did. She made life fun and enjoyable.

It was the balance I needed when it felt like the rest of my life was in shambles. In the last two years I'd been promoted to Vice President of the Devil's Psychos and my sister had moved away. I had known stress growing up with a single mother, but I felt like life had been throwing me punches left and right lately.

Kara had met her father and transferred to Harvard to finish her undergrad. It had broken my heart. Vince Carmichael had reached out to her shortly after her junior year of college had started and presented Harvard on a silver platter. Kara had been all too happy to have finally connected with her missing parent—especially after the death of our mother—that she had been over the moon and accepted his gift quickly.

I knew that gift would come with strings.

All gifts did. Especially from rich and powerful men.

Kara had disagreed with me about Vince and his intentions, and our relationship grew strained through the distance. It was better if I didn't even ask Kara about her father and just let it go. I still got better updates through Maya, considering the girls were still best friends, but even Maya was noticing the strain on her friendship with Kara.

Maya couldn't tell Kara about the club, so she found it difficult to share much of her life with Kara when there was a blazing wall in between them. At least, that's what she told me. I could understand her frustration too—I'd only been keeping that part of my life away from my baby sister for years.

The music changed, something harder with a heavier beat pounded out of the massive speakers around the club house. Across the room, I saw Dagger's eyes light up with mischief as he cut his conversation short.

Dagger danced his way through the naked bodies fucking on every surface they could, and shimmied through the bodies grinding on the dance floor until he sidled into Maya's space with feline grace.

From my spot across the room, I could see Maya's sultry smile as she reached up and wrapped her arms around Nico. With Jason at her back and Nico pressed against her front, she was sandwiched between them and looked utterly happy.

Contentment rolled over me as I settled back in the recliner I'd been lounging in for the last hour, just happy to watch my girl with my two best friends.

Life might have been stressful, but this wasn't.

Maya made everything about life better.

Chapter Twenty-Three

Maya

I YAWNED AS I pulled my coat on. From my brief glance out of the hospital window as I had headed to the locker room earlier, I saw that rain pummeled the pavement, a constant deluge that flooded the streets.

I'd just gotten off a fourteen-hour shift in the emergency department at Mourningside General—a shift that should have ended two hours ago. My replacement had shown up late, claiming car trouble from the rain. It was probably the truth, but I was tired and cranky and just wanted to go home.

It was just after two in the morning and I should have been in bed already. My phone had been blowing up all night with messages from my guys, until I finally caught a bathroom break and called them back.

Jason had promised me a spanking for ignoring his calls, but I hadn't been in the mood for him. I was exhausted and had witnessed a small child come in with multiple gunshot wounds to the torso. An alleged mistake from his slightly older brother. I didn't know what to believe, as the mother was inconsolable and the father was absent.

I had used my safe-word mid conversation with my boys, effectively cutting off their bickering. My men had remained silent while I had explained my night and then they told me that they loved me and to get home safe.

Two years into our relationship and our dynamic had transformed into a full-time twenty-four-seven d/s relationship. I had thought that I'd never commit to a full-time dynamic, but it had progressed so naturally, that when Jason had brought it to my attention one day, I had just smiled and shrugged.

They were my Dom's and I was their Sub—that was all that mattered to me. I enjoyed them taking charge and taking care of me. Following their rules was such a turn on for me. Most of the time, we were on the same page about our relationship, and when we weren't, we paused and spoke about our feelings. If one of us really wasn't listening, then we used a safe-word, my guys included.

Since I'd been at work when I had used my safe-word, it was more of a wake-up call to my overprotective and very worried

Dom's. They knew my job could be crazy and unpredictable. They were just worried that I wasn't home. It was late and the weather was crap and we lived in an unsafe world.

So when I texted our group chat at two in the morning, I was not surprised when I immediately received a response from Nico, to get home safe in the rain.

Maya:

Finally clocking out and headed home

Nico:

Get home safe Little Dreamer. Shit went down at the clubhouse. We'll be home late.

I was a little surprised that they hadn't come to pick me up, but his text was all I had to go off.

"Night Dwight," I mumbled to the night-shift security guard as I walked by, finally headed for the main door of the hospital.

"Goodnight, Miss Maya. You have a safe drive home now." The older man gave me one of his bright white smiles.

I returned his easy smile and wondered if I should just wait out the rain a couple hours, maybe find a supply closet that one of the residents had carved a sleeping cubby into.

As quickly as that thought entered my mind, I dismissed it. I'd just finished a fourteen-hour shift, at the end of a six-day run. I was about to be off for the next eight days and I was more than ready to be home and in my own bed. I wouldn't even bother showering until I woke up.

A crack of lighting flashed across the sky, followed quickly by a booming blast of thunder that rattled my bones and the windows. "Shit," I muttered as I paused at the door. My Honda Civic was parked somewhere in the middle of the employee lot, a good hundred yards away from the door. There was no doubt about it, I was getting soaked.

I pulled the hood of my sweatshirt up over my head and muttered, "Fuck it." I darted out into the night and the torrential downpour, praying I didn't slip and fall.

When I was finally safe in my car, I started the engine before I stripped off my soaking wet hoody. I grabbed a dry one from the mountain of laundry that was tossed in the back seat, still there from the weekend before when I'd planned to go to the laundry mat, but never made it.

Now I was grateful for the dry clothes as I waited for my car to warm up in the early spring night. While I waited, my car made a dinging noise and I groaned when I saw the gas light had come on. "Motherfucker," I sighed.

Annoyed, I pulled out of the parking spot and fixed the radio as I pulled out of the lot. I headed down the road toward home, hoping that the twenty-four-hour gas station by the house wasn't closed because Barry decided to drink on the job and locked up early.

Ten minutes later I pulled into the well-lit gas station and sighed. It was still raining torrentially and the overhangs didn't help when the rain was blowing sideways. I was the only car in the lot though. I quickly got out my car and did the deed of paying with my credit card before I put the nozzle in my tank, then rushed back into the car.

I was just settling in when two cars raced into the parking lot, a fancy BMW coupe and a late model Buick LaSabre. The LaSabre roughly cut off the BWM, boxing it in between me and pump. I watched in horror as an older white man climbed out of the BMW and started shouting at the driver of the LaSabre.

My blood chilled in my veins as the driver of LaSabre opened the door and stepped out. Dressed in black from the hood on his head, to the heavy black boots he wore, the man that stepped out was broad-shouldered and tall. Much taller than the older white man that had stepped out of the BMW.

One look at the man covered in black clothing, had shivers running down my spine. He may be some twenty feet away and in the pouring rain, but the man was intimidating as hell, as was the Glock 9mm he pulled out of the back of his pants.

I gasped, watching the scene unfold before me, like watching a car crash—I wasn't able to look away. Lighting flashed as thunder rolled through and the black-clad man fired off the 9mm several times.

The older white man jerked back violently, as his body absorbed the bullets.

I covered my mouth to keep myself from screaming, as the shooter pumped several more rounds into his victim, and he fell backwards onto the hard pavement.

There was no doubt in my mind I had just witness a hit—this was an outright assassination. And I was in the wrong place at the wrong damn time. Motherfucking shit.

I couldn't move. I couldn't breathe.

There was a loud thump as the gas pump finished filling my Civic. I jumped in my seat, startled and drew the attention of the shooter. That intimidating man, dressed in all black, turned my way. He gave just the slightest tilt of his head, as he acknowledged my presence.

"Shit, shit, shit," I gasped, fumbling for the lock on my car door. I couldn't drive away; the nozzle was still in the gas tank.

Slowly, oh so slowly, the man in black turned and stalked toward me. In no time at all, he was before me, stopping right outside my driver's side window, towering over my car. He placed a hand on the roof and leaned down to face me, using the Glock to knock on the window to get my attention.

I jumped at the sound, even though I watched his every move.

He motioned with the gun for me to exit the vehicle.

My heart pounded in my chest as blood rushed my ears. *Fight or flight, bitch! Fucking move!* I thought about just driving off, letting the gas nozzle rip out of my tank as I drove away. A bit of damage to my car and maybe ripping off the gas line out was the least of my problems, right? Not when there was a dead body on the pavement some twenty feet away. The station had to have insurance, right? I could drive off and live to see another day.

He knocked on the window with the gun again.

I scrambled for the door handle, already cursing my decision. So much for fight or flight.

The man barely stepped back as I stepped out of the car. He was in my face, in my bubble a moment later. His breath was rancid, smelled like stale cigarettes and whiskey. There was a thick, jagged scar that ran down the left side of his face, almost half an inch thick. It was raised and puffy, and sliced through his eye. The iris on his left eye was a pale blue, almost gray, probably blinded from the injury.

I forced myself to look into his right eye, the iris almost as dark as night.

He watched me silently, his gaze roaming over my face. He reached out and pulled my clipped-on work badge off my shirt. "Maya Henderson," he said coldly, his voice a nasally rasp as he read my name tag.

I shivered, not only from the cold and rain, but from the way his voice skated over me. His voice was higher than I thought it'd be, not like the deep scary killer he appeared. I'd never heard anyone sound like he had before...it was almost unhuman.

"Please don't kill me," I murmured, shivering. "I promise. I didn't see anything. I won't say anything."

He struck before I even saw him move. His massive hand wrapped around my jaw, gripping me tightly. He shoved my face backwards, my head slamming back against the side of my car as he forced my face to look up at him. His fingers dug in harder, nails puncturing my skin. "You saw nothing, Maya Henderson, because nothing happened," he growled in my face.

I whimpered as he squeezed my jaw even harder, before he slammed my head back against the car again. My ears rang as I lost my focus on him towering above me. Pain radiated through my skull and down my spine as my teeth clenched painfully in my mouth. I let out a stifled whimper when he leaned even closer to my face.

"I'll be watching you Maya Henderson," he rasped, his face inches from mine. "Your family, your coworkers, even your little dog won't be safe from me, if you tell a single soul what happened here tonight."

I nodded as much as he would allow with his fingers still painfully grasping my face. "No one," I muttered.

"I've got your name, your place of work, and your license plate," he rasped again, an amused air spreading across his face. "Soon, I'll know everything about you."

I trembled as a shiver ran down my spine that had nothing to do with the cold.

He chuckled darkly and finally let me go.

I scrambled to get my feet under me before I fell to my ass on the wet pavement.

"Get home, little rabbit," he chuckled, before he turned away.

Then he was gone, climbing back into his LaSabre and easing out of the gas station parking lot, like a man with all the time in the world—not like a man who just murdered in cold blood.

My hands shook as I quickly pulled the nozzle out of my gas tank. I screwed on the gas cap and shut the metal cover. I was back in my car a moment later. I didn't wait to stop shaking. I had to drive away. I couldn't be here. I needed to be far, far away from the scene when it was discovered, and who knew when Barry would wake up from his little nap behind the counter.

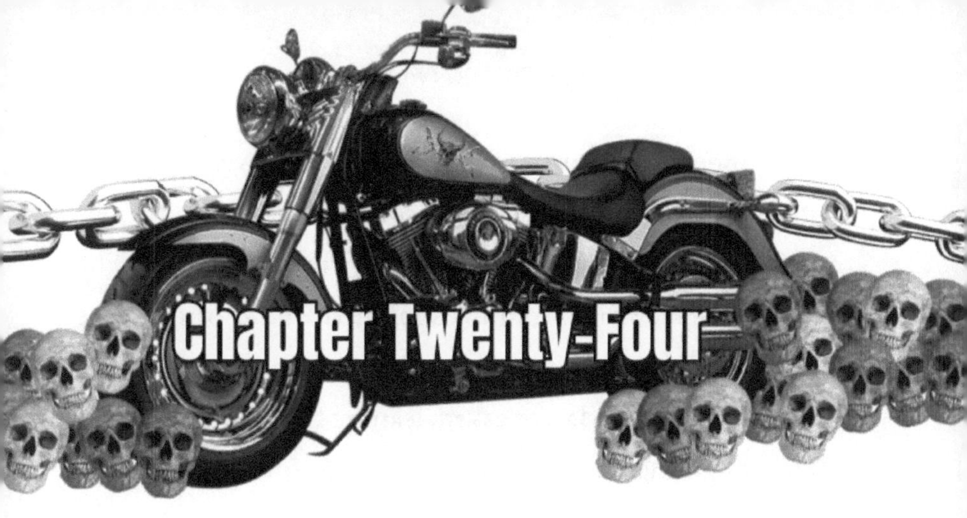

Chapter Twenty-Four

Jason "Stone" Langford

I SIGHED IN RELIEF when the text from Maya hit the group chat that she had made it home safe from her shift at the hospital. I hated that she worked such long and hard hours. She made good money and she loved her job, but she came home utterly exhausted and often fell into bed for over twelve hours after a working a week of twelve-hour shifts.

I was even more pissed that I wasn't home, waiting up for her, to help her shower off her shift and tuck her into our bed. The bullshit that had popped off with the club couldn't wait though, and when our president called us all in, there was nothing we could do.

Club came first, always.

Maya understood how it was, and while she never voiced her frustration, I knew it bothered her sometimes.

"Someone killed the mayor tonight," President Larry "The Butcher" Buckley said from his spot at the head of the large table that made up our church.

"What the fuck?" Marcos asked, leaning forward in his chair.

"He was gunned down at Barry's gas station about an hour ago," Buckley said.

I frowned, "But you called us here before that happened."

Buckley grunted. "Yeah. We were raided tonight."

The men around the table—all of our brothers present—roared with fury. "Why didn't you lead with that?!" My father shouted. He didn't bother to hide his glare at our president.

Buckley did a downward wave motion with his hand, cutting off the roaring rage around the room. "I think they're both connected. Whoever raided us, I think they also set the hit on the mayor."

"Why do you think that?" Bear asked, crossing his arms over his wide chest. The man was huge—bear like—with a mane of dark black hair that fell around his broad shoulders and a thick black beard that covered most of his face. He was stacked with muscles on top of muscles, and tattoos covered most of his skin from the neck down. The dude even had the word *Bear* tatted over his left eyebrow.

"I got a call from Sanders down at 501, that our warehouse had been hit. Someone walking by happened to call in that they witnessed someone trying to break in," Buckley said.

I crossed my arms over my chest, narrowing my eyes on Buckley. Detective Sanders from precinct 501 was a long-time friend of the Devil's Psychos, his friendship with Buckley had gone back decades to their grade school days. If Sanders said someone called in the break in, then the information was legit.

But why? And who the hell broke in to our warehouse?

"We need to go down there and secure things—"

"Then why are we here?" Nickle interrupted everyone shouting.

I eyed the newly patched brother with interest. Nickle usually went along with anything Buckley said, loyal to the fault. He was still so green; he didn't question things yet—until now.

"Because we gotta let things lie low, until Sanders says the coast is clear."

"So we're just letting whoever raided us, take everything? The fuck?" My dad bit out.

"The hell we are!" Dagger growled.

"Enough!" Buckley roared, slamming the judge's gavel down on the wooden table top—effectively silencing the arguing men around the table. "It's done. Sanders is watching the place, back up had already been called in before he got there. The police are turning the place over now. There's nothing we do—the shipment's lost."

"How does this have to do with the mayor?" I asked.

"Sanders called, saying that Barry saw a snake tat on the neck of the guy who gunned down the mayor, but didn't see anything else," Buckley answered. "And the witness from the warehouse also saw a snake tat on one of the guys."

"Las Serpientes—aren't they a street gang from the south side of Chicago?" Marcos asked.

Axel, Phoenix, and Blaze shifted in their seats, suddenly on full alert. I cocked an eyebrow, not that the three men noticed.

"Yeah. They've been here for years now, but it seems they're making a play for Creekton and being bold about it too," Buckley grumbled.

"How the fuck did they find out about the warehouse?" Bear asked.

"Unclear, but masked fucking Las Serpientes were running all up and down the block," Buckley said.

"Jesus fucking Christ," Axel muttered, shaking his head, before he shot Phoenix and Blaze a look of contempt.

"We gotta do something about them." There's a fire in Blaze that I hadn't seen before.

The usual laid-back trio were fired up and raring to go, like Las Serpientes were a personal afront to them or something. Definitely something had happened that those boys weren't talking about.

I shared a look with Marcos, who raised an eyebrow. Yeah, we'd talk about it later. For now, we needed to figure out our next move and convince Buckley that sitting here on our fucking asses was not the way to go about things.

"Alright, so how we hitting the snakes?" Nico asked.

"Let's just go burn down their house," Blaze growled.

I stifled a laugh. Blaze and fire... yeah, it was too easy.

"Now hold your damn horses," Buckley grumbled. "We gotta be smart about this. Can't go in half-cocked."

I watched our president as he slowly scratched his eyebrow... like he was stalling. Was Buckley stalling? I had no proof, just a hunch, and staring at Buckley—who was usually a hot head and cocky—being utterly calm was telling.

I didn't know what it told though, just that something was up with our president.

"We should be smart about this," My dad spoke up, agreeing with Buckley.

I looked at my father to see him eyeing the table carefully. It wasn't lost on him either then, that Axel, Blaze, and Phoenix were acting differently than normal. I would have to make a point to speak to my dad away from the club to garner his insight.

"What do we know?" Bear asked.

We spent the next two hours planning on how we were going to take down the snakes, only for Buckley to hmm and haw over it. It was some fucking bullshit.

Frustrated beyond belief when we finally got out of church, I didn't stick around to speak to my dad. My girl was home alone in the middle of the night. All I wanted to do was get home, shower and slip into Maya.

Sleep would come after, much, much, after.

As expected, the house was dark and quiet when we walked in. We shed our boots in the mudroom off the kitchen before we moved through the house to the stairs, climbing them quickly.

We found Maya in our large bed—two king mattresses pushed together—sleeping naked as she usually did anymore. I loved how our relationship had evolved over the last two years and how Maya had evolved. Gone was the shy girl just learning BDSM and negotiations, now we had a spit-fire of a submissive that wasn't afraid to try new things and often brought up ideas out of all the smutty books she read.

It was a dream come true. I couldn't imagine ever being happier.

Well, I would be in about thirty seconds when I slipped my rock-hard cock between Maya's slick folds. I quickly stripped off the rest of my clothes and headed into the shower. It had been a long day and the last thing I wanted to bring anything from work into our bed.

Nico tried to push me out of the way as I headed for our ensuite bathroom, but I beat him there. "Fucker." He chuckled under his breath. There were two other showers in this house, those two could wash off elsewhere.

I made quick work of soaping up and rinsing off. After a quick towel off, I left the bathroom naked, not bothering to cover up. In the bedroom, Marcos still hadn't moved, he was standing at the end of the bed, watching Maya sleep. His hand was moving slowly over his jean covered cock. "Shower's free," I muttered.

Marcos nodded absently, still stroking himself through his jeans while he stared at Maya. She was sleeping on her back, half the covers pulled off of her, either by her own wiggling or Marcos's interference, but one tit was out and half her belly was showing. "So fucking perfect," Marcos groaned.

I nodded, my naked cock growing hard.

"I'm gonna knock her up," Marcos declared.

My jaw dropped open and I jerked my head to look at my brother in disbelief. "What?"

Marcos nodded absently, his eyes never leaving Maya. "Yeah. I've been fucking with her birth control. Giving her the sugar pills when she's not paying attention."

"Dude, the fuck?" Nico said from the doorway behind us.

I glanced over my shoulder to find my Nico with his hair dripping wet, as he walked into the bedroom naked.

"Mmhhmm," Marcos murmured. He was utterly lost to the bomb he just dropped onto us. "She'll never leave, then."

I cocked my head at Marcos, confused. I was so used to seeing Marc—*Killer*—with his head on straight. He was usually wound so fucking tight and so in control, that he made me look flighty. Where the hell was this insecurity coming from? And why the hell were we just now hearing about it after being in a relationship with Maya for two years?

I knew that Marcos's possessiveness was off the charts—shit, so was mine—but Marcos was acting completely out of character.

"Since when are you worried that she's gonna leave?" Nico asked, voicing the same concerns I had.

Marcos shrugged a shoulder and then sighed softly. "I don't know... since my Mom? Since Kara left? I don't know. Two of the three women in my life that meant anything to me are gone...Maya can't leave me if she's carrying my—our baby, right?"

I sighed deeply. This was some heavy shit. "Nah bro," I agreed quietly. "She can't leave if she's having our baby."

Nico walked further into the room to stand shoulder to shoulder with Marcos. I moved closer to be right next to them as well. "Well, what are we waiting for? Let's knock up our woman."

I chuckled dryly, *leave it to Nic to make a joke during a heavy moment.*

"I'm gonna hit the shower," Marcos muttered. He jogged for the bathroom, a new determination in his gait. A moment later, the water was turning on.

I shared a look with Nico. "You sure about this?"

Nic's answering grin is sheepish. "She's mentioned how she's wanted kids one day."

I laughed softly and shook my head. Looking at our girl, I was slightly surprised that she hadn't woken yet, but at the same time, I knew after a week of twelve-hour shifts, she was always beat. She'd be dead to the world, unless we got too loud or jostled her too much.

I walked over to the bed, deciding to get things started. She was ripe for the taking, naked skin peeking out from under the covers. Her nipple pebbled in the cool air. I leaned over her and sucked her nipple into my mouth. In the two years we've been together, I still hadn't lost hope that one day I'd convince her to pierce them.

One day, after she had a baby, apparently. I'd take her down to Slade, myself. But that day was still a long while off and knowing Marcos had been tampering with her birth control pills, there was a good chance she could already be pregnant with how often the three of us fucked her.

She rarely told us no. If she was too tired, she just rolled over and closed her eyes while parting her legs. Maya really was the best thing that ever happened to the three of us. Every day we grew closer to inking her, making her our old lady permanently.

One of these days Marcos was going loose his control and bring her down to the courthouse to marry her. I doubted she would get much say in the matter. She could have whatever wedding ceremony she wanted after the fact, but on paper, she'd belong to our vice president.

I heard the water shut off in the bathroom. Marcos wasn't playing around, if I wanted to go first, I needed to get a move on. I kissed my way down her bare belly, pulling the blanket out of the way as I went. Moving slowly, I made sure not to jostled her. I wanted to savor this, make it last.

Usually somnophilia was Marcos's thing, but the appeal had grown on me in the last couple years, with how deeply Maya slept. She never complained about it, either. She never complained about a lot, period.

"Utterly perfect," Marcos murmured, as he walked back into the bedroom. I glanced at him out of the corner of my eye; he was still toweling off.

I moved my way between Maya's legs, parting them. I settled onto the bed on my stomach and began to feast on her cunt. My hands held down her hips as I went to town. I was only half worried about her staying a sleep, mostly for her sake though. I knew how utterly exhausted she was. She deserved her rest. I just needed her more.

When I was sure she was wet enough, I kissed my way up her body until I was hovering over her and my rock-hard cock was gliding through her folds. I slid in slowly, breathing hard. God, I would kill to just fuck her hard as I wanted to.

Once I was fully seated inside her wet hot heat, I snaked my hand beneath her back and cradled her against me, before I smoothly flipped us so I was lying back in bed and she was draped over my torso. Her legs fell to either side of my hips and I stilled, waiting to see if she'd wake.

When it was clear that her breathing was even and she wasn't moving, I tilted her head to the side so her cheek was resting on my shoulder facing away from me. I knew one of those guys would be using her mouth, regardless of her being awake or not.

Nico headed for the bedside table and grabbed the lube we didn't even bother to hide in a drawer. Nic tossed the lube to Marcos, knowing exactly what he needed, before he kneeled on the bed next to me and stroked Maya's face with a tattooed covered hand. Nic leaned down and pressed a gentle kiss to her lips. "So fucking perfect, Little Dreamer."

I held still as Marcos squirted lube along Maya's cunt, not even bother to aim for her ass. Cool lube pooled around my balls and I had to stifle a moan. "You joining me?" I asked my brother, already knowing the answer.

"Have to. We're getting her pregnant. No more wasted cum," Marcos said. "Nic, don't come until we're done. Save it for her pussy."

Nico chuckled under his breath before he lined up his cock with her lips and smeared his pre-cum all over them, painting her with it. "So fucking perfect," he murmured again.

I waited, my cock throbbing painfully, as Marcos slowly lined himself up against Maya's cunt. Pressure built around my dick while Marcos pushed forward, popping his head into the tight wet heat that was Maya's pussy.

"Fuuuuck," Marcos groaned the word out. Loosing a breath, he panted.

I slid my hands over Maya's back, admiring the smooth blank skin there. It was just begging to be inked. I imagined a gothic scene of demons and angels fighting across her back, something that warred with the two halves of Maya that made her whole.

Marcos thrusted in further, only to stop and groan. We hadn't done this before—both of us in her pussy together—Maya hadn't wanted to try it. For some reason the idea made her nervous, even if she had initially said she wanted to during our negotiations. We respected her decision when she was awake.

"Fucking hell, bro." Marcos panted and pushed in further. "I can feel every damn one of your bar bells."

I groaned as the friction of Marcos cock against mine while surrounded by Maya's cunt was almost enough to push me over. "Stop," I groaned.

Marcos chuckled under his breath. "Gonna blow, bro? I'm not even all the way in yet."

Nico laughed and pressed his cock between Maya's lips. He was monitoring her breathing, making sure she wasn't waking up. Not that it would matter, I thought. We wouldn't stop, but it was an extra layer of suspense, trying to do all of this while she was still sleeping. A thrill, if you will.

I grunted as Marcos bottomed out inside Maya. Taking a deep breath, I closed my eyes and counted to ten. I almost wished Maya was awake for this. Having her writhing and moaning between the three of us would have made this not such a bro-fest.

Marcos didn't give me any warning before he pulled out halfway and thrusted himself back in hard. "Oh fuck," Marcos panted. "Dude, you close, man? I'm not gonna last long. Your fucking piercings."

I panted and nodded. I was barely holding back myself. "Yeah man. Let go."

Picking up speed, Marcos grunted while I groaned. Marcos's thrusts were short and deep and I couldn't take it anymore. I came with a low growl, clenching my teeth as Marcos let out a deep moan, his hips shuddering to a stop. Marcos hunched over slightly, catching himself on the bed as his knees gave out.

I could only lay there, body twitching as I recovered from the intense orgasm and tried to catch my breath.

"My turn," Nico muttered, pulling our attention back to him.

Looking down at Maya, she was still passed out and breathing evenly. I had no fucking clue how. *Did she take something?* It wouldn't be the first time she took a sleep pill after a long shift. It wasn't something she did often, but she was known to take one once in a while.

"Yeah man," Marcos muttered. He let out a hiss as he slowly pulled out of Maya.

I grumbled, but I too pulled out, and slowly rolled over so Maya was laying on her side in the center of the bed. It took me a minute to untangle our limbs, but eventually I was able to shift backwards away from her.

Nico walked around the bed and climb in on the other side, crawling across the bed until he glided in behind her prone body. Once he was seated in her warm sheath, he rolled her onto her belly and carefully maneuvered her head so she could breathe easy while passed out.

I rolled off the bed, intending to go clean up, when I saw the amber colored prescription bottle on the nightstand, with a note beneath it.

I took one.

Use me.

Love you.

"No, shit." I chuckled and pulled the note from under the pill bottle. I handed it to a curious Marcos, who had glanced away from watching Nico and Maya.

Marcos's grin is diabolical. "She wanted to be used tonight, Nic. Have at it. She's out."

Nico only grunted as he picked up speed, pumping into Maya's heat. "Fuck, she's perfect," he said for the thousandth time that night. "So fucking—," he grunted as he came, hips freezing in place, "perfect."

Maya

I WAS FREAKING OUT; I didn't know what to do. Dax Hillcrest had made it very clear that should I tell my boys—tell anyone—there would be hell to pay. I spent the week after my late-night encounter trying to act as if nothing was wrong, but my insides were eating me alive—as was my guilt.

I'd never kept anything like this from my guys. Ever.

We didn't do secrets between us, even with club shit, my guys told me everything. I was all in, there was no half-ways in this life, it was how people got killed. The club was dangerous, because they had dangerous enemies and I needed to know so I could stay safe. Also, so I could keep an eye out myself in the hospital—I could come across anyone at any point.

Here I was though, keeping something so fucking huge from my men. Details like this could change their war. Someone had hit their warehouse the same night and time that someone had killed the mayor.

I knew who killed the mayor, yet the rest of the world didn't seem to know—my guys included.

I was going to be in so much trouble when my guy found out I was kept this from them. This could break us. The last thing I wanted was to lose them—Marcos, Jason, and Nico were the world to me. My entire life revolved around them. I had my guys, my sister, and a handful of close girlfriends, and that was it.

My stomach rolled again at the thought of my massive betrayal.

"Hey Miss Maya, you clocking out for the day?" Dwight the security guard called out.

I jerked my head up and looked around, realizing I was in a daze as I was leaving the hospital. I shot Dwight an apologetic look. "Hey Dwight, yeah, I'm out of here." I had just finished a rare day-shift and my mind clearly wasn't in the right place.

"Well, you have a good evening now," Dwight smiled.

I grinned back, loving my comradery with the older gentleman. Dwight was a kind-hearted man that made sure to know the name of every staff member that entered through the hospital. He kept a bucket of candy on the desk and his wife made Christmas cookies every year to share with all those that stopped by. It had become a meeting place amongst the nurses who need a sugar fix in the middle of a long shift.

"I am out of here," I announced a broad smile on my face. "I'll see you in a week!"

"Have a great vacation," Dwight replied with a smile.

I pushed out of the hospital, a smile on my face as I tilted my head up to the sunshine. *Is this what it's like to work day shift? I could get use to this.* The thought made me chuckle. As much as I enjoyed getting off in the sunshine, the tension of admin and staff that weren't there at night, had made the day drag on forever.

It had also made my nerves worse.

I had too much on my mind and kept getting distracted; which was evident a moment later when I realized I couldn't find my car. The lot that morning had been packed and I hadn't been able to park in my usual lot.

Sighing, I realized I had to trek the half mile to lot C—the overflow lot. On my walk over, an unsettling feeling rolled over me. I'd been so out of it all day, but now I felt the weight of the secret baring down on me.

In the naked light of day, my decisions were detrimental to my relationship. There would be no coming back from this. It was a betrayal. I knew it in my heart—my guys would see it that way as well.

After two years together, it was killing me.

I had to come clean.

Tonight.

Lost in thought, I made it to my car without realizing. Only to jolt out of my thoughts when I saw the bouquet of flowers on the hood of my car. I whipped my head around, looking for anyone out of place in the parking lot. I was mostly alone, though. Other hospital workers were headed to their cars as well, but nothing seemed out of place.

I looked down at the massive bouquet on the hood of my Honda Civic. It wasn't your standard flower arrangement. It was utterly breath taking, but it was made up of Snapdragons and begonias and black dahlias. I knew from a literature class in college that there was a whole flower language back in the day.

I pulled out my phone and quickly looked up what each flower meant. Begonias were thought to symbolize caution, Snapdragons meant deception and concealment, and black Dahlias were the symbol of betrayal.

Motherfucker.

My heart exploded in my chest. Was this from my guys? Did they somehow find out? Were they breaking up with me?

My hand fluttered as I reached for the note that accompanied the flowers, it was tucked up under my windshield wipers.

A little birdie told me you's was acting suspicious. A little 2 obvious that you're hidin sumthin. People catchin on little whore... like the 3 men you let fuck every hole you got. It would be a shame if sumthin were 2 happen 2 one of them guys... someone else might have to step in, 2 fill your holes.

At the bottom of the note was crude drawing of the Devil's Psycho's logo.

My whole body ran cold as my spine locked in place. It was from Dax. The flowers, the note, the fucking threat, it was all from Dax fucking Hillcrest.

A frighten sob tore out of me before I could stop it. I slapped a hand my mouth and quickly stifled any noise I could make before anyone from work could suspect something was wrong. Suddenly, there were too many people around.

I grabbed the note and the flowers, unlocked my car, and shoved it all in the passenger seat as I quickly sat behind the wheel. Once I was locked inside the vehicle, I needed two hands to get my shaky key into the ignition. I had to get away from work, fast.

I flew out of the parking lot, barely paying attention to those around me and sped away from work as fast as traffic would allow. Tears poured down my face as I finally let myself cry.

I was so totally fucked. Dax made it clear he knew who my guys were. The biker gang he had just started a war with when he sent his crew to steal from their warehouse, all while he was killing the mayor, someone also instrumental to their work.

My breathing grew erratic as I began to hyperventilate. I had to pull over quickly. I found a park in the neighborhood not far from the hospital and quickly parked in the lot. I buried my face in my hands and sobbed my heart out. My entire body shook with the force of my sobs.

I'm so fucking, fucked!

I had to come clean. I needed to go home and wait for my guys to get back from work and tell them everything. They would be upset, but I would have to bear the consequences. There was too much riding on them not knowing.

Resolved to a plan, I focused on getting my breathing under control and calming down. I wiped my face with my hands and cleaned up as best as I could. Checking my make up in the rearview mirror, I swiped away the ruined mascara and eyeliner, before I reached for my water and took a long gulp of the cool liquid.

I sat there a moment longer composing myself. I took deep breaths and let them out slowly. Just as I was getting ready to leave, my phone rang. My eyes flashed to the phone screen in my cup holder. FUCK! I hadn't texted that I was leaving work!

Nico was calling me.

I quickly picked up the phone and cleared my throat before I answered it. "Hey baby."

"Maya! Thank God." Nico sighed in relief. "Are you almost done with work? Marcos and Jason have been shot!"

My heart fell into the pit of my stomach. "What?" I gasped, disbelief and understanding sunk within her. Dax. This had Dax written all over it.

"Look, they're ok, but they could use your medical expertise. Are you coming home soon?" Nico's voice was calm in my ear, steady.

"Yes. Yep. Clocking out. I'll be there soon."

"Good. Love you, Little Dreamer."

"Love you too," I choked out. I hung up my phone and set it back in the cup holder. Taking a deep breath, I checked my reflection in the mirror again and wiped away another tear. I needed to get home and get to my guys.

Glancing over at the flowers on the passenger seat, I grumbled, "Fucking hell." Making a snap decision, I grabbed the bouquet and threw open the driver's side door. I walked over to a garbage can in the park and tossed the flowers. "Bitch up, Maya. We've got shit to do," I told myself.

At home, I find both Marcos and Jason sitting at the kitchen table holding dish rags to bleeding wounds. Marcos's was pressed against his calf and Jason's was held against his left bicep. Once again, my heart stopped in my chest, and my breath hitched as I gasped.

My guys were hurt.

"Come here, Mia Vida," Marcos murmured, holding an arm out to me.

I walked slowly, tentatively toward him; my eyes darting to Jason as well. Jason gave me a tight smile and reached for my hand as I slid onto Marcos's thigh. Perching on the leg that wasn't injured, I looked up at Marcos and frowned. "What happened?"

"Las Serpientes," he replied immediately. He sighed. "Their leader Dax Hillcrest is looking to make a move in Creekton. Starting with trying to take out the Psychos."

I swallowed thickly. I could feel the blood draining from my face. Slowly I turned to take in Jason. He was pale himself, but still he reached out to me with his injured arm and looped our fingers together loosely.

Nico stepped in beside me and rested his hand on my shoulder, massaging gently. "Don't worry about the snakes," he muttered. "We'll take care of them."

I could only nod my head, my voice unreliable. My loss for words didn't seem to bother my guys, though. I swallowed thickly again and looked down at Marco's calf. His jeans were a bloody mess and he was dripping onto the tile floor. "Shit," I swore. I dropped Jason's hand and slid from Marcos's lap.

I bumped into Nico as I tried to back away and he wrapped his hands around my hips. "Easy, little Dreamer."

I took a deep breath and tried to steady my nerves. I had work to do here. "I need my bag," I muttered, mostly to myself.

"Right here," Nico said from behind me.

I glanced over my shoulder, to find my medical bag sitting on the counter, already open. The three of them were oddly calm, for two of them just being shot. Realizing I was probably in shock, I slowly stepped away from Nico and walked the short distance to my bag.

"How did this happen?" I asked again, my mind struggling to keep up. I started pulling out gaze and iodine, forceps and suture kits.

"The other night he went after our warehouse, raided us. His crew took an entire shipment of both weapons and drugs. We went after his crew tonight, took a little pay back," Marcos answered.

I gasped, immediately dropping the supplies I had gathered from my duffle.

"Shh, little dreamer. It's ok," Nico murmured. His warm hands enveloped mine, steadying my shaking fingers.

I squeezed my eyes shut, wrapping my fingers around his, stealing his strength.

Nico pressed a kiss to my temple before he murmured softly to me. "They're ok. We're all going to be ok. I promise you."

I let out a shuddering breath.

"Darlin, be a good girl, now." Jason's voice was a soft croon that sent shivers down my spine for a different reason. After two years together, the man's voice could still affect me. He knew exactly what he was doing to me too—it was a weapon he honed to his advantage.

I took a deep breath before I shot him a withering glare.

His answering smirk was hot as fuck. The little quirk of his lips in the corners, his eyes crinkling. God damn, even dripping blood, Jason Langford was sexy as hell.

"Fucking hell," I muttered. His little trick had worked though; I managed to clear my mind and snap out of my funk. I was able to gather all of my supplies quickly, before I gloved up and got to work.

Maya

THE GUNSHOT WOUNDS HAD looked worse than they actually were. *Flesh wounds*, as my guys had called them. Jason's had a deep graze through the side of his bicep, while Marcos's was a fairly simple through and through in his calf muscle.

I had patched them, stitching and bandaging them, before ordering them to rest.

Resting, turned out to be a joke for men like Marcos and Jason, though. I had managed to keep them home and in bed for day and half—mostly with bribes and blow jobs. Half way through the second day, they compromised for the couch, but I knew after that, I would lose them.

It was for the best, though. I was going stir crazy myself. I was still trying to figure out if I should come clean, especially now that Dax knew who my guys were. There was too much pressure. Too much riding on me keeping my mouth shut.

Dax was dangerous. His threats were real. I could lose my men. They'd already been shot.

What would he do if he found out I told them about the mayor? As far as I knew, my guys had no idea what I had witnessed. What would happen if they found out Dax was threatening me?

They would go after him. Harder than they already were now. And he would kill my guys.

No, I decided. I would not be telling my men. I could only pray that this skirmish with Las Serpientes would be the last one. They got their pay back for their missing shipment and raided warehouse. That was it, right?

I paced the empty living room, deep in thought.

Marcos, Jason, and Nico had gone to the clubhouse, despite my pleading that they stay home. Apparently two days home was enough to heal from gunshot wounds.

I shook my head. I couldn't stay home. I had too much restless energy. It was a Friday night, so I pulled out my phone and made a call. It had been too long since I last saw my friends Arturo and Karma and the whole gang anyways.

Karma answered on the second ring, loud music pumping through the phone. "Yo, Maya!" she yelled.

I laughed and wiped away tears that had immediately welled up in my eyes at the sound of my friend's voice. "Hey girl! It's been too long!"

"Fuck yeah, it has! What are you doing tonight? Come on through!"

Again, I laughed. "Hell yeah, that sounds great! Give me an hour, and I'll be out that way!"

"Right on!"

Smiling and suddenly excited, I hung up the phone and headed for the stairs. I needed to change my clothes and order a ride share. There was no way I would be driving tonight. I'd be breaking one of the cardinal rules in my relationship, but I found that I couldn't bring myself to care.

The party blazed on around us, just like old times as I sat in an Adirondak chair in front of the roaring fire. Music pounded from speakers on the back deck and people milled about the huge yard. Next to me, both Karma and Stephanie were smiling and sipping drinks as Arturo told a riveting tale of an architect design fail that had happened on the job, that was funny enough with how Arturo told stories.

Kyle and Travis were manning a beer pong table on the deck and shouts could be heard as they closed in on their opponents.

It felt like old times. Only person missing was Kara. Well, and Terri and Hunter, but I hadn't talked to them in the last two years. Terri was abroad traveling most of the time and Hunter moved out west for med school.

My heart clenched at the thought of my best friend. Phone calls had grown more distant in the two years since Kara had moved to Harvard. Kara's relationship with Marcos was rocky, and it made it difficult for Kara to speak to me some days. There was too much emotion there.

Just like it was hard for me to constantly lie to Kara when we spoke. There was too much I couldn't tell her about: the club, the guys being shot, the threats and stalking. It was all just too much.

I forced myself not to think about it all. I downed the rest of my drink and laughed loudly at Arturo's story. This, I could handle. My friends, this party, this night; I could handle this.

Knowing what would be waiting for me when I finally went home? That was a problem for another time. My phone had started blowing up about an hour ago. It was going on one a.m. so that was typical for my men.

I hadn't texted them that I was leaving. I left a post it note on the counter that I was going out with friends. They didn't need to know I went to Karma and Arturo's. This was my little slice of heaven—my safe space from it all.

I would allow myself to have this for tonight, and tomorrow I would face the consequences of my actions... namely the ride share I would be taking while I was fucking wasted in a couple hours.

It was going on three-thirty in the morning when the car pulled down the long driveway of our rental house. I was struggling to stay awake in the back seat. In the back of my mind, I realized how dangerous of a decision this had been, but I was home safely now and that's all that mattered.

I was a little surprised that my men didn't come running out of the house the second the car pulled up, though. I could see all the lights on in the house. They were clearly still awake.

Dread settled into my gut as I climbed from the back of the car. I mumbled something to the driver, before I stumbled into the house.

The house was quiet. Utterly quiet. Though every light blazed on, not a sound could be heard. "Fuck," I muttered to myself. The silence made my struggles all the more defending as I fumbled with the knee-high boots I was wearing.

Why the hell would they leave all the lights on, if they had gone to bed?

I started shutting the kitchen lights off as I headed out of the room, then the dining room. When I got to the living room, I jumped back in fright, letting out a high pitch shriek as I found all three of my guys sitting on the couch.

Jason, Marcos, and Nico were lined up on the sectional, elbows on their knees and heads bowed as they waited for me to come home. All three heads slowly raised to meet my gaze as they took me in.

"Fuck," I muttered again. I could feel their disappointment radiating off them in waves, the heaviness of it weighing on their shoulders. My own shoulders slumped upon taking in their disappointment. "I'm sorr—"

"How'd you get home?" Jason spoke over me, cutting me off. He stared at me emotionlessly, almost coldly.

I swallowed thickly. "Rideshare." I barely mumbled the words.

Nico hissed, shaking his head.

Marcos growled low in his throat.

Jason continued to stare at me with that unattached gaze in his eyes. "Go to your room. We'll talk about this tomorrow."

"But—"

"Tomorrow." Jason lowered his voice, deepening it.

I gulped. Nodding blankly, I fought back tears as I headed for the stairs. I knew they would be upset, but I'd never seen the three of them like this before. It was almost enough to push me to using my safe-word. Something I hadn't had to do in a very long time in our relationship.

No, I decided. *I made my bed, now it's time to lie in it.* I made my choice earlier in the evening—a very sober choice—I would face my consequences head on and accept whatever punishment my men deemed fit. As was the nature of our dynamic. We chose this lifestyle. I made my choice to use a rideshare, not once, but twice tonight.

I slept fitfully, waking up cold several times—not used to sleeping alone—before I finally gave in and got up around six-thirty. I hoped to make my guys a big breakfast before they had to leave for the day.

Instead, I found the house empty. They had left already. Or had they even gone to bed? I couldn't remember what time I had gotten in, but I knew it was late.

On the kitchen counter I found a note, though. Jason's neat slanting script was evident even from across the room. My heart sank as I slowly walked across the kitchen, dreading what it might say.

You will clean the entire house today. We want it spotless. The floors should be good enough to eat off of. Every single room will shine. You will be naked and waiting on your knees in position one, when we get home this evening. Don't worry about dinner, we'll be home late. Make sure you are showered and shaved. On my dresser are the implements of your punishment. We reserve the right to add more if we feel like it later. The plug you will wear immediately upon reading this note. Prep yourself THOROUGHLY, I don't want any messes.

I let out a shuddering breath. It was impersonal as a note could be. No name, no other emotion giving away his feelings, besides the all caps and underling of *thoroughly*. I knew what he was hinting at there, how he expected me to clean my asshole in prep for their punishment tonight.

It was another little punishment that I would be expected to carry out myself: an enema.

God, it was embarrassing. The thought alone had my face turning red and my body heating. My heart sped up. It wasn't my first time doing an enema. With all the anal we did I had looked into ways to keep things cleaner while playing. I usually did one every couple of months, discretely, on days I knew they wouldn't be home.

I kept the supplies in a storage bag under the bathroom sink and my guys only knew about it because said sink had leaked at one point and they had to clear out everything to clean. Thankfully my stuff had been in a sealed bag and hadn't gotten dirty, but I still made sure to thoroughly clean everything before my next use.

After a brief conversation about what had been in the bag, they let the topic go. Nico occasionally bought me new tubing or inserts, but they showed up in packages under the sink, and no one spoke of them.

This was the first time they were using it as one of my punishments, though. It was the first time I was being directed to cleanse myself so thoroughly. My heart raced as I reread the note from Jason.

I had a busy day ahead of me, I better get started.

I was shaking slightly as I filled the one-liter enema bag with distilled water. After a full day of cleaning, I had forgotten to eat. It had been for the best, though. I had a cup of coffee to cure the slight hang-over I had woken up with and then hit the ground running, cleaning every square inch of the house.

After my body had had its regular bowel movement post coffee, I figured it was time to clean myself out. Filling the liter bag, I set down the jug of water and then pinched closed the top of the blue medical bag I had filled. The bag was hanging from a hook I had attached to the towel bar and I had the anal probe attachment clipped to the side of the bag with a binder clip as to not fall and get dirty. The probe was attached to a six-foot clear tubing that ran up to the blue medical bag full of water.

I laid a couple towels down on the floor, just to be safe, but at this point I was confident I wouldn't need them. I was pretty much a pro at holding things in by now—both figuratively and physically.

Unclipping the anal probe—a narrow four-inch hollow cylinder with a slightly flared opening with a small hole for the water to pass through—I laid myself down on my left side and slid my right leg forward. Not bothering with lube, I ran the probe through my slit, gathering my own juices, before I brought it back to my ass and slowly slid it inside my asshole.

The idea of this being used as a punishment, both degraded me and turned me on. I always got off on the idea of enemas before I started doing them to myself. The idea of it was degrading and embarrassing, but I couldn't help that the process of it turned me on.

With the probe fully inserted, I reached back for the stop lever on the tubing and slid it open. I moaned softly as the cool water invaded my bowels, filling me. This part was always nerve wracking. How much could my body take? Would my stomach expand?

I had worked myself up to a full liter of water in the time I'd been doing this, but it still was uncomfortable the more the bag emptied inside me.

Breathing through the coolness as my intestines slowly began to cramp, I glanced back at the bag to see it was almost done, almost completely inside me. I took another deep breath as the bag emptied, before I slowly pulled the probe out of me. I had to clench down to hold the water inside of me, knowing it would be more beneficial to the cleansing process if I held the water in as long as possible.

I had read many medical articles regarding safe enema use, knowing full well the risks of the procedure. The kink community websites I followed also drilled in the importance of safety, while understanding the benefits of *cleaning*. In the end, I had found a safe balance of when to use and how often.

After a full ten minutes of holding in the water, my stomach was cramping hard and I barely had time to stand and move to the toilet to empty myself. In the end, the pain, hassle, and the mess were worth it. When I was fully empty and cleaned up, I inserted the lubed up, bejeweled stainless steel butt plug into my now cleaned ass, and groaned as I got used to the stretch.

Jason had set out the largest of the plugs that we owned, meaning he fully intended to be inside me later that evening, Jacob's Ladder and all.

The day dragged on, my body aching from both my hang over and lack of sleep. My anxiety weighed on my mind. Intrusive thoughts got the better of me as I thought of just how disappointed my men had been when I came home the night before.

Once again, I thought about coming clean about Dax and then warred with myself over keeping quiet and keeping my men safe. I had made myself so nervous that anytime I tried to eat, even a piece of toast, my stomach rolled and I couldn't do it.

By the time dinner rolled around, I was a mess. The house was spotless, though. Had probably never been cleaner in the two years that we lived there. But I was a mess. Exhausted and sore, I muscled through my shower, washing everything and thoroughly shaving every nook and cranny before I rinsed off and wrapped a towel around myself.

I had enough time to soak in our large free standing bath tub before the guys got back home, so I fully intended to. Now that I was shaved and fully clean, I could lay back in the hot water and soak away my worries—or try too at least.

Without knowing exactly when the guys would be home, I couldn't risk falling asleep, not if I wanted to try and get on their good side—and I would need to try to get on their good side if I wanted to survive tonight's punishment.

I had a feeling it would be worse than anything I'd been through before. I could only hope that our relationship would survive it.

Jason

I GROUND MY MOLARS as I clenched my jaw. To say I was upset about Maya's disregard for her own safety the night before was an understatement. She had broken one of the fundamental rules of our relationship. We didn't have many for her, but we expect the ones we had to be followed.

It was never a good practice to administer a punishment while angry. I knew that. I'd had all day to cool off. When she had come home at almost four in the morning, I sent her to bed, alone. I left her a written list of instructions for the day, along with a list of household chores I wanted completed, while I went to work with Marcos and Nico.

I had taken my time driving home from our job that day—a protection run that Marcos had taken me and Dagger with him on. Knowing our girl was waiting for us, I had purposely dragged out our drive home, stopping for food and gas.

When the three of us had finally gotten home, the house was spotless. It smelled amazing and Maya's favorite candles were burning in glass jars around the living room and kitchen. Her finishing touch whenever she finished cleaning.

We set the food down in the kitchen—we'd eat after we finished punishing our girl. None of us could wait any longer to punish her, though. It was all we'd talked about all day.

Upstairs in our rental house, we found Maya right where I expected her to be: on her knees, on the floor in front of the bed and facing the door. Her spine was straight, her shoulders back, plump tits pressed out and hands flat on her thighs, palms up. She was utterly breathtaking.

"Good girl," I said as I walked into the room.

Her belly quivered as her breath hitched. Her eyelids fluttered. I smirked, knowing just what my deep voice could do to her.

"The house looks really good, Dreamer," Nico complimented her. "Good to know you can follow directions."

A blush creeped over her chest and face, but she kept her mouth shut and her eyes down.

"I think you've forgotten how things are done around here," Marcos said in a deep rumble. "Think we've grown too lax with you."

I circled her kneeling form. A shiver went down her spine as her lowered gaze tracked my feet. The blue jeweled plug was nestled between the rounded globes of her ass, looking utterly fuckable.

I reached over her shoulder and palmed a heavy tit. I pulled it up and squeezed it roughly, until she was hissing slightly from the pain of it, but she didn't say a word. I let off my rough treatment of her breast and rolled her nipple between my thumb and forefinger. I grabbed her other breast and gave it the same treatment, squeezing it until she was hissing, before letting go and rolling the nipple between my fingers.

I pulled on her nipples, pulling up and out, squeezing tight until she was hissing again. She was panting when I finally eased off, but she never said a word. "Maybe we need to pierce these," I said softly, my mouth inches from her ear, my breath hot against her skin.

She shivered and closed her eyes as goosebumps bloomed across her flesh.

"Pierce them, then hang weights here." I tugged on them again, pulling them down this time. "We could put a chain between them," I continued, dropping my voice lower, making it huskier.

She gasped as her tongue darted out and wet her lips.

"I think you like that idea," I murmured moving closer. I nibbled on her ear as she let out another small huff of breath, still not making a sound. "Good girl," I growled into her ear.

Her thighs clenched and her belly quivered from the force it took to stay still and silent, but she was holding strong.

"Spread your thighs," Nico ordered from where he leaned against the wall, facing her.

Maya did so slowly, spreading her thighs wide, while still sitting on her heals, forcing her lower body into a butterfly position.

"Look at that dripping cunt," Marcos murmured.

I trailed a finger from her breast down her soft belly and over her belly button. I toyed with the piercing there before I dipped my fingers lower and slid through her soaking wet folds. "Soaking wet, boys," I muttered.

"Like a good little whore should be," Nic replied.

I circled my finger through her folds and around her hole, gathering her fluids and dragging them up to her clit. I circled her clit before I pinched it between my fingers and brushed my thumb over it, strumming the taut bud like a guitar string.

Maya's breathing grew labored and eye lids clenched tightly closed as she tried to remain in control. She knew the consequences of coming without permission. "Hmm," I hummed. "Maybe a piercing here too."

"Fuck," Marcos groaned as he reached down and adjusted his dick in his jeans.

A shiver racked Maya's body and I smirked, as her pussy gushed. "Oh, little darling," I crooned softly in her ear. "You and I are going to discuss this again, I think." I bit down on her earlobe, startling a gasp out of her. "Time for your punishment."

Maya's eyes flashed opened and I had to hide my smirk at how blown her pupils were. The caramel irises were almost completely covered by the black pupil. She blinked as she took in her surroundings, her eyes unfocused and darting between us.

"Stand up," I murmured in her ear, before I backed away. I took a seat at the edge of the king bed and spread my thighs. Nico walked over and sat down in the window seat while Marcos stayed where he was, leaning back against the wall, near the door.

It took Maya a moment to unfold herself and stand. I could see her edging on subspace, eyes blown, waiting to tip over. I wasn't going to let her, though. Tonight was a punishment; I was going to keep her present as much as I could. "Come here," I ordered, lowering my voice again, knowing how it drove her wild.

She moved immediately, stopping right in front of my spread legs. I patted my lap and she swallowed audibly, before she bent over my thighs, positioning her breasts on the mattress. The gap between my thighs made it harder for her to brace and relax, with her legs being shorter than mine, it kept her on edge and uncomfortable, everything I was looking for in a punishment.

Pressing her breasts against the mattress, I pushed her down between her shoulder blades and held her in place, positioning her how I wanted her. I rubbed my hand over her exposed ass, warming the skin for the beating it was about to get. "What are my rules?" I asked her.

She let sucked in a soft breath of air before she started speaking. "Never lie, always text the group chat when I'm leaving work, call for a ride if I'm out drinking without you, no rideshares ever, never wear panties unless I'm on my period, and don't speak unless given permission during a scene."

I smirked as she rattled off my—our—rules, while I continued to rub her ass cheeks. "For your indiscretions last night and your overall disregard to your safety, you will receive ten lashes by hand..." I trailed off watching confusion furrow her brow. "And ten lashes by an instrument of our choice." She relaxed against him, thinking I was finished, so I continued. "Each."

She gasped and tense up on my lap. "But that's sixty lashes!" she exclaimed.

"Do you want ten more?" I questioned her, my voice stern. I landed a warning smack to her ass causing her to yip.

"No, Sir," she answered immediately.

"You don't seem to realize how disappointed we are," I growled, my voice low and deep. I watched the goose bumps break out across her back as a shiver went down her spine. "You blatantly broke one of our rules."

She remained silent, her breathing hitching in her throat.

"Not only did you break our rules, but you put your life in danger," I growled, anger rising up in me again. I needed to get myself under control. I couldn't let my anger rule me, not when I held her vulnerable before me. I would never hurt her, not irrevocably.

"We will each spank that ass, Little Dreamer," Nico said, his voice soft. "Then we will each choose a toy of our choice to whip that ass with. You will count each strike and apologize for putting your life in danger last night. Do you understand me?"

"Yes, sir," she answered immediately.

"Your ass is going to be so sore by the time we're done, you're not gonna be able sit for a week, Mia Vida." *My life*. Marcos grunted, crossing his arms over his chest.

Maya turned her head on the bed to look at him.

Marcos stared her down, his jaw ticking as he watched her spread on my lap.

"Shall we begin, darling?" I asked, smirking slightly, as if she had a choice in the matter.

"Yes, Sir," Maya murmured.

I didn't give her another minute to brace. I smacked my heavy hand down on her ass with a loud resounding smack! She jumped in shock, but she didn't cry out as her body pressed against my rock-hard cock. "One. I'm sorry for putting myself in danger last night."

"Good girl," I praised her, rubbing my hand over her heated skin, soothing the sting of my first hit. It was the only reprieve she was going to get for the next few minutes.

I landed another blow. "Two, I'm sorry for putting myself in danger." Smack. "Three, I'm sorry for putting myself in danger."

She was panting slightly and I decided she wasn't sorry enough.

I smacked her ass harder and faster. "Four, I'm sorry I put myself in danger. Five, I'm sorry I put myself in dang—" Her yelp of pain, interrupted her apology. "Six, I'm sorry I put myself—"

Smack, Smack, Smack.

She yelped again as I landed blows to her unsuspecting thighs.

"Keep counting," I snapped.

"Seven, I'm sorry, Sir. Eight, I'm sorry I put myself in danger. Nine, I'm sorry I made you worry."

I landed a particularly harder blow to her inner thigh.

"Shit. Ten. I'm sorry I didn't call."

I rubbed my hand over red ass. It was warm to the touch, but nowhere near how warm or red as it would be later. I nodded to Nico who was sitting at the window seat. I pointed at the red handled wooden paddle sitting on top of the dresser, the one I had pulled out earlier, in preparation for this evening. The one she had to move in order to dust the dresser.

I smirked, knowing she had picked it up and set it back in place after she cleaned. The bedroom was immaculate, as was the rest of the house.

Nico grabbed the paddle and walked over, handing it to me. I eyed the wooden paddle with a grin. It was heavy in my palm. Leather wrapped around the handle, giving it a better grip than wood beneath it. The handle flared out to a wide three-inch wooden paddle with holes drilled through it, to allow for airflow to pass through it as it swung through the air. It allowed the user to hit faster. One side of the paddle had a cushioned pad covering the wood, while the other side was bare wood, ready for maximum damage.

I like to use both side on Maya. I especially enjoyed the pink round circles the holes in the paddle would leave behind. I loved marking her skin. Her creamy skin turned the most delectable shade of pink.

"You will say, 'I'm sorry, Sir,' after each hit," I told her, before I smacked her hard with the padded side.

"One. I'm sorry, Sir," she said immediately through a gasped breath.

I started at a gentle pace and continued to rain down blow after blow. Each time she apologized and gave me a count. She was squirming slightly in my lap, but I knew this was all just a warm up for her. For as angry as I had been, Marcos was the one who had really been upset when she hadn't called. Especially after we had stayed up waiting for her.

On the seventh hit with the paddle, I turned it over, so the bare wooden side would hit her and I aimed my blow for her upper thighs. She jumped in my lap and cried out at the unexpected change. "Seven, I'm sorry, Sir," she gasped.

I did eight and nine back-to-back, one on each thigh. "Eight, I'm sorry, Sir. Nine, I'm sorry, Sir." Her sentences were rushed and clipped as she tried to power through the pain.

I landed one last blow, my hardest one yet, to her bare ass and she cried out in pain. I had to hold her upper back down, to keep her in place. Her body shuddered as her breathing came out in violent pants. "Ten, I'm sorry, Sir." Her voice breaking at the end.

I set down the paddle and slid my hand over her warm skin, soothing away the sting of the paddle. "Shh," I murmured, as I caressed her bottom. "You were so good," I praised her, knowing exactly what she needed to hear. "My good girl."

I gave her a minute before I helped her to her feet. She wobbled slightly when I released her, but Nico was there, gathering her into his arms. "Easy, Little Dreamer," he murmured.

I stood up from the bed and headed for the recliner in the corner of the room, giving Nico space for his turn with our girl.

"Drink some water," Nic muttered to her, holding the straw of her stainless-steel cup to her lips.

Maya took careful sips as I sat back and adjusted my cock my in jeans. Her ass was a sight to behold: pink and plump with white circles dotting the juicy canvas. I just wanted to sink my teeth into her round globes and eat her up.

After Nico finished tending to our girl, he had her lay down in the center of the bed. Nico wasn't big on punishment, he knew it was a necessary evil, but he wasn't a Sadist like Marcos or I. Thankfully Maya wasn't a bratty sub, so punishment wasn't something we usually had to dole out.

I watched Dagger circle the bed, watching Maya all the while. She was panting slightly still, but her breathing was slowing down. Finally coming down from the spanking she'd received.

Nico set down her cup on the bedside table before he walked over to the end of the bed and took a seat. Maya was still laying in the middle of the bed, facing away from him, so he snapped his fingers loudly.

After two years together, Maya's training was perfected. She knew how to read us, knew what we needed before we asked, and knew if we snapped our fingers that she needed to move her ass into position. Immediately, she got up on her hands and knees and shuffled on the bed, crawling over to Nico and across his lap.

She settled across his thighs, bracing on her elbows with her ass draped over Dagger's lap. "You know I don't like having to do this, right?"

Maya sighed, her head hanging low. "Yes, sir."

"You will count after each one and say 'I'm sorry, sir'."

Maya remained quiet, until Nico slapped his palm against her ass. "I'm sorry, sir," she murmured softly.

Nico made quick work of her spanking. He wasn't one to dole out punishments, so he never drew them out. Maya counted and apologized after each one, gasping for breath with each hit. He may not have liked punishing her, but he didn't let her off the hook either, each blow would be painful.

When he finished with his hand, he tapped her thigh and she crawled off his lap. Nico stood up and went into the closet. He rummaged around in there for a few minutes before he found what he was looking for and came out—a cane held in one hand and a pair of handcuffs held in the other.

A low whimper escaped Maya's lips as she took in the items in his hands. Yeah, Dagger might hate punishing her, but he would still do it thoroughly so she'd never forget their rules again. A shiver ran down Maya's spine and I shifted in my recliner, waiting for her to break another rule.

She kept quiet though and stayed still while Nico cuffed her wrists together, then pulled her arms up toward the headboard. He grabbed a length of chain they kept attached to the backside of the headboard and pulled it through the space between the headboard and mattress. He quickly attached the end of the chain to the loop between Maya's cuffs with a small carbineer.

"Are you going to be a good girl, or do I need to tie down your legs?" Nico asked.

Marcos moved from the wall he'd been leaning on and walked over to the nightstand. He pulled a length of rope from the drawer and tossed it on the bed. "She doesn't get to make choices tonight."

Dagger didn't need to be told twice, he wound the length of rope around Maya's ankles and tied them tightly together, before he pulled on the rope and yanked her body down the mattress, pulling her arms tight, and tied the rope to a hook under the bedframe.

Maya couldn't move, and she didn't make a sound, while Dagger stepped back and surveyed his handiwork. Maya's back rose and fell with each breath, as she panted, her skin pebbled with goosebumps.

Dagger rounded the foot of the bed and climbed up on the mattress from the side. Maya turned her head to face him and waited, while Dagger stared down at her, while he kneeled next to her on the mattress. "You will count these after each hit, and when I'm finished with all ten, you will thank me for your punishment."

Maya nodded and kept quiet.

The cane in Dagger's hand was red with a black leather handle, it was a quarter inch thick and made of fiberglass. It was designed for pain and punishment. Just what Maya needed.

I shifted in the recliner, adjusting my very hard cock beneath my jeans. Maya hated the cane with a passion; she could never handle it without using her safe word. I wondered how many whacks Dagger could get in before Maya called him off.

Without warning, Dagger brought down the red cane in a fast crack against her flesh. Her ass jiggled from the impact, the line of red flesh bloomed immediately, and Maya let out a whoosh of breath in a loud gasp. "One, I'm sorry sir." Her voice was choked with pain already.

I undid the zipper on my jeans and pulled out my cock, stroking myself while I watched Dagger hit Maya again with the cane. "Two. I'm sorry sir." Even from across the room I could see the tears falling down her face.

The next hit, Dagger landed to her upper thigh, leaving a nasty red welt across the tops of both thighs and making her cry out between clenched teeth. I gripped my cock harder.

"Three. I'm sorry sir." Maya's voice cracked at the end of her apology.

Marcos shifted from where he was standing against the wall, making me wonder if he would intervene. Marcos only crossed his arms, though, and settled back in.

Dagger rained down two fast blows, making Maya cry out. Her breath caught as she sobbed. "Four, five. I'm sorry sir."

Her ass was bright red, as were the tops of her thighs. I wondered how much longer she had in her.

A coat of sweat clung to Dagger's forehead and he wiped it from his brow before he hit her with another smack of the cane—this time to the middle of her thighs. She jolted and arched against the bed, as much as she could while restrained and sobbed loudly.

Dagger didn't wait for her to count. He gave her another fast rap of the cane, this time lower, to her calves.

She shrieked in agony.

I waited for the safe-word to fall from her lips. She sobbed uncontrollably, her breathed ragged, but still no safe-word.

Dagger gave her a minute to sob. He didn't try to sooth her or rub away her pain, he just let her sob into the mattress.

"Six, seven." Her voice was muffled and thick with tears, but even I heard from her across the room.

"Good girl," Dagger murmured, his voice low. "Three more." He struck her again to middle of her ass.

"Eight. I'm sorry sir."

Dagger rained down the last two blows in quick succession.

Her screeching yells that pierced the air, had me pausing mid-stroke of his cock. We'd never heard Maya wail in pain like that before. The soul crushing agony in those yells would stay with me for a long time.

Dagger didn't wait for her counts, nor did he wait for the thanks he had demanded from her, instead, he tossed the cane to the floor and pulled his pocket knife from his jeans and quickly sliced through the ropes around Maya's legs before he pulled out the keys to the handcuffs and uncuffed her.

He slid down on his side, on the mattress next to her, and pulled her into his arms. "Shh," he murmured, rubbing her back. "You did so good, baby. Such a good girl."

I felt my cock soften, knowing our girl was in pain. I tucked my dick away and stood from the chair. I turned to the door as Marcos pushed off the wall with a booted foot. I followed Marcos out the bedroom door and into the hallway.

Silently, we both went down to the kitchen and filled zip lock bags with ice. I pulled out a frozen hand towel we kept in a bag in the freezer and unfurled it. It was hard and crispy, not malleable, but I was able to pull it part. I draped it over my shoulder and grabbed a bag of ice, before I headed back up to our bedroom.

Maya was still crying, quieter now, and Dagger was still whispering softly to her.

I slid on the mattress behind her, pulling the frozen towel from my shoulder. I pushed it against her red skin, making her yelp. Marcos laid the Ziplock bags of ice over the frozen towel before I laid down beside her, rubbing her back. We stayed that way for several minutes, icing her bottom and murmuring our praise to her.

When Maya eventually began to shift, she rolled over so she could face us. "So good for us," I muttered.

"Ready for more?" Marcos asked.

Maya nodded slowly.

Jason

I SHIFTED ON IN the recliner in the corner of the room, watching as Maya choked on Marcos's cock. He hadn't punished her yet tonight, for her transgressions, even though Nico and I had already.

Marcos would, but he liked to handle things differently with Maya.

Where I was more strict and harder on her and Nico was more loving and gentler, Marcos ventured somewhere else on the scale. His creative punishments often ventured into a psychological torture that even unnerved me.

His methods often worked, though. I thought it was Marcos's methods that lasted the longest with Maya. It was rare if she repeated the same mistake after a punishment, but if Marcos really trapped Maya into a punishment, it was guaranteed she wouldn't repeat it.

It was why we didn't need many rules for her. It was also why, we rarely needed to punish her at all. Instead, we preferred to play primal games with her, making her run through forests naked while we chased her.

We had a wild sex life and we loved every minute of it.

The sounds of Maya choking on Marcos's dick was making my own cock hard again. She always made me so hard.

She wouldn't come tonight; we would make sure of it—despite her moans as she choked on Marcos's dick.

"Time to say 'night-night'," Marcos crooned darkly, his voice melodic as he pulled a syringe from the back pocket of his jeans that were still bunched around his thighs.

Even from across the room, I saw the moment Maya realized what Marcos meant. Her whole body froze, tensing up. With her mouth still around Marcos's cock, he took advantage of her startled state and gripped her by the hair, shoving his cock further down her throat.

She immediately sputtered and gagged, slapping at his thighs, trying to push him away. He held her tighter and brought the cap covered syringe up to his mouth. He bit off the cap, before he brought the syringe down to her neck.

Maya struggled against him, now using both hands to try to push him away. It was no use though; Marcos had already stuck the needle into her neck and pressed the plunger. Her struggles grew weak as the sedative kicked in.

Only when her hands slid off his body, did Marcos pull his cock out of her mouth.

"Please," she murmured, as Marcos slowly and gently pulled her body backwards, so she fell languidly against the mattress with her head on the pillows.

There was a moment of silence as the three of us watched as her eyelids flutter closed and breathing evened out. When Marcos started pulling up his jeans and tucking his dick away, Nic spoke up from where he sat in the window seat. "What's your plan?"

Marcos looked up from Maya, a slight smirk on his face. "We're gonna tie her up in the woods out back."

I grinned wickedly. My brother was as psychotic as they came, even if he kept it under wraps.

"It's sixty degrees outside," Nic said, rubbing his knuckles over his trim blond beard.

"She'll be fine." Marcos shrugged a shoulder and picked up his shirt from the floor.

I got up from the recliner and headed into the walk-in closet. We would need ropes and blankets. Maybe even the whip. Marcos still hadn't spanked her for her lack of judgement. She would learn, though, the hard way.

Twenty minutes later, we had Maya wrapped in thick blankets as we trudged through the deep forest that surrounded our rental house. One day, I hoped we had the money to buy the house from the owner. The unincorporated lot had everything we had wanted and the forest surrounding it kept prying eyes away.

Nico carried a sedated Maya, almost reverently, as we followed Marcos to the spot he had picked out. He must have had this idea for a while, because when we got to a small clearing, there was already a fire ring made from small boulders and a heavy tarp laid over a mound of fire wood.

"Boy scout much?" I taunted my brother.

Marcos looked over at me and smirked. "Don't be jealous."

I just shook my head as I took in the rest of the clearing. Three large logs were standing on their ends, set up as stools around the firepit. There was another tarp tied down over a stack of chopped wood, stacked and ready for burning, with a pile of kindling next to it. The man had even made a make-shift table out of a large log that he'd cut to waist height and nailed a four-foot by four-foot sheet of plywood on top.

He had literally thought of everything.

Marcos pulled off the backpack he had slung over his shoulder and set it on the table.

I walked over with my own bag that contained the ropes we would use and set it down. "What tree are you using?"

Marcos pointed to a thick limb of a nearby maple tree. The tree itself was almost three feet around. It was old and thick and the limb Marcos had pointed to was almost a foot in diameter itself and some forty feet in the air. "We might not have enough rope," I commented.

Marcos shrugged, seemingly unbothered as he reached for my pack and started pulling out heavy bundles of rope.

Nico continued to hold Maya bridal style against him. The three of us had opted to not put sweatshirts on over our T-shirts. If our girl was going to be utterly naked in the cold, we wouldn't be warm either. We needed to be able to gauge the cold on our skin ourselves, in order to keep this safe for her.

We might be borderline psychopaths, but we had heavily negotiated our scenes far in advance. This particular scene we were about to play out, Maya had whispered to us in the dark one night. She'd been black out drunk after a club party and hadn't remembered it the next day. The three of us had each questioned her about what she remembered in the days that followed... and she never admitted it.

This was dubious consent at best.

We would have to watch her carefully when we roused her, make sure she was truly on board before we moved forward.

"Start a fire," Marcos said and headed for the maple tree with a bundle of rope.

Ten minutes later, a healthy fire roared in the pit and Nico was setting Maya down on the ground. He opened the blanket that was bundled around her and Marcos kneeled down next to her, getting to work with the Shibari ropes.

I helped hold Maya up and position her for Marcos, while he wrapped the ropes around her chest and arms. We positioned her arms so she was holding each elbow behind her back and Marcos looped the rope around her chest and arms, creating a harness we would suspend her by.

After Marcos had her upper body tied up in an intricate design of knots and loops, he moved onto her legs. He wrapped the rope around her upper thighs, and over her hips, but leaving plenty of room to spread her wide open and access to spank that glorious ass.

He bent her knees and tied her ankles up at her thighs, before he made another harness around her hips that he would also use to suspend her with.

A few moments later, using heavy carabiners, we tossed two ropes over the limb and quickly attached them to the harnesses.

Once Maya was fully suspended and the ropes tied off to the trunk of the tree to hold her in place, we both stepped back to admire Marcos's handiwork. "Goddamn," I breathed, taking in Maya's naked body.

She was not a skinny woman; she was thick in all the best places. Her heavy tits swung down, resting against her face, as her head lolled listlessly. The rolls on her belly were only accentuated by the rope harnesses and her thighs bulged between the ropes weaving up her thighs. She was an utter work of art and my dick had never been harder in my life.

Nico pulled out his phone and started snapping photos as she spun slowly. The fire light danced on her creamy flesh, highlighting all her beauty. "Bro, you had a good idea about piercing her tits. Fuck me," Nic groaned and stepped closer to Maya, reaching out and squeezing one heavy breast. The rope harness had spun in between, above, and below her tits, forcing them up and out from her body—forcing more blood into them, making them plumper. "These would look amazing with a weighted chain hanging between them."

I grunted in approval. We would need to see to that ASAP.

Marcos reached into his pocket and pulled out a pack of smelling salts. He broke one open and shoved it under Maya's nose. "Wakey, wakey," he crooned, as she sputtered into consciousness. "Welcome back, whore."

Maya gasped as true consciousness settled into her. Her head snapped up and she frantically looked around the clearing. Nic and I stood back, our backs to the fire, warming ourselves. She most likely could only see our silhouettes in dark night with the light at our back.

Marcos stood in front of her face and Maya stopped her struggling when her eyes landed on him. Marcos's fingers laced through Maya's hair at the base of her skull, using her ponytail and pulling, he yanked her head back roughly so she was forced to stare up into his eyes. "I will ask you one time, and one time only," Marcos's voice was a deep gravelly sound that almost sounded animalistic in nature. "Do you need your safe word?"

Even from thirty feet away, I could see the goosebumps spread across Maya's skin as a shiver went down her spine. She licked her lips slowly, her eyes wide, before she shook her head briefly. Her lips curved as she let out a quiet, "No, sir."

Marcos chuckled darkly pulled a handkerchief from his back pocket. He wrapped it around her eyes, blindfolding her, and tied it tight behind her head.

Maya's chest heaved as she panted harshly.

I had to adjust my cock in my pants. It throbbed; I'd never been so hard in my life. Our girl was fucking breathtaking. I wanted nothing more than to sink my cock into her hot cunt.

Maya

I felt like I was floating, literally. Hanging by ropes, from a tree in the woods, I was floating above the ground. Besides the weightlessness, I was experiencing that floating feeling in my mind, almost as if I was disassociating: sounds muffled, smells grew sharper, and my body numb.

My tongue felt heavy in my mouth. I swallowed thickly, wondering what they were waiting for—what Marcos was waiting for. Jason and Nico had already punished me for taking the rideshare home, but Marcos had been biding his time.

The sedative had been a surprise. We'd spoken in great length about adding drug use to our play, but I never imagined the lengths that Marcos would go to. Waking up in the woods tonight, naked and hanging from a tree in the middle of the night, hadn't on been on my bingo play card. This was something out of one of my dark romance novels.

My guys took my safety seriously—only they were allowed to put my life in danger. Taking a rideshare while intoxicated at two a.m. hadn't been smart. It was dumb and reckless, beyond careless, and just plain stupid. Why would I pay for a rideshare, when I could have just called one of my guys? They would have gladly come to pick me up.

All I could do was take my punishment. Or safe-word out. But I agreed to this dynamic between us—I craved it—so I would hold strong and endure my penance.

Someone circled me slowly; I could hear their feet crunching in the fallen leaves. A shiver slid down my spine as a cool breeze danced across my skin. I heard a whistle of wind before I felt the stinging bite against my ass. I yelped and tried to jerk away. I couldn't see, I had no idea what I was hit with, but it fucking hurt.

"Quiet," Marcos barked, from my right.

I took a deep calming breath and let it out slowly, forcing myself to relax.

"You still have twenty lashes coming. Ten will be from this switch." He ran the thin switch over my backside. It felt rough, like tree bark. *Did he seriously find a switch from forest to punish me with?* "And ten from my hand. You will count and thank me for punishing you, after each hit."

I kept my mouth shut and braced for impact. I was expecting the switch first, like he'd teased me with. I jumped slightly when his hand came down on my ass, my cheek jiggling with the impact. "One. Thank you, sir."

"Thank you for what?" Marcos ground out.

"Thank you for punishing me, sir."

Marcos didn't waste time with the spanking. Each hit was firm and bruising—measured. He gave me just enough time to name each count and thank him for my punishment before he landed the next blow.

I was gasping and panting by the time we reached ten. A sheen of sweat covered my body and my pussy was clenching. There was something so erotic about being strung up in the woods, for anyone to see, while my man spanked my ass.

I knew he was just warming up for my true penance: the switch. Marcos was always harder on me than the other two—even Stone, for as much as a hard-ass as he came off. No, Marcos like creative discipline that I would remember—and feel for days.

"We all waited up for you last night, you know? Waited for a text to come get you." Marcos's voice was low and deep. It sent a shiver down my spine.

I hung there in silence, not really hearing what he was saying. I was floating in my body again, floating and slipping through my own thoughts. I already knew my crimes. I only had ten more lashes of the sixty to go, before I was finished. And I wasn't counting that warning hit with the switch earlier—oh no. I knew my man, that one wouldn't count toward the grand total.

"Maybe we need to reevaluate our relationship? Maybe it's time to renegotiate things? Because this isn't working on our end."

I snapped my head up, trying to look at him as fear raced down my spine, but I was still blindfolded. There was a murmuring behind me, I couldn't hear what they were say. Did Jason and Nico agree? *Do they want to break up with me over a damn rideshare?*

"Do not speak." Marcos spat out, inches from my face. "You don't get to defend your actions. And if we want to renegotiate, that's our decision."

I opened my mouth and quickly closed it. He was right. He could renegotiate at any time, all of them could. But why was he bringing it up now in the middle of a scene? *Had I really fucked up that badly?* My heart pounded in my chest, as my thoughts whirled a million miles an hour.

The first whack of the switch didn't even register until a blinding pain burned along the back of one of my thighs. I'd already been paddled and caned tonight, but the switch was by far the worst.

I yelped and arched, trying to reach for my thighs with my tied hands, but unable to. I didn't even remember to count before Marcos's wrapped his fingers around my ponytail and roughly yanked my head up.

"Count." He growled.

"One. T-thank you f-for pun-punishing me, s-sir," I stuttered. My body shook as pain radiated across my body, spreading out from where I'd been hit.

He forcefully dropped my head, and I was already so weak, so let it fall limply—hanging from my shoulders almost painfully.

I took ragged breaths, forcing myself to calm down. I had nine more fucking hits to go before I would be finished. *Then we can have a fucking conversation about whatever the fuck Marcos is talking about! Renegotiation my fucking ass!*

The next smack of the branch wasn't any easier than the first, even if I was expecting it this time. "Two. Thank you for punishing me, sir." I managed to keep my voice steady, as I spoke the words through clenched teeth.

I could survive this. I would survive this.

Jason

I WATCHED MAYA SLOWLY succumb to the pain of her lashing. The thin reed-like branch Marcos had found was torturing her more than the cane—and she hated the damn cane.

I shifted on my feet as Maya sobbed deeply. I was honestly surprised that she hadn't used her safe-word yet.

Nico shifted beside me, running a hand through his blond mane. He genuinely hated the punishment aspect of our dynamic. As much as he got off on the power plays, when it came to discipline, Nico preferred not having to administer it period. It was why he chose the cane. Something that would stick with her and she'd hopefully remember down the line, and not fuck up again.

I was somewhere in the middle between Marcos and Nico. While tonight I'd gone easy on her with the paddle, I'd known vaguely what Marcos had been planning for her.

"Dude." Nico grumbled under his breath.

Maya's sobs got louder as the branch whipped across her breasts. Bound between woven lengths of rope, her glorious tits were firmly squeezed and extra plump from being confined. They had to be painful enough, before Marcos's cruel torture.

Marcos waited until Maya finally spoke, voice broken between gasping sobs. "Ei-ei-eight. Thank you f-f-for my pun-punishment, s-s-sir." She was shivering uncontrollably at this point.

I shifted on my feet; my body blissfully warm near the raging bonfire.

Marcos finally took pity on our girl and gave her the final two blows in a quick succession that left her screaming in pain.

I was glad for the woods and the lack of homes near us. The last thing we needed was someone calling the cops and them stumbling on the scene.

Marcos dropped the switch and pick up Maya so they were chest to chest, with her head cradled in the crook of his neck.

Her whole body was shaking and I worried about hypothermia. I wasn't sure if it was cold enough for it, her body had suffered a trauma and it was a chilly September evening.

"Need you to say the words, Mia Vida." Marcos's voice was low and sensual as he held her body upright, as much as the ropes would allow.

Dagger pulled and buck knife from his belt and walked over to them, while I picked up one of the blankets.

Maya continued to sob against Marcos's neck. Dagger hovered just steps away from her. We couldn't be finished with the scene, until she said the words.

"Nine. Ten," she choked out.

Dagger walked another step closer.

Marcos smoothed a hand over her back, at least the couple inches of bare skin he could reach between the two rope harnesses he had created to suspend her from the tree. "Come on, Mia Vida," he murmured softly.

"Thank you-you for my punishment, s-sir."

The moment she finished speaking the words, Dagger cut away the length of rope hold Maya's feet up. Marcos scooped her into his arms, while Dagger worked on the length holding her upper torso airborne.

I spread open the blanket as Marcos turned to me, passing Maya. Marcos helped to get her wrapped in the blanket and I wrapped her tightly in my arms, before I turned toward the fire and walked over. I sat down on another blanket and arranged Maya on my lap as I held her tightly against me, near the fire.

"You did so good tonight," I murmured softly to her. I pressed a kiss to her temple and pulled her closer, her body trembling in my arms. "So good, darlin'."

Her sobs wracked her body, almost uncontrollably. It made me nervous that she might hyperventilate. "Easy now." I forced my voice to stay calm. I'd never seen her like this before.

We still needed to unravel the ropes still tied around her, but I needed a moment to hold her. I glanced over my shoulder at Dagger arguing with Marcos. I couldn't hear what they were saying, but I knew Dagger didn't like how far Marcos took things tonight. Neither of us did.

When she started coughing—deep gut-wrenching coughs—my heart dropped. She didn't have asthma, but she was clearly struggling to breath. I felt her body tense up, before I heard it—her gagging as her stomach clenched and her body doubled over in my lap.

"Shit," I swore. I struggled to turn her, while still tied up, as she dry-heaved several times. Nothing but bile escaped her, though. *Had she not eaten all day?*

"A little help over here," I snapped at Marcos and Dagger.

Dagger finally stalked away from Marcos, storming toward Maya and I. He took a deep breath before he kneeled beside us. "Can I cut you free, little Dreamer?" His voice was soft as he slid a finger along her cheekbone.

She nodded, as tears silently streamed downed her face. She still hadn't said a word since being cut down, but she finally stopped gagging.

Maya slowly stopped shivering as I kept up a string of encouraging words. "Such a good girl. Always so good for us. I love you."

Her eyes were closed, her breathing still erratic.

I met Dagger's eye; the pain evident in my brother's stare.

We had taken things too far tonight.

Dagger cut the ropes from her body and I tried to keep her as warm as I could, moving the blanket out of the way while Dagger cut.

As the ropes fell from her body, Maya slowly opened her eyes. They were glazed over. A dazed express—subspace or shock—had settled over her.

I felt a chill run down my spine. I had never seen her like this before. It made my stomach roll.

We had fucked up.

I had to do something, pull her out of this somehow. I slowly unwrapped the blanket from around her and stood up, settling her on her feet.

I was grateful when her legs held her weight and her body kept her upright. I kept my voice low as I spoke to her. "On your knees Little Dreamer," I said, my voice deep as I commanded my little Sub to drop to her knees. I watched her carefully, noticing every breath and twinge of pain that crossed her face.

Her breath was still erratic, but she gracefully slid to her knees before me. She straightened her back, only wincing slightly as her bare ass hit her feet. She pulled her shoulders back and slid her hands on her thighs, palms up, and dropped her gaze to the ground. There was still a dazed expression in her eyes though, like she was going through the motions of muscle memory and not truly in the moment.

Once she was fully in position, I nodded once, even though she couldn't see my face. "Good girl."

A warm blush coated her blotchy cheeks, as her breath caught in her throat. Good, she's still in there. Maya had a praise kink a mile wide. I smirked, knowing just how easily I could wrap her around my fingers, or my dick.

"Why were you punished tonight, slut?" I asked. I needed this more now than anything else.

Maya trembled. "I didn't text you for a ride when I was leaving the party. I took a rideshare instead. I put myself in danger while I was drunk." Her voice was hoarse; she'd been screaming and sobbing for hours now.

Finally, I felt the tension drain from my body. She understood her transgression and had paid for it dearly. She was also not as out of it as she first appeared. I felt my own anxiety over her well-being loosen the hold around my heart.

"And will you do that again, Maya?" I purposely used her name, ending the scene.

Her head shot up and her wide-eyed stare flew to mine. "Never. I promise." Her head whipped around to look for Marcos and Nico, but both men had come to stand on either side of me. Her eyes were wild as she tried to make eye contact with each of them. "I promise you; I will never do that again." Her voice was raw, her breath hitching as she spoke, as another sob threatened to tear out of her.

I believed her.

I opened my arms to her, blanket held aloft in one hand—it was all the invitation she needed. She tried to fly up into my arms, had managed to stand, before she pitched forward, her legs crumpling beneath her.

I barely got my arms under her and cradled her to my chest, before she passed out.

"Maya!" Nico shouted.

Maya's head lolled back on her neck, completely unsupported—she was unconscious.

"Fuck," I cursed.

Marcos moved in behind her, easing her back and pulling her up into his arms bridal style. "Check that she's breathing," he ordered.

I slid my fingers along her neck and felt for a pulse, while also watching her chest rise and fall very, very slowly. "Heart beat is weak, breathing is slow. She's likely hypothermic. We need to get her warm, now."

The urgency in which we moved was unprecedented. Never behind had one of us had a medical emergency during a scene—let alone Maya. Never before though, had we taken a punishment so far.

Nico managed to get the blanket wrapped around Maya while in Marcos's arms. My heart lurched in my throat as Marcos took off running through the woods towards the house.

Thankfully, we weren't all that far away.

Nico and I chased after them. I barely thought about the fire still burning in the pit—something we'd have to come put out at some point—all I could worry about right at that moment was Maya.

I tore up the stairs to our bedroom on the second floor, where I found Marcos had set Maya down on the bed and was already stripping himself of his clothes. "Bare skin," he barked at them.

I immediately pulled my cut, hoodie, and t-shirt over my head in one swift yank. I didn't even bother with resting my cut on the chair in the corner—it wasn't important right now. Nothing mattered more than Maya. Nothing.

Together, we pulled her under covers and sandwiched her between our naked bodies. We maneuvered her onto her side so we could press as much of our skin to hers. "Darlin', I need you to open those eyes for me." I spoke softly, brushing her hair out of her face.

"Come on, Mia Vida. Time for you to yell at me," Marcos said.

"We took it too far tonight," Nico said from somewhere in the room. He sounded far away and despondent. "It was too much."

As much as I agreed, I couldn't think about that right now. All that mattered was Maya.

Nico

I PACED THE BEDROOM, my heart racing. Marcos and Jason had Maya sandwiched between them, buried under the blankets, but she was pale and still unconscious.

Muttering to myself, I tried to make sense of the situation. "We took it too far tonight. It was too much."

I felt like I was spiraling. My head was a mess. "It wasn't right. I should have safe worded."

"Dagger, man," Marcos snapped. "Get it together."

I shook my head, running my hands through my long-disheveled hair. I had heard of Dom-drop before, but I never experienced it. I never thought it would happen to me.

Maya let out a low whimper that had me spinning on my heel. I could barely see her though, Jason and Marcos had her so thoroughly surrounded. I moved closer, trying to catch a glimpse of her beautiful face.

I moved toward the bed as Maya lifted her head, looking around. "Nic," she murmured.

"I'm here, little dreamer. I'm here." I kneeled on the bed and reached for her hand. She laced her cold fingers through mine and held on weakly.

"Here," Marcos said. He nodded toward his spot.

I didn't ask questions, I ripped my shirt over my head and immediately shimmied out of my jeans, before I quickly changed places with Marcos. "Hey, little dreamer," I murmured. I found myself feeling better, now that I held her in my arms.

"Hey Nic." Her voice was low, sluggish; her speech slightly slurred.

I was so fucking scared. "We should take her to the hospital."

"She'll be fine," Marcos snapped. "Just keep her warm."

I shook my head, but did as I was told. I hugged her close to my naked body, as shivers slowly wracked her body. She was warming up. She would be ok.

She would be ok.

Maya

I woke slowly the next morning, feel disorientated. My head was pounding and my mouth was dry. I rolled over in bed, surprised to find myself alone. *What the fuck?* I remembered Marcos carrying me inside last night after our scene in the woods, remembered how freaked out my guys had been, Nico especially.

Why the fuck weren't they still in bed with me?

I reached out for my phone on the nightstand, finding it plugged in, in its usual spot. I typed in her passcode quickly and checked the time. Ten-thirty a.m., on a Friday. Did my guys go to work and leave me alone?

There was a text message on my phone, so I quickly opened it, hoping it was from one of them. Sure enough, a message from Marcos was sitting there.

Marcos

> Sorry to not be there this morning, Mia Vida. Duty calls at the club. We'll see you tonight for the party at the clubhouse.

I huffed and tossed my phone. Straight to the point with him. No point arguing or writing back. Club came first for my guys. Always.

I laid back down, my body achy and feeling weak. Tears welled my eyes at the thought of being alone and unable to make it to the bathroom. I was so thirsty and my head was killing me. I just wanted some water and ibuprofen, but the bathroom was so far away.

Marcos's words popped into my head at that moment. *"Maybe we need to reevaluate our relationship? Maybe it's time to renegotiate things? Because this isn't working on our end."*

Is that why they weren't here? Did they need space? Away from me? Did I fuck up that badly, that they really wanted to renegotiate things? And what wasn't working for them? The whole thing was so out of left field to me. We had been SOLID for the last two years. Never fought, never really even argued.

Marcos could be a controlling hot head sometimes, but I usually just safe-worded him back into the realm of decency. It was a wake-up call for him when he was getting a little too over the top possessive.

Jason too could be a little much too, though he usually saw reason without me needing to safe-word out of our twenty-four-seven dynamic.

Nico though, Nico I didn't have to do anything special to get him to understand when things were just too much. I was surprised by him the most. Why didn't he tell those guys to fuck off? Why wasn't he here this morning?

The club. The Devil's Psychos Motorcycle Club always came first. Always.

I had been mostly ok with it, until now. It had never come first before something as monumental as *taking care of me post hypothermia* though.

My stomach rolled. I was going to be sick. I lurched out of bed, barely managed to grab the small bedroom garbage can before my stomach heaved. I didn't have anything in my belly though, other than stomach bile. My entire abdomen clenched in pain as I continued to dry heave. I was sobbing by the time I finished. I needed water, I was so dehydrated.

Moaning, I forced myself to my feet. If the guys weren't here to help me, I would have to help myself. First, I needed to brush my teeth, drink a gallon of water, then raid the medicine cabinet. From there, I needed a shower and food. I would put on my big girl panties, and bitch the fuck up.

Then I would tear into my men when I next saw them. How dare they leave me alone like this. There would definitely have to be some renegotiations and reevaluations of our relationship, for sure. Otherwise, I wasn't sure this would be working out much longer for me.

Today was unacceptable.

"Well, well, well, what do we have here, Little Rabbit?" His nasally voice sent shivers down my spine. I froze where I stood in front of the freezer section of the grocery store.

After managing to shower and ingest an IV bag of saline from my medical kit, I felt good enough to grocery shopping and pick up a couple things for dinner. Because low and behold, there wasn't anything to eat in the house. If I didn't shop, there was no food.

The very last thing I needed was to run into the very man who had shot two of my guys, just a couple days ago. Ice chilled my veins as I looked over my shoulder to find Dax Hillcrest in the flesh. Turning, so he wasn't at my back, I realized he had boxed me in against the freezers.

Towering over me, Dax looked menacing as hell in his black hoody and jeans. Even his boots were black. There was a black bandanna around his neck, like he had pulled it down from around his face, so I could see him clearly. The bright florescent lights of the grocery store glinted of the milky white of his ruined eye, the jagged scar still as puffy and red as it had been the night I saw him kill the mayor—worse, if possible, under the lights.

Terrified and still not feeling great, I didn't have my guard up, my shields in place. I was not ready to deal with this man. "What do you want?" I asked, my voice cracking.

He chuckled softly. "Besides your boyfriends dead?"

I gulped as tears began to well in my eyes.

Dax reached out and ran a finger along the low cut of my tank top, his rough finger skimming across my skin. "I could settle for you." He smirked down at me.

Repulsion ripped through me. I fought off the urge to gag as my stomach rolled. I ground my teeth, forcing myself to breathe, to think. *Come on, Maya.* Reminding myself I was still in the middle of a grocery store, I pushed passed Dax, hitting him with my shoulder. "You wouldn't know what to do with a woman like me."

His deep answering laugh was the thing of nightmares. Something I was sure would stay with me for years to come. "I know exactly what to do with a whore like you. My crew is begging me to let them have you. You like multiple men at one time, right? Sounds like I'd be doing you a favor. Give you a real gangbang."

I gulped, terrified.

"Or you could leave town," he continued, stepping closer. "You leave town, leave those three guys behind and never look back. Then I will stop messing with you, and I won't kill the three of them... or your parents."

A gasp left my lips as my eyes widened.

"What do you think of that idea, Little Rabbit? Starting to see the bigger picture yet?"

I nodded minutely. I was starting the see the bigger picture here and I knew my men were not safe if I stayed.

"You have two days to decide. After that, I'm going after all three of them." Dax backed away then, turn away and leaving.

My body shook as I stood there, utterly lost. Fight or flight, huh? What about utterly frozen and helpless? I knew for certain though, Dax Hillcrest would kill my guys and my parents if I didn't leave.

I had to make a choice: tell my guys, or leave them forever.

After I made sure to eat something, I dressed into something sexy—at least as sexy as I was feeling at the moment. Still feeling lethargic and not right from the scene the night before, I had a feeling I was deep into sub-drop after not receiving the proper after-care from my guys. Even with adequate after-care, there was a chance that I still might have dropped due to the intensity of the scene.

I dressed in a slinky silver top that was cut low but still hugged my tits, despite the mostly open back. I paired it with a pair of leather pants, as I wasn't in the mood for a skirt. I had a feeling I would be grabbing one of the guys' sweatshirts from their dorm room at the clubhouse anyways.

I drove myself to the party at the clubhouse. I didn't like having to rely on the guys for a ride, especially if they started drinking and couldn't take me home. Lots of party nights they hosted out of town clubs, which made it impossible for them to leave. My work schedule was always funky, so I didn't always want to spend the night, knowing I wouldn't get a good night's rest.

The clubhouse in downtown Creekton was run down and lit up like the fourth of July. Patched bikers were milling around the main parking lot and down the sidewalk. Music blared from speakers inside and scantily clad women walked around in sky high heels. I didn't usually feel out of place, but tonight with my mood, I really wasn't feeling this place.

I hadn't heard from my guys all day. Nothing past the text from Marcos, telling me to be at the party that night. From the looks of things, there were a couple out of town clubs in town. It always made me uneasy when other clubs were in town and I walked through the clubhouse alone.

I still wasn't inked with the guys' names—something that was a slight contention in our relationship. I didn't see what the big deal was, they felt like it was a marriage proposal, so they weren't there yet.

Another thing, I might have to reevaluate in our relationship.

Entering the clubhouse, I was hit with a wall of heat, that immediately made my stomach clench. Hot and sticky was the last thing I wanted to deal with tonight when I already felt like shit. I should just turn around and go home, text my guys that I didn't feel well and call it a night. They could get over themselves.

Instead, I powered on, weaving through the maelstrom of bodies as I searched the room for my three men. It wasn't long before I found them holding court around a pool table in the corner. There were a couple guys around them, joking around and playing pool as well, but the kicker, the real fucking kick in the stomach for me?

The blond bimbo that was hanging off of Marcos's arm and his crooked ass smile as he stared down at her, entertaining her. Dressed in nothing but a string bikini top, and the shortest damn jean skirt I had ever seen, the bitch was looking for an easy fuck.

And Marcos was entertaining her. Allowing her to touch him.

Over my dead body.

At my absolute wits end, I stormed across the clubhouse barroom, not giving a flying fuck who I bumped into as I charged toward Marcos and the fucking whore hanging off his arm.

It happened fast, before Marcos could even realize I was there. I grabbed the bitch by a fistful of hair and yanked her backwards away from Marcos. Yells went up around us, but the blond turned on me, sneering, and pushed me away.

"Well, well, well. If isn't the Psycho's whore," the woman spat. Her brown eyebrows didn't match her hair—typical. "I hear half the club's been between your legs."

I growled at the skank. "Bet half the city's been between yours."

The skank tried to push me backward, but I stood my ground, waiting.

"Why would I, when I already have a man?" She chuckled softly, circling me. She kept her voice low so no one around us could hear.

I turned with her, never taking my eye off the bitch. Out of the corner of my eye, I could see Marcos crossing his arms over his chest as he took in the scene before him; Jason and Nico beside him, both men watching carefully.

"Maybe you're familiar with him? He's awfully interested in making you his play thing." She laughed again.

I narrowed my glare at her as I froze up. I had a feeling I knew exactly where this was going.

"Caught on, did you? Yeah, Dax said he saw you today. Said you looked really nice, all frozen like a deer in the headlights at the grocery store... kinda like you are right now."

Her little smirk set me over the edge. I growled, baring my teeth.

"Yeah, he said he can't wait to kill your guys, so he can share your skanky body with his crew."

The words barely left the bitch's mouth, before I was charging her. I tackled her into the pool table, slamming her twig body hard against the graphite surface before I pounded her face with my fist. Hit after hit, I rained down on the stupid bitch, until I felt something give way beneath my knuckles. An orbital socket maybe?

Someone was screaming as hands grabbed me roughly, yanking me off the beat-to-shit whore on the table. A pool of blood spread around her head. She wasn't moving. I didn't care though. I wrestled against the three guys pulling me away, until I was pulled out a fire exit and pushed into the cool night air of the parking lot.

Someone was still screaming. It took me a moment to realize it was me.

"Enough!" Marcos roared, getting in my face.

"Fuck you!" I roared back, pushing him in the chest. "Fuck you! Red! Fuck you, I'm done." I backed away from him quickly.

"Maya!" Jason shouted, stepping toward me.

"I said Red. No. I'm done with this shit. So fucking done." I shook my head, catching Nico watching me solemnly.

"Maya," Nico murmured almost inaudibly.

"Fuck you too," I spat at him.

I turned away from my men, hair whipping in the wind, and stormed off toward my Civic. Not for the first time that day, I wondered just what this meant for our relationship.

Reevaluate and renegotiate.

Chapter Thirty-One

Marcos

I STOOD IN THE parking lot of the clubhouse, dumbfound-ed. I stared after where Maya had been standing, wondering what the fuck had just happened.

"What the fuck?" Jason let out a slow breath, his voice full of the disbelief I was feeling myself.

"What was that about?" I asked.

"That was you letting some whore hang off you, disrespect-ing our girl," Nico replied.

I snapped my head up to look over at my buddy. Nico hadn't been right since the night before, not since he thought that I had taken things too far with Maya's punishment. Nico had been downright pissed at me when I made him leave Maya this morning, to greet the incoming visiting clubs.

But Nico was also right. I had let some whore hang off my arm for too long. I hadn't expected Maya to walk in when she had. She'd been later than normal and things had gotten out of hand.

"That was more than that," Jason said. "She's beaten girls before for getting too close to us, but never that badly. She might have killed that girl."

A gun shot went off in the clubhouse.

We whipped around to see what was going on, but there were too many people standing in the doorway. Pushing my way through the door, I led the way inside, to see what the fuck was going on.

President Buckley was standing over the body of the blond that Maya had beaten to holy hell. His gun was still aimed at the girl. She had to have gotten up at some point, because she was slumped over sideways now, with a bullet hole in her forehead.

"What the fuck?" I asked.

"She was Hillcrest's girl. She came here to spy," Buckley replied, anger pinching his face. He slowly lowered his gun, still glaring down at the blond.

"What?" I asked dumbly. Had Maya known?

"Looks like your girl got a head start on her," Buckley said.

"Yeah," I muttered, still in utter disbelief. *What the fuck was said between them?*

"Lina heard what Tish said to Maya. It was not good. Dax threatened to give Maya to his crew to use, after he killed the three of you," Bear said.

"She woke up long enough to laugh and say that Hillcrest would level the club," Buckley added, sliding his gun back into its holster. He walked away like it was nothing.

I swallowed thickly, my mind reeling. We had a fucking spy in our clubhouse? "Get rid of the body. Toss her on Hillcrest door step," I ordered a couple prospects.

Turning, I found Jason and Nico standing near the front door speaking with Buckley. On the same page, I headed for my friends and president. We needed to get out of here and find our girl.

We had made a grave mistake tonight.

It took longer than I had hoped to get out of the clubhouse. Buckley wanted us to stay and smooth things over with the visiting clubs. As Vice President, it was part of my responsibility. I had tried to get Stone and Dagger to leave without me, to go check on Maya, but they both insisted she needed time to cool down.

I didn't like it. Too much had happened in the last twenty-four hours. I'd never seen Maya so fucking wild, so damn angry. She looked sick, as well. Pale. Something wasn't sitting right with me.

It was going on six a.m. when the three of us finally pulled in the driveway. "This is fucked." Jason's low sigh was a punch to the gut for me. I was already feeling the guilt, but hearing it in Jason's voice as well, I knew I fucked up.

"We shouldn't have left her alone yesterday. She was hypothermic. She woke up alone. We're fucking lucky she even woke up," Nico spoke the words that were weighing heavily on my mind.

I hung my head, still seated on my Harley.

"She looked pale," Jason added.

"Yeah." I agreed.

"Let's go face the music," Nico said, sighing softly.

I could only nod, as I slowly dismounted from my bike.

As we walked into the kitchen, we were greeted with the tell-tale sound of someone throwing up in the hallway bathroom. "Shit," Jason swore, then headed quickly in that direction.

I looked around the kitchen space, seeing Maya's medical bag open on the counter. Next to it, was an empty saline IV bag—like she'd used it. My eyebrows furrowed together as I tried to make sense of what I was seeing. Why would she need a saline bag?

My muddled thoughts couldn't keep up, as there was a banging on the front door. "Police! Open up!" a male voice shouted.

"Fuck," Nico said.

I barely had time to look over at the door, before Nico was opening it to show two uniformed officers standing there. "Nicolai

Gage," one of the officers spoke up, his voice deep. "We have a warrant for your arrest."

Maya and Jason choose that moment to walk out of the hallway bathroom and into the living room. Her face was pale and she was dressed in blue hospital scrubs. She cried out, reaching for Nico as the uniformed officer roughly turned him around and cuffed him on the front porch.

Jason had to wrap his arms around Maya as she tried to run to Nico. He held her back, picking her up off the ground as she began kicking and screaming Nico's name.

Nico's face was solemn as he watched Jason drag Maya away, before the officers cuffed him and dragged him out of the house.

I stood frozen, watching as my life descended into chaos around me.

I had fucked up.

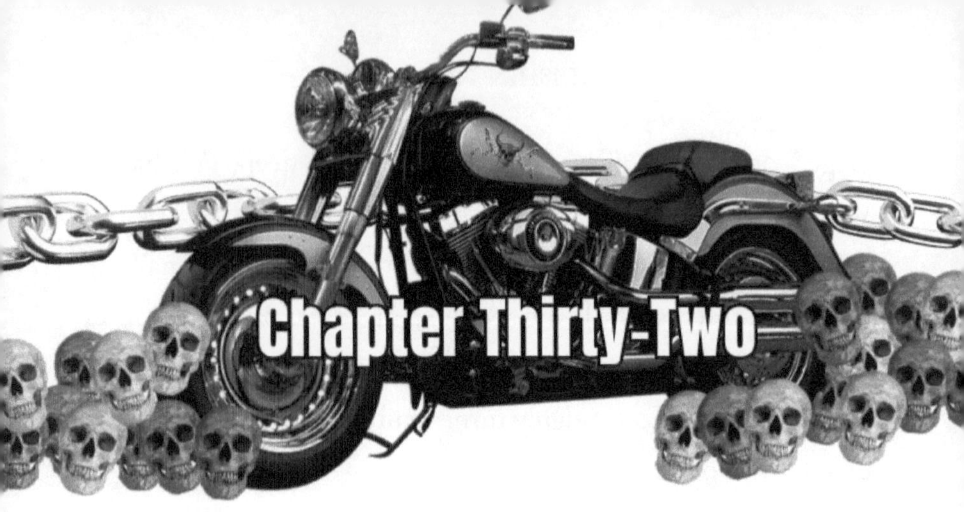

Chapter Thirty-Two

Maya

He was framed. Hillcrest planted evidence.

ANOTHER FUCKING TEXT MESSAGE from Marcos. Another morning alone after everything went to complete and utter hell. I stared around the empty living room, after rereading the text from Marcos for the hundredth time. Him and Jason had left immediately after Nico had been arrested.

They promised to call, to keep me updated, to come fucking home as soon as they could.

They hadn't though. Three hours later and all I had gotten was a text.

A fucking text that Dax Hillcrest had planted evidence to frame Nico. Just days after Hillcrest had shot both Marcos and Jason. After he sent his whore of a girlfriend into my men's clubhouse to make a point.

He was fucking everywhere. He could and would do anything to get to us.

Get to me.

I wasn't safe. My boys weren't safe as long as I was here. For whatever reason, Dax had it out for me. It had to be more than just witnessing him murder the mayor. He was growing obsessive in his pursuits.

I couldn't stay here. I had to leave.

Decision made, I headed upstairs and quickly pulled out my suitcases. I would pack as much as I could, as fast as I could. It wasn't the first time I had to move quickly. I learned a couple tricks after moving out of my parents' house two years ago. I could do this just as quickly on my own.

Jason

I groaned as Nico climbed off the back of my bike, finally able to stretch out. It was hard riding with a dude behind me. But I was grateful to have my brother back. Our lawyer had worked his magic and at least gotten Nico out on bond for the time being. He wouldn't be able to go far, but he was home.

Maya would be happy about that.

"Fucking hell," Nico groaned. "You couldn't have gotten a fucking car to pick me up in? Could have taken Maya's car."

"She's at work," Marcos grunted.

Nico sighed. "She should have called in."

"I don't think she wanted to see us," I said.

"Even if she was pissed, she'd want to see that I was back home safe," Nico grumbled and headed for the back door.

Marcos and I followed slowly, bodies aching after being awake for a close to thirty hours. We never had gone to sleep after we punished Maya Thursday evening. Now it was Saturday morning and we were dead on our feet.

"What this?" Nico asked, holding up a sheet of paper that was sitting on the counter, next to what appeared to be a used saline bag.

I narrowed my eyes on the bag, confused, before I looked at the note.

Reevaluate and renegotiate.

Red.

"What the fuck?" Nico asked, whirling on Marcos.

I could only stare blankly at the paper, my mind still trying to process. Maya's neat cursive handwriting was on that paper, but the words didn't make any sense.

Marcos swore under his breath, before he took off running for the stairs.

"No," Nico gasped, before he quickly followed after him.

My heart dropped into my stomach.

Red. As in her fucking safe word. She fucking wrote us a note with her safe word and then my guys had flown up the stairs.

"NOOOO!" Marcos's deep cry of agony filled the house.

"No," I muttered, my eyes still on the note. "No."

"She's gone," Nico said, coming down the stairs. "She left. All her stuff is gone."

I sank to my knees, my eyes falling from the note, to the empty saline bag and used needle on the counter, wondering what the fuck had happened.

Chapter Thirty-Three

A week later

Maya

I PUSHED MYSELF UP from the floor of the bathroom, reaching up to the flush the toilet as I wiped my mouth. At the sink, I quickly washed my hands before rinsing my mouth out.

After I brushed my teeth, I took a deep breath and stared into my reflection in the mirror. I felt like shit. I hadn't been sleeping and I was throwing up every day. I could only image how much weight I'd lost in the last week of being at my sister's.

"How you doing?" Jenna asked as she came to lean against the door frame.

I dragged my tired eyes over to my sister, just in time to watch Jenna set a pink box onto the counter top. A pregnancy test. "Fuck." My heart sank upon seeing the box. The realization rolling over me.

"Yeah," Jenna murmured.

"Fuck," I repeated.

Jenna nodded. "That's usually how it happens."

I couldn't even crack a smile at the off-hand joke. In my mind, I just repeated the word: Fuck. *This couldn't be happening!*

"I'll give you some privacy," Jenna said, after she pulled a paper dixie cup out of the medicine cabinet.

I nodded numbly.

Jenna left the bathroom.

All I could do was stare at the box. Fuck.

This was it. All my hopes and dreams, all of my plans, all laid out before me, about to change. Everything was about to change. I didn't need the test to know the answer.

In my heart, I already knew the answer.

I was pregnant.

To be continued...

Check out Brandishing Betrayals,

Devil's Psychos MC Book 2.

Coming August 1st!

412

Coming Soon....

Loved the Devil's Psychos?

Please take a moment leave a review on amazon here!
Sign up for my newsletter here, for the latest updates and sneak
peeks on what I'm working on.
Follow me on social media!

amazon.com/author/methornwood

facebook.com/methornwood

instagram.com/midnightdreamingwriting/

goodreads.com/author/show/45144764.M_E_Thornwood

tiktok.com/@me.thornwood.author

https://twitter.com/ME_Thornwood

Ready for more Marcos, Jason, Nico, and Maya?

Pre-order book 2 today!

Brandishing Betrayals:

Devil's Psychos Book 2

Brandishing Betrayals takes places ten years into the future, after the events of Embracing the Consequences.

Haven't Read the Ravager Knights MC yet?

Brandishing Betrayals takes place six months after the events Embracing the Consequences.

You do not need to read it to read Brandishing Betrayals, but I recommend that you do!

Brandishing Betrayals

Maya Henderson

I slammed my eyes shut as I crashed into a brick wall. Not an actual brick wall, if the muttered, "Shit," was anything to go by. Heavy hands landed on my upper arms, steadying me.

I snapped my eyes open and gasped when I saw the leather motorcycle cut with the patch on the front that read Devil's Psychos.

Fuck.

My heart pounded in my chest and blood rushed my ears. My eyes widening in disbelief. How was this possible? I looked up into the darkest brown eyes I'd know anywhere.

"Maya," Marcos Candella breathed, his grip on my upper arms tightening. Astonishment and disbelief filled his face as he stared down at me.

"Marc," I whispered, unable to gather words. I looked up at the love of my life, with wide eyes. I trailed my gaze over him, taking in every detail. His hair was still buzzed short against his skull, his eyes were such a dark brown they were almost black, and a dark goatee framed his plump lips, looking every bit as kissable as I remembered.

My gaze raked over him, before I glanced over his shoulder and saw another sight that sent my heart racing. "Jase," I gasped softly, my eyes raking over the second love of my life.

"Hey, Darlin'," Jason Langford drawled smoothly as ever. Whether he had been affected by my sudden appearance or not, he didn't let on.

His steely gray eyes bore right through my soul. He was tall, a good foot taller than my five-three frame. He was lanky too, with a slim muscular build. Athletic build. His blond hair was cut short and styled into a messy, bed-head fashion that suited him. He wore a silver chain around his neck, and a plain, gray fitted t-shirt under his Devil's Psycho Cut. A barbell was pierced through his left eyebrow. There were gauges in his ears, along with several other piercings.

He was still as fucking hot as he was ten years ago, even if he did seem to have more hardware. He had aged well and his face was clean shaven. His smooth voice made me shiver, like it always used to. It was like honey, a smooth drawl that set my core on fire. Always had.

"What are you guys doing here?" I asked, looking between the two of them. My heart racing.

"Dagger's in surgery," Marcos answered softly. He finally let go of my upper arms and I felt cold and unbalanced, immediately missing his touch.

I shivered slightly and tucked a stray hair behind my ear. "Is he okay?" I asked, fear plaguing my heart. The third and final love of my life was hurt and in surgery.

"He'll be fine," Stone answered, giving nothing away.

My eyelids fluttered; his voice always got to me. For a man that didn't talk much, he used to have me eating out of the palm of his hand whenever he spoke softly to me. Some ten years later and his voice was still napalm to my soul.

"Mom!" a young boy's voice called out from behind me, breaking me out of my stupor.

I froze, my heart pounding in my chest. Blood rushed my ears, as my whole world was caving in around me. I didn't want them to find out this way. I had planned on telling them, telling Marcos, but I wasn't ready yet.

"What the *fuck*?" Jason's voice was a booming crack in the silence.

I jumped, not used to hearing that tone from Jason, *ever*, even Marcos startled at his tone. Marcos stared over my shoulder, in disbelief and awe.

"How?" Marcos asked, his voice soft. His eyes locked on my son, Lucas.

I squeezed my eyes shut in panic. How the hell would I ever explain this? I needed time. *This wasn't supposed to happen this way!*

"Mom," Luke called again.

I quickly glanced over my shoulder to see my little boy, staring at me with wide eyes. He had dark black hair and deep brown eyes, just like his father. His left arm was in a sling, and he was sitting back on the hospital gurney he'd been brought in on from school.

I gave him a pained smile. "Just a minute, honey," I said.

"Maya?" Marcos's voice was sharp, my name a question.

"Mom, I want to meet him," Lucus said. His voice was steady and sure. He may be just a nine-year-old boy, but he knew what he wanted.

I closed my eyes and took a deep breath. *Fuck.* I needed more time. I couldn't do this. They were going to hate me. When I opened my eyes, I couldn't meet Marcos's gaze. "Would you like you meet your son?" I asked him softly, staring at the Devil's Psycho patch on his cut.

"I would love to meet my son," Marcos said softly. He brushed by me without saying another word, and walked into the exam room beyond.

I watched him extend his hand to Lucas and introduce himself. "I'm Marcos, what's your name?" he asked gently.

"Hi," Lucas said. He put his hand in Marcos's and maintained eye contact while he shook his father's hand. "I'm Lucas, my friends call me Luke," my son answered.

I gasped softly and quickly covered my mouth, as tears welled in my eyes. I'd always known Marcos would be a great father, I felt horrible denying him all these years. I would never be able to explain why.

"What the fuck is this, Maya?" Jason growled quietly. His hand wrapped around my bicep and pulled me toward him.

I faltered as I was jerked forward. Jason Langford was not one to fuck around, *ever*. My heart raced; I couldn't do this.

"Did you know you were pregnant when you left us?" Jason demanded, cutting right to the heart of the matter, his slate gray eyes bore into mine.

I gasped at the intense anger I saw in those eyes; anger, hurt, betrayal, all of it clear as day on his beautiful, handsome face. At least it was to me. I'd always been able to read him when no one else could. The club had given him the road-name of Stone, because he was usually a stone-cold mask.

I'd always been able to read him, though. And he always saw through my bullshit.

Until now.

I nodded slowly. "Yes," I murmured and lifted my eyes to meet his gaze. I needed him to believe the worst in me. I needed him to want nothing to do with me. It was safer that way, safer for all of us.

His glare intensified, the vein in his jaw throbbed as he clenched his teeth. Even after all these years, he was sexy as hell when he got worked up. "Why?" he snapped.

"Do I need a reason?" I shot back and raised an eyebrow at him. I put my hands on my hips, brushing off his grip on my bicep, and glared up at him. I knew I was being unfair. It had been ten years since I last saw him. I didn't know anything about the man before me, not really, not anymore.

Jason growled deeply again. He never was one for game playing. He had patience for a lot of things, but lies and bullshit were not one of them. "You've changed," he snapped, his gray eyes rolling over my face.

I rolled my eyes and shrugged a shoulder. "Sure have," I said, nonchalantly.

"Not for the better," Jason added, his eyes narrowing in contempt.

I glared back him. I forced myself to appear angry and disgruntled, rather than the hurt and anguish I really felt. All I wanted to do was lean into him and let him wrap those strong arms around me. I wanted to hear him tell me everything was going to be okay and that he would take care of me, protect me from here on out.

Instead, I met his glare and crossed my arms over my chest. I squared off with the big bad wolf and steeled my spine. I had to keep the distance between us. My safety and my son's, depended on that distance. "Don't worry, *Stone*," I drawled. "I'm not here for you."

He stepped closer to me, like he was trying to intimidate me. "Don't worry about that, doll face. You proved your worth in the end. Less than nothing."

It took everything inside me to not break under those words and his distance. The pure venom in his tone rattled me to the core. This was not my Jason. My Jase, would never look at me with such contempt in his gaze.

Tears welled in my eyes at his words. Pain stabbed my chest, like a physical blow, as my heart shattered into pieces over his words. Thankfully I was saved from answering as the doctor walked up, clipboard in hand.

I turned from Jason as the doctor glanced my way and nodded once, before he walked into the exam room.

"Alright little dude," the doctor spoke loudly. "Are we ready to get a cast on and get out of here?"

Luke looked at the doctor nervously.

I walked over and grabbed my son's hand. "We sure are, aren't we Luke?" I said and forced myself to push through the pain and tears and smile at my son. I could be strong for him. I would be, strong for him. I had to be. I had no other choice.

Luke eyed me, seeing my pain. He squeezed my hand before he turned to the Doctor. "Let's do this," he nodded.

"That's what I like to hear. Why don't we get out of here? I'll wheel you out, your parents can follow me and we'll head up to orthopedics on the second floor," the doctor said.

No one bothered to correct him.

I held my son's hand as the doctor wheeled the gurney out of the exam room and they headed for the elevator.

Halfway down the hall, when it was clear that Marcos wasn't following, Luke told the doctor to wait.

I glanced back to see Marcos and Jason in a discussion, before both men did a manly hug with a back slap, before Marcos was striding toward us.

Jason didn't follow.

Haven't Read the Ravager Knights MC yet?
Brandishing Betrayals takes place six months after the events Embracing the Consequences.
You do not need to read it, to read Brandishing Betrayals, but I recommend that you do!

Also By M.E. Thornwood

Missed out on the Ravager Knights MC?

Start with Courting the Consequences!

Check it out here!

Choices have consequences, and some consequences cannot be undone.

FIGHTING TO SURVIVE IS all Kara Carmichael knows. Whether it was surviving the streets as a poor kid on the southside of Mourningside, Illinois or fighting the legal injustices in the court room, Kara prides herself on her ability to fight and win.

She also knows that every choice you make, has an outcome or consequence.

As the managing partner of the most prestigious law firm in the city, Kara had fought her way into a good life. She had made all the right choices.

Or so she thought.

When the Ravager Knights MC rolls into her law firm and kicks up trouble, Kara has a choice to make.

Fight the soul burning attraction of three rough and tumble bikers? Or fight for the prestigious job and gilded lifestyle she worked her entire life building?

Check out Reconciling the Consequences here!
Make a choice. Consequences be damned.

Kara made her choice, and the consequences of her choices left her burned and beaten.

After her father's hitman failed to kill her and her ex-boyfriend carried her body from the burning house, Kara wakes up in hospital...

her ex-boyfriend carried her body from the burning house, Kara wakes up in hospital... alone.

Without a home to return to, and her father still out for blood, Kara has only one choice left... beg for forgiveness from the three men whose hearts she deliberately broke. Or die trying.

Will Johnny, Derrick, and Kevin accept her apology and move on? Or will Kara have to face the consequences for her choices and save herself from her father?

Check out Embracing the Consequences here!

Not all consequences are bad. Some consequences are meant to be embraced.

Kara Carmichael knows first-hand that not all consequences are bad. She never would have met her boyfriends had her father not framed Mac Taylor for embezzlement and the list of other alleged crimes.

With her father locked away, Kara and her guys are faced with a new reality and a new family dynamic.

But when new threats and old enemies rear their ugly heads, new challenges are once again thrown their way.

Can Kara embrace the consequences for her actions or will it all come crumbling down around her?

Check out Brandishing Beginnings here!

They say trouble comes in three... as in the form of three rough and tumble bikers.

They make my heart race and my skin sizzle. They push my boundaries like no one else, introducing me to the dangerous world of the *Devil's Psychos* motorcycle club. And they're completely wrong for me.

When my college friend invites me to her family's home for the holidays, I didn't expect to see her brother Marcos—a gorgeous man I haven't been able to stop thinking about since we met—and he didn't come alone. His two best friends are hot as hell and downright dangerous... and they all want me.

One night I give into temptation. They teach me to submit, and it's hotter than I ever could have imagined.

Afterwards, I try to dismiss our passion as a one-time thing. But

I can't stop thinking about Marcos's demanding presence and chiseled jaw. And Jason and his sexy piercings and sultry voice. And I miss the way Nico seemed to balance the two and always make me laugh.

When I need a place to stay, they take me in, and things heat up quickly. It turns out the three of them really like being in charge... and I find that I like that, too.

But a dangerous encounter reminds me of the risky world they live in—a world that could make me a target. For these guys, I'll risk losing my heart, but could that mean putting my life on the line as well?

Acknowledgments

OMG! Thank you to all my readers! Thank you for reading!

As always, thank you to my husband. You are my rock, without you, I wouldn't be able to do this.

To Jessica Baker! Thank you for always listening to me rant and ramble!

To my bestie. My sister from another mister. I love you darling! We need a spa day!

To my girl Megan at Cantina Book Club! Thank you for being my friend for the last 20 years!

Once again you readers, thank you so much for reading my books! I appreciate each and every one of you!

M.E. Thornwood is a contemporary Why Choose romance author that enjoys writing about dark themes, thrilling suspense, and hot hot spice. She loves her alpha males and the women who don't put up with them. Writing has been her passion since she was a little girl.

She lives in the Midwest with her husband and two children. When she's not writing, she's enjoying camping with family and friends, hiking with her kids, and reading books with her loveable fat cat Midnight.